To my wife, Andrea
May this book be but a chapter in the
life I've dedicated to you

THE WRECKING CREW

TAYLOR ZAJONC

Blank Slate Press | St. Louis, MO

Zajonc

Blank Slate Press
Saint Louis, MO 63116

Copyright © 2016 Taylor Zajonc

All rights reserved.

For information, contact:
Blank Slate Press at 4168 Hartford Street, Saint Louis, MO 63116
www.blankslatepress.com
www.expeditionwriter.com

Blank Slate Press is an imprint of Amphorae Publishing Group, LLC
www.amphoraepublishing.com

Manufactured in the United States of America
Cover Design by Kristina Blank Makansi
Cover art: 123RF and iStock
Set in Adobe Caslon Pro and Aachen BT

Library of Congress Control Number: 2015959849
ISBN: 9781943075164

CHAPTER 1

The Dassault Falcon sliced through the sky, triple Pratt & Whitney jet engines rocketing a sleek windowless fuselage over endless miles of lawless Somali coastline. Inside, Dr. Fatima Nassiri's eyes drifted across the panoramic view, a clever combination of powerful exterior cameras and curved video screens. The projected illusion was breathtaking, transforming the interior into an impossibly lifelike 360-degree view. If she let her busy mind drift away from the technological complexity for a moment, it almost felt as though she were floating among the clouds.

It was a great step up from her previous Somali expedition. Grant money was tight, so she'd crammed herself into an aging Mitsubishi MU-2 turboprop, elbow-to-elbow with her graduate students as they conducted their fifteen-hour data collection missions in a sweltering, unpressurized cabin.

While outside the African sun beat down on the fuselage like a blacksmith's hammer, Dr. Nassiri sunk deeper into her plush leather seat, enjoying the gentle air conditioning with a hint of lavender perfume. Funny what happens when a Bahraini billionaire loses his favorite fishing spot to red tide—the trickle of research money became a flood, only this time with the added perk of a private jet. She was determined not to allow the opportunity to slip through her fingers—every dollar counted, every dollar brought her inches closer to understanding the growing red tide infecting the Horn of Africa like a plague.

Even now, she could peer at the high-resolution display and watch the spreading plumes of algae swirl like finger-paint in the deep turquoise of the shallow coastal ocean. At sea level, the thick, maroon intrusion stank of death as poisons asphyxiated the lowest single-cell rungs of the food chain, permeating through the food web to fish and mammals. Sea life could swim and starve or stay and suffocate.

Dr. Nassiri sighed. She was too old to cry over dead fish and dying dolphins and starving African fisherman.

The young, ponytailed graduate assistant to Dr. Nassiri's left reminded her of herself in younger days. She was an environmentalist, a scientist, and a true believer in the power of good intentions. Dr. Nassiri would never admit it to anyone, but the student was her favorite, the type of girl she'd always secretly hoped her son would someday marry. The other, a heavyset young man sitting further up the cabin, was a top pick from her university's oceanography program.

Security was the overriding concern, so the scientists dropped transponders according to a specified grid pattern. The plane would swing wide on the way south, considerably circumventing the coast of Somalia. The pilots would only hug the coast on the return route and never exactly the same course twice. No sense in telegraphing predictable movements. Somalia was bad territory, red zone, no place for a forced landing. At an altitude of only two thousand feet, their presence was close enough to annoy the pirates, some of whom occasionally fired a haphazard hailstorm of small-caliber fire skyward, or even the rare slow, arcing rocket-propelled grenade.

A flashing indicator on the closest screen interrupted her rambling, boredom-induced thoughts. She pressed the communication button on her gold-inlaid, wood burl armrest to reach the cockpit.

"We're coming up on coordinate zero-zero-five-one," she said. "Prepare for the drop."

"Roger," whispered the pilot over the silky intercom connection. "Go ahead."

Dr. Nassiri motioned to one of her two graduate students. "Ready transponder zero-zero-five-one."

The young man nodded and punched in the code to his computer console.

"Reaching coordinates in ten ... nine ... eight," he counted. "Preparing to release ... four ... three ... two ... mark ... release!"

Dr. Nassiri pressed the release button on her wall screen, allowing a wing-mounted transponder to drop into the airstream. It would be a few moments before the tumbling instrument impacted the ocean below. They were designed to record all data before reaching a modest crush depth of just a few hundred feet. The Falcon shuddered, the finicky aerodynamic trim of the craft disrupted by the drop. Soon enough, the transponder came alive as it sunk through the water, transmitting a host of high-speed oceanographic and chemical data.

"*Holy shit*," exclaimed the female graduate student, pointing to the curved screen on her side of the plane.

"These readings are off the charts. Do you think we dropped a dud?"

The doctor tipped her glasses and glanced at the live data stream. Heavy metals, exotic chemicals, radioactive isotopes ... a veritable toxic soup of deadly man-made materials. Her mind flashed back to a rumor she'd heard years ago.

The very thought made her shiver. *Mertvaya Ruka*— could this be the first evidence of the Dead Hand? The Dead Hand was a legend spoken only in hushed whispers among her fellow faculty, and even then, most often followed by a shrug or dismissive wave. But whenever she read about a flock of seabirds plunging dead from the skies, three hundred porpoises beaching themselves on rocky shores as their organs dissolved, or entire fishing stocks collapsing without warning, she'd wonder if a single tendril of the Dead Hand had escaped its coffin. And then there were these off-the-charts readings, data that seemed as if she'd dropped the transponder into the well of Hades.

Or it could be just a dud, an expensive transponder down the drain.

"Alright, let's circle back around to the last position," she said. The pilots obliged, tilting the aircraft into an elegant turn. The young man resumed his countdown as Dr. Nassiri prepared to release another transponder.

As her graduate student prepared the drop sequence, she stopped suddenly—a strange black vessel materialized a thousand feet below the Falcon, clearly visible on the high-resolution video screen. It cut through the water like a surfaced shark, the prow underwater, but with a stubby central tower rising well above the waves. It looked like no fishing boat she'd ever seen. Two black-clad men stood in the tower. One of them lifted a long, tubular instrument towards the plane. Then a flash from below, a bright light trailing smoke. It circled, rapidly climbing towards the aircraft.

My god—is that—?

"Mi—*missile!*" screamed Dr. Nassiri. "Missile!"

Even if the pilots could hear her, they could do nothing. First it was a thousand feet below, just a speck of light followed by a plume of white smoke, and then—*good god*, it was fast—the missile detonated against the port jet engine with a blast like the entire universe had collapsed inwards on itself in an instant. The pressure wave tore through the passenger compartment, blowing out Dr. Nassiri's left eardrum before she even heard the sound. The wall screens went dark, leaving the length of the windowless fuselage dark save for electrical arcs and daylight streaming through the gaping holes in the aircraft's thin skin. Wetness streamed from her nose as a tearing pain bit at her chest and wrist.

The plane heeled over like a bird with a shot-gunned wing, and the young man to her right was sheet-white, open-mouthed and bleeding, holding onto one shredded arm with the other. She couldn't hear his screaming over the wounded roar of the surviving engine.

Flames—she could see *flames* through the perforated carbon fiber fuselage of the dying jet. The exploded turbine had turned the plane's composite skin into a ragged mess. Heat and wind and sound flooded the cabin with unimaginable ferocity. Twenty million alarm bells went off through her mind as the jet tumbled through the air, all of them screaming *going to die, going to die, going to die.* Through the shrapnel holes she saw sky, water, sky, water as she tumbled too fast to even catch a glimpse of the horizon.

The jet hit an updraft, slamming her down into her

plush leather seat with monstrous force, pinning her down. To her right, the young man's eyes rolled into the back of his head. Too much blood lost in just moments, his body simply shut down. The jet screamed, the whistle of wind through the fuselage blending in with the shrieking engine, a perfect maelstrom of mechanical distress. Then a *wham*, like getting hit with a blindside rugby tackle, like missing a step and taking that first big hit falling down the stairs, the jet bounced off the first of the whitecaps. Her entire chair tore loose, spitting sheared bolts and metal fragments as the aluminum mounts ripped free. Debris cartwheeled through the air, cracking Dr. Nassiri on the side of the head. Her vision swam gray.

The jet struck the water again, off-center, and toppled to a dead stop, slowly rolling over to total inversion, wrecked and flooding. Dr. Nassiri hung upside down, watching helplessly as a collapsing bulkhead fell onto her young female student, pinning the woman against the bench. Dr. Nassiri released her safety belt, tumbling helplessly through the air before splashing into the gathering flood of ice-cold seawater over the thick carpet. The freezing water was a gut shot, a snap back to technicolor reality. The aircraft was filling—rapidly.

She couldn't tell if the body to her right—no, it wasn't a body, it was her student—she couldn't tell if he was living or dead, but he wasn't moving and there was blood and—

A single image froze in her mind ... exposed pink brain matter leaking from his crushed skullcap as angry, foaming seawater flowed over his motionless mouth and nose. Dr. Nassiri pushed herself to her knees, reaching with a shaking hand towards the collapsed instrumentation panel. The young woman hung upside-down in the leather seat, pinned down by the bulkhead. She whimpered as the rising water floated her long, sweat-soaked ponytail in a wet pile. Dr. Nassiri tried to push the debris off her, but it wouldn't budge, wouldn't even tremble.

"Help me," moaned the young woman. "Please, help me, *please, help me, please!*"

It was then that Dr. Nassiri caught a glimpse of the jagged carbon fiber strut sticking not into but *through* the girl. She couldn't bear to make eye contact; she could only see the terrible wound torn through her pupil's chest. The girl probably couldn't even feel it through the rush of endorphins and adrenaline.

Dr. Nassiri tried to speak, and then the water was over the young woman's face, her dying student bubbling ineffectually beneath. Her ears popped with the pressure of the rising water. This couldn't be it. This couldn't be the last few seconds of her life.

Water flooded the interior with renewed force, pushing Dr. Nassiri upwards into a rapidly shrinking air pocket. The plane was upside down, everything was wrong. Pushing with her legs—and she treaded water now—she could just reach the manual release lever of the emergency door. She yanked on it, once, twice, to no avail. Horror flooded over her, as the last remaining vestige of rational thought told her *too much exterior pressure.*

The plane would need to flood and equalize the pressure differential before she could release the door. Her tiny air bubble would disappear—and then how long until the end?

She had no time to think, no time to consider any other options, she took one ragged, burning breath of jet fumes and smoke and thin air and ducked underwater as the last of the air bubbles flowed through a lattice of shattered carbon fiber and streamed to the surface. She fumbled blindly for the lever and—

And then it was free, just like she'd done a dozen times before. The door swung open. Her clothes caught on jagged metal as she squirmed her way out of the tiny opening. *Freedom*—kicking her legs, she pushed for the glistening surface, breaking into thick, smoky air. Sunlight streamed through her burning eyes amid a growing slick of flaming aviation fuel.

My lamb, my little lamb!

With three more kicks of her legs, she swam underneath and away from the field. She popped out of the water, gasping for breath. The stinging seawater cleared from her eyes just enough for her to slowly turn around, treading water. She saw no land, nothing but endless rolling waves and the burning fuel slick. No sign of the mysterious vessel that had sent the beautiful jet spiraling from the sky.

My little lamb, my beloved only son.

But then something in the distance—incoming boats, attracted by the smoke. Three of them, lost in the heat of the day as they sped towards her. Three low, fast fiberglass hulls, unpainted, filled with dark faces and bristling with weaponry.

Do not search for me, my son.

And then the pirates were upon her.

CHAPTER 2

Jonah Blackwell suspended himself from the ceiling of the chain-link cell, his eyes shut against the red tones of the rising sun. His fingers and toes wrapped around the steel links, holding his too-thin form in the air as he slowly lowered and raised his body against the force of gravity, letting his muscles clench, then release, each contraction bringing him a few inches closer to the unbounded brilliance of the cloudless sky.

He'd do a thousand repetitions this week. He planned a thousand more next week, maybe a thousand and one the week after. Finishing his quota for the day, he allowed his calloused feet to drop to the dirt floor of his cell. Jonah crouched, his bare knees reaching far past the ragged cuffs of his western-style khaki shorts. At a lanky six feet two inches, the ceiling of his cell was too low for a proper pull-up. Never mind that—with the protein-poor diet served to the prisoners, he could maintain little but lean, stringy muscle.

Prison 14 scarcely stood out from the endless drab brown desert landscape of southern Morocco, just two dozen buildings behind concrete blast walls and concertina wire. A tiny outpost of misery marooned in a sea of desert, leaning guard towers held silent sentry over a large courtyard ringed by rows of auxiliary tents and trailers. A ragged motor pool held a dozen decrepit pickups, each modified with military paint and human cages. The main gate opened to the desert and a disused perforated concrete pad complete with a skeletonized helicopter, long since stripped of any salvageable parts.

The prison had been hurriedly built to house a few dozen inconvenient reminders of an attempted coup. It now held nearly five hundred religious dissidents, misplaced progressive idealists, and disgraced political apparatchiks. The temporary outpost had long since become permanent, at least as permanent as anything in the Sahara. Past sandstorms scarred every building as the thick bulwarks slowly lost a long war of attrition with the desert wind and sand.

Prison 14 of the Moroccan Directorate of Territorial Surveillance did not officially exist, nor did the indistinguishable, ragged men housed in the endless rows of eight-by-eight chain-link cells. The designation of the prison, the numeral 14, was an intentional affront to logic, seemingly conjured by the desert itself as a cruel joke—there was no Prison 13 any more than there was a Prison 15.

No roads led in or out of the compound, the location only a string of geographical coordinates in an ocean of heat and sand. By helicopter it could be estimated as about eighty miles south of the Guetta Zemmur, itself a miniscule township in the Moroccan-administered territory of the Western Sahara. But by land it was a step off a single-lane dirt road and into the largest nothingness on earth.

The camp wasn't built to punish, but to warehouse. By the time a shackled, defeated man reached its razor-wire walls, the secret police had long since demanded their last answer and the torturer delivered his final electrical shock. Prisoners were left here, perhaps to live, perhaps to die, but always to be forgotten. Morocco's Directorate of Territorial Surveillance ran the prison with a sort of backwater bureaucratic indifference, with no more humanity than whim demanded and a laxity borne by profound boredom. The real authority of Prison 14 came not from chain-link cages, steel shackles, dogs, or rifles; it came from the eight million square miles of desolate, pitiless Saharan desert surrounding it, a body of shifting dunes and drought aged three million years, born before the faintest glimmer of humanity graced the face of the earth and destined to outlive it by time immeasurable.

Jonah ran a hand through his close-cropped blonde hair, releasing a halo of dust. Breakfast would be served soon, announced with no more pomp or circumstance than the click of magnetic cell locks. It was almost time for the weekly shower, practically the only form of timekeeping in Prison 14. Between his tanned skin, gaunt muscles, and strong features, Jonah could almost be mistaken for attractive. Not yet thirty, he'd become a man who filled silence with silence and wasted few movements.

Some of the political prisoners, Marxist student activists mostly, liked him, if for no other reason than his occasional patience for English tutoring. Jonah actually felt a bit of sympathy for the young prisoners of conscience. The journalists, bloggers, and activists typically came from middle-class backgrounds, and were largely unprepared for the exacting machinations of state-sponsored terror.

They thought if only they could reach the West, make them care—this of course, was the reason for the English lessons—then something would be done. The grand injustice performed upon them would be rectified and the foundational tenets of a just moral universe restored.

Jonah did not believe this. He knew that some things just were, just as they'd always been. Perhaps the long arc of the universe bent towards justice, but it bent further towards indifference.

The electronic locks clicked, releasing the door to his cage. Shabby, barefoot men shuffled from their rows of cells, joining the stream of broken humanity towards the cafeteria tent in the center of the square. Jonah held back. It wouldn't matter if he bolted to the front or stood last. Besides, it was more difficult to put a knife in the back of the last man in line.

It did not matter to the fundamentalists that as far as most Americans were concerned, there was no hangman's scaffold too high for a Blackwell. Son of an embezzler, son of a rapist or an addict or a murderer ... all these lineages could be overcome by the eternal cycle of American reinvention. But there would never be redemption for the son of a missing American traitor.

A commotion rippled through the line as convicts moved or were shoved aside. A large, unkempt man pushed himself against the stream of prisoners. Jonah scowled, recognizing him as Umar, a low-level Rabat gangster whose weaponry sideline with the Islamic fundamentalists finally landed him in the ghost prison.

Umar was distinctly malodorous and dirty in a way that stood out even among the filthy detainees. He'd never cut his hair or beard since arriving and preferred to shower fully clothed. The gangster spotted Jonah and grinned, revealing a wide yellow smile speckled with gold and rot. Sensing something amiss, the last of the other inmates crowded and pushed their way free, only to join the circle forming around both men.

Umar was the sort of convict who managed to remain quite fat despite the limited diet of the prison. The guards realized early on he was a man without ideology, the sort of man they could use to strengthen their grasp within the walls. He never seemed susceptible to the despair that plagued even the most hardened of the religious fundamentalists; he was a rat that found comfort in cages as if he'd never known life without them, a rat that murdered other rats for sport.

Jonah attempted to slip past, but Umar sidestepped to block him, knocking one of the younger prisoners into a row of razor wire. The prisoner didn't wince, didn't shout—just yanked himself off the hooks and, head down, shuffled away as quickly as he could. Umar smiled again and said something in Darija, the local dialect of Moroccan Arabic. Despite his many months in prison, Jonah had a difficult time with the accent—something about a man's beard?

He'd only had trouble with Umar once before. Months earlier, the gangster had started trying to corner one of the political activists, a slight, former photographer from one of the wealthier families in the Moroccan city of Meknes. When Umar leered and smacked his thick lips to the activist in front of Jonah during a pinochle game, Jonah tossed the nine of hearts at Umar's feet. Unknowing of the meaning of the gesture, a confused Umar bent to pick up the card. Before he could even look up, Jonah viciously kicked in the gangster's face. His shinbone shattered Umar's eye socket and knocked him unconscious for eight full minutes.

Umar spent the next two weeks in Prison 14's rudimentary medical trailer nursing a swollen face and very specific notions of revenge. That was until Jonah snuck in and delivered him a hand-carved mortar and pestle, made from the rocks found in the prison yard. Jonah showed Umar how to grind out his pills into a thin white line. The primal memory of addiction took over, making the gangster's next week the most fun he'd had since he discovered the joys of street heroin in the slums of Rabat. It wasn't as if all was forgiven—forgiveness does not exist in the Sahara— but Umar now recognized Jonah as a man who knew his place in the prison ecosystem and decided to allow him to continue his existence as a low priority target.

Jonah watched as Umar reached up to stroke his beard again, saying the same phrase in Darija again. Louder, but still friendly, the gangster again tried to prompt Jonah. What was it? A joke about his face?

The American unconsciously reached up with his right hand to touch his own thick beard. With lightning speed, Umar threw his entire body towards Jonah, a feint concealing a hand darting towards Jonah's abdomen. Jonah saw the glint of a steel blade for the fraction of a second before it was driven into his gut, just below his ribs.

Shit. Apparently Umar had reassessed his priorities.

Pain washed over Jonah, focusing him. Umar struck hard, but too hard; the fat gangster wobbled off balance, vulnerable. Jonah whipped his right fist across Umar's face with a brutal right hook, catching the previously injured eye socket with full force. Then he saw it for the first time— Umar's dilated pupils, darting eyes. The gangster was jacked out of his mind. He'd need to beat the man unconscious, maybe to death. Umar wasn't going to back down, not this time, not even for a shattered eye socket, not for a broken bone or dislocated joint, not even a brain-rattling concussion.

So it was going to be a real fight, no posturing, not a lesson or a warning or boredom, but a blood-in-the-sand fight to the death.

Jonah winced as his abdominal muscled spasmed with pain. His mind raced, calculating his next move. Umar grabbed his shirt and Jonah clapped the big man's ears. It would have ended the fight for any normal opponent, but Umar just laughed and threw him into the fence, the gangster's inner ears already wet with blood. Jonah struggled to his feet and looked down. The knife had worked its way free but he didn't have time to look for it, didn't have time to turn the weapon against his massive foe.

Umar threw a wild punch and Jonah ducked, coming up underneath the gangster with a blow to his jaw, dislocating it. Fear entered Umar's frantic eyes. Jonah doubted the man could feel the pain, but that some deep part of Umar's lizard brain screamed at him through the fog of the drugs that something was very wrong. Screaming at him that he'd need to finish the fight.

The gangster straddled Jonah and drew himself up to a sitting position, aiming a meaty fist at Jonah's face. Jonah raised his arms in a boxer's defense, but the punch blew through, a crushing strike against the side of his head. A second blow from the other side violently knocked his head the other direction and his arms fell limp to the ground. He knew he was losing the fight, losing badly.

The blows didn't stop, and Jonah's rattled mind spit out garbled, conflicting instructions. Only one thought rose to the surface.

So this is it.

He didn't feel anger or sadness. But he did feel a twinge of surprise, as if sitting down to a novel and finding it stopped halfway through, the rest of the pages blank. Three years was a good run, sometimes the music stops and you don't have a chair. Umar's ruined face stared back at him, jaw hanging to the side, nose shattered, eye drooping as the gangster raised his fists back and prepared for the final blows.

A single gunshot rang out, and Umar jerked in surprise. He twitched for just a moment, then slowly tilted back, collapsing to the ground. Jonah crawled out from underneath his twitching form, dragging himself away without looking back. Adrenaline coursed through his veins like a raging river, as did anger—anger at the brutality, the suddenness, the unfairness, and most of all, the sheer randomness of the attack.

The silhouette of a man holding a pistol stood between him and the sun. Armed prison guards flanked him, each with varying degrees of disinterest painted on their face.

"Bring him to my office," said a voice in clipped Queen's English. "Gently."

Several guards grabbed onto Jonah's arms and torso. He allowed them to lift him to his feet, and even placed his arms across their shoulders as they walked him through a door in the fence and towards the medical trailer. The other inmates knew better than to watch, but Jonah did catch the worried look of one of the activists. It was never a good thing to leave the grounds of the courtyard, not even for a visit to the infirmary.

With the sun no longer silhouetting his form, Jonah got his first good look at the man who'd saved him. He recognized him as Dr. Hassan Nassiri, a man who no more belonged in the blight that was Prison 14 than did an orchid in the Sahara.

Dr. Nassiri had arrived the prior evening to great commotion and speculation among prisoners and guards alike. Most hoped he'd come to replace the current director, a drunken army medic with a penchant for thick-needled penicillin shots and a strong reluctance to distribute even the most innocuous of narcotics, much to the impotent rage of Prison 14's addict population. By stark contrast, Dr. Nassiri was a military surgeon building a lucrative part-time private practice in Tangiers. In the prime of his mid-thirties, with clear, olive skin and long, dark hair framing a sharp, well-proportioned face, he was one of the finest examples of well-to-do Moroccan lineage, a product of generations of commingling between brilliant, wealthy men and beautiful, equally wealthy women. Though such families had long ago exited the aristocracy to the professional academic and medical class, everyone wondered what had brought such a man so low. What could possibly have reduced him to the purgatory of Prison 14? Incompetence? Heartbreak? Punishment?

The adrenaline from his fight wore off, and Jonah's knees buckled. "Careful," Dr. Nassiri said as the guards caught him. Following in the doctor's footsteps, the guards half-carried, half-dragged Jonah past the medical tent toward a small mobile trailer parked at the far edge of the camp. Dr. Nassiri opened the door and the guards propelled Jonah inside.

Jonah stepped into a world of shapes and colors he never thought he'd see again. The trailer was richly appointed, with thick, comfortable carpeting, a single examination table and an imported Spanish-style writing desk. Dr. Nassiri took a seat in a comfortable green leather chair behind his desk, allowing the guards to unceremoniously deposit Jonah on the examination table.

"You may leave," said Dr. Nassiri without looking up. The guards nodded and exited the trailer. Dr. Nassiri unlocked the lowest drawer on his desk and removed his pistol from his waist holster. Jonah caught his first look at the pistol that had taken the life of his attacker—an Italian-manufactured Beretta 92FS with markings of the Moroccan internal security forces, a simple 9mm firearm ubiquitous to governments and police forces worldwide.

Dr. Nassiri clicked the safety on and placed it in the lowest drawer, locking it. He took his medical kit from behind the desk and walked up to Jonah. He snapped latex gloves on his hands. "May I examine your wound?" he asked.

Jonah looked down at his stab wound for the first time in a few minutes, and was surprised to see that the bleeding had already begun to subside. He nodded, giving permission. Dr. Nassiri leaned close, probing at the ugly puncture. Jonah smelled expensive cologne.

"A small blade, the wound does not appear too deep." Dr. Nassiri took an antiseptic sponge from his bag and began to clean the area. "And as to your face—I imagine you've taken worse blows during your incarceration. Any dizziness? Fatigue? Nausea?"

Jonah shook his head. He felt he'd just gone through a washing machine with a set of bowling pins, but only the stab wound concerned him. Dr. Nassiri produced a syringe from his medical satchel and filled it. He smiled apologetically and stuck it into Jonah's side. Immediately

Jonah felt the numbness spread as the local anesthetic took hold around the wound.

"This will need stitching, my friend," Dr. Nassiri said.

Jonah met the statement with silence.

"You do not wish the stitches?"

"Give me the needle and thread," Jonah said. "I'd prefer to do it myself."

"I assure you, I am quite artful with such minor procedures."

Jonah weighed raising a fuss, but didn't see the benefit. The last man to sew him up was the drunk medic who'd done the job with rough, shaking hands. Jonah had the scars to prove it.

"Lie back, Mr. Blackwell," Dr. Nassiri said. "This will take but a moment."

Dr. Nassiri possessed the practiced, smooth mannerisms of an experienced surgeon, and accomplished the stitching with no pinching or pulling. When finished, he slipped off his gloves, washed his hands, and took two bottles of Pellegrino sparkling water from the fridge, giving one to Jonah.

"I've read your file, you know," Dr. Nassiri said.

"Yeah? What does the DST have to say about me?"

"Thirty years of age. You come from … interesting … family stock. Your father, Donald Blackwell—"

Jonah gritted his teeth. It wasn't the first time his traitorous family history had been thrown in his face. When his original DST interrogators initially discovered his identity and family lineage, they'd treated it as a grand coup and confirmation of his inherent criminality. And thirty? He still thought he was twenty-nine. He must have missed his last birthday.

"Your father, Donald Blackwell," continued the doctor.

"CIA station chief with two decades of service. Highly decorated. That was, of course, until he vanished when you were … seventeen, I suppose? Eighteen?"

The doctor pronounced CIA like *see – aye – eh*, letting each syllable drip off his tongue like poison.

"He was a diplomat," said Jonah, repeating his childhood cover story by pure instinct. The truth was more complicated. One day his father was there, the next he wasn't. Over the next two years, concern became suspicion became accusation, each falling domino driving Jonah further from home.

"You were born in Beirut? Three days before the 1983 American Embassy bombing?"

"Does it matter?"

"Your mother is conspicuously absent from your file."

"I was hatched."

"You traveled a great deal in your youth."

"Saw a lot of third-world shitholes growing up. Are you going somewhere with this?"

Dr. Nassiri pushed the file aside and looked directly at Jonah.

"I need you, Mr. Blackwell," the doctor said.

Ah, the pitch. Here it comes, thought Jonah. An opportunity to collaborate for some small creature comfort or empty promise. Jonah crossed his arms, already refusing in his mind. It was bad enough to be alone in a room with one of them this long; every action would be suspect for months, assuming he'd survive the retaliation of Umar's friends.

"I understand you are an accomplished marine diver," continued Dr. Nassiri. "You studied for two years at the college of Marine Design at Glasgow University but did not complete the program. Dive instructor in Thailand, then volunteered for the British Embassy relief effort in recovering drowning victims after the tsunami. Saturation dive certification in Norway, several shipwreck and oil rig projects, and from all appearances the beginnings of a lucrative career."

Jonah uncrossed his arms. This he did not expect. Even remembering what it felt like to dive was like another stab wound, throwing him out of his prisoner's hardened mindset.

"You came to specialize in saturation diving, including commercial salvage and well inspection and repair work for the oil and gas sector," continued the doctor. "You were one of the first divers onsite at the *Costa Concordia* disaster—under a false name, of course. And this is not to even speak of your rumored treasure hunting. Spanish galleons, Roman caravels, Phoenician traders. It's theorized that some of your activities and relationships ended in violence. There are gaps in the record, but I understand the DST was very curious as to whether you'd pursued a certain sunken Moroccan transport plane rumored to have carried a king's ransom of cultural artifacts."

Jonah frowned, signaling his unwillingness to rehash his arrest in Moroccan waters. He knew exactly what had pushed him from legitimate work and into the shadowy world of criminal treasure salvage. Survival, plain and simple. Once the news broke that his father wasn't just a disappeared spy but a suspected traitor and double-agent, Jonah's world shrank considerably. Sure, it looked bad from the outside, but the minute-by-minute decisions were clear from his perspective.

"Get to the fucking point," said Jonah.

Dr. Nassiri smiled, ready to set the hook. "Six days ago, a jet aircraft was lost off the Horn of Africa, sinking a few miles from the coastline of Somalia. This plane carried a scientist and her two assistants, as well as a great deal of oceanographic research. I thought it lost forever, but our civil communications network has picked up a transponder signal emanating from the wreckage. I believe the aircraft has come to rest, in perhaps three hundred, three hundred fifty feet of water."

"Which is it? Three hundred or three hundred fifty?" asked Jonah. "It makes a difference."

"I do not know," admitted Dr. Nassiri. "The transponder has been communicating, but we do not believe it will continue to do so for long before the batteries expire. I must begin a recovery of the data and the bodies of the personnel immediately."

Jonah cocked his head, not bothering to ask the obvious question.

"You are pragmatic," said Dr. Nassiri. "As am I. I feel that this service will outstrip your transgressions, and I am willing to have you released from custody. The proper bribes have already been set into motion. This is your chance at a new life, Mr. Blackwell."

"What's to prevent me from telling you to shove it the second we leave Moroccan soil?"

The doctor just smiled. "A new identity," he finally said.

"What?"

"While I cannot prevent you from breaking terms, I have come up with a method of incentivizing you to fulfill your obligation. Specifically, I understand you are not currently welcome in the United States, the nation of your citizenship."

Jonah said nothing. He had no family there, no friends, not anymore. And to step foot in the United States as a Blackwell would only serve to reopen one of the more painful wounds in recent American political history, to say nothing of his probable arrest.

"Anyone can buy papers."

"Who can offer a solution to facial recognition? Fingerprinting? My friend, I specialize in these areas of microsurgery!" Dr. Nassiri opened his arms wide, and began to talk excitedly. For the first time, Jonah felt as if he was seeing the real man behind the doctor's façade, a man who prided himself in the expertise of medicine. "Why, facial recognition is the easiest. I will do this personally. You need not fool any persons anymore, merely the machines. For them, it is simply the matter of moving the location of specific data-points. I could move one ear up a millimeter. Bring in your nose just in the slightest; reshape the left eye socket to more closely match your right, the more attractive of the two. Just enough to nudge the data points and you are a new man as far as any software is concerned. The fingerprints are even easier ... just a matter of the surgical incision and the creation of several subdermal fissures under the fingers. Two weeks later, your fingerprints will be unrecognizable. They will have no hallmarks of change, but be so different as to bear no association with your previous identity. Work history, identification papers, this is easy by comparison. Keep in mind that very little must be changed to make you undetectable as your former self. I'd recommend you stay away from major airports, untrustworthy past acquaintances, and the borough of Manhattan, but otherwise you would have the chance to start again."

"Would I need to return to Morocco for the procedure?"

"No. We could rent all necessary space and equipment in Thailand."

Jonah nodded, considering the offer. Changing fingerprints and facial hallmarks seemed simpler than the gender reassignments Thailand had become renowned for. As if there were anything to consider—he'd been gone for too long already, only collaborators conversed with prison personnel in private.

"What would you need to undertake the recovery?" asked Dr. Nassiri, signaling that the pitch was over. No negotiation, Jonah could take it—or die in prison.

"I'm familiar with the area. I worked on a sunken World War II civilian transport some years back. A lot of ammunition and a stash of silver coins. Aircraft are manageable. I could probably do this one alone, and with a minimum amount of equipment. I would be alone, correct?"

"We would like to keep our footprint as small as possible."

"I'd need a full set of trimix rebreather gear. Recovery liftbags. And a ship. You know much about the pirates in that area?"

"I assure you, we will be well-defended."

"I'm going to take that as a no," said Jonah. He sighed, collecting his thoughts. "Forget being well-defended. Be fast. They are devious, they are sophisticated, and they are organized. If they run into trouble, they don't retreat. They call in reinforcements. I don't care how well-defended you are, you'll run out of ammo before they ever run out of pirates."

Jonah could tell Dr. Nassiri was not a man used to being challenged or overruled. The handsome doctor paused just a little too long before graciously accepting the correction.

"See, you are already proving your value to me," he said. "This is excellent."

Both men sat back in their chairs for a moment to consider each other.

"I've been in prison a long time," said Jonah. "I need to hear the catch."

"I left out … details … about the scientists in the lost plane," whispered Dr. Nassiri. "They are of no interest or consequence to my government. I have no sanction or backing from the Directorate or any other organization. The scientist is my mother. She was in Somalia studying a massive new red tide. She's dedicated her life to her research. This project cost her her life. I must recover her body; I must recover her life's work."

"What if I'd rather shoot my way out of here?" asked Jonah. "I don't think you'd be able to stop me if I wanted to take that pistol of yours for a last stand."

"You're my last hope," said Dr. Nassiri. "I'm begging you. I'm at your mercy. I've tried to hire divers, mercenaries. No one will work in those waters for any price. And then it occurred to me to check prisoners, find a man who could be motivated. And then I found you, Mr. Blackwell. I swear to you I'll do what I said. Believe me when I say I gave up everything—everything to come to this prison to meet you."

There was something different about the doctor now. No more clipped formality, no more deception, the Moroccan's once-arrogant face radiating the one emotion Jonah could truly identify with—pain.

"No backing—no support—so what's the big plan for getting me out of here?" asked Jonah.

Dr. Nassiri gingerly opened a desk drawer to reveal a single pre-prepared syringe. "I will give you a powerful sedative," said the doctor. "I'll declare you dead from the fight, a cerebral hemorrhage. I'll drive you overland to Marrakesh in a body bag. I've already hired a ship in Casablanca."

"Your ship won't work."

"But—" protested the doctor.

"There's only one ship in the world that's fast enough," said Jonah. "And she ain't for charter."

"I'm afraid I'm in no position to purchase a yacht."

"That's fine," smiled Jonah. "Because we're going to steal it."

CHAPTER 3

Charles Bettencourt loved speaking at Ivy League business schools. A beautiful aura of greed hung in the air, so thick he could smell it—hell, he could swim in it. These soft-handed, sharp-minded children of privilege read *Liars Poker* like an instruction manual, idolized bronzed Wall Street movers, and wanted life fast, dirty, and rich. They wanted to be the masters of the universe. They wanted it all.

He never did this pump-'em-up, leave-'em-wet speech for anything less than a full crowd, hungry adulators packing every available seat. Leaning forward in his too-small folding chair on the stage, he squinted his eyes at the darkened auditorium.

A self-made billionaire, Bettencourt was at the top of his career and he knew it. His adherents called him the man who'd conquered Silicon Valley, but his detractors preferred nicknames like 'Pink Slip Charlie,' 'Bastard Bettencourt,' or sometimes the unwieldy 'Charles Wins-in-court'. So what if he'd jumped ship from hedge funds and cut a bloody swath through the California tech industry? Mergers, acquisitions, hostile takeovers, and financial maneuvers were all part of the game. Disruption wasn't just for blue-collar autoworkers in Michigan anymore; the nerds had it coming just as much as anyone else. But to the media, Bettencourt was a dyed-in-wool, true-blue, goddamn American golden child. His prominence in tech had grown to prominence in everything—private security, energy, global freight, anything that mattered to the world he intended to shape in his own image.

The speaker—some Harvard blowhard who hadn't been real-world relevant since the '90's tech bubble—was wrapping up a second lap on his effusive and wholly unnecessary introduction, lapping up the impatient attention of the audience as if it was his own.

Besides him, a well-coiffed lawyer leaned over to whisper in Bettencourt's ear.

"I know this is bad timing," said the lawyer, "but the Conglomerate needs to talk. Soon."

He frowned deeply. He'd rather stay in the moment, look across the audience, see all the young people who wanted to found the next billion-dollar empire. Even the mention of the word *Conglomerate* sent a feeling through his spine with which he was thoroughly unfamiliar—fear.

"Make an excuse."

"They don't like excuses," protested his lawyer. "You know the types of people we're dealing with here."

"Make a *convincing* excuse," Bettencourt snapped.

"And with no further ado or apologies," said the speaker with a flourish. "President and CEO of Bettencorps, Charles Bettencourt!"

The crowd didn't applaud. They roared.

Bettencourt rose to his feet, his handsome face catching every ray from the expensive stage-lighting system. He flashed a white grin—not Hollywood white, but white enough to pop in press photos—and waved at the audience with one expansive flourish. Catching the eye of an attractive blonde in the front row, he winked, enjoying her reaction as she visibly blushed.

"I was a marine archaeology undergrad," he began. "Never mind that only about one in twenty of my cohort would even get a faculty position, and the rest of us would spend the rest of our lives selling life insurance and arguing about feudalism with all the other former humanities majors."

He knew exactly what to say, just the right mix of self-immolation and cruelty. Every word hurled right into the audience's ears to rattle around for a millisecond before being pumped out into their brains as *the next billion is yours*.

"So the US Navy had recently declassified a treasure trove of bathymetric data of the deep sea. I'm talking really deep, like two, sometimes three miles beneath the surface. My academic advisor was determined to suck all the grant money out of this great white elephant he could. He puts these old—and I mean old—printout data sheets through the computer, and the computer starts spitting out possible archaeological shipwreck targets. I mean, we had an entire storage locker of these rolled-up photo-paper printouts, so I'm stuck feeding these through the scanner for an entire summer.

"And then we find something, a great target. It's on the old Spanish treasure routes. We don't know much, but the computer says two important things. One—this target is made of wood. Two—this target is old. We had ourselves a mission.

"So the professor sets me on a two year circle-jerk, where I spend sixteen hours a day writing grant proposals, analyzing depth charts, scoping equipment, busting my ass to try to get an exploration mission on the water. We scrimp, save, steal, and borrow, and eventually put together about two and a half million dollars. By the way—who here has a bigger trust fund than that?"

Nervously looking at each other for approval and laughing, a number of the students in the back slowly raised their hands. Legacies—he loved them, one big fat slab of cocky around a tiny-weenie bit of insecurity, all of them. Like they had to get permission from their neighbor to be wealthy. *Wait for it. Here comes the punchline.*

"Keep those hands up, you rich fuckers. OK, next question. How many of you got that trust fund because your parents were archaeologists?"

Yeah, they were laughing now, especially the jacket-wearing, dinner-club legacies in the back.

"So we raise our two and a half million dollars, which, incidentally is peanuts money, and we book this ancient Ukrainian deep survey vessel and a couple of rusting Russian mini-subs and take them into the middle of the ocean. I get to be on one of the first dives to see this wreck. Naturally, I'm creaming my khakis for a chance to see this target, the deepest wooden shipwreck ever discovered. We launch this old submersible into the water. Takes five and a half hours to descend to the bottom of the ocean. We reach about 17,000 feet deep and start searching for our shipwreck site. Another three hours pass, batteries are already about halfway expended. It's like an alien world down there, rolling dunes of mud and silt, not much visibility, a bunch of weird fish all around, not that we cared about them. That's how narrow-minded I was. I was probably surrounded by species that had *never been discovered before* and may go extinct before they're ever classified, and I didn't give a shit because I was an archaeologist, and all that weird fish stuff was for biologists.

"After about three, three and a half hours of searching, eating nothing, breathing stale air and pissing into bottles, we see the shipwreck. It's like the greatest moment of my life, right? Like my first cigarette, my first lay, and my first time behind the wheel all in one, right?

"Let show you what I was looking at," he said, and clicked the massive projector on. It hummed for a moment and a grainy, low-resolution image flickered onto the screen. The audience strained to make out the foggy picture. It was still from one of those old analog magnetic tapes, bad quality made even worse by time. Squinting, one could sort of make out the curve of a rotten ship hull, green coppering and exposed nails from where the wood had been eaten away. Rum bottles and preserved coconuts spilled out of the bulging, disintegrating hull.

"Well, we found a ship's chronometer, a few gold and silver coins, a 'brace' of pistols—that means a pair, future MBAs—and a telescope. And a bunch of other junk, the historic equivalent of a Walmart delivery truck."

He clicked the remote rapid-fire, snapping through photos of all of the described artifacts in front of bland white backgrounds with tiny rulers for scale.

"I actually had all these artifacts tracked down and bought recently. When the invoice came in, I realized I'd spent more on a 1945 Chateau Mouton-Rothschild Jeroboam wine than I'd spent on the entire collection. At least I drank the wine with an excellent steak tartare. This shit just takes up wall space in the bathroom of my yacht."

Even Bettencourt couldn't help but chuckle at the laugh line, but the audience positively loved it.

"But none of that is important to my story," he continued. He clicked the projector off for dramatic effect. "The first thing I saw wasn't this three-hundred-year-old wreck. It was this—" He clicked the projector back on. The new image was an extreme close-up of the underside of the shipwreck's hull. A single modern-day aluminum can was nestled underneath the decaying wreck.

"That, my friends, is called intrusion. Some hapless jackass finished his soda and tossed it off the side of his fishing boat. It filled with water and fell three miles until it hit a three-hundred-year-old-wreck. Bull's-eye!"

The audience chuckled a little, but they held back. They couldn't tell where he was going with the story. Were they supposed to be dismayed at the sacrilege?

"Suddenly, it all made sense," he said. "There is nothing untouched by progress. That Pepsi can represented more accomplishment than I'd ever make as an archaeologist. Should that wreck be there in another hundred years, the archaeologists won't explore it. It will be explored by the industrialists, people like you and me, because it will be our machines that we build down there. The humanities are a true Darwinian dead-end; they do nothing for social progress. The Sistine Chapel may be old, but who cares? A static, moldering monument. Sure, it may be pretty— but I'd tear it down in a second to build a skyscraper. Give me industry, give me progress. In a thousand years nobody will remember the writers. Nobody will remember the philosophers, or the soldiers, or the doctors. They'll only remember the entrepreneurs. Those who build the future, not those who navel-gaze about the past."

He stopped for the reaction this time. Smile. Deep breath. He always loved the part where he got to Anconia Island, his crowning achievement.

He'd built a world free of bureaucratic interference, free of governmental taxation and confiscation, free of judicial malpractice and corruption, free of parasitic collectivism, and the thick, chafing ropes of anti-capitalistic leeches. His world, one of truly unleashed free enterprise, embodied by a glittering man-made island rising from the ocean. True creation, an act reserved for the gods alone.

Of course not every potential financier could understand the project, nor stomach the risks. Enter the Conglomerate.

Ah yes … the Conglomerate. An organization of a thousand shifting faces, shell corporations and nested subsidiaries, offshore bank accounts and untraceable assets.

Truth be told, Bettencourt knew only three things about the Conglomerate. First, they operated with total anonymity. Second, they had unimaginable quantities of money. And third, they were very serious. Serious in the *wake-up-dead* sense of the word.

He purposefully directed his mind away from his increasingly impatient backers to continue his blockbuster speech.

"Okay, everybody wants to know about the Anconia Island project, right? It's the culmination of everything that Bettencorps is about. You know we do tech manufacturing, we do contracting, subsidiaries, private security, blah, blah, blah. But what we really do is globalization. Products, talent, energy—anything that needs to be moved from one place to other. From supply to demand, it's really that simple. But what does that all have in common?"

He pursed his lips, allowing the question to linger on

the audience. *Energy?* Some of them whispered to each other. *Communication? Or maybe the information economy? That had to be it—*

"Security," he announced. "Security is the lynchpin, the prerequisite, the quintessential element to the structure of economy and existence."

He didn't wait for a reaction, just clicked the projector forward again. A grainy cell-phone video played, the lens wet with ocean spray. The shaking image showed a shivering, pale young man as he bled out onto the black carbon-fiber deck of a sleek experimental trimaran racing yacht.

"My name is Klea Ymeri," spoke a tinny voice through the projector's speaker. Her voice shook in time with the shaking of the camera—the voice came from the woman filming. The camera panned up, and the audience could now watch the experimental racer cutting through crashing waves on the open sea with dangerous speed. Too fast for the video compressor to keep up, the camera whipped around 180, spotting two grainy skiff speedboats in hot pursuit. Muzzle-flashes erupted from the closer speedboat, followed by the sharp crack of high-powered rifles. The camera hit the deck as splinters of carbon fiber cut through the air in sharp relief against the spray of the ocean. Suddenly, Klea's face occupied the entire camera frame— too close, too intimate for the silent audience. Though a pretty girl with short dark hair and a soft pale face, the look in her eyes brought the shocking intensity of the video to an uncomfortable level.

"My name is Klea Ymeri, aboard the vessel *Horizon*," she repeated with more urgency this time. "We're under attack at ten-mark-seventeen-mark-fifty-four north, fifty-six-mark-forty-seven-mark-twenty-one east. Kyle Harrison and Molly-Anne Ivanovich are dead. Colin White is badly wounded and I can't stop the bleeding. We won't be able to hold out long, they will overtake us in minutes. By their actions I do not believe they mean to take us alive. It will be over soon. Tell my family I love them."

The transmission ceased, leaving her terrified face frozen in the frame.

"Clever girl," mused Bettencourt. "Her presence of mind is amazing. This took place off the Horn of Africa, a few hundred miles from the failed nation-state formerly known as Somalia."

The audience murmured, not sure if he'd made a joke or not.

"She stuck the phone in an empty mayo jar," he explained. "Tossed it overboard. The US Navy traced the signal, found the phone. She's been missing and presumed dead for about four years now. That vessel? You may not remember, but the *Horizon* was an MIT project, an electric-biodiesel hybrid meant to set a round-the-world record.

"And the handsome young man bleeding to death in the first frame? He'd proposed to her the day the *Horizon* left port. They were going to have their engagement party the day they arrived in back in Bordeaux. Presence of mind, intelligence, bravery, and devotion … this means nothing if you don't have security.

"So we played this to the International Mercantile Shipping Association. Got us the first contract to secure the area with a private security force."

He let the crowd sit for a moment as he prepared to change the subject. Too easy. He could make them feel sadness just as quickly as ecstasy, fear as quickly as hope.

"Think these pirates respect international waters?

Hospital ships? Missions of mercy or exploration? No, they respect force. A borderless world, that's where we're headed," he mused.

"What about territorial integrity? The rights of the indigenous peoples?" shouted a female voice from the audience. Bettencourt snapped around, but couldn't identify the source of the interruption. He smiled.

"Sister, the automobile was tough on the carriage industry."

"What about quality of life? Raising social standards?" she shouted back. Ah, yes—the attractive brunette near the back. Why did the activist types always wear glasses?

"I love this topic," he shouted. "Let's pretend we focus on social justice nonsense. Bettencorp's medical subsidiaries start paying their janitors enough to drive a Cadillac and retire at fifty-three. Guess what? We just made less profit. That means less investment. That means we don't come up with a new cancer treatment. We don't add the next drug to the AIDS cocktail. But at least you feel good about it because our low-level staff drive caddies they didn't earn."

"But—"

"One more word from you, young woman," he said, pointing. "And I'm going to have to hire you. Then you'll really be in trouble. Look, you're also entitled to believe the world is flat."

Wait for it—line it up—get ready to take that swing—

"And when you make your first billion, I'll let you debate me all afternoon." He shrugged at the chuckles and flipped to the next slide, the big reveal. It was a beautiful shot of open ocean with a massive city rising up out of the water like the lost civilization of Atlantis. He'd paid top dollar for the shot, flown the film crew out from Tokyo, put them on a top-of-the-line helicopter with a gyroscopically stabilized camera mount and high-definition video system. Light glinted off the ocean waves like rolling gold. It was, in a word, perfect.

Bettencourt spoke as the camera rotated around the oceanic megatropolis.

"This is Anconia Island. Started initially out of the security concerns we talked about earlier. The goal was to have a stable, permanent presence off the Horn of Africa—one that could provide economic opportunity, private security, and a workforce free of national interests. These structural underpinnings were actually three different massive oil-drilling platforms at one point, all scheduled for decommission. We dry-docked them in the South Pacific, decontaminated everything, stripped all the equipment off and built these office-building and condominium-style high-rises.

"Don't let the glass fool you, these are built for tsunamis, lightning strike, even a class-four typhoon. Each building has a specialized function. We have our own greenhouse and hydroponics gardens. We have deep-water portage and a jet-rated floating runway. We've already developed plans to expand that runway to accommodate passenger aircraft. Communication to the outside world is handled by a dedicated communication satellite, capable of supporting sustained traffic of 800 megabytes per second *per terminal*—that's right, per terminal. That's a must-have, considering that the population of Anconia is now approaching 3,000 souls. This includes a large contingent of IT personnel supporting Fortune 500 companies nationwide, including offshore software development, banking and data-storage. All of this in a non-extradition, non-national, untaxed environment where nobody can be involuntarily subpoenaed. We sublet fully forty percent of our facilities to like-minded corporate interests, and we intend to double the size of Anconia Island every five years for the next two decades.

"Anconia Island is already a shining beacon of security and prosperity for a lawless region. The local Somalis are a little slow to get on board, given a complex combination of political and cultural factors. But Bettencorps has a standing invitation to the Somali people. If you remember nothing else, remember this—we want them to be a primary beneficiary of this great endeavor. We intend to train them, we intend to employ them, and unlike the UN and their revolving-regime neighbors, we're in the region to stay. Already we've set forth several strategic alliances with the local powers and engaged in some of the first sustained economic development in Somalia in more than a decade.

"I have a vision," he said. "I want masses of Somali professionals commuting to Anconia Island for extended rotations. I want satellite facilities on the Somali mainland. I want white-collar workers, blue-collar workers, green-collar workers. I believe the people of the Horn of Africa are the single largest, untapped economic resource on the planet and they're just waiting to be unleashed on the world."

Time for the big wrap-up. He had them all, every single wide-eyed student.

"And here's why I think this. You want to leave an impact on the world? Don't write a textbook; invest in a company you believe in. Don't graduate and become a literary critic; quit school and start a business. Don't be an academic; be an entrepreneur. You, quite literally, own the future. And the only type of progress is economic progress."

Cheers streamed from the audience, and he raised both hands in triumph. He wouldn't be taking any questions, not today.

"Thank you everybody!" he shouted. And with that, Charles Bettencourt took three steps down to the auditorium floor. The pressing crowd surrounded him, massing together to try and get an up-close look, a handshake, the chance to shout a too-brief question.

A tiny, unwelcome thought crept into the back of his mind. Unknown to the enthralled crowd, the success of Anconia was far from assured. The glittering skyscrapers atop the island were still less than half occupied and the entire project painfully over-budget. To make matters worse, the Conglomerate had begun to demand certain … concessions.

An attractive young woman—a blonde? No, there were too many people for him to get a good look—pressed her entire soft hand into the immaculate woolen pocket of his tailored designer suit. She left something small and crisp behind as she withdrew her hand, no doubt a phone number.

Through the questions, the handshakes, the congratulations and the half-joking job requests, Charles couldn't help but notice that nobody asked him what the local Somalis called Anconia Island.

They called it the Death Star.

CHAPTER 4

Inky-blue waters lapped against seawalls and along the length of the city's largest dock. Glittering like a jewel in the warm Mediterranean night, the perpetually lit skyline of the grand harbor of Valletta, Malta was an ancient collection of baroque steeples and domes coupled with a rarified concentration of affluence few harbors could boast. Preparations for the Rolex-sponsored yacht race were in full swing, and the dock, wide as a three-lane highway, held the parked Bentleys and Maybachs of old money, the Ferraris and McLaurens of the more ostentatious. Each flashy supercar lay parked beside the long gangplanks before a line of custom-built megayachts. They were of every construction, flagged from Paris, Dubai, New York, Sydney, Tokyo, London, Shanghai, Venice and other far-flung centers of power.

High-speed police zodiacs patrolled the harbor while bulky, humorless security officers paced the dock, discrete submachine guns folded under expensive suit jackets. Submerged lights illuminated the dark waters below, lighting the massive white-hulled queens from beneath. The dock was peaceful, quiet, and still. A few of the older guests had gone to bed, as well as a few of the early risers and the jetlagged. Though already two hours past midnight, the majority of the revelers had not returned with their entourages from an exclusive party at the extravagant city-center Hotel Phoenicia.

The crown jewel of the collected ships gently rocked at the end of the long dock, as if every other yacht were but a court valet, and this the empress herself. Sleek lines suggested a vastly different intent of construction than the other bulbous, glitzy cruisers that surrounded it. This was not just any plaything of the ultra-wealthy; this was the *Conqueror*, the fastest superyacht ever constructed, a coiled spring, a loaded .357 magnum with a hair trigger. Her sleek 140-foot carbon fiber underhull gently rose and fell with the lapping waves, the moonlight glinting off the laminated strands of ultra-strong synthetics. The skin hid a true technical marvel of exactingly designed structural honeycombing, and her upper works were constructed of high-quality aluminum and ceramic composite, interrupted only by blacked-out lightweight privacy glass. Even while docked, her lines whispered sweet nothings of speed, a barely restrained surging velocity.

Clad in black diving gear, Dr. Nassiri concealed himself behind a rock jetty two hundred meters from the long dock. Jonah treaded water beside him, fussing over last-minute adjustments to the doctor's buoyancy compensation vest.

"I told you I'd never scuba dived before," Dr. Nassiri said.

"Yeah, well I figured you'd at least be able to put your flippers on the right feet," Jonah said.

"Are you quite, quite certain no charter vessels will work for our mission?" Dr. Nassiri tried, but failed to conceal his anxiety.

"The *Conqueror* is the only ship in Malta that can outrun pirates," said Jonah. "If I wanted to get myself shot, I would have gotten it over with in prison and saved myself a trip across the desert in a body bag."

"So it must be the *Conqueror*?" repeated Dr. Nassiri.

"She's a thoroughbred," said Jonah. "She's got twin Purcell engines and a TF80 diesel turbine making over 20,000 horsepower. She tops 80 knots at full speed, and the only thing faster on water is a US nuclear submarine. If the pirates catch us in that, we deserve to be caught. We need her ... and she ain't for sale."

"She looks as if she could outrun a fighter jet," admitted Dr. Nassiri, admiring the yacht from the distance.

A third diver surfaced in a wreath of bubbles. Youssef "Buzz" Nassiri, the doctor's cousin, dropped the regulator out of his mouth.

"You pussies ready?" asked Buzz, glaring at Jonah.

Buzz, simply put, was a bully. He'd been a bully since he and the doctor were children, and would probably always be one. But if there was a place for bullies in this world, stealing a yacht likely was it.

Jonah ignored him, but Dr. Nassiri popped in his regulator and nodded. Just remember to breathe, he reminded himself.

The trio slipped beneath the waves, following Jonah. The American seemed even more comfortable beneath the waves than he did above, allowing himself long, lazy kicks, propelling himself forward with minimal effort. By comparison, Dr. Nassiri clawed and kicked at the water, trying to maintain his balance as he followed, dragging a large mesh dive-bag behind him.

Jonah did a long, slow barrel roll, turning belly-up to

look at the surface, then flipped back again. Buzz followed closely, too closely, and Jonah aimed a sharp kick at his head, nearly knocking his facemask off.

Buzz waved his middle finger at Jonah, who shrugged in return and pretended the kick was an accident.

The underwater illumination nearest to the stern of the *Conqueror* flickered as the trio approached from just under the surface. Small bubbles drifted upwards through the shallow water, silently breaking as they surfaced. Jonah's neoprene-encased hand stealthily emerged from the water, grasping the polished aluminum handrail to the stern sundeck. The wetsuit-clad American cautiously raised his head just above water. From below, Dr. Nassiri watched as Jonah pushed himself belly first onto the fine-grained teakwood deck and peeled back his wet goggles. The doctor following closely behind him.

The doctor's pulse pounded, unpleasant quantities of adrenaline coursing through his system. He was jittery, paranoid. Strange to think his career depended on his ability to make snap decisions, to stay cool and dispassionate, and to operate with a steady hand on even the most traumatically injured patients, and yet stealing a boat unnerved him so completely.

It's the rules, he thought. He'd always been the type of person who understood and adhered to the rules. It's what made him successful. It's what gave him comfort. As a surgeon, he could inadvertently allow a patient to die, abysmally fail at the repair of a wound or the removal of a tumor. But that was still within the rules. Stealing wasn't.

After taking a moment to see if anyone had noticed his incursion, Jonah Blackwell wriggled free of his bulky air tanks and buoyancy-compensation vest, securing them in a hidden compartment underneath the deck and out of sight. He pulled a plastic Ziplock bag from his weight belt, and noiselessly dropped the lead weights onto the deck.

Wasting no time, Jonah tore open the bag, letting the squared-off polymer composite pistol inside tumble into his dominant hand. He pulled back the slide, racking a .40 caliber round into the chamber. It was a debate giving him the gun—not a debate Jonah was party to, but a debate nonetheless.

Youssef emerged from the water. Bracing his feet, Jonah reached into the water with his left hand and gripped Buzz's forearm, pulling him onto the low deck. With more flash than necessary, Buzz rolled onto the deck, theatrically covering possible ambush points with an amphibious-modified Soviet-era bullpup rifle, complete with an integrated grenade launcher.

What a joke, Jonah had whispered to Dr. Nassiri when Buzz first proudly revealed his new toy. *Is your cousin expecting underwater frogmen?* Grenades for that piece of junk rifle hadn't been manufactured since the Reagan administration.

Jonah had taken a disliking to Dr. Nassiri's cousin from the moment they'd been introduced, despite the doctor's glowing introduction. Buzz was ex-special forces, trained by Americans for Moroccan internal anti-terrorism and counter-insurgency operations. A real hardass, as Jonah might say.

When he'd first met Jonah, Buzz didn't even acknowledge the American, just gave Jonah an icy *so-this-is-the-fucking-prisoner* look that would have not been out of place at an all-girls prep school.

Buzz stripped his neoprene hood and shed his tanks

onto the slipway. He was built like his gun, squat and ugly, with almost as many scars. He'd shaved his head that morning and glared at Jonah with open malevolence, anger flashing behind his dark brown eyes.

"You fucking stupid or something?" Buzz demanded with a whisper. "I told you I was first on deck. You going to clear rooms with that plastic peashooter, you deaf Yankee fuck?"

Jonah replied with a masturbatory gesture.

"I don't have fucking time for this," said Buzz. He shouldered the weapon and disappeared into the main cabin.

Dr. Nassiri shrugged off his equipment. He felt quite relieved that the underwater portion of this particular plan had come to an end, despite the fact that the dangerous phase had not even yet begun.

The doctor's large mesh diving grab bag was stuffed with two bulky shrink-wrapped cubes. While Jonah raised his head over the deck to spy on the guards, Dr. Nassiri slung the bag over his shoulder and ascended the boarding ladder and off the slipway.

Leaving the doctor behind, Jonah crept the exterior length of the ship holding a titanium dive knife, slipping the razor-sharp blade through one mooring line after another. By the time he'd reached the final thick nylon line, the massive yacht had already begun to pivot away from the dock, carried out into the harbor by the receding tide. Buzz silently joined Jonah at the bow, the best vantage point to the dock and still-inert patrol boats. Buzz gave Jonah a curt nod and took up a position, intending to stay there. Jonah shook his head in irritation.

Automatic sliding glass doors silently opened in front of Jonah. Just inside the foyer, Dr. Nassiri stashed the mesh duffle underneath a curio table and unwrapped his black Beretta. Jonah and the doctor covered each other as they moved on tiptoes across the colored marble floor of the foyer, leaving behind splotchy wet footprints.

Passing between twin faux Greek columns, they entered into the salon, scanning the dark burlwood fixtures for signs of occupancy. They passed beside the chef's kitchen, then descended the stairs to the four unoccupied staterooms and the locked crew cabins. The owner, infamous for his all-night parties, had not yet returned. Jonah cracked the door to the crew cabin then closed it again.

Stepping into the engine room was like stepping into a space station. The compartment reserved for the massive turbine engines dwarfed every other cabin within the entirety of the vessel. It was truly the beating heart of a beautiful mechanical organism. The turbine system required endless rolls of neatly secured insulation, and a bank of computers were set aside to monitor system statistics and operations. Dr. Nassiri imagined that even at a comfortable cruising speed, the *Conqueror* was designed to inhale a prodigious amount of expensive high-octane fuel. Unlike the sumptuous old-world tones of the rest of the yacht, this room was pure tech.

"I have to credit the owner for this marvel," said Dr. Nassiri.

"Yeah, but can't say I feel much guilt for stealing it," mused Jonah.

The doctor agreed. That morning at their hotel, he'd done a little investigating on his own. The *Conqueror*'s owner was a retired CEO, one of the pioneers in the practice of chopping up subprime mortgages and selling them for cheap, tanking the American economy, and nearly taking down the world with it. Still, his taste in yachting could not be denied.

Jonah stripped off his hood to reveal a sharp face, newly cut short hair, and a closely trimmed blonde beard to top his tall but still-thin, muscled frame.

"Last chance to call it off, Doc," he said. "Ditch the guns, jump overboard, and we haven't done anything that can't be walked back with a sincere apology and a good lawyer."

"Thank you for the consideration, Mr. Blackwell," Dr. Nassiri said with a grim smile. "But my commitment to see this through remains unchanged." He stripped off his hood as well, revealing tussled black hair that framed his dark eyes and classically handsome features.

"We're stealing a yacht together," Jonah said with a laugh, slapping the doctor on the back. "If that doesn't put us on a first-name basis, I don't know what will. Call me Jonah."

"I suppose it goes without saying that I have much more to lose than you," Dr. Nassiri said, intentionally refusing the familiarity.

"If you say so."

Dr. Nassiri had known full well that his mission would likely require some bending of the rules, but he hadn't truly come to terms with the magnitude of the criminality until he had slipped into his wetsuit and slid into the dark Mediterranean Sea. Since removing Jonah from Prison 14, the doctor had come to realize that the American was the type who figured any problem that couldn't be solved with a sledgehammer, could be solved with two sledgehammers or a roll of det cord. Dr. Nassiri knew Jonah wasn't a criminal, not in the traditional sense, but despite his protests, Jonah appeared quite comfortable with the criminality at hand. And the more at ease Jonah was, the more Dr. Nassiri ached to get the whole thing over with, salvage what he could of his mother's research, find her body, and take her home. And then to return to his real life.

The doctor busied himself with his duffel, removing two massive cubes of shrink-wrapped euros. Jonah looked over his shoulder as the doctor handled the 500-euro notes, the chosen vehicle of international financial smugglers. The sum total of the Nassiri family fortune and a decade of savings, it amounted to more than a million euros.

A strange enterprise, this, thought Dr. Nassiri. Stealing a yacht while bringing enough money to charter one free and clear.

"See something you like, Mr. Blackwell?" asked the doctor, feeling Jonah's eyes on his money.

"Yeah, I'm looking at your money."

"It'd be easy," said Dr. Nassiri. "You have me dead to rights with that German pistol of yours. You could end this fool's errand right now."

"Don't tempt me. And the story about your mom better not be bullshit."

The doctor sighed and stood up. Jonah followed him to the bridge, both abandoning the money in the center of the foyer.

"Go secure that cash," said Jonah. "I think it's in everyone's best interest if it's not just laying around. Oh, and your cousin? I think he's going to be butthurt if he doesn't get the chance to blow someone away."

"Don't worry about Youssef," said Dr. Nassiri. He stuffed the Euros back in the duffel and slung it over his shoulder. "I remind you that he can handle himself, thank you."

The doctor followed as Jonah led the way back up to the bridge. He was not disappointed in the layout of the command compartment—three leather bound racing seats, futuristic joysticks, monitors, and control panels surrounded by steep-angled windows, none of which would have been out of place on a sci-fi movie set.

Dr. Nassiri knocked on one of the side windows, getting Buzz's attention, who then relinquished his position on deck and entered through a side door.

"We're drifting away from the dock," said Buzz. "It's time to deal with the crew." With that pronouncement, Buzz chambered a round to his ridiculous assault rifle for effect. Jonah scowled, and Dr. Nassiri joined him in the displeasure. The doctor didn't like the idea of killing anyone, and certainly not over a yacht.

"Cousin Hassan, you take a position on the bridge," said Buzz. "Blackwell and I will take the crew quarters one at a time. He'll cover the door while I subdue and zip tie the crew. We're outnumbered here—so don't take shit. Somebody yells, somebody resists, put them down quick, move on."

Jonah stopped paying attention and began scanning the lengthy control board, brushing against the custom-milled aluminum buttons with outstretched fingers.

"Now after we take the first room, some of them may get wise and—Blackwell, am I fucking boring you here?"

There it was—the American had found whatever he'd been looking for. Jonah cleared his throat and pressed a shipwide intercom.

"Captain to the bridge, Captain to the bridge," said Jonah into the intercom.

"Are you fucking insane?" snarled Buzz.

"What are you doing?" demanded Dr. Nassiri, horrified. This was the moment he'd dreaded—the moment when Jonah Blackwell betrayed them. It was too perfect. Dr. Nassiri kicked himself, realizing he'd allowed Jonah to set up every aspect of the operation.

"Chill out," said Jonah. "Especially you, Buzz. Go stand in the corner and put your rifle away, you're embarrassing yourself. Just stand there and look scary or something. And for fucks sake, lower that muzzle and don't shoot anybody."

Dr. Nassiri was too baffled to even react. Realizing he was now bound to Jonah's plan, Buzz angrily lowered his assault rifle.

Jonah leaned across the control panels and picked up a pair of Leica binoculars from the dash. Looking out, it appeared that the tide was pulling them out to sea faster than he'd expected. They were now nearly a hundred and fifty meters from the dock. Security personnel milled around the empty berth, confused. Some of them waved or radioed to the patrol boats, but there was no coordination and the zodiacs had not yet mobilized after the drifting yacht.

Footsteps sounded from behind the trio. Jonah lingered on the binoculars for a few extra moments before putting them down and turning around. A befuddled captain stood in the entrance to the yacht's bridge wearing a white terrycloth robe. His charge adrift and his bridge occupied by wetsuit-clad strangers had temporarily paralyzed his faculties. The white-bearded captain stood still at first, silent, before composing himself just enough to demand answers.

"What is this?" he shouted. "Who are you people?"

Jonah plastered a giant smile on his face and walked up to the captain.

"We're from Global Repossession," said Jonah, openly grinning as he gave the bullshit story. "So nice to meet you, Captain … ?"

"Robinson."

"Captain Robinson, a real pleasure. Always wish it was under different circumstances. I'm Jonah Blackwell, and I'd like to introduce you to my team, Hassan and Youssef Nassiri, the two gentlemen behind me."

Jonah snuck a glance to see how the doctor and his cousin would react to the use of their real names. He was not disappointed; Dr. Nassiri's was rigid with utter horror and Buzz looked angry enough to snap Jonah in half where he stood.

"Now I don't know if you're in the loop on this," continued Jonah, "but the owner of this vessel is about eight months behind on payments, forcing the Royal Bahamian Bank to issue a repossession order. They subcontracted the job to Global Repossession, my employer."

"But—" sputtered the captain.

"Nobody told you? Well, I'm afraid that's more the rule than the exception, captain. As I'm sure you're aware, once I've taken position on the bridge with a valid repossession order, I've established mastership of this vessel."

"This cannot—"

"I think you'll find all the paperwork in order," said Jonah. He reached inside his wetsuit and produced a thick stack of soggy, dripping, illegible paperwork and slapped it on the chart table. The captain looked as if he'd just been handed a soiled diaper. He grimaced as he picked at the water-soaked documents with two pinched fingers.

"All is in order?" asked the captain, reluctant to examine the documents himself.

"Subcontracting agreement, mastership order, ship's papers with updated ownership and licensing documentation, the works," answered Jonah.

"Well …," Captain Robinson said, begrudgingly resigning himself to the inevitable.

"The good news—well, not good news for the owner, but good news for you—is that the Royal Bahamian Bank has already found a potential buyer out of Dubai. This goes down smoothly and there's a good chance you'll be retaining this post. If you're interested, of course."

"I suppose—"

"But short-term, we've got a situation to deal with. I need the crew dressed and at muster stations in five minutes. I need everybody on the ships' launch and back in Malta. I'll take the *Conqueror* to Gibraltar to work out the last of the paperwork. Hopefully we can smooth things out to fly the crew there to meet the new owners. Sound like a plan?"

The captain crossed his arms, uncrossed them, and crossed them again.

"It's your bridge, Captain," said Jonah. He saluted the captain, standing at attention, waiting for him to act. Dr. Nassiri and Buzz awkwardly followed, botching the salutes in their haste. Jonah quickly motioned for the cousins to put their hands down. Dr. Nassiri complied, embarrassed.

The captain sighed, adjusted his terrycloth robe, and stepped up to the control panel. The moment his back was turned, Jonah rested his palm on the pistol. Dr. Nassiri had the distinct impression the American was ready to club the captain should he raise an alarm.

The captain stepped up to the intercom, switched the knob to general broadcast.

"Crew of the *Conqueror*, crew of the *Conqueror*, this is a general alarm," he began.

Jonah silently unholstered the pistol, preparing for the unexpected. He hesitated, waiting to hear the captain's next words.

"Please muster at the rear launch. Wear your emergency gear and bring all personal effects and medications necessary for the next seventy-two hours."

Jonah reholstered and concealed the gun, both he and Dr. Nassiri sighing in relief. Buzz still looked like he could pop a blood vessel.

"Sorry I can't allow you to pack larger bags," said Jonah. "Can't have the crew taking the silverware, can we? I promise we'll catalog everything and get it to the owners. I will personally supervise the process to make sure it gets done right."

"This isn't the first yacht I've had repossessed from underneath me," said the captain. "I understand you can't just have us walk away with all the table settings and artwork."

"Well, maybe a few spoons," cracked Jonah. Both he and the captain shared a congenial laugh.

The captain exited the bridge and went below. Jonah and Dr. Nassiri looked at each other.

"So you think he believes it?" whispered Dr. Nassiri.

"As long as he doesn't look too closely at the documents I gave him," mumbled Jonah. "Stay on the bridge. I'm going to supervise the exit of the crew."

On the rear deck, the well-trained crew collected by the ship's single launch boat. Several stewards, two cooks, the engineer, and officers prepped the craft for deployment. The vessel would be crowded but serviceable. Twenty-two feet of carbon fiber and polished aluminum, she was custom-designed to complement her mothership. The crew of the *Conqueror* boarded and Jonah began the automated launch sequence. Two large winches slowly rose from their hidden compartments in the deck, lowering the lifeboat over the side and into the ocean by two thin woven-steel cables.

The now-former captain of the *Conqueror* unrolled the soggy documents into his hands and absentmindedly examined them. He started slowly at first, and then rapidly, angrily shuffled through the papers.

"These … these … are *menus!*" he shouted at Jonah from across the narrow chasm.

Jonah pressed the emergency release and the tender dropped the last four and a half feet into the waves, knocking every crewman to the deck as the launch splashed down in the ocean. Jonah sprinted back to the bridge, took the center console and began the engine startup sequence.

"That was somewhat brilliant," said Dr. Nassiri grudgingly as he took the chair to Jonah's left.

"Yeah, never steal something with a gun that you can steal with paperwork," said Jonah. "Buzz, how are we doing here?"

Buzz peered through the Leica binoculars and looked at the dock. "It's getting busy," he said. "A yellow Lamborghini has arrived at the *Conqueror*'s berth. Looks like the driver is doing a lot of pointing and shouting."

"That would be the owner," said Jonah. "He always had a thing for Italian supercars. And shouting."

Dr. Nassiri picked up a second pair of binoculars and took a look for himself. "Is he supposed to be that orange?"

he asked, referring to the former CEO's obnoxious fake tan.

"You're the doctor, you tell me."

"Security personnel are boarding the patrol boats," said Dr. Nassiri. "I believe it is likely that the captain has radioed for assistance."

"We're running out of time," added Buzz with a snarl. "This wouldn't be a problem if they were all zip tied below decks."

"Still not a problem," said Jonah. "I just have to bypass the security lockout." His fingers danced across the console, pulling up systems schematics across the screens. "Too bad … I really wanted to see the expression on his face when I stole his boat."

"I assure you, its quite apoplectic," said Dr. Nassiri dryly. Neither one of the Nassiri cousins could tear their eyes away from the binoculars and the mobilizing security forces.

The engines sputtered, turned over, and stopped.

"Shit," said Jonah. The computer had locked him out again and automatically cut the engines. He tried pushing through another subroutine, searching for a back door into the core systems.

"We are now dangerously low on time," said Dr. Nassiri. "Are you certain you can do this?"

"I can do this," said Jonah through gritted teeth. There it was—the software back door. The console in front of him lit up like a Christmas tree, a thousand individual indicator lights flicking to life at once. The engines roared, nearly knocking Buzz over as the entire yacht jolted forward. Jonah throttled up, breathing life into the massive machine. She was a thing of beauty, surging forward, slowly at first, the powerful engines kicking out a churning wake almost as long as the ship herself. The patrol boats were blinded by the spray, knocking into one another behind the speeding yacht.

Dr. Nassiri clapped a hand on Jonah's back, smiling with the pure pleasure of escape and success—and relief. Jonah couldn't help himself. With his hand on the tiller of the most beautiful ship he'd ever had the pleasure of stealing, he grinned from ear to ear.

The indicators passed fifty knots, then sixty, before topping out almost to eighty. Even the untrained ear could hear the engines singing in beautiful harmony and rhythm, perfectly tuned, precisely attenuated for the task at hand. The howling engines drowned out all else but the starry night sky as Malta disappeared behind them.

"So tell me, what did you have against her previous owner?" asked the doctor.

"That's a story for another day," answered Jonah.

CHAPTER 5

Dr. Nassiri hung from the back deck of the *Conqueror* on an improvised climber's harness, swaying as the ship cut through the tranquil blue waters of the eastern Mediterranean. He leaned back, bracing his feet against the stern, closing his eyes as he allowed his face to soak up the sunlight. A bundle of steel wool swung from a string, attached to his belt loop. Combined with a carefully applied series of caustic chemicals, he'd found the wool more than adequate in removing the namesake *Conqueror* from the stern of the yacht. The next task was infinitely more pleasing, painting a new name with a set of artist's oils.

Despite the rocking of the yacht, he found his surgeon's hand well equipped for the task. Shirtless, he moved with the waves as he held the rope with one hand and painted with the other, using the inside of his free forearm to dab off drips from the brush. He hadn't painted anything in years, despite the deeply loved pastime. Appropriate for a surgeon, he preferred nudes from life, his brush deliberately reproducing the human beauty of anatomical musculature.

Jonah and Youssef were in another section of the ship,

disguising it further for the eventual passage through the Suez Canal. The labor required whiting out an entire row of glass windows with thick marine paint, removing distinctive superstructure indicators and disabling the marine transponder. Between the disguise and false paperwork, Jonah believed they'd have the cover necessary to pass through the Suez Canal and into the Indian Ocean.

When Dr. Nassiri expressed his concerns, Jonah said it would have worked a couple of years ago. He couldn't say for certain now.

"The worst they can do is throw us in prison," Jonah had said, laughing. "Status quo for me."

It was then that Dr. Nassiri decided he'd rename the megayacht *Fool's Errand*. Maddeningly, Jonah's alpha-male swagger actually worked on Youssef. The soldier started following the disagreeable American around like a lost puppy. Youssef delighted in the fact that Jonah actually called him "Buzz," a nickname first given to his cousin by an American training officer.

Dr. Nassiri found the nickname deeply shameful to his family, an affront to both his culture and his cousin's dignity. The nickname had not been ordained with affection. Youssef earned it during a morning engagement drill when, returning from a piss, he'd managed to entangle a rat's nest of pubic hair into the zipper of his combat trousers. The resulting yelp had alerted opponents to his team's position, losing the exercise and earning him a vicious beating by his own team. Both ailments sent him to the infirmary, whereupon the American training officer took one look and dryly told him to "buzz that shit," to prevent a reoccurrence.

A series of ringing shotgun blasts rattled Dr. Nassiri's thoughts, shaking him out of his gloomy reflection. He froze.

Several more shots from the bow. Then, another sound entirely—could it be laughter?

Dr. Nassiri pulled himself away from the incomplete project and scaled the ladder up to the rear deck. He smelled the thick, acrid scent of expensive cigars. Walking up the exterior passage past the bridge, his eyes first fell onto a blanket laid out on the bow deck, covered corner to corner with a wide assortment of antique weaponry and ammunition. A pearl-handled Colt 1911 lay next to several Remington shotguns, .38 snub noses and two fully-automatic Thompson machine guns straight out of a 1930s Chicago gangster movie.

Youssef and Jonah ignored him. Jonah balanced a drum-magazine Thompson machine gun in his hands, practicing shouldering and lowering it while Youssef rooted through a crate of expensive wines and liquors, looking for an appropriate vintage.

"Pull, motherfucker!" shouted Jonah to Youssef.

Youssef laughed and grabbed a bottle of Bollinger Blac de Noisrs Vieilles 1997. He leaned back and hurled it like a Molotov cocktail. It spun through the air beautifully as Jonah opened fire, sending up arcing lines of bullets after the spinning bottle. Dr. Nassiri plugged his ears, and on the third burst of bullets, Jonah finally caught a bottom corner of the bottle, exploding the $10,000 champagne in a shower of white foam and green glass.

Dr. Nassiri glanced over the spread. In case the hooligans ran out of bottles before bullets, Youssef had helpfully gathered a large pile of silver serving dishes.

Dr. Nassiri loudly cleared his throat, and then again. Nothing. Neither of the shooters wore any kind of ear protection, they simply hadn't heard him. In frustration,

Dr. Nassiri kicked the pile of silver, and it clattered to the deck. Jonah and Youssef whipped around to face the doctor.

"I do hope you are not intoxicated," said Dr. Nassiri in the most openly patronizing tone he could muster.

"Join us—have a stogie," said Jonah, waving the acrid cigar in the doctor's face.

"What if we are discovered?" said Dr. Nassiri.

"We won't be," stated Jonah. "They'll think we're getting it chopped in Sicily or Algeria. End of story. That's where yachts go when they disappear in the Mediterranean."

Dr. Nassiri frowned, turned and walked away in a huff. It wasn't long before the gunfire resumed.

Solace wasn't hard to come by on the *Fool's Errand*. Dr. Nassiri found a fresh linen suit in one of the crew compartments. Alone on the bridge while enjoying a sparkling water, he amused himself by watching the tiny green blips travel on the radar screen. The gunshots subsided when Youssef and Jonah finally lost interest. Youssef snuck off to nap or loot and Jonah began pacing the entire length of the ship, as if the sheer openness of the vessel were the most pleasurable thing in the world.

The bridge door slid open behind him, but Dr. Nassiri didn't bother to look up as Jonah slumped into one of the racing chairs beside him. The American had his index finger curled around a plastic ring of an inexpensive six-pack. By the look of things, he was on his second. Dr. Nassiri silently questioned the choice given the king's ransom of top-shelf wine and liquors for the taking.

"Must you?" he asked.

"What?" said Jonah. "It's just beer. I'm not getting fucked up."

Dr. Nassiri grunted his continuing disapproval.

"You want one?"

"No."

"You observant?" asked Jonah.

"Not especially."

Both men allowed silence to linger between them.

"Why are we doing this, Doc?" asked Jonah. "I've got to say, I've worked a lot of recoveries. We know your mother is dead. That's not a mystery. And I hate to say it, but body recoveries are ugly business. You're probably not going to want to see what I pull up."

"I've seen bodies before."

"This is your mom we're talking about."

"You needn't spare me."

Jonah frowned.

"Why are we doing this, Doc?" the American repeated. "Islam considers burial at sea consecrated; we're not putting her spirit at rest by disturbing her grave."

"Mr. Blackwell, we are not here to put her spirit at rest. You mistake the priorities of my intentions."

"So correct me," said Jonah. He stifled a small belch.

"Some days previous to her disappearance, my mother contacted me. She said she'd found traces of something terrible in the Horn of Africa, something that changed her understanding of the region. It was a discovery that would be vital to oceanographic research for a generation, a discovery with global consequences. She would not tell me what it was."

"And then she vanished."

"That's right. And then she went missing. I must complete her—"

Jonah waved him silent with a hand and leaned forward in the racing chair to scowl at an instrumentation panel.

"What's wrong?"

"Hold that thought," said Jonah.

The doctor realized the American wasn't meaning to be rude, something was happening. Jonah flipped between a series of menus, continuing to scowl.

"We may have a problem," Jonah said. "Somebody is messing with the fuel/air mixture of the engines."

"Sabotage?" asked Dr. Nassiri.

"That's the strange thing; I really don't think so. They're messing with the parameters, but if I'm reading this correctly, they're improving engine efficiency at cruising speed. This is definitely not a latent script running under computer control. This is a person."

"Could it be Youssef?"

"If it's Buzz, I'm feeding him to the sharks. But does tuning the fuel/air mixture really sound like your moron cousin?"

"No," admitted Dr. Nassiri. "No, it does not."

Beers in one hand, pistol in the other, Jonah stood up. Dr. Nassiri chambered a round and prepared to follow him.

"Should we get Youssef?" asked Dr. Nassiri.

"Not enough time. Besides, I'd rather not have anyone get shot. I want to find out what's going on first."

Dr. Nassiri nodded and allowed Jonah to take the lead down to the engine room.

Jonah opened the heavy metal fire door to the engine compartment and locked it open. Pistols in hand, both men slowly made their way into the chamber. Jonah stopped at the first intersection of gangplanks and ducked his head around the corner towards a row of computer servers. He pulled back, frowned, and tucked his pistol behind his waistband.

"You'd better take a look at this," whispered Jonah.

Dr. Nassiri peeked around the corner. With a laptop resting on long tan legs, a young blonde woman sat cross-legged on the steel-grate floor next to the computer servers, trendy headphones over her ears, bobbing her head to an unheard beat. She was totally oblivious to the two baffled men watching her. Dr. Nassiri fought back an urge to straighten his shirt, run a hand through his thick black hair, anything that might make a difference in her first impression of him.

"Excuse me," said Jonah, then repeated himself a little louder.

Still nothing. Six-pack in hand, Jonah waved both arms until her peripheral vision caught the motion. Startled, she yanked off her headphones and looked up.

"Um, hey," she said, with the slight twang of a Texan accent.

"Hey, yourself," said Jonah.

She stared at the two men for a moment. The compartment was silent except for the low humming of the engines. Dr. Nassiri cleared his throat. He wanted to say something, but all he could think about was her freckles, blonde hair, those long legs disappearing into short shorts—

"You need something?" she finally asked. "Usually Frank does the tours. I'm kind of in the middle of something, but I'm almost done."

"Who's Frank?" asked Jonah.

"Frank, the chief engineer?" she answered. "I'm Assistant Engineer Andrews. Frank usually does the engine compartment tours. So how was the big shindig last night?"

"It was a nice distraction," said Dr. Nassiri dryly. He found it difficult to imagine how she'd missed all the commotion of the previous night. And yet, here she was.

Jonah snorted, trying to fight down laughter at the doctor's wry comment.

"I hear a lot of stories about those fancy parties," said Andrews. "I'd love-love-love to attend one someday, but they're not really for the crew."

"What's your name?" asked Jonah.

"Alexis," she answered, more than a little taken aback.

"Listen Alexis. This is a little awkward, but where have you been over the last twelve hours?"

"I don't understand."

"Let me rephrase. How did you spend your last day or so?"

"Um ..." began Alexis.

Dr. Nassiri could tell she would have preferred to know where the line of questioning was headed before answering. She glanced at Jonah and then the doctor, then back to Jonah, leaving Dr. Nassiri to wish she'd held his gaze for just a moment longer.

"I've mostly been working the big software patch," she said.

"Updating the fuel/air mixers?" said Jonah.

"Yeah, that's it. Frank told you about that project? I didn't think he'd paid it much mind."

"Sure," said Jonah. "Let's assume Frank told me."

"So I was a little late turning in," she continued. "Got up early, and I've been in here for the last ... jeez, five hours or so. Kind of feel like I'm the only one working today, to be honest. Where is everybody?"

Jonah and Dr. Nassiri both joined her in the uncomfortable laughter.

"Here's what I need you to do," said Jonah. He pulled one of the beers off the plastic rings and tossed it to her. Alexis fumbled as she caught it, almost dropping it to the deck. "I'm going need you to wrap up what you're doing, drink at least one of these, and come join us in the galley. No need to chug, just do it at your own pace."

"But—"

"I already okayed it with Frank," said Jonah. "See you in a few minutes."

Dr. Nassiri followed Jonah up the main staircase, back towards the bridge. "Are you certain it's a good idea to leave her down there by herself?" he asked. She hadn't seemed to catch on to the hijacking, but all the same …

"I don't think she can fuck with anything I can't fix," said the American.

"Are you certain about that?"

"No."

"What if she doesn't go along with the plan?"

"Then we'll be the bad guys. Let's hope it doesn't come to that."

Jonah slumped into a comfortable chair while Dr. Nassiri leaned against the wall, both men waiting. Within a few moments, Alexis poked her head in the door.

"Seriously, where is everybody?" she asked, still holding the unopened beer in her hand.

"My name is Jonah," he said. "This is Hassan. We have borrowed the *Conqueror*."

"Borrowed …?" she asked.

"Let's drop the euphemisms. We stole it. Don't worry, everybody's fine. We hustled the crew into the launch and they're back in Malta. We're currently on a course to Sicily, but that's mostly to throw off the authorities."

"Oh," said Alexis, stunned. She popped the tab of the beer and took a very long drink.

"I wanted to hire a boat instead of hijacking one," said Dr. Nassiri. "For whatever that's worth."

"I can't believe this is happening," mumbled Alexis, more to herself than anyone else. "This is my first job out of grad school."

"What a coincidence," said Jonah. "This is my first job out of prison."

Alexis's eyes widened and she looked at Dr. Nassiri.

"We're very sorry you're here, Alexis," he said. "We explicitly told the captain to muster everyone for evacuation. He must have missed you in the count. We'd had no intention of shanghaiing you."

"It's not shanghaiing," corrected Jonah. "That's when you capture someone on land and force them onto a ship. If anything, she's more of a hostage."

"Hostage!?"

"But hostage taking necessitates intent," argued Dr. Nassiri. "This was quite without."

"Wait, are you guys *pirates*?"

"Technically yes, I suppose," said Dr. Nassiri. "But what we can all agree on is the fact that you are not a prisoner."

"But you are somewhat stuck with us for the time being," added Jonah. "So, yeah, you basically are a prisoner."

"I'm still a little concerned here," said Alexis.

"Ten days ago, my mother went missing off Somalia during an airborne oceanographic research expedition," said Dr. Nassiri. "I believe her plane crashed. All of her scientific data, her research—her life's work, really—is aboard that plane. I recruited Mr. Blackwell—"

Jonah snorted, loud enough to interrupt. The American

clearly found the word *recruited* quite amusing given the context at hand.

"I'm so sorry about your mother," said Alexis. She shot Jonah a nasty look for his poorly-timed interjection.

"I recruited Mr. Blackwell as a recovery diver," continued Dr. Nassiri. "We intend to first traverse the Suez Canal, then berth at Anconia Island for supplies."

"You mean that libertarian oil platform city? The new nation, data haven, all that stuff?"

"I've made arrangements," said Dr. Nassiri. "We will source all necessary diving equipment at that location and Mr. Bettencourt's private security forces will provide us with protection as we excavate the underwater crash site. For a fee, of course."

"And where do I figure in?"

"You are welcome to disembark at Anconia. Alternatively, you may see us through on our mission, allow us to make landfall, and disappear. Then you may take command of the *Conqueror* and do with her as you see fit."

"And how do I know you're not just selling the *Conqueror* to the nearest shady shipyard?"

"Because if that were the case, you'd already be shark chum," interrupted Jonah. "Besides, ninety percent of the *Conqueror* is custom, made to order. You can't move custom parts that hot on the black market."

"Quite," said Dr. Nassiri. "And upon completion of our mission, the gentleman and I intend to part company."

"As friends, of course," added Jonah, with more than a hint of sarcasm.

The two men stopped trading further shots as Buzz hurtled down the main staircase towards them with such speed, he almost tumbled rather than sprinted. Buzz stopped dead in his tracks, dumbfounded as he stared at Alexis. She gave him an awkward little wave.

"Who the fuck is this?" the soldier demanded to his cousin. "Forget it—we have an incoming radar contact. Computer says it's on an intercept course."

Jonah leapt to his feet, knocking over his chair. He ran up the stairs three at a time towards the bridge with Dr. Nassiri, Alexis, and Buzz following.

The American slammed himself in the chair, eyes already glued to the radar screen. Without looking away, Jonah placed the radio headphones against one ear and turned the dial towards the upper frequencies.

"What is it?" Dr. Nassiri hissed.

He could see it now, too, a fast-moving green speck growing closer with each radar pass. The predictive route calculated an intercept course. Jonah moved the radio dial upwards, then stopped as he found the frequency.

"Jonah—" began Dr. Nassiri, but Jonah cut him off with the wave of a hand, still listening to a faint transmission.

Jonah slammed down the headphones. "I need a pencil. Or a pen," he said. "And paper."

"But—" said Dr. Nassiri.

"Now, goddamn it! Now!"

Alexis threw open one of the nearest drawers and slapped a pad of paper in Jonah's lap. He began furiously scribbling equations with a fountain pen.

"Time to tell us what the *fuck* is going on," yelled Buzz.

"That radar signature," said Jonah, not looking up from his calculations, "is a Bell AB 212 helicopter, deployed by Malta's Coast Guard. She carries a three-man fast-rope strike force and a door gunner. We're about to be boarded."

Jonah returned to his work, checking his numbers. Dr.

Nassiri briefly wondered if the American was having some kind of nervous breakdown. But Jonah didn't seem the type.

"Looks like it'll be a proper gunfight," said Buzz, a strange combination of grimace and smile on his face.

Alexis audibly gasped. "No way," she blurted.

Buzz pushed himself past the other two and reached for the throttle to increase speed. Jonah slapped his hand away.

"We must increase to top speed!" said Buzz.

"I'm inclined to agree," said Dr. Nassiri. "Increase the speed."

"Do not touch that throttle," ordered Jonah. "We can't maintain eighty knots. We won't even make it to Suez if we start sucking down fuel like that."

"Fuck this," said Buzz. "I'm going to shoot that fucking chopper down."

"No you're not," said Jonah. "I need you to throw anything that floats overboard—the life rafts, kayaks, life rings, pool toys, all of it."

"Are you *crazy*?" demanded Buzz.

"Just do it. Alexis, I need a full security-lockout of all systems. Can you do that while still maintaining engine speed?"

"Yes, but—"

Angry, frightened, and feeling ignored, Buzz shoved Dr. Nassiri aside and drew a .38 revolver. He aimed the handgun at Jonah's head and cocked back the hammer. Jonah didn't wait, didn't even flinch—with one smooth motion, he parried the gun and kicked, knocking Buzz's legs out from underneath him. The former soldier crumpled to his knees, one hand on the console, and the gun tumbled away from his grip. Jonah slammed his fist against the side of the soldier's face, knocking him flat on his back.

Buzz issued a howling, mournful protest tinged with equal portions embarrassment and pain.

"Dr. Nassiri," continued Jonah, returning to his seat as if nothing had happened. "I need you to throw everything that floats overboard. Alexis, I need a full security lockout of all vital systems without affecting our heading or speed. When you're finished, which needs to be *immediately*, you meet me just outside the engine room. Understood?"

Shaking, Alexis furiously typed at the nearest console. Dr. Nassiri stood frozen, staring at his cousin's bruised face.

"You going to pull a piece on me again?" Jonah shouted to Buzz. "Or are you going to start listening?"

"I will *kill* you," growled Buzz through clenched teeth, holding his bruised face with one hand.

"Nobody dies today," said Jonah.

Dr. Nassiri rushed out of the door and yanked the quick-release strap of the first life raft. It bounced off the side of the *Fool's Errand* and tumbled into the ocean. As he struggled with the second, Jonah appeared beside him to help. In the distance, both men noticed a faint dot just above the horizon, and the distant *whop–whop–whop* of rotor wash.

"Doc, we're out of time," said Jonah as the second raft dropped. "Alexis!" he shouted. "Get below decks. Now."

Dr. Nassiri and Alexis followed Jonah down to towards the engine compartment, past the heavy steel fire door. Buzz stood in the corner, bent over, still wincing as he held his hand to his face. Jonah opened the nearest supply locker and searched desperately. Dr. Nassiri watched his face light up when he came across three air bottles and a child's Minnie Mouse snorkel. The bottles were each the size of a canteen, only with a built-in breathing regulator instead of a cap.

"I do not understand your plan," protested Dr. Nassiri. Madness, all of this, letting the prisoner take charge with some strange course of action, a course of action he refused to fully explain.

"He's fucking mental!" shouted Buzz. "He punched me!"

Jonah ignored both men, reached down and pried open a heavy floor hatch. Below it lay a massive cistern of filmy water holding drainage from the showers, kitchen sinks, dishwashing, and laundry, more than large enough to fit four persons. Dr. Nassiri suddenly realized the need for the pony bottles and the snorkel.

"That's the greywater system," said Alexis, still confused.

"Everybody in," said Jonah.

Even over the engines, Dr. Nassiri could now hear the sound of the approaching helicopter. Looking at the water, the doctor saw Alexis transition from frightened to completely terrified.

Nobody moved.

Jonah cleared his throat with barely restrained fury at having to explain himself.

"Given our distance from Malta," he began, each word dripping with anger, speaking as though to a small, disobedient child, "and the weight profile of a loaded Bell A212, the incoming helicopter—which will be over us in *less than sixty seconds*—has only fifteen minutes of hover time. That means that if the team onboard can't fast-rope down, clear every room, and bring the ship to a halt within that time, they'll be forced to re-board and clear out."

"You want them to find a ghost ship," said Dr. Nassiri, grasping Jonah's plan. "No persons onboard, no life rafts, no way to change course, no way to escape, no way to stop the engines!"

"Exactly. And by the time they mobilize a second helicopter, we'll be well out of range. Everybody in the tank—now."

Dr. Nassiri took the first pony bottle from Jonah's hands and bit onto the regulator. He breathed in, experimentally at first, and felt the cold hiss of pure air flow into his lungs. The oily water was actually a more pleasant temperature than he expected. Inside, the claustrophobic compartment was nearly completely dark save the light through the hatchway. There was nothing to hold on to as the tank rippled and jostled with the motion of the yacht.

Alexis slid in next to the doctor, her breathing short and choppy. Buzz splashed in next, grunting as he did so. He stuck the regulator to his pony bottle in his mouth and immediately ducked his head completely underwater. Dr. Nassiri saw Jonah save the Minnie Mouse snorkel for himself.

Jonah reached up and pulled the hatch shut, turning the interior of the compartment into a perfect inky-black as they heard footsteps on the deck above them. Dr. Nassiri's under-stimulated brain played tricks, sending little imaginary flashes of light into his vision, the type of hallucination only seen in pure darkness. The doctor had to restrain himself from reaching up to test if the hatch could be re-opened from the inside to assure himself they would not be doomed to asphyxiate in a greywater cistern, clawing at the unyielding metal ceiling.

Dr. Nassiri felt motion swirling through the waters next to him, then Alexis's hand as she grabbed his, intertwining their fingers. He tried to give her a little reassuring squeeze, but it was returned with a deathly tight grip. Her fright permeated the compartment, rapid breathing, short, twitchy movements, all the indicators of near panic.

A small splash and then a mumble.

"Oh, no," whispered Alexis.

She'd dropped her pony bottle, leaving her to push her face into the air pocket at the ceiling of the tank.

Dr. Nassiri released her hand and touched the ceiling, pressing himself beneath the surface. He felt through the dirty water, pushing through food particles and grit until his fingers brushed against the smooth bottle. He slowly surfaced, and slipped the bottle into the engineer's outstretched hand.

"I'm not so great with tight spaces. Or the dark," Alexis whispered.

"It will be over soon," said Dr. Nassiri. Bedside manner was never his forte. And why even comfort her, this strange female mechanic he'd known for mere moments?

"Thanks," said Alexis. She took one deep breath, but it barely registered. She was still too tense. Her hand reached out, finding his again. Dr. Nassiri willed himself to be calm, to send a sense of peace flowing from his body through his fingertips and into hers.

Footsteps again, faster this time. The soldiers on deck were running out of time. Dr. Nassiri heard the fire door to the engine compartment open with a loud grinding noise. If they were able to stop the engines—if Dr. Nassiri and the other hidden passengers were discovered—he tried not to consider the possibilities.

Splashing noises came from the other side of the tank as Buzz surfaced and popped the regulator out of his mouth.

"I have to pee," he announced to nobody in particular. Dr. Nassiri winced. Alexis giggled next to him, her teeth chattering with fear.

Jonah spoke next, his voice low and resonate with

measured fury. "You all—everybody talking right now—you're breathing my fucking oxygen. That's what your air bottles are for. *Stop talking.*"

More footsteps, stomping. And the muffled echoes of men shouting at each other. Dr. Nassiri prayed for the hum of the engines to remain constant, just a little longer. The *whop-whop-whop* of the helicopter rotors returned for minutes but it felt like the sound lasted hours. And then, nothing. Nothing but the vibration of the engines, the faint splashing inside the tank, and the hiss of regulated air exiting the pony bottles.

"I goddamn hope you held it," said Jonah, jabbing Buzz in the ribs with a finger.

He straightened himself up and cracked the grey-water tank hatch open a hair. Light sliced through the opening into the chamber, almost blinding Dr. Nassiri. In turning away, he caught a glimpse of Alexis, her blond hair dark and plastered to her face, her wide, beautiful eyes staring into his. Her gaze penetrated him more than the sudden blinding light, forcing him to look down and away. And then the moment was gone.

"All clear," announced Jonah.

He flipped the hatch open and climbed out, followed by a wincing Buzz.

Dr. Nassiri held Alexis by the waist, helping her out of the tank, then climbed out himself. He smelled of a strange mixture of expensive soaps, laundry detergent, and fish. It was decidedly unpleasant, but dealing with it would have to wait. He followed Jonah to the bridge, passing Buzz as the former soldier cleaned his injured face in the galley sink.

Looking at the radar screen, Jonah nodded. The

helicopter was heading back to Malta; they'd not succeeded in cutting off the engines despite their efforts.

"We're receiving broadcast radio telemetry," said Jonah, squinting at a computer screen. "They're re-classifying the *Conqueror* as a hazard to navigation and recommending sea-based interception. We're in the clear."

Despite Jonah's proclamation, Dr. Nassiri felt anything but safe.

CHAPTER 6

His face creased into a deep scowl, Charles Bettencourt stood on the far corner of Anconia Island's floating jetway with arms crossed as the cold sea air brushed over the tarmac. The imposing oceanic city rose behind him, glittering tower blocks of glass and steel on three massive platforms. His lawyer stood beside him, mimicking his concern with similarly crossed arms.

Then he spotted the helicopters, five Blackhawks coming in low. Still distant, they flew in an attack formation, tight, fast, and on an intercept course with the long jetway. Chaos erupted. Medical personnel popped up gurneys and IV lines, stacked bandages, and checked oxygen lines. Volunteers with medical experience stood out of the way as best they could, rocking from foot to foot with evident tension. Dozens of armed security personnel clustered in small groups, each decked in a collage of armor and weaponry.

Behind him, a single Gulfstream G-4 jet spun up engines to a screaming pitch, forward thrust pushing against orange plastic stop-blocks. The aircraft bucked and vibrated, engines drowning out all other sounds as the assembled personnel covered their ears. It was his, or at least it should be. Today, it would be a medical transport, rushing the wounded to a Level I trauma center in Munich.

Bettencourt didn't even want to think of what blood would do to the made-to-order Venetian carpeting he'd recently had installed. Perhaps some good would come out of the situation and he'd finally have an excuse to get that Gulfstream G-650 he'd had his eye on.

The five helicopters drew close; he could hear the dull thumping of the rotors slicing through the African air.

"Should we help?" asked his lawyer. "When they come in, I mean. Do you think they'll need us to unload the wounded? Assist the medical personnel?"

"You're wearing a $15,000 suit," snapped Bettencourt. "A suit *I* bought you."

One of the helicopters dropped from formation, gradually losing ground and altitude to the other four. Harsh white smoke poured from the engine compartment, trailing behind the machine. The rear tail kicked out like a drift car in a hairpin curve, pulling the airframe into a flat spin. And then it simply dropped out of the sky, nosing down, smoke trailing, violently smacking into the ocean. The blades chopped into the waves, splintering as the engine ground to a halt, leaving the stricken hulk to bob in ocean whitecaps.

Many of the civilians stood frozen, but several of the soldiers leapt into one of the nearby tenders, one of which roared to life and sped towards the stricken airframe. It appeared to Charles that they'd reach it before it sank. Either way, the helicopter was well insured. That would go a long way to mitigate the disaster with the Conglomerate.

The remaining four helicopters approached the

jetway, flared, and landed hard. Bettencourt put his hand up to protect his face as dust and debris washed over the collected personnel. An IV bag stand fell to the ground, its bag splitting open, spilling saline solution over the thin layer of asphalt.

The helicopters bore witness to the battle: shattered glass and blood stains, punctured aluminum pockmarked with bullet holes and burn marks. They'd been in a hell of a fight.

Colonel Westmoreland, chief of security operations, stepped from the nearest helicopter and into the chaotic scene. He was a massive man, made all the more massive by his Kevlar/ceramic armor and heavily customized G36 assault rifle.

Bettencourt's lawyer approached Westmoreland first, ducking under the still-spinning rotor blades.

That's probably a mistake, Bettencourt thought with a flicker of amusement.

Sure enough, Westmoreland shoved the lawyer with almost enough force to knock him down. The lawyer didn't wait to see what would happen next and turned tail to sprint away. Westmoreland took off his Kevlar helmet and hurled it at the lawyer, narrowly missing his heels. His closely shaved head matched the starkness of his callous expression.

The men in the tender managed to pull one last soldier from the drowning helicopter before it turned belly-up and slipped beneath the surface, disappearing from view. The tender spun around and buzzed back towards the pier.

Colonel Westmoreland pushed his way past the medical personnel and reached into the lead chopper. The mercenary dragged out his struggling prisoner, a shabbily-dressed Somali, hands bound, black hood covering his head.

"He's captured one!" said the lawyer. "One of the pirates!"

"Not sure why," mused Bettencourt. "They don't bargain for their own."

Ignoring the chaotic scene, Westmoreland dragged the struggling man away from the crowd and towards the side of the pier. Bettencourt followed him, watching as the colonel put the man on his knees at the edge of the pier, whipped off his hood, and placed a 9mm pistol against the back of his head.

"Bad day, Mr. Westmoreland?" Bettencourt asked, approaching him from behind.

Colonel Westmoreland turned to face his boss, shook his head, and turned back. The man at gunpoint wasn't a man; he was a *boy*, maybe only fourteen or fifteen. His small frame, clad in filthy, threadbare rags, quaked with fear.

"Hey," Bettencourt said to the kid. "You speak English?"

The pirate said nothing. Bettencourt slapped him lightly on the side of his face. "English?" he asked again.

"Fuck your mother!" shouted the pirate in a voice nearly an octave higher than expected. Bettencourt chewed down a snicker; the kid sounded like a Brooklyn cabbie who hadn't been tipped. Not great at making his own case for survival—maybe too young to realize that capture and a bullet to the back of the head meant more than a red splash screen and a re-start from the last save point of his video game. He shook his head at Westmoreland and stepped away from the edge.

The colonel holstered his pistol and yanked the hood back over the boy's face, ending any further conversation. Behind them, the doctors and volunteers continued the grim task of triaging the wounded; some turning their attention to the mangled, bloody men zipped inside black plastic bags.

Bettencourt put an arm around Colonel Westmoreland's massive shoulders. It was the sort of consoling gesture he imagined might be appropriate for the occasion.

"What happened out there?"

"Dalmar happened." Westmoreland practically spat the words. "Dalmar fucking Abdi happened. Come with me, I have something to show you."

Grabbing the hooded prisoner, Westmoreland stomped off the jetway with Bettencourt and his lawyer following close behind. Bettencourt's jaw clenched, his deep scowl returning.

Dalmar fucking Abdi indeed.

The free-flowing spigot in Bettencorp's bottom line, the cocksucking jackal of the high seas. Nobody even knew who the bastard was. One rumor said Dalmar Abdi was the son of Mohammed Farrah Aidid, Somali warlord and illegitimate self-declared president of the country, a man who picked a brutal close-quarters fight that claimed two American helicopters and eighteen servicemen. Supposedly, Dalmar Abdi, all of six years old, rusting Kalashnikov rifle longer than he was tall, lead a company of ten children against an American rescue convoy.

Another said that he was the son of a Mogadishu soft drink magnate, educated in Rome before returning to his homeland as an aid worker. Once discovering the state of the country and the vicious campaign against it by western powers, he rose up, gathered supporters and became the most feared pirate in the region.

It was probably all bullshit. Dalmar Abdi was

just another pirate, albeit an exceptionally gifted one. Bettencourt rankled at the fact that he'd made Dalmar rich, not just Somali rich, but coke-off-a-model's-tits, soccer-franchise, private-island rich. Four years ago, Dalmar and his crew captured a Ukrainian transport loaded with Soviet-era tanks and self-propelled artillery, enough firepower to redraw the entire region. It wouldn't have mattered except for the fact that the transport was under Bettencorps protection and Bettencourt had personally guaranteed safe passage to some notably humorless Russian plutocrats. It wasn't just a matter of honor that the weaponry be returned. Bettencourt had little interest in waking up one morning staring at the wrong end of a Makarov pistol.

So he'd dug deep and paid. A lot. Low nine figures, to be precise. He was hoping it was enough for Dalmar to re-consider life in Somalia and go retire to some Swiss chalet like so many of the other political figures of the region. Hopefully a place where he could send a trusted asset to personally extract a refund for the ransom.

But then Dalmar did something completely unexpected. He gave it all away, some to the construction of a local hospital, and the rest to the locals themselves through a network of warlords and tribal leaders. Bettencourt realized he'd inadvertently kick-started the creation of one of the larger private militaries in the region, most of whom were volunteers. Abdi recruited from multiple tribes, continued taking ships under Bettencorps protection, and ransoming, stripping, and sinking them. Despite Bettencourt's hopes, Abdi stayed out of Somalia's territorial squabbles, content to simply pay off huge swaths of the country. He became the golden goose, a scrappy pirate with no visible manifestation of his staggering wealth and power. Perhaps Abdi knew that you can't put a self-guided bomb into a man's mansion if he didn't have a mansion.

The tide didn't turn until Bettencorps purchased a fleet of heavily armed helicopter and jet drones, enough firepower to keep the Somali shark at bay. They'd acquired the wealth of armaments from an American Department of Defense grant after a great deal of arm-twisting by a legion of extraordinarily expensive lobbyists. They'd needed an excuse, which Bettencourt was only too happy to provide—fudged satellite and high-aerial surveillance supposedly linking Abdi's brigands to Al Qaida of Africa. A little bad press, it seemed, was enough to get the big guns.

Colonel Westmoreland scanned his security badge against a massive hangar door built into one of the four main circular steel pylons holding up the largest platform of Anconia Island. The marine equivalent to an underground vault, the doors opened wide to reveal an immaculately clean, white circular room filled with endless rows of humming black computer servers. The colonel led Bettencourt, the lawyer, and the prisoner into Anconia Island's command and control system.

"Give me the room," the mercenary barked to the assorted white-coated network engineers and programmers. It didn't matter what they were working on, they took one look at the hooded prisoner and filed out wordlessly, heads down. Westmoreland pushed the boy into a chair and told him to stay put. The boy obeyed as Bettencourt and his lawyer found seats.

Colonel Westmoreland dug through the boy's pockets. Finding a few trinkets, he slammed a pack of gum, a few

7.62mm shell casings, and a plastic card onto the nearest desk.

Bettencourt reached for the laminated card. On one side was the Batman comic book logo, one of the older ones before the latest redesigns. He flipped it over. To his surprise, he found a smiling digital picture of the boy on the other side.

Official Member, Batman Hero's Club. The boy had scrawled his name on the card, *Jaff Suliman*. Bettencourt frowned and passed it over his lawyer, who typed the name into his smartphone.

Colonel Westmoreland dug into his vest and produced a small half-terabyte solid-state memory card. He plugged—no, jammed it into the command and control computer. The lights to the server farm dimmed and a video flickered, projected larger-than-life on the nearest wall.

Taken from Westmoreland's perspective, the video began in the bay of one of the Blackhawks, shot from a camera mounted to the side of the colonel's helmet. The helicopter swooped low over a Russian transport ship as she tossed in the waves far from the coast.

"It was a fucking ambush," narrated the colonel. "They love these Russian transports for some reason. I don't know what the thinking is; we're never going to put any heavy weaponry within 2,000 miles of these animals."

"What did this one carry?"

"Grain. Mostly."

"Anything belonging to the Conglomerate?"

"No. Thank God for that."

"Are you sure we should be talking in front of the prisoner?" asked the lawyer.

"Fuck him," Colonel Westmoreland said. "He's never seeing daylight again."

"Fuck your mother!" shouted the prisoner from inside his hood. Westmoreland aimed a half-hearted kick at him, still almost managing to knock the boy out of his chair.

"All we knew is that we got a distress signal from one of our client vessels," said the colonel. "We were showing up to assist, maybe do a little turkey shooting if we found any pirate skiffs nearby."

Bettencourt smiled at this. He'd had a turn on one of the new miniguns when they'd first arrived at Anconia. Epic. The sheer amount of fire the guns laid down was second to none, long, scorching lines of bullets so hot and thick they glowed like lasers in mid-air, brighter even than the midday African sun.

The video continued, Westmoreland's chopper leading the other four in a swooping arc around the transport.

Bettencourt felt a little dizzy as he watched Westmoreland's disembodied hands reach for the rope, then slide down onto the deck of the transport. The camera took a position behind one of the ventilation funnels as men dropped all around him.

"This is about the time things start going wrong," Westmoreland said.

On the video, a figure moved onto the outside staircase adjacent to the bridge, a towering monolith located on the rear of the transport, rising nearly four stories over the relatively flat deck. Westmoreland aimed his rifle at the figure, then lowered it as the man began to wave both arms. He appeared to be one of the sailors, beckoning the mercenaries towards the bridge.

The colonel took three steps forward when the entire

bridge and every portal in the four-story high structure lit up like a Christmas tree with muzzle flashes and incoming bullets. The sound was deafening, even over the PA system of the audio/visual room, so loud that the speakers cracked and went to static, unable to convey the full auditory violence of the gunshots.

Westmoreland's video flew to one side, finding cover. The man beside him fell, hit, while others returned fire. The helicopters flew in circles, trying to find an appropriate target on the transport superstructure.

"Holy shit," exclaimed the lawyer.

"If it weren't for those helicopters, we'd be dead or captured," said Westmoreland.

"Was Dalmar on board?" Bettencourt asked.

"How should I know? We don't even know what he looks like. But if he was, there's a good chance we got him. The pirates may have scored a victory, but it cost them."

"He probably wasn't onboard," said the lawyer. Westmoreland turned toward him and glared. "No really—think about it. When was the last time we had a confirmed report he was a part of one of these raids? My intel guys think he's directing from landside."

"Your intel guys," chuckled Westmoreland sarcastically.

"Yes, my intel guys," the lawyer said, chin jutting out in defiance. "With respect, most generals don't serve on the front lines, Colonel. Why would Dalmar risk it?"

Westmoreland turned his back on the lawyer and resumed the video. The three men watched as the mercenaries charged up the stairway through a hail of bullets, fighting their way to the bridge. The two lead men threw grenades through the doorway. The bridge exploded, glass shattering and tumbling onto the deck. The last wounded man tumbled through the door to the bridge, collapsing at the base of a navigational terminal, blood pooling around his feet and ankles. Behind them, more pirates poured from below, materializing like ghosts, capturing the deck where they'd been moments before.

"We had to turn the bridge into an unassailable position," said Westmoreland, narrating the video as it continued. "Once the last man was in the bridge, we torched the exterior stairway with thermite."

Westmoreland's video turned back to the bridge, a scene of perfect chaos. Wounded men struggled, attended to by their comrades while others shoved the crumpled bodies of hostages into the corner. Helicopters strafed the decks below.

Three pirates burst through the door to the interior stairwell, catching the mercenaries by surprise. Westmoreland was first to return fire, but the pirates vanished before any were hit. The pirates hung back, probing the weaknesses of the impromptu fortress, never staying long enough to give the mercenaries a clear shot. They'd learned to fear the fixed guns of the helicopters, but at such close range the heavy weapons couldn't be brought to bear without wiping out the mercenaries as well. Every bullet expended brought more pirates, peeking, crouching, whistling to each other as they advanced. Westmoreland was losing.

Fuck it, said a voice over the video. The green flash of an unpinned grenade flew through the air and down the stairwell. With a concussion too loud for the video to capture, the weapon detonated with a blinding flash, collapsing part of the interior staircase.

And then an AK-47-wielding boy stepped into view of the helmet-cam. Charles instantly recognized him as the colonel's prisoner. In the video, Westmoreland dove to the floor, reached into the compartment below and dragged the boy out by his collar, punched him squarely in the face, ripped the rifle from his grasp, hooded and zip tied him within seconds. Bettencourt felt genuine amazement at the speed of the capture. From the boy's perspective, he may have well been abducted by aliens, a single hand reaching down from above and dragging him upwards and away.

The men pushed their way up a ladder and onto the roof of the ship, kicking and breaking off radio antennas and radar units, trying to make enough room for their escape. The first of the helicopters flew in for a dangerous one-skid landing, allowing Westmoreland's men to pile aboard. Westmoreland practically threw the prisoner into the chopper, then dove in after him. The helicopter took off, rejoining formation while a second repeated the rescue.

The two lead helicopters broke formation, backing away for an attack run, then strafed the entirety of the ship, firing countless rounds into the waterline of the ship. The transport started to list almost immediately, taking on water into every below-deck compartment.

Bettencourt didn't know if any crew survived the encounter this far, but he knew none of them would live for long. The Russian transport heeled over but refused to sink. Above the bridge, the last of the shot-up mercenaries were loaded. The helicopter accelerated, gaining speed as it escaped the wounded ship, chased by three long-tailed rocket-propelled grenades—the pirates fired one final salvo, one last attempt to inflict damage.

Two missed, but the third impacted the rearmost chopper, halfway back to the tail rotor. The craft spun, losing control, but the expert pilot righted her, re-gaining trim and putting her back into formation. The last clip of the video showed the fleeing helicopters moving away as the Russian transport, burning, rocked in the lapping waves.

"We have to strike back," said Westmoreland, yanking the memory card out of the computer. "At this moment, Anconia Island is on war footing."

Bettencourt frowned, the offshore bankers, software developers, data miners and other denizens of Anconia wouldn't like that kind of talk. They weren't soldiers. Before he could formulate his response, his lawyer interrupted.

"You're not going to believe this," he said. "But I think I found our prisoner's Facebook page."

The lawyer synced his phone into the nearest terminal. Sure enough, the young prisoner's image flashed into view, maybe a year younger, proudly wearing a Batman T-shirt and holding an RPG.

"Cute kid," said Bettencourt.

"Holy shit, I think Dalmar has a page, too," said the lawyer, bringing up the pirate's stark rifle-crossed emblem.

"I hope you're not using your personal account."

"No, I'm using corporate. What should I do?"

Westmoreland simply crossed his arms, not approving but knowing too little about the process to actually protest.

"Hell, I don't know," said Bettencourt. "Friend him. The Public Relations department will throw a shit fit when they find out, but do it anyway."

The lawyer pressed a few keys, all three men waiting for a moment.

"I sent the request."

"War footing," said Westmoreland, intending to return the discussion to a subject with which he was eminently more familiar.

"Um, sorry to interrupt," said the lawyer. "But he just friended me back."

"Already? The fucker must live on Facebook."

"He just might," mused the lawyer. "He actually has more followers than our corporate site ... hold on ... now we're getting a video chat request from him."

"Seriously?" Bettencort said.

"Agree to it," said Colonel Westmoreland. "We have a prisoner. That's something worth talking about. Can we trace the source? I want to know *exactly* where that fucker is holed up."

"Trace it? Are you kidding me?" said the lawyer. "This is Facebook we're talking about."

"Despite your shitty attitude," said the colonel, "I still don't know if that's a yes or no."

"Let me put it this way, do you want some pedophile tracing your kids?" said the lawyer, shaking his head. "No, you can't trace somebody using Facebook."

"Well, stop fucking around and start the feed," said the colonel.

"Put it on the main screen," Bettencourt directed.

The lawyer swept the page up onto the server farm's main screen. and with a jab of his index figure, accepted the video chat request. A few seconds later, an image formed on the big screen and Dalmar Abdi filled the display, a dark, intense, handsome face staring directly into the camera. Bettencourt found himself wishing they'd picked a smaller screen; Dalmar dominated the room like the Wizard of Oz, while the room's fisheye camera rendered him and Westmoreland as small, slight figures.

Dalmar was transmitting from a nondescript bedroom, a simple mud-walled space with a single bed. A second man, tall, muscular, bare chested, slept soundly wrapped in the sheets, blissful and unaware. So the rumors were true—Bettencourt could practically smell the sex through the video connection.

"Colonel!" announced Dalmar with practical glee and in near-perfect English. "I missed you! Get it?"

With that, Dalmar threw his entire head back and laughed the deepest, purest belly laugh, his shiny white teeth blinding, his echoing voice booming over the room's PA system.

"Mr. Abdi," said Charles.

"Oh, I see Charles Bettencourt is with you," said Dalmar, still smiling with the last remaining chuckles. "And his pet lawyer. All of my friends are here! All of my friends, the men who give me so much money and such endless fun."

"How many men did you lose today?" asked Colonel Westmoreland with a sadistic smile.

"None!" shouted Dalmar, his smile never wavering. "I have never lost a man. Those shot, rise as the sun sets; those drowned, swim to shore, those burned and maimed—"

Unwilling to listen to the ranting another moment, Colonel Westmoreland grabbed the prisoner by the neck and threw him to center of the camera's view. Hands still tied behind his back, the boy stumbled and collapsed in a heap as the mercenary straddled him, yanking off his dark hood.

"And who is this?" said Dalmar. Unmoved by the display, he seemed genuinely curious.

Blinking in the sudden artificial light, Jaff immediately affixed his stare to Dalmar's image. His eyes went wide, his mouth hung open. Celebrity? Hero worship? Was Dalmar actually Jaff's Batman?

"Ah, I can see now!" said Dalmar. "It is my best soldier, Jaff!"

Jaff mouthed words, but no sound came out. *He knows my name*, the boy seemed say.

"Jaff, I am very proud of you," said Dalmar.

"But I was captured," the boy whispered, not certain his idol could hear him.

"There is nothing you could do that would make me disappointed in you," responded Dalmar. "After all, what do we say to our captors?"

"Fuck your mother!" shouted Jaff.

"Very good! Very good! My friends, let us put my best soldier aside for a moment. We have business to discuss. Jaff, I promise you that your moment will come."

Jaff bowed deeply, his face aglow with a burning pride.

"I'll begin," said Bettencourt. He stood up and adjusted his suit. "Dalmar, I'll admit it. I'm impressed. They said nobody could take a vessel traveling faster than eighteen knots, and you took one. I can't get you to retire—"

"And you cannot kill me."

"But let's not get bogged down in semantics," the CEO continued. "What's it going to take? I feel like I don't even have a starting point with you here. Give me a number. Ask for the world and we'll see where the negotiations take us. What do you say?"

"You wish to *negotiate*?" asked Dalmar, theatrically incredulous. "How does one negotiate with death? You, you people, you bring death with you. Death to our people, death to our seas, death to our hope. And I am the death-killer. I *pray* for your massacres, for the poisons you pour into our waters. For every Somali you kill, I raise an army of their brothers and husbands and sons."

Bettencourt's phone rang, and he found himself absentmindedly checking it. Lucianna … goddamn it, every time he missed one of her kickboxing lessons she blew up his phone like some crazy stalker. Annoying as hell, almost not worth it—

"Am I boring you?" Dalmar's voice boomed over the streaming video. Bettencourt realized the room had gone absolutely silent.

"What the hell, boss?" Westmoreland demanded. Even his lawyer seemed irritated.

"Shit, I'm sorry. It's my kickboxing instructor, goes bonkers every time I skip my personal training session."

"Are you screwing her?" asked Dalmar.

"Well … yeah."

"That's your problem right there, Boss," muttered Westmoreland. The lawyer nodded in agreement.

"I understand, my friend," said Dalmar, jabbing a thumb over his shoulder to the sleeping man in bed behind him. "This one is *unbelievable*. Always wants to upgrade, whatever that means. Wants a nicer house, a nicer car. I cannot win."

"Now do we get to talk about the prisoner I'm about to fucking execute?" asked Colonel Westmoreland, clearly annoyed.

"To business then," said Dalmar. "I am willing to speak of Jaff, my best soldier. My best soldier knows, as all the best soldiers know, that their commander only asks one thing of them."

Dalmar's dark eyes pierced through the video feed, focusing all his energy on the young, enraptured pirate.

"Jaff, do you know what I am going to ask?"

Jaff shook his head.

"I only ask you *die well*."

Jaff nodded in complete focus and agreement. The boy spun around and suddenly *his hands were free* and he launched himself at Charles Bettencourt like a cannon shot, as if the entire universe had shrunk to a singular nothingness between two immovable objects. Something glinted in his hand and Charles's brain sputtered and spit something out like *knife*. The worst part was that he just stood there with his mouth hanging open like some thoughtless dumbfuck begging to get his gut slashed open. Just as fast, Westmoreland had his hands around the boy's neck, throwing him to the ground.

Out came the colonel's custom pistol, and it popped once, twice, three times directly into the boy's chest, deafening in the small room. The boy sputtered once, gurgled, dropped the knife, and died.

Dalmar let out a long sigh and shook his head. "Missed again." He smiled one last time, a wide, sad smile and said, "Until next time." Then he closed the feed and all that remained on the screen was his main Facebook page.

"You're welcome, Boss," Westmoreland said.

Bettencourt didn't look up. He was distracted, staring at his shoes around which a puddle of blood was forming. Jesus. *But probably not the first pair of Pradas to walk through blood,* he thought. *And no, I do not need to thank you, Colonel. That's what annual performance bonuses are for.* He glanced up at the screen and then turned and headed back out to the landing deck with his lawyer, as usual, on his heels. Westmoreland's cruel smile followed them to the massive door, disappearing only as it slid shut behind them.

Something about the sea air centered Bettencourt, putting him back into his proper alignment. It wasn't the blood or the boy or the gunshots—not even Dalmar's superior taunts. It was the surprise, a sensation he felt deeply unused to. He hated it.

"Walk me through my afternoon," he said to his lawyer. He leaned against the nearest railing and peeled off his bloody shoes, holding them to his side, standing on the rough metal grating in his socks, watching the waves below.

His lawyer pulled out a Blackberry and scrolled through the new messages. "Well, the Russians are trying to get in touch. They're pissed about the transport; want somebody's head on a platter. It's going to take some serious kowtowing to get out of this one."

"I'm not in the mood. What else?"

"Um, this is a little weird, but the *Conquerer* is arriving in the next couple of hours. At least I think it's the *Conquerer*."

"I'm not following."

"Let me put it this way. It sure looks like the *Conquerer*, but the pilot is calling her the *Fool's Errand*. Somebody named Dr. Nassiri is in command, says he knows you. Says you have some kind of arrangement."

"Hmmm …" Bettencourt racked his brain for some reference to Dr. Nassiri without success. He threw his shoes over the railing. They tumbled through the air and disappeared into the ocean.

"Set up the appointment."

CHAPTER 7

Dr. Nassiri stepped off the *Fool's Errand* and onto the concrete pier of Anconia Island. It certainly *felt* like land, without the nearly imperceptible sway felt even on the largest ships. From this angle it was difficult to appreciate the true proportions of the oceanic city. A triad of oil platforms rose from the sea like a cliffside, far above the lapping waves of the Indian Ocean. Anconia was an entire metropolis perched on top of the pillars, easily amounting to three massive city blocks. Looking up, he felt the same way he'd felt when arriving at Casablanca the first time, amazed—and maybe even a little proud—at the scale of human endeavor demonstrated.

He heard footsteps behind him as Alexis practically skipped down the gangplank to join him. "Jonah said he'd check in and do the docking paperwork," she said. "Ready to see the city?"

"Of course," said Dr. Nassiri. "Off to see the Wizard."

Waving her forward, he followed her toward the main harbor elevator. He adjusted the strap of his duffel bag, trying to find a comfortable place on his shoulder, but there was no proper placement given the bulky contents.

With some difficulty, Dr. Nassiri had found another linen suit aboard the *Fool's Errand* and resolved to keep this one in better repair than the previous.

Alexis had changed into her "civvies" as she called them, a charming term for a tight tank top and designer jeans. She'd also liberated a fashionable pair of Manalo Blanhnik heels from the megayacht's master cabin, wearing them with total confidence, despite their impracticality.

Dr. Nassiri had made a half-hearted attempt to get Jonah and Youssef to accompany him to the city. Jonah simply grunted, a gesture Dr. Nassiri took as a no. Youssef did the same, his unabashed admiration for the American having metastasized to hero worship after realizing his belting to the face probably saved them all. This hero worship had more recently evolved into outright duplication, forcing Dr. Nassiri to grit his teeth as his cousin, unconsciously or not, aped the American's verbal idiosyncrasies and obnoxious swagger.

Still, he was glad they had opted not to join him. This meant he'd have Alexis to himself. Since she was discovered onboard, he'd had several chances over the last four days to talk with her, but had shied away every time an opportunity arose. He didn't want Jonah or Youssef around and was a little anxious, even if he didn't want to admit it, about the small spark that lit up inside, a feeling he'd almost forgotten existed, whenever he saw her easy smile or heard her delightful Texan accent.

He'd carefully choreographed the minutia of their conversation in advance and yet now, as the elevator rose through the air on its programmed ascent from the dock level, he forced down a twinge of panic, realizing he had forgotten what he had planned to say. An awkward silence hung over them both. He glanced down at her and flashed a somewhat uncomfortable smile that he hoped didn't look like a grimace.

"So what do you do?" asked Alexis. "For a job, I mean. Other than hijacking ships and kidnapping girls."

She'd meant it to be funny, but Dr. Nassiri felt the need to defend himself.

"I didn't mean to kidnap you. Or steal the ship. That was Mr. Blackwell's—"

"I know," she said with a genuine smile and a reassuring pat on the arm. "He calls you 'Doc'—what type of doctor are you?"

He drew in a breath. "I'm a surgeon."

"Like …?" asked Alexis, putting two cupped hands just away from her breasts.

"No, not at all," he laughed. "Military surgeon. But I worked part-time in a private practice where I performed a number of cosmetic procedures."

"But no tits."

"None to date."

The massive elevator jerked to a halt, far above the artificial jetty below. From here, the *Fool's Errand* looked like little more than a model ship rocking gently in the waves.

Dr. Nassiri and Alexis stepped off the elevator and into the center of Anconia Island's main courtyard. The experience was slightly uncanny, as if they'd emerged into the center of a modern-day California office park. Green grass and plants covered most of the area, surrounded by tall buildings and walking paths. A few white-collared workers milled about or sat on comfortable aluminum benches. It was, in a modern way, beautiful.

In the center of the complex rose a single main building,

a massive glass structure fully ten stories higher than the next tallest. Dr. Nassiri didn't need to ask anyone directions to know that was where he was headed. One could typically find the king in the highest tower.

"Wow," was all Alexis could say as they entered the lobby.

Dr. Nassiri looked around for an information desk or security guard. But the art-deco styled lobby was empty. No guards, no metal detectors, no badge system or front desk sign-in.

"Guess they don't need much security," he said. It occurred to him that such exercises would have been totally superfluous. This wasn't some regular city office building, but rather a mere appendage of a larger body, that of Anconia Island itself.

"Yeah," Alexis said, looking around. "If they let you berth or land here, you've probably already been checked out."

According to the placard above the elevator bank, only a single elevator at the far end of the lobby rose to the penthouse. Dr. Nassiri pressed the gold-plated button, and the brass-inlaid doors opened with a soft *whoosh*, beckoning them into the elevator. The doctor was briefly seized by an urge to take Alexis by the hand and lead her in. He snuck a glance and got the strong sense she may have appreciated such a bold move. But he kept his hands by his side.

The door slid shut. Inside, the elevator had no buttons, just cloudy glass walls lit from behind by some unseen source. An invisible panel in the wall flickered to life, revealing a previously-hidden video screen. Dr. Nassiri had the uncomfortable feeling there were also one or more hidden cameras trained on them.

An attractive red-headed woman in an elegant business suit appeared on the display, looking in Dr. Nassiri's direction with a tight, professional smile.

"May we help you?" she asked. "It does not appear you have clearance to the selected level."

"Dr. Nassiri to see Charles Bettencourt," said the doctor. "By appointment."

"Of course," said the young woman. She turned away from the video display for the barest of moments, leaving Dr. Nassiri to wonder if he was in the right place after all.

Without a sound, the display flickered off, disappearing as if it'd never existed.

The elevator rose, then gained speed as if pulled upward on a silk thread. It didn't stop at any floors, it wasn't the type of elevator that served a building, it was the type that served a single man. The cloudy glass walls faded to invisible, going clear as the elevator appeared to burst free, soaring over the skyscrapers of Anconia. The effect was incredible as the machine climbed the last ten stories towards the penthouse, rising over the oceanic city, sunlight glittering on the steel and glass skyscrapers, glancing off the rippling waves far below.

Before he could finish appreciating the view, the elevator slowed to a smooth stop and doors behind him separated and opened. Dr. Nassiri and Alexis exited into an angled, glass-roofed penthouse, complete with a helicopter landing pad extending off the side of the structure. The far end of the room was dominated by a massive oak desk with a solitary, high-backed chair, turned to face away from them. Beside him, Alexis sucked in her breath with a quiet whistle. It was an art-deco cathedral, an information-age throne room for a god of modern capitalism.

Flanking the elevator stood a corridor of free-standing glass panels entombing ancient Japanese parchments. Swirling, colorful designs depicted dragons, samurai, Kraken, and beautiful geishas in some of the most intricate patterns Dr. Nassiri had ever seen. As Alexix gaped at the view, he bent closer to inspect one of the panels, staring in fascination as he realized the parchments were not paper.

They were human skin.

He stood abruptly and moved away before Alexis could turn her attention to the parchments and make the same discovery.

He recalled learning about this practice some years ago. Upon death, a poorly-favored or debt-ridden yakuza gangster might be flayed and tattooed, as their skin, in samples as small as postcards, were highly prized by dark-spirited collectors. Bettencourt's collection must have been years in the making—entire bodies, male and female alike, skinned and stretched out like human canvas, encompassing necks, back, buttocks, every tattooed inch of flesh. What these macabre artifacts said about their collector, he did not know. And did not want to find out.

The high-backed chair swiveled to face them, revealing Charles Bettencourt. He rose and walked around the desk to greet the pair, wearing a wide smile and no shoes. "Welcome to Anconia Island," he said.

Jonah Blackwell stretched out on a deck chair of the *Fool's Errand*, adjusting his position for optimal sun absorption. Beads of sweat wept from every pore, drawn out by the intense heat. He'd already gained a few pounds, filling in between his stringy muscles, giving him a fuller, healthier look. It wasn't like he needed a tan. Prison 14 had many things in short supply, but sun wasn't one of them. He just liked the feeling of freedom.

He took another bite of the bacon sandwich he'd prepared for himself. It'd been too long since he'd felt the satisfaction of a full stomach, but for some reason it also bothered him. It made him feel lethargic, dull-edged. The skills imperative in prison—observation, speed, brutality, paranoia—were all unnecessary here.

Buzz lay on the deck chair beside him, snoring loudly while wearing Louis Vuitton sunglasses appropriated from the master cabin. Jonah wondered if Youssef knew they were women's. Or maybe they weren't, Jonah wasn't exactly up on the latest fashions.

Buzz yawned and stretched, slowly waking up from his midday nap. Over the last few days, he'd practically inhaled a case of Bollinger champagne and endless cigars, so much that he'd developed a budding alcohol-plumped belly. It wasn't enough to be distracting, but it did look just a little out of place on the former soldier's otherwise athletic frame.

Without missing a beat, the ex-soldier reached over to a small glass table next to the deck chair and retrieved a silver cigar case. He opened it, ripped off the end of a cigar with his fingernails, and tried to light it.

"Motherfucker," he mumbled with irritation as the lighter sputtered twice before catching. Succeeding, he sucked in two big lungfuls of cigar smoke and coughed as he exhaled.

"Too bad we don't have some *em-jay*," he said to Jonah, waving the cigar theatrically. "Razor this shit open, get our smoke on for *reals*."

"Buzz, that's a $600 cigar," said Jonah.

"Mother ... *fucker* ..." mused Buzz as he considered the expensive cigar with no small measure of respect. Jonah realized the Moroccan would probably still razor it, even if all he had on hand was a dime bag of skunk.

Before Jonah could respond, a loud crashing sound emanated from below decks. Both Jonah and Buzz froze cold, staring at each other, listening. It sounded like an entire rack of glass dishes had suddenly hit a tile floor, too loud to be an accident.

"You suppose Hassan and Alexis are back?" Buzz said, his voice low.

Jonah shook his head, picked up the pearl-handled 1911 pistol from the side table and secured it in the small of his back.

Unarmed, Buzz allowed Jonah to lead as both men carefully tread down the stairs towards the main galley. A massive man with a shaved head stood next to the bar, his back to the pair. Easily six foot six, his swollen shoulders, arms, and neck gave him the look of a man who could knock down buildings with his bare hands and pull apart rail cars with his teeth. A trail of dirty footprints marched across the expensive white carpet, and a customized Kevlar and ceramic plate vest had been tossed over the back of the nearest chair. The man's muscles flexed underneath his sweat-soaked shirt as Jonah and Buzz approached from behind. He didn't turn around.

The man stumbled from foot to foot, humming to himself, infusing the air with the distinct malodor of expensive booze as he casually mixed himself a White Russian from too much Swedish vodka and too-old milk.

Jonah took a closer look at the bullet-proof vest and realized he could make out colonel's bars, completely out of place on a mercenary. The live grenades dangling from the vest seemed much more apropos, enough explosive power to sink the *Fool's Errand*. Drawing the 1911 pistol from his waistband, Jonah kept it in his dominant hand and leaned against a wall, concealing the weapon from the uninvited guest.

"You lost?" asked Buzz.

The intruder hesitated for a moment, and then slowly turned to face Jonah and Buzz. Jesus, he looked like hell. And he was drunk.

"I am not lost," he answered. With a broad, cruel smile and dirt, rust, a thousand scabbed-over cuts, and sweaty, unwashed clothing stained with blood, the colonel looked like he had just stepped off a battlefield. Maybe Anconia Island wasn't libertarian Disneyland after all.

"Then what are you doing here?"

"A janitor tried to kick me out of a bar. Something about them not being open. I told him to mix me a drink anyway." He brought the glass to his mouth and sucked down half the liquid in it, then held it up in a mock toast. "He was stubborn, though."

The colonel's hand was bloody and busted open along the knuckles. A chill shot down Jonah's spine. Buzz flinched. "So I asked myself," continued the colonel without waiting for any further prompting, "where would be … the best place … to get milk?"

Facing them, the colonel leaned back up against the wall. He held the White Russian in one hand and a H&K pistol in the other. Jonah kicked himself for not noticing it sooner.

"Buzz," said Jonah, more to his companion than the stranger, and without ever taking his eyes off the colonel. "Fuck off."

Buzz didn't need to be told twice. The only one in the room without a weapon, he ducked his head and retreated back up the main staircase. Neither the mercenary or the former prisoner spoke until the footsteps faded.

"I don't think your friend liked me," said the colonel.

Jonah still couldn't tell whether or not the he was trying to pick a fight. Safety off, his finger rested on the trigger. He didn't want to put odds on it, but guessed he could probably outdraw a drunk.

"What do you want?" asked Jonah.

"Didn't I tell you? I needed a proper drink."

With that, the colonel slurped down the last of his White Russian with one gulp and tossed the empty glass on the floor. It bounced a couple of times on the carpet and rolled under a chair. The smell of bad milk again reached Jonah's nostrils.

The colonel shrugged and pulled out another bottle, tequila this time, slapped two glasses on the bar and poured two overflowing shots. Holding his pistol with one hand and the shot glasses in the other, he stumbled towards Jonah.

"Gutsy move, parking a stolen boat on my island."

This is it, Jonah thought. His hand tensed around the hidden pistol, preparing to aim and fire. The colonel leaned in close, too close, giving Jonah an uncomfortably clear look at his blood-flecked face. Backspatter, the forensics experts called it. The signature blood spray found on an executioner, the blood found on a man who'd just shot someone at point-blank range. The colonel pressed a shot glass into Jonah's hands, dripping tequila onto the floor.

"Let's toast," said the colonel, swaying slightly, "to death. The one thing that keeps us men."

"To death," said Jonah. Both men downed their shots without breaking eye contact.

"You must be Dr. Hassan Nassiri."

Dr. Nassiri bowed ever so slightly and extended his hand to the CEO.

"A pleasure to be here, Mr. Bettencourt," said Dr. Nassiri. "Thank you for agreeing to this appointment."

"Please," said Bettencourt dismissively. "Just call me Charles. And who is this lovely young woman?"

The CEO fixed his sight on Alexis, nearly burning a hole through her with his intense gaze.

"Alexis Anderson." Alexis reached her hand out to take Bettencourt's. He shook it with both hands, completely covering hers, staring directly and deeply into her eyes.

"I'm so happy to welcome you both to Anconia. I know you're going to have a wonderful time during your stay here. I do hope it's not too brief."

"What you've accomplished here is … incredible," said Alexis. "I had no idea it was of this scale."

"Isn't it?" said Bettencourt, moving back around to the other side of his desk. "I'd like to downplay Anconia Island, but I simply can't. We've not only created the first truly new nation to grace the face of this earth in two centuries, we've created the very foundation it lays upon."

"Quite an achievement," said Dr. Nassiri with admiration.

"Indeed, indeed. I regret I can't give you the full tour today. Our security forces had a bit of a skirmish earlier, and I'm afraid I have to deal with the aftermath."

"I'm very sorry to hear that," said Dr. Nassiri.

"Just part of life on the frontier," said Charles, waving off the concern. "Can't live out here without weathering an occasional pirate raid." He turned his laser-like attention back to Alexis.

"But I prefer to concentrate on the positives of Anconia Island. For instance, we grow our own food in state-of-the art greenhouses and hydroponics gardens. What few fish we can't farm in our oceanic pens, we can capture with our small fishing fleet. It's a little hard to get a steak around here, but I can promise you the best marlin you've ever had."

Alexis smiled and a faint blush rose to her cheeks. Dr. Nassiri found himself feeling a pang of—jealousy? He couldn't quite place it, but knew he didn't like Charles Bettencourt now, and liked him less with every word he spoke.

"Anconia Island is perched on fully functioning deep-sea platforms," Bettencourt continued. "We have solar panels, of course, and wind turbines built into the superstructure and the rest of our energy needs—which are substantial—we extract from natural gas in the shale deposits on the continental shelf. Total self-reliance is our overriding philosophy, and we are determined to meet our goals. I admire determination in others as well ... which brings us to our business." He gestured toward the duffel bag. "Dr. Nassiri, what have you got for me?"

Dr. Nassiri took the duffel bag off his shoulder and placed it on Bettencourt's desk. Unzipping it with a flourish, he reached inside and pulled out three massive blocks of euro banknotes and set them on the desk. "I trust this will be to your satisfaction," he said.

"Start talking," Bettencourt replied. "You have my undivided attention."

"A small jet plane recently disappeared a few miles off the Somali coastline. My mother was aboard. I do not believe there were any survivors." He could feel Alexis's eyes on him as he spoke and felt that she intuitively understood his pain. "However, not long after the crash, the plane's emergency transponder began communicating. Because of this, I have both the location of the sunken aircraft and a belief that my mother's research, her life's work, will have survived. She would have wanted me to recover it if at all possible; the last time we spoke she said she was close to an important discovery."

"And her body?"

"I intend to recover it."

"So how can I help?"

"Security. I have no intention of being captured and ransomed during this expedition."

"Let's start with the location," said Bettencourt. He paused for a moment, then gestured to the money spread over his desk. "And I have to say this is an excellent start, a real show of good faith."

Dr. Nassiri pulled his smartphone from his pocket, and pulled up a digital map showing the location of the transponder, and handed it over. "This is where we intend to dive."

Bettencourt squinted at the map for a moment, and then placed the smartphone on the oak desk. The surface desk sprang to life, revealing that the oak pattern was just an illusion, an elaborate and convincing façade. The desk pulled the image off the smartphone—leaving a slightly uncomfortable Dr. Nassiri to wonder what other details the system had liberated from his mobile device—and displayed it on the desk, stretching the map from edge to edge. The tiny transponder signal silently blinked in the center of the display.

"Here's the problem," Bettencourt said. "Your signal is deep in the red zone." He pressed the touch-sensitive screen, overlaying it with a second map, showing roughly the territory that Anconia Island controlled. "We have sea patrols," he continued. "But the footprint is too big, and they're not fast enough. They attract a lot of organized pirate attention, putting my men in danger of attack by overwhelming forces. The true power in this region is my helicopter fleet, but your transponder signal is out of their operational range. I can't station a patrol with you."

"I don't believe you need to," said Dr. Nassiri. "We have a fast ship and good radar."

"So I hear," Bettencourt said, with a knowing smile. "Even the fastest pirate skiffs can't catch anything faster than about forty knots, and from what I understand, forty knots is just getting started for your ship."

"Here is what I propose," continued the doctor. "We will go into your 'red zone' unescorted. If we are approached, we turn tail and run towards Anconia. I want helicopters waiting for us once we're within fuel range."

"Deal," said Bettencourt. He pointed to the blocks of cash. "What is this? A million euro? You may be a little short."

"One and one-half million," said Dr. Nassiri.

"That will buy you *one* trip into the red zone. My helicopters aren't cheap."

Dr. Nassiri pursed his lips in thought and then nodded. "Agreed."

Bettencourt sighed, sat, and leaned back in his chair, looking from Dr. Nassiri to Alexis and back. "Are you sure you want to do this? There can't be anything on that plane worth your lives."

"I'm well aware of the risks," said the doctor.

The CEO flicked off the desk display, returning it to the oak pattern. He pulled open a drawer and produced a small letter opener, cutting a long slit into one of the blocks of money. He pulled out a single crisp 500-euro note and snapped it between his fingers.

"Did you know you can fit €150,000 into a cigarette box? Amazing." A wide smile formed crinkles around his eyes. "This note has been banned in Italy and the UK due to its favor with organized crime. And for good reason. A million American weighs forty-four pounds, but look at this! A million and a half Euros weigh practically nothing! More wealth than most men could earn in a lifetime, and you carried it in here in a single duffle bag."

"I'm pleased we've reached an arrangement," Dr. Nassiri said, anxious to escape Bettencourt's company. The way he had looked at Alexis was bad enough, but the way he looked at the money was positively grotesque.

"I'll have my assistant send you the contact information for my chief of security, Colonel Westmoreland," said Bettencourt. "All arrangements will go through him."

"Thank you," said Dr. Nassiri.

"And how about you, my beautiful Alexis?" said Charles. "We have a fabulous seafood restaurant in the southeast corner of Anconia and they serve the best mussels I have ever tasted, plucked fresh from the sea every day. A little butter and they practically melt in your mouth. I've set aside a very particular bottle of 1973 Red Mountain for a special occasion … rich, balanced, not too fruity and with a very nice finish. Tell me, are you the kind of girl I can meet over business in the afternoon and take to dinner that very night?"

Dr. Nassiri and Alexis sat together on the edge of a raised concrete flowerbed in the center of the Anconia Island courtyard. They'd decided to share an Ethiopian fit-fit stew on flatbread, but neither could manage to do more than pick at it. Alexis was uncharacteristically silent and contented herself to halfheartedly watching people walk from building to building.

"You can stay here, you know," said Dr. Nassiri. "In fact, I'd like you to stay here. I never planned on your presence, and I never intended to take you with us beyond Anconia."

"Since you haven't ransomed me and I haven't escaped, I guess I'm stuck," said Alexis with a tiny smile.

"I'm serious," said Dr. Nassiri. "You should stay here, not leave with us."

"Do you want me to stay here?"

"It's selfish to ask you to come, it's simply too dangerous."

"Dangerous?" She rolled her eyes. "If I stay here, I'll probably have to go to dinner with Charles Bettencourt." His heart gave a little *thud*, and the urge to feel her fingers twined with his swept over him, but she kept going. "Besides, who will run the engines? If you don't have someone constantly adjusting for power loss, cavitation—"

"But if the pirates—"

"If the pirates catch us," Alexis interrupted. "We deserve to be caught. Nothing can outrun the *Conqueror*." She let the name of the stolen yacht hang in the air.

"We should go back to the ship," she said. "Big day tomorrow."

"That money, the money I gave Bettencourt," Dr. Nassiri said. "I need you to understand that was everything to me. Everything. My father died years ago, and I mortgaged my childhood home, I sold every stick of furniture, my car, my property, my business investments. It all went into that bag. There is no backup plan. The oceanic research work was my mother's life and the only way to do honor to her is to finish it."

"And Jonah? How does he figure into this master plan? What if something happens to him on the dive?"

"I found Jonah in a prison, the type of prison for men who are meant to die incarcerated. I'm giving him another chance at life, perhaps more of a chance than even I will have once this venture is completed. I have committed resources to allow him to begin his life again. But in the meantime he's expendable. If he doesn't know this, he has no one to blame but himself."

"That's not how we treat friends where I'm from," said Alexis.

"Jonah Blackwell will never be my friend."

Dr. Nassiri followed Alexis as she ascended the gangplank to the *Fool's Errand*. He allowed himself one momentary glance at her once they were onboard, but she did not return the look, instead staring forward, expressionless. He didn't understand why, but whatever he'd said about Jonah bothered her, so much so that she disappeared down the main staircase towards the engine room without so much as a goodbye.

Dr. Nassiri shook his head, more in frustration with himself than her. Despite her obvious anger, she hadn't said anything to rescind her offer to accompany the *Fool's Errand* on the final leg of the mission. Whatever tomorrow brought, apparently the Texan's code of honor went very deep.

Passing by the bar, Dr. Nassiri noticed open, half-empty liquor bottles, dirty footprints on the carpet, and several dishes on the floor. He snuck a glance behind the bar, and it looked as if an entire row of bottles had been dropped onto the tile floor, leaving shattered glass everywhere.

"Animals," he muttered to himself. The last thing he wanted was have to babysit two grown men, men upon whom he had to depend. With dread in his step, he headed for the back deck where, sure enough, he found Youssef and Jonah exactly where he'd left them, spent cigars surrounding their sleeping forms as they baked in the African sun. Right then and there, he decided he would have to have a very serious conversation with his uncle regarding Youssef's future as soon as they got home. Something would have to change if his cousin was to ever make anything of himself.

Charles Bettencourt stood at the corner of his office, observing but not enjoying the most spectacular view in the city. He'd summoned his chief of security more than thirty minutes ago, and he still hadn't shown himself or reported in. Charles hated being kept waiting. There was no good reason—or for that matter, way—to disappear in a nation measuring just a few city blocks.

The elevator doors chimed in the far end of the room, and he turned as the doors slid open and out stumbled a very drunk Colonel Westmoreland. To his supreme displeasure, Charles observed that the mercenary had not bothered to remove the live grenades from his vest.

"You ever run a business?" asked Charles, disgust lacing his voice. "Was there ever a little bald-headed Colonel Westmoreland running the world's angriest lemonade stand in suburban Topeka, or wherever the fuck you're from?"

"I did lawns," answered the colonel, returning the smirk.

"What?"

"Lawns," said Westmoreland. "I mowed lawns. Pulled weeds."

"And if some other kid came sniffing around your customers?"

"I'd beat the shit out of him."

"Doctor Hassan Nassiri is sniffing around my business, and he doesn't even have the respect to do it in a ship that belongs to him. If I'd been able to reach the owner of the *Conquerer* I'd have given him an opportunity to buy his yacht back and deal with the hijackers personally. As it is—"

"What do you want me to do?" asked the colonel.

"Kill them," Charles said. "Preferably before the Conglomerate catches wind. If the Conglomerate thinks Anconia is compromised, they're going to start dropping bodies."

"How do you want it done?"

"They're about to leave Anconia Island in an attempt to retrieve the data from Professor Fatima Nassiri's aircraft. Put the ship and crew on the bottom. Make it look like pirates."

CHAPTER 8

Alexis scanned the control panels of the *Fool's Errand*'s engine room. Green across the board. A true rarity for an engine room so complex. The humming Purcell engines were finicky at best, demanding the same exacting attention as a fussy derby stallion. Take your eyes off them for too long, and, well, something was bound to go wrong. Even the wrong toned hum in one of the turbines could mean the system was about to throw a blade, leaving them dead in the water. But for now, all was in working order.

She tiptoed over to the main door and checked the access hallway. Empty. She pulled the door shut, hurried to the nearest computer terminal, and pulled up a hidden subroutine, her way of tapping into the internal security system to keep an eye on her new shipmates. Though she'd long known about the vulnerability, she'd never had a reason to exploit it before. She'd buried her new code under half a dozen unrelated protocols, even masked the signal by passing it through a data conduit normally reserved for air quality analysis. Too bad she didn't think to do a little investigating on the suspiciously quiet day before she found out she'd been stolen along with the *Conqueror*. Even so, Jonah seemed like a pretty sharp guy. She didn't know what he'd do if he found out. Best to keep it secret. Maybe he'd shrug and wander off without saying another word. Maybe he wouldn't. She'd seen his scarred-over knuckles, the residual hardening around his eye socket and jaw. This was a man who knew violence intimately, a man capable of inflicting it as well.

She sat back in her chair and folded her legs up underneath her. So far, being kidnapped hadn't changed much except that she was in charge of the engine room now and there was no dress code. She wore a pair of cutoff jean shorts and yoga tank top that would have been expressly *verboten* under the no-nonsense chief engineer of the *Conqueror*. The outfit didn't exactly go with her steel-toed workboots, but who cared? Dr. Nassiri certainly wasn't paying attention, not since their awkward little moment on Anconia Island. Or maybe he was paying attention, just in the sense that he went out of his way to avoid even crossing her path.

Dr. Nassiri. She needed to flat-out stop thinking about him, stop hoping she'd run into him on her way to the bridge, the kitchen, her bunk, or hell, even the head. She wasn't about to go full circle back to her upbringing in Amarillo, Texas, a town where the general consensus was that big hair and long legs would get a girl a lot further than what was between the ears. Still, she did wonder about him. For instance, she genuinely couldn't grasp his need to rename the ship *Fool's Errand* of all possible new names, especially since going after his mother's body and recovering her research didn't sound very foolish. It seemed noble, somehow. Not a fool's errand at all. And although she realized a stolen ship would need a new name, to her, it was and always would be the *Conquerer*.

Men, she thought. Her dad would tell her to forget about them, that her job was to look after herself and keep the engines purring. Her mother would find the whole thing hilarious—well, not the kidnapping and pirate stuff—but that Alexis was worried about what some Moroccan doctor thought of her. They'd always been the kind of parents who went their own way, that gave a tomboy the latitude she needed to pursue whatever interested her. And here she was, an engineer on a beautiful ship in a dangerous part of the world, occupying herself with thoughts of a moonlit evening on the high seas with Dr. Tall Dark and Handsome. *Jeesh*.

The surveillance system blinked to life on her screen. Alexis hopped up and took one last look down the hall to make sure nobody was coming to check on her. Paranoid much? Probably, but she liked her life like she liked her engine room, with as few loose bolts lurking around as possible.

The screen flicked over to the bridge. Dr. Nassiri stood lone watch, binoculars in hand. How old was he, maybe early to mid-thirties? A bit older than she was, but not ridiculously so. He certainly wore it well—smooth skin, high cheekbones, intelligent, dark eyes. She'd already recognized the initial fluttering of attraction, and had told herself, in no uncertain terms, to get real. Maybe this was what Stockholm syndrome felt like, but she doubted it. Sometimes a handsome doctor was just a handsome doctor, even if he did inadvertently kidnap you.

The screen flipped over to the galley.

Hellooooo Jonah.

Jonah Blackwell stood in the center of the dining area completely naked, his collection of diving gear spread across the floor in neat, squared-off little piles, wetsuit carefully folded on one side. Alexis hit the *stop* button almost unconsciously, preventing the camera from switching away from the voyeuristic view.

He stood without moving, gaunt, tanned muscles glistening, even in the grainy display of the surveillance system. She watched as he gathered the folded wetsuit in his hands and stepped into it. Her friends at home would be swooning at his lean body, broad shoulders, and fuck-all-y'all attitude, but Alexis felt something entirely different when she looked at him. Danger—a trait she found very unattractive.

Leaning in closer to the screen, she caught a brief glimpse of stitching under his left ribs as he pulled the wetsuit up his abdomen and over his shoulders. Holy shit, it looked like someone had stuck a knife in him, and recently.

Alexis flicked through the other screen views, passed on the option to watch Buzz, binoculars clamped to his face, scanning their wake for company, and then flicked to the bridge with an overhead view directly down at the consoles. Jonah, now dressed in the wetsuit, placed his hand on the finely-machined aluminum and carbon fiber joystick as he wordlessly piloted the yacht. According to the high-resolution digital nautical charts displayed on the consoles, the ship and her illegitimate crew were now well into the lawless Red Zone.

Earlier in the day, Jonah, Buzz, and Alexis had cleaned, loaded, and test-fired all of the weapons in the collection. They wouldn't fend off an attack for long. She wished they could have picked up more weaponry at Anconia Island, but the security forces weren't selling. Frankly, the crew of the *Fool's Errand* were better set to defend a Chicago bathtub distillery than a megayacht.

In the surveillance screen, Jonah picked up the walkie-talkie from the console and pressed the button to talk.

"How we doing in the engine room?" Jonah's voice, crackled over the speaker making Alexis jump—for a moment it sounded like he was right beside her.

"We're five-by-five down here," she said into her own walkie. "Barely ticking over. When you need power, you'll have it."

"Nice work, Alexis," Jonah said.

Over the surveillance screen, Alexis caught Dr. Nassiri glaring at Jonah's back. The doctor obviously didn't appreciate the familiarity with which he'd spoken to her. What, was he jealous? An unbidden smile spread across her face. Flattering, yes, but the timing really sucked.

Jonah put his hand back to the joystick tiller and snuck a glance at the radar screen. Alexis pulled up the radar feed on her own system but saw nothing but coastline. Good. They were close, maybe just a few minutes away from their destination.

Jonah disappeared from the screen and Alexis flicked over to the dining area again. He walked into view and she watched as he programmed his dive computer and then went out to the back deck of the ship where he arranged his tri-mix SCUBA gear, including several tanks of different air mixtures, lift bags, high-intensity xenon lights, reserve-air pony bottles, vest, weights, and multiple regulators. Since it was newly purchased from Anconia Island, he was triple-checking everything—even though she could tell it was all top-of-the-line and meticulously maintained.

Jonah had explained the plan. It was simple, he'd said, a 300-foot plunge to the bottom as fast as possible while using the transponder signal to stay on station. He called it a "bungee dive," and said planes were easy to get into. Big sections of the thin carbon fiber skin were most likely weak or missing. He'd get inside, grab the transponder, hard drives, and whatever else he could find and stick it in the lift bag. Dr. Fatima Nassiri's remains as well, assuming he could get to her. Maybe the other ones, too, but that would be seriously pushing his eighteen-minute bottom window. Just in case, he and Buzz cleared out enough room in the walk-in freezer of the *Fool's Errand* to fit all five bodies.

Alexis hoped Dr. Nassiri was ready to see his mother in a bad way. A month on the bottom of the ocean didn't do a body good. She'd seen it before, when the *Conqueror* assisted with a drowning recovery. She shuddered just thinking about it.

Dr. Nassiri appeared next to Jonah. Alexis could tell he was tense. The doctor began to open his mouth to ask something, but then—Alexis couldn't put her finger on it, but something was just wrong.

She took a step back from the console. The engine pitch had changed. In fact, it wasn't just the engine, it was the entire acoustic signature of the *Fool's Errand*, a change so imperceptible Alexis could scarcely drag it into her conscious mind. Nothing on the radar—but something was still wrong.

Acting on instinct, Alexis changed the feed channel to an external view, flicking through the screens as quickly as possible. Nothing whatsoever, then—

Holy fucking fuck there it was, a shape just a hundred feet off the starboard quarter, a long, dark streak under the water paralleling the course of the *Fool's Errand*. It resembled a shark or a whale, only much too large. The craft didn't move with the flow of an organic creature; it moved unnaturally straight and parallel to the yacht. Alexis felt a sudden chill come over her, as if they were being stalked.

"Is that—?" she started to say, as the conning tower of a massive, matte-black submarine sliced through the waves, parting a frothing white-foam bow wake. The submarine rose, revealing itself to be even longer than the *Fool's Errand*, stretching well beyond the aperture of the surveillance camera. The bow broke from the water as one last wave crashed over the deck. A massive four-barreled anti-aircraft weapon grew from a rear-deck raised platform just behind the stage. This was no pleasure craft, the submarine was built to intimidate, every line deliberate and menacing, more than enough firepower to take on even the largest pirate mothership.

Alexis snatched the radio in her hands. Shit, she knew she had to call this in to the bridge. *Shit*, they were going to know she had access to the surveillance cameras. *Shit. Shit-shit-shit.*

"Unidentified contact!" she shouted into the radio. "Port side aft!"

Alexis opened the surveillance feed to the bridge on a secondary monitor, watching as Dr. Nassiri briefly froze, unsure. She could see behind his eyes as he dug into the dark recesses of his brain to remember which side was port and which was starboard. Jonah didn't hesitate; he stuck his head out the window immediately, cocked it briefly, then returned to his station and snatched the marine radio.

"Unidentified submarine," said Jonah into the microphone. Alexis heard the call over her systems. "This is the yacht *Fool's Errand*. Please state your intentions."

The radio crackled, but no answer returned. Alexis bounded up the main staircase, just in time to hear Jonah repeat his hail over the emergency frequencies. Hell, it didn't even matter if the submarine could hear their radio calls or not ... the pirates certainly could, and were no doubt already mobilizing to investigate the sudden electronic chatter deep within their territory.

"Who are these people?" she demanded, clad in her cutoffs and tank top and self-consciously smelling of high-octane marine fuel and engine lubricant. "Why are you breaking radio silence?"

"Alexis, I need you back in the engine room."

"Why?" she retorted.

"Alexis!" shouted Jonah, loud enough that Alexis flinched. "Engine room! *Now!*"

Without another word, she turned and practically sprinted back down the stairs. She allowed herself a single backwards glance at the bow, where Buzz stood like a mermaid figurehead, his weird soviet SCUBA-gun in hand, leaning far over the railing as if pressing himself over it could somehow allow him further sight. Even with her limited knowledge of firearms, she knew the Russian weapon belonged in a museum, not on the deck of a ship plunging headlong into the most dangerous waters on the planet. At least Buzz looked scary as hell, with his scarred-up shaved head and weirdo assault rifle.

Alexis threw herself back in front of her console station, just in time to see a single figure emerge from the top hatch of the submarine. She squinted at first, then realized what she was looking at. The man looked like one of the Anconia Island mercenaries, a welcome sight. An intense wave of relief washed over her as the soldier smiled and saluted the *Fool's Errand*.

On the bridge, Dr. Nassiri smiled and waved. Jonah

yelled at Buzz to stop pointing his 'fucking rifle' at the new arrivals.

Alexis allowed herself a little smile as her tension faded; the cavalry had made quite an entrance. It appeared Dr. Nassiri's money went further than expected; this was a brilliant show of force. In fact, it probably didn't even matter that Jonah had broken radio silence. If any pirates showed up, the mounted cannons could open up and it'd be over before it even started.

"Unidentified submarine, we're happy to see you," said Jonah over the radio. "Appreciate the escort, we will stop engines and stand by for instructions."

"Roger, stand by," confirmed a harsh voice over the radio.

On the bridge monitor, Dr. Nassiri stopped his schoolboy waving, but kept the foolish grin plastered over his face. Alexis brought the engines to full stop, feeling the slight vibration as they spun down to idle.

Over the video feed, a single shaved-head mercenary, rifle slung behind him and armored vest heavy with equipment, removed the stoppers from the barrels and connected the weapon to an unseen ammunition feed in the deck. He swung the quad-gun back and forth towards the horizon, testing the articulation of the impressive weapon.

Alexis froze as the gunner suddenly swiveled around, training the massive quad-barrels on the bow of the *Fool's Errand*.

"What the hell—?"

The gunner fired, blinding the security camera with light, noise deafening as the four barrels of the anti-aircraft weapons lit up in succession and laser-like tracer rounds ripped through the unprotected engine room of the *Fool's Errand*. Fire blasted apart the thin carbon-fiber skin of the yacht and cut the supporting rib structure to pieces as Alexis held her hands over her ears and screamed. Overhead florescent lighting flickered and died as daylight streamed through the Swiss-cheese hull and deafening ricochets tore through the upper structure of the megayacht. Alexis instinctively hit the deck as a hail of broken glass, splintered fiberglass and red-hot aluminum shrapnel rained down around her. She couldn't think, couldn't move, her entire adrenaline-compromised perspective a grey, gun-slit view of her own hands as the console behind her exploded in a shower of flames and molten glass. The monitor bank on the console tipped and fell, slamming into the unyielding metal grating with a flash of electrical arcs.

The live feed from the bridge continued to play. Dr. Nassiri curled up in a fetal position soundlessly screaming on the monitor.

Oh great, thought Alexis. I'm going to die watching television.

In slow-motion, Jonah scrambled to his feet, trying to reach a walkie-talkie as a second barrage tore through the bridge.

From the bow feed, Alexis watched as Buzz jumped to his feet, Soviet rifle already shouldered as he stood on the extreme end of the bow, possibly the most exposed position on the entire ship. The submarine crossed their bow, firing as Buzz leaned over the bow railing.

"*Run!*" screamed Alexis at the security feed. She realized she could scarcely hear her own voice in her blast-deafened ears.

On the bridge, Jonah tried in vain to impart the same message. *Find cover, you stupid fuck*, he mouthed, waving his arms, oblivious to his own safety.

Buzz didn't hear Alexis, didn't hear Jonah, could not have possibly heard them. Alexis saw the Moroccan man in fragments, tiny mosaics as the engagement played out. Buzz's face, dripping blood from a massive cut across his forehead and scalp. His hands, grainy specs over the security feed, aiming his strange rifle at the submarine's conning tower. Buzz pulling the trigger, firing a single ineffectual burst towards the man at the quad gun.

He held down the trigger, muzzle climbing as the continuous burst of fire danced across the hardened steel skin of the submarine, missing the anti-aircraft gun entirely and spilling bullets ineffectually into the ocean. The mercenary turned—those *reflexes*—and took aim.

Pulling his own trigger, the gunner emptied bullets into the bow of the *Fool's Errand*, obliterating it. It was almost as if Buzz had said, *and for my next trick, I will disappear* as he was enveloped in a cloud of fire and pink mist. And that was that, he was just gone, along with the entire bow of the ship, both taken off the face of the earth as if they'd never existed.

At least Jonah still appeared to have his faculties. Alexis saw him find the pearl-handled handgun with one hand and jam it into the belt of his wetsuit. And then he called her over the radio.

"Full power to the engines!" he shouted. She noticed a brief silence—as far as the mercenaries aboard the submarine were concerned, the *Fool's Errand* was a burning, shattered hulk. The one remaining console to her right flashed bright red; half of the compartments on the port side were taking on water as one critical system after another died in a cascade of technological failure.

The turbine engines roared to life, propellers supercavitating seawater into frothing bubbles as they spun up to a screaming pitch. Perhaps the *Fool's Errand* had a trick or two yet—the props bit into the sea, throwing Alexis to the deck of the engine room as the yacht leapt forward, narrowly cutting across the stern of the attack submarine, full power to the engines, lazily wallowing to starboard as seawater rushed into the lowest deck.

The Somali coastline loomed in front of the bow feed as hurricane-force headwinds and roaring seawater ripped through the bullet-shattered hull of the engine room. Behind them, the submarine took lazy potshots against the stern of the vessel, forcing Alexis to duck as they ripped through critical systems.

She wrenched valves and switches, bodily throwing herself at the remaining hydraulic controls, trying to correct for the highly compromised hydrodynamics of the rapidly leaking hull.

"Come on you bastard!" she screamed at the controls.

Just moments, that's all she needed. Just moments to get them close to the coastline, away from the submarine. And then probably get captured and executed by pirates. Goddamn fantastic.

The massive turbine engines of the *Fool's Errand* sputtered once then caught again. Shit, fuck, shit shit *SHIT!* The coolant system was shot to pieces, no pressure, the engines already reaching critical temperatures. If one or both of them went—well, the resulting explosion wouldn't just leave them dead in the water, it would turn the entire stern of the *Fool's Errand* into a smoldering ruin.

"Alexis, what is happening down there?" shouted Jonah into the radio. Over the bridge security feed, Dr. Nassiri was on his feet, shell-shocked, staring empty-eyed at the gaping maw that was once the bow.

"It's bad!" she yelled into the radio.

She realized she sounded scared, terrified. Not the impression she wanted to convey. He could probably hear the screaming mechanical distress of the engine room over the radio. Jonah would know whatever was happening down here couldn't be good.

"Report!" he shouted.

"We're shot to pieces!" said Alexis, her own voice distant over the sound of the wind. "All coolants systems are gone; we're taking on water fast. I've bypassed every safety system just to keep us moving but we'll be dead in the water in seconds."

Silence over the radio as Jonah weighed his options. No lifeboats; but they'd just be floating orange target practice anyway. The submarine wasn't here to take prisoners, that much was clear.

Jonah hadn't released the transmit button on the walkie, and Alexis could hear Dr. Nassiri on the marine radio, screaming out a jumbled distress signal for anyone who would listen, anyone who would help. He pleaded with the submarine to stop the attack, to take mercy on the mortally wounded ship. Alexis could see he wasn't even transmitting, the marine radio had taken a stray bullet, spilling the electronic guts of the device halfway across the shattered bridge.

"Give me one last burst of engine power," growled Jonah over the radio. "Anything she's got left I'll need over the next fifteen seconds."

Jonah thrust the joystick to port, bringing the *Fool's Errand* around in a violent buttonhook, throwing Alexis to the deck again.

Last stand, thought Alexis. There wouldn't even be

anything left to bring to Texas, she'd just be some dumb American girl who disappeared from a godforsaken part of the world she was never meant to be in the first place.

With immense calm, Alexis bypassed the last of the safety measures and set the engines to full power. She dropped to her knees as the *Fool's Errand* thrust forward, ruined bow pushing upwards into the sky as the turbines howled with fury. The *Fool's Errand* completed the turn as unrelenting thrust accelerated the burning hulk forward.

It was funny how the mind remembered the little things in a time like this. Like when she first stepped foot on the *Conqueror*. A few days after walking up on stage to get her diploma for a masters in mechanical engineering with a focus in naval architecture. She'd read about the ship porting in Galveston, so she drove her shit-box car there, stepped on board, demanded to see the engineer and told him she could increase the power of the engines by 8.5%. The moxie got her an interview; an 11.3% improvement got her the job. She wondered if her car was still parked at the dock, rusting and moldering away unattended, windows clouded with dust, tires flat, batteries long since dead. She probably should have sold it.

The *Fool's Errand* bore down on the submarine, gaining speed. Her instincts were right. Jonah was not a man who liked to lose. Over the video feed, she could see him crouched by a console, Dr. Nassiri at his side.

Surprised by the suicidal act of its cornered prey, the fire from the submarine stopped as the gunner took stock of the changed situation. The moment was all Jonah needed as the *Fool's Errand* surged toward the submarine, passing sixty knots in speed, bearing down like a freight train.

"Brace for impact!" shouted Jonah over the radio,

his voice echoing through every compartment of the stricken ship. Dr. Nassiri crumpled into a ball and rolled underneath the nearest console as tracer fire arced over the ruined bow and lit up the bridge and engine room with brutal intensity, raining sparks and metal fragments onto Alexis as she tried to find a position where she could survive the coming crash.

The destroyed bow of the *Fool's Errand* dropped as the yacht reached hydrofoil speeds, the ship skipping across the water as it zeroed in on the submarine. The gunner froze as the *Fool's Errand* threw her keel across the platform, a symphony of destruction. The impact hurled Alexis forward, smashing her face and head against a bullet-riddled console.

For a brief moment, all was silent as Alexis struggled to remain conscious. Her gray, swimming vision lied to her, and she stumbled as she reached for something to hold on to. Her fingers tapped across the deck grating, touching burning lubricant and broken glass. The acidic smell of leaking fuel filled her nose and lungs. Nevermind that … the entire ship had shattered itself across the back of the submarine just aft of the conning tower, large scarred patches of the matte-black steel skin of the sub showing through gaping holes in the *Fool's Errand's* hull.

She crawled up the main staircase, trying to keep underneath the growing billows of black smoke. Her fingers touched the Winchester shotgun as if it'd been placed there as a sign from the Almighty himself. God wanted her to fight.

Rolling on her back and cradling the shotgun in her arms, she racked a round into the chamber. She pushed herself to her feet and made her way to the bridge, surveying the jungle of hanging wires and wrecked consoles around her. Dr. Nassiri looked up at her, eyes wide, still in shock.

"What do we do?" asked Alexis. Jonah was already gone, to where she did not know. But some part of her knew he had a plan.

"We follow Jonah," croaked Dr. Nassiri. He glanced at her shotgun, then down at the 9mm pistol he had in his own hand. Billowing black smoke filled the bridge, and Alexis tried to force open one of the doors. A twisted frame kept it jammed in place.

Dr. Nassiri didn't wait, he crawled on top of the consoles and through the shattered front windscreen. Alexis followed, more falling than stepping out of the window towards the bow of the crashed yacht, shotgun in hand, intense sunlight splaying across her face as she stepped outside. The yacht had obliterated the quad gun and gunner.

Alexis kicked a deck chair out of the way, winced and pulled a piece of glass out of her leg. At least she wasn't hit, not as far as she could tell. Adrenaline could do funny things to the brain, she actually felt pretty fucking good right now.

Jonah's SCUBA gear lay scattered across the deck. One of the anti-aircraft rounds had pierced the rear of a tri-mix tank in the ensuing chaos, detonating it and putting a massive splintered crater in one corner and embedding jagged shrapnel in the deck, bulkheads and chairs.

And then there he was. Jonah stood perched on the side of the yacht, 1911 pistol in hand, taking a perfect overlook position on the conning tower at just ten feet away. He took a bead on the hatch, waiting for it to move, twitch, anything that would justify sending a hollow-point round through the brainpan of first man to pop his head out like a whack-a-mole.

A wave of uncontrollable laughter washed over Alexis.

Sorry Dad, her brain spat out between shaking giggles. *Accidentally wrapped the family Volkswagen around a telephone pole.* It didn't make sense, which made it all the funnier, so much that her eyes teared up and every impulse to fight the inappropriate laughter just made it that much more intense.

Apparently sensing a moment to prepare, Jonah unzipped the front of his wetsuit halfway down his chest, grabbed a pressurized pony reserve bottle of pure oxygen from the deck, and stuffed it in.

Taking a position behind him with Dr. Nassiri at her side, Alexis sincerely hoped if Jonah was shot, it'd be in the heart or head, not in the pony bottle. An explosion like that, so close to his soft tissue and hollow organs would blow him to pieces. Hell, it would be pretty spectacular, probably enough to kill her and the doctor as well. The potential energy stored in air tanks, even in the little ones, was substantial.

The hatch in front of him flew open, articulated by an unseen hydraulic system. All Alexis could see was a Yankees ballcap. The mercenary didn't even make it to eye level before Jonah pulled the trigger. There was no way Jonah could miss, not at this range. The shot impacted just above and to the left of the white Y, splatting skull against the back of the hatch. The body tumbled down and out of view, landing below with an audible, sickening thump. Jonah hurled the pony bottle after him, hoping it'd go unnoticed with the chaos of a dead man dropping in from above.

Fucking whack-a-mole, thought Alexis as she watched Jonah take a step back, launch into a running start and leap though the air towards the conning tower, gun in hand. He landed with difficulty, catching the railings right in his ribs, knocking the wind out of his lungs. He slid over the hatch entrance and looked down, handgun at the ready. She watched as he took aim at the pony bottle and fired and could feel the shock wave from fifteen feet away as the conning tower shook and belched out a big cloud of white oxygenated vapor.

Jonah stole one glance towards Dr. Nassiri and Alexis with an intense look that made Alexis cold and hot all over, and then he disappeared into the submarine. She heard gunshots, multiple weapons of multiple calibers. The American was in it now, a straight-up, close-quarters, old-school gunfight.

"What do we do?" asked Dr. Nassiri.

Alexis didn't know and knew the doctor didn't either. She looked behind her. The ragged hulk of the *Fool's Errand* had already given up the ghost, its shattered frame slowly slipping beneath the waves and pulling the submarine down with it. They wouldn't have their little perch for long.

"We follow Jonah," said Alexis. Forcing her muscles to unfreeze, she pushed herself back, launched into a run and leapt for the conning tower. Unlike Jonah—and with no small amount of pride—she landed perfectly, both feet on the tower, one hand on the railing and one on the shotgun. Must have been all those dance and cheerleading practices before she knew how explain to her mother that she loathed everything about them.

Twelve feet below, in the red-lit control room of the submarine, the mercenary with the Yankees hat lay on his back, one dead, accusing eye staring directly up at Alexis. An entire quarter of his head was completely missing, as his still-struggling heart pumped a seemingly endless supply of blood into a gathering pool. Dr. Nassir made the leap too, landing awkwardly beside her and almost losing his handgun in the process.

Alexis straddled the hatchway, crossed her arms like a mummy, and simply allowed herself to drop. This was going to hurt, a lot.

She fell fucking hard, landing awkwardly on top of the body of the head-shot man, rolling to the side, trying to take some of the momentum laterally without breaking an ankle.

Beside her writhed the two sailors Jonah had hit with the exploding bottle trick. Both were dead, but they didn't know it yet. They trembled on the ground, mouths foaming with pink-flecked bubbles, lungs destroyed by the concussive force. Alexis had never seen it before; but some deep part of her knew the men had seconds before they lost consciousness, minutes before they were dead. The horror overwhelmed her, and in that moment she would have done anything in her power to save them.

Alexis heard movement from her right and swiveled the shotgun to take aim at a young man, dressed in the horizontal stripes of a Russian sailor's uniform halfway slumped over a pilot's console. The young man held his chest, eyes closed in pain, unarmed. The Russian sailor was a slight, good looking man, the type that could have modeled if he were taller. A picture of him wearing a vintage sailor suit in a Ralph Lauren ad flashed before her eyes. Jonah had put two rounds directly into his sternum, throwing him back against the instrumentation panel with a violent impact, splattering blood across the dials. He sputtered, coughing up blood, as he compulsively touched his wounds, stared at his hands, and touched his wounds again.

"Alexis!" shouted a voice from above the conning tower. She looked up to see Dr. Nassiri leaning in like he were at the top of a wishing well. Too scared to shout back at him, she urgently waved him down. She heard a gunshot, felt the fragment of lead fly by her face, heard the zing of a too-close bullet. Gunshots chattered away from the unseen bow section of the submarine. Some of them sounded like automatic rifles—Jonah wouldn't last long against that volume of firepower.

Dr. Nassiri slid down the ladder, dropping down beside her. She watched as he holstered his pistol and triaged the head-shot man and the two now-silent, foam-spitting sailors, no hope of survival. His eyes fell on the handsome Russian with the two chest wounds, and his training took over. Dr. Nassiri put both hands on the slight man, dragged him to his feet and slammed him on top of a chart table, then went to work to save his life.

"Give me the medical kit from the wall," he ordered.

Alexis looked over and saw it—it was one of the massive full-emergency-care ones, including emergency oxygen facemasks and splints. But the nature of his demand completely baffled her as gunshots continued to echo through the claustrophobic chamber.

"Are you for real?" demanded Alexis.

"Please!"

With no time to protest, Alexis crawled across the compartment, grabbed the medical kit and heaved it towards the doctor.

"Thank you," said Dr. Nassiri, ignoring her glare.

Jonah started shouting at them from two chambers up in the bow, his words scarcely intelligible over the din of the fighting.

"I've got two pinned down here in the bow!" he shouted. "Alexis, Doc—if you're alive, I need you to capture the stern!"

Alexis racked another slug into the shotgun and considered his words. *Goddamn fucking motherfucker.* She really didn't want to do this and certainly not alone. She was fucking scared, really fucking scared. And there was the doctor, wrist deep in one of their enemies, trying to save a life while bullets rained down around them.

"Doc, you hear that?" she shouted. "Let's go, let's move!"

Doctor Nassiri ignored her. She could see on his face that he'd completely fallen back on his training. Maybe he couldn't even hear her. In the midst of the carnage, he had become a battlefield surgeon once again.

Screaming inside her own head, Alexis grabbed the 9mm out of the back of the doctor's waistband and stuck it into the front of her cutoff shots.

And there she was, shotgun in hand, skinned-up knees, and wet, tangled hair. At least she had on her utility boots. Weapon leveled, she charged back into the throbbing engine room. Movement on her left—she fired, blasting apart a chunk of the battery bank, spitting debris in all directions. The sailor—maybe an engineer?—swore and twisted away, trying to escape the leaking acid. She fired again, the slug ricocheting off the interior walls of the submarine. Movement, and she fired again, blasting apart an instrumentation panel. And there he was, an older, darkly tanned man with a gaunt face and a buzz cut holding a steak knife.

Alexis took aim and pulled the trigger, but the shotgun clicked empty. Knife in hand, the engineer lunged towards her as she dropped the shotgun, drew Dr. Nassiri's pistol and traced five shots into his upper chest.

Alexis burst in through the next hatch, 9mm raised, fully expecting to find herself in a hail of bullets. In most military submarines, this compartment would have been the aft torpedo room, perhaps with a few bunkbeds. Instead, Alexis found herself within the most spectacular armory she'd ever seen—even better than a Texan gun emporium—rows and rows of German assault rifles, handguns, grenades, breaching charges, all manner of armor, and both engineering and combat SCUBA gear.

Gunshots rang out from the command compartment, two compartments forward. It sounded as if Jonah had been forced to retreat, assuming he was still alive. She knew he wouldn't last long, not with a rapidly diminishing supply of ammunition and two trained men after him.

Alexis snatched the nearest weapons she could find, a phosphorous grenade and a breaching explosive, then charged headlong out of the compartment towards the command compartment. Bullets zipped around her, as expertly-placed shots rang out from the forward bunkroom, the last stand of the surviving crew of the submarine. She headed back toward Dr. Nassiri, and fired a few shots at the unseen attackers as Dr. Nassiri just stood there, not ducking, not even wincing at the loud retorts.

Jonah was still a chamber forward, no help to her. And there was no way she could get the grenades to him without being shot herself.

As if to add to the perfect scene of chaos, a thousand gallons of freezing seawater poured down the conning tower ladder, gaining momentum like a flash flood down a box canyon. The cold water jolted Alexis out of her shock. She leapt to her feet and ran over to the control console, fingers dancing over the complex, seemingly endless control schematics, looking for a solution to the rapidly filling submarine.

"Are we sinking?" shouted Dr. Nassiri. At least he'd found his wits.

"I found it!" sounded Alexis. With a mechanical whine, the hydraulics to the hatch kicked in, forcing it shut. The massive surge of water cut off immediately, leaving a strange silence as seawater dripped from the closed hatch. Then more gunshots. Jonah shouted something to her, but she couldn't make it out.

The submarine creaked loudly, a metallic moaning sound ringing throughout every compartment, structural members shifting and settling as the pressure around the vessel increased.

"I think we're still sinking," said Dr. Nassiri, quieter this time. Alexis looked up, seeing an analog depth gauge central to the command panel where the Russian sailor had been shot. The needle of the gauge edged slowly to the right as the submarine plunged ever deeper. They were sinking fast—too fast. Eighty feet. A hundred. The ribs of the submarine shuddered with the rapidly increasing pressure. Alexis heard a loud scraping sound, and the entire submarine shuddered again.

Then she realized what was happening. It was the wreckage of the *Fool's Errand*, still clinging to the submarine, dragging all aboard into the crushing abyss.

CHAPTER 9

The submarine plunged into the depths, steel hull groaning with long, low rumbles, creaks, and the pinging of re-settling rib joints. As gunshots continued to ring out within, Dr. Nassiri hunched over the chart table in the command compartment, his forehead sweating the type of itchy beaded sweat that only forms when your hands are inside the chest cavity of a living patient. The young man in front of him, mid-twenties at most, stared up at him, passing in and out of consciousness.

My kingdom for an anesthesiologist, thought Dr. Nassiri. But this was battlefield medicine in all its butchery, a fight between him and hemorrhaging wounds. No intubation, no ventilators, just a blade, bandages, and bare hands.

His young Russian patient came round into consciousness with an ugly, violent flailing that knocked off his own oxygen mask, gasping, wheezing, spitting up foam and blood. Sometimes they did this towards the end. Eyes wide, the man screamed in Russian. Something-something-something-*babushki*. Dr. Nassiri tried to translate it in his mind, but only recognized the word *grandmother*.

The Russian didn't have enough undamaged lung tissue to spare, and his left lung immediately began to collapse. He lapsed into unconsciousness again.

The doctor snuck a glance towards the gunshots echoing from the corridor leading towards the bow. Jonah and Alexis had taken cover behind a locker. Through the open hatchway, Dr. Nassiri had seen Jonah turn and catch his glance for a moment. Jonah's look wasn't judgmental, it was a quizzical *what the hell are you doing?* Why help a man who tried to kill us? Jonah would have no idea as to why he'd even attempt to save the Russian—after all, Jonah had done his utmost to put the man down for good. But when bullets started flying, all Hassan Nassiri knew to do was save lives.

A barrage of small arms fire rang out, and he heard Alexis cursing like he'd never heard a woman curse before. He wished he hadn't allowed her to take his sidearm. Still, his gun was best with her—he preferred the knife if it came to that.

Another round of fresh creaking and groaning filled the air around them, echoing like a cathedral antechamber.

"We're sinking," announced Alexis, as if she hadn't already said it just moments before, as if the ongoing gunfight was not enough to worry about.

More bullets flew down the corridor, bisecting the space between Dr. Nassiri and the two Americans.

"Want to take a stab at the crush depth?" asked Jonah without turning around.

"No idea," said Alexis.

"What do we do?" shouted Dr. Nassiri to the Americans through the hatchway.

"Glad you could join us on Planet Earth," said Jonah.

"We can't fight our way out, not unless they get sloppy."

"Are they getting sloppy?" asked Alexis.

"No," answered Jonah over the seemingly nonstop din of incoming bullets.

Theoretically speaking, they had to run out of ammunition at some point. *No—no—no*—more blood from some unseen nicked artery. Dr. Nassiri pressed his fingers deeper into the wound, trying desperately to find the source, somehow stop it.

"Hey fuckers!" shouted Alexis at the two mercenaries holed up in the forward bow. "We're sinking! Cut this shit out!"

Jonah waved his hand in the corridor; the mercenaries tried to blow it off. Apparently they weren't in a talking mood.

"Jonah, I have grenades," said Alexis. "Two of them."

"That's a terrible idea," said Jonah, smirking. "Worst I've heard all day."

Without another word, he yanked one out of her hands and chucked it down the corridor.

"Cover!" screamed the mercenaries in near-unison.

The guns-for-hire dove into the far forward section, too fast for Jonah to get off an accurate shot, and slammed the heavy steel door behind them. Before they could change their minds, Jonah bolted after them, caught the handle and held it shut. Dr. Nassiri adjusted his body so he could watch the developments down the accessway while still keeping pressure on the Russian's wounds.

"Is this your plan?" asked Alexis as she went after him, picking up the grenade. "I think you're supposed to pull the pin."

"I'm not suicidal. Fire in this compartment could set off

the whole ship," Jonah said. He winced and braced himself against the kicking door as the two men inside struggled to get it open again. Jonah had the upper hand, not from raw strength, but because he'd managed to brace himself in a way where it'd take a hydraulic press to budge it from the other side.

Jonah took his free hand and pointed up at a series of metal tubes running between their compartment and the barricaded bow compartment.

"Alexis, get an axe," shouted Jonah. "And Doc, get the fuck in here, I need a hand."

"I'm a bit busy," snapped Dr. Nassiri from down the corridor.

Alexis pulled a fire axe off of the nearest wall.

"Hassan, I put two shots in his chest," shouted Jonah, getting angrier by the second. "I assure you, he will die in minutes. I need you right-*fucking*-now!"

"I'm good with an axe," said Alexis.

Dr. Nassiri glanced up as Jonah stared him down. It wasn't as if the American could march over there and make him give up his patient. The door kicked again, almost opening enough to see moving shapes on the other side. Either Jonah was weakening or the men inside were getting desperate.

"Knock out that ceiling pipe," ordered Jonah, pointing above his head.

Alexis took a single wild swing at the overhead pipe and the axe head clanged off, sending the uncontrolled blade flying downwards, embedding itself in the deck between Jonah's legs just inches from his crotch.

"Try again," said Jonah. "Aim for *that* pipe."

Alexis scowled as she took aim at the overhead pipe.

The mercenaries behind the door heard the axe-on-metal clanging and renewed their efforts to escape.

Alexis swung the axe a third time, burying it into the pipe. Jonah plastered a wolfish grin on his face, excited by her initial success.

One more shot to the pipe and it came free, exposing a small opening into the other compartment normally reserved for air flow.

"First grenade, no pin pulled," said Jonah. "Far as you can shove it in."

Alexis pushed the first phosphorous grenade into the air pipe, bracing herself in the air so she could reach in almost to her shoulder.

"Good," said Jonah.

"Now what?"

"Now we give them a chance to surrender. Ever seen video of what white phosphorus does to the human body? We put a live grenade in their compartment, it's going to light up the whole forward like an industrial oven."

Jonah adjusted his position, still bracing the hatch shut.

"Hey assholes!" shouted Jonah through the heavy hatchway. "Time to pack it in. You're cornered. You're outgunned. How about I open this door and see you on your knees, facing me with your hands raised? It's either that or I swear to god, I will turn you into a smudge on the deck plates."

The pressure on the other side of the door eased. They'd stopped trying to force their way through.

"What do you say?" yelled Jonah.

"Standing down!" rattled a voice from the other side of the hatch. "We're standing down!"

Jonah stepped back from the hatchway and allowed it

to open slightly only to see the black barrel of an assault rifle jammed through the opening.

"Shiiiiit!" he stuttered and kicked the barrel back into the forward compartment. Using all his strength, he dragged the hatch shut again with a ringing clang as the assault rifle shot twice, bullets ricocheting against the deck and through the accessway.

"Fuck these guys," he growled, checking himself and Alexis for bullet wounds. "Get the second grenade. Pull the pin; shove it in deep into the pipe, past the dividing wall and into the forward compartment. Close the valve. Can you do that in the six seconds before it detonates?"

"Yes," answered Alexis.

"Six seconds," repeated Jonah.

Alexis stared daggers as she yanked the pin and plunged the grenade into the air pipe. She wrenched the pipe valve with all her strength, nearly succeeding in closing it when the explosion went off, shooting a five foot long jet of hot phosphorus flame out of the pipe and shaking the submarine to the keel. Alexis reached up again and just managed to cut off the jet before it set the nearby bunk beds on fire.

From the other side of the steel wall and three hatchways compartments forward, two men screamed as they burned alive. Ammunition cooked off with dull pops, precipitating a secondary explosion and more screaming. Jonah held the door closed against one last kick, waiting for the sickening silence.

Still bracing the door, Jonah grimaced and Alexis shuddered. Dr. Nassiri had seen burn victims, even treated a few; he couldn't imagine celebrating anyone dying that way, not even a mortal enemy. And what of this supposed victory? Were they victorious in the fact that they would die moments after the mercenaries instead of moments before?

Dr. Nassiri glanced up at the depth gauge as they passed a thousand feet. The very thought of it gave him chills, water the distance of three football pitches weighed down on them. How much could the hull of this vessel take? Probably not much more, judging by the creaking and pinging sounds echoing through the submarine.

Jonah held the door shut for one more minute, then let it go. No sounds came from the compartment; his hands were bright red from the searing heat. The smoldering bodies of the mercenaries in the bow would have to be considered a loose end, at least for now. If the jet of white fire shooting out of the pipe was any indication, death would have been fast, a bright white light searing heat, a few screams and— once the brain cooked or blood boiled—nothing.

Jonah scrambled to the control panel followed by Alexis, both now intimately close to Dr. Nassiri in the tight quarters of the command compartment. Dr. Nassiri kept his back turned—a few more staples and the bleeding might actually be under control—

"Blowing ballast tanks," said Jonah. He inputted a series of commands into the controls console and was rewarded by a loud hissing sound as the external ballast tanks filled with air, displacing the heavy seawater and lightening the entire vessel. The depth gauge slowed as all three watched with held breath. The gauge just edged barely past fifteen hundred feet, almost stopped, then continued deeper and deeper, once again picking up speed. The groaning of the structural members continued with renewed intensity.

"This is not good," Jonah said. "There's too much weight from the yacht pulling us down. Alexis, give me engine power. Let's push this ship off our backs."

"Me?" Alexis looked at him as if he'd sprouted horns.

"You're my engineer."

"But I've never—"

"What happened to their engineer?" Dr. Nassiri asked.

"I think I shot him." Alexis said.

"Dead man's boots." Jonah pointed at the controls. "You're my new engineer."

"Shit. Shit. *Shit!*" Alexis kicked the empty chair in front of the control panel, sending is spinning.

"I need you." Jonah said.

"Fuck you." Alexis said as she stilled the chair and sat down. Fingers flying, she pulled up a series of menus and engine diagnostics. "I can give you sixty seconds of full battery power," she said. "Maybe ninety, then we're running off emergency reserves."

"Sixty?" demanded Jonah. "That's it?"

"I may have also shot up the battery compartment," she admitted.

"Can't do anything about that now. Put the pedal to the metal."

Alexis winced as she inputted the command. The long driveshaft of the submarine spun to life, chewing at the dark water, trying to gain traction. The entire vessel shifted, the bow rising as the stern fell, putting Dr. Nassiri in the uncomfortable position of hugging his patient to prevent him from sliding off the chart table.

The semi-conscious Russian hugged him back, and Dr. Nassiri could have wept with joy—with the bleeding contained and with the IV bag the Russian still had enough strength to move. The doctor took the opportunity to listen to both lungs. It wasn't good news, but total lung collapse had been prevented. If they lived through the next sixty seconds, the Russian might just make it.

"Come on, you *bitch*!" Jonah shouted as the submarine shuddered and bucked under the intense power of the massive rear propeller. "Come on!"

One loud, long scraping sound, peeled along the skin of the submarine, and then another—the yacht wreckage above them was moving, but not enough. Not more than thirty seconds into the exercise, the engines died amid the howl of emergency warning klaxons.

"What happened? That wasn't sixty seconds!" yelled Jonah over the cacophony.

"It's the drag, we sucked down too much power," shouted Alexis. "We're down to emergency reserves. The computer is locking me out of throttle controls."

"Down to bare knuckles and swingin' dicks," mused Jonah as the now unimpeded depth gauge rolled past 1700 feet. "Fill the ballast tanks, make us heavy."

"What?" said Alexis.

"Fill them. I want to hit the sea floor with enough impact to knock this wreckage free. Doc, I need your help here. Fuck that guy—he's already good as dead."

"But we have no idea how deep the bottom is!" protested Alexis.

"You got a better plan?"

Dr. Nassiri ignored both Americans. There it was, the last bandage put in place.

"Am I going to have to put a fucking bullet in your patient's head?" demanded Jonah. "If I kill him, will you please fucking help me?"

Dr. Nassiri cleared his throat, loud enough for Alexis and Jonah to look up from their stations. "Please allow me to assist," said Dr. Nassiri. And with that, he took a massive syringe loaded with a bear shot of amphetamines and adrenaline and jammed it into the Russian's heart, pushing the plunger fully down.

The Russian's eyes jumped open, wide enough to see the whites around all sides. Nearly crazed, he yanked the syringe out of his chest and tried to jump to his feet while screaming in Russian.

"English!" shouted Dr. Nassiri.

"Who fuck you are?" he yelled, his thick accent tumbling out of his mouth for the first time.

Dr. Nassiri glanced down at his name patch—Vitaly Kuznetsov.

"Vitaly, we're the ones your crew tried to kill," said Dr. Nassiri. "All your comrades are dead and we're sinking."

"Is submarine. Is *designed* to sink," said the Russian, as if this would be obvious to anyone.

"We're passing eighteen hundred feet," said Jonah. "What's our crush depth?"

"Difficult to say until actually crushed, no?" Vitaly gurgled. He dragged himself up against the wall, his head lolling.

"Fucking *guess* for me," said Jonah, frustration building again.

"Maybe two thousand five hundred? What big deal, just blow ballast, make us very light for emergency surface."

Nobody had to tell Dr. Nassiri that they were already past two thousand and still rapidly descending. Five hundred feet to go, maybe less given the violence of the collision. How long would it take, a minute, maybe two? At least the end of the ride would be quick enough, a sudden bang, a rush of water.

"We blew the ballast," said Jonah. "We've got three hundred and seventy tons of yacht wreckage fused to the upper deck pushing us down."

"No good, no good," Vitaly said, realizing the predicament for the first time over the powerful combination of endorphins, pain, amphetamines, and adrenaline. "Battery power?"

"Down to reserves," said Jonah, scowling at the man he'd shot. "We were going to try to drive the submarine into the sea floor, knock off the wreckage that way."

"No good, no good," said the Russian. "Your idea terrible. We must *roll* submarine. You certain everybody dead?"

"Your comrades are dead," said Jonah. "How do we roll? Is that even possible?"

"I believe rolling only option. But rolling submarine only tried one time. Black Sea, nineteen-seventy-three by Russian Navy."

"Did it work?" asked Alexis.

"Everybody die," Vitaly said. "My father lose two cousins."

The Russian threw an arm over Dr. Nassiri's shoulder. The doctor guided him to the helmsman's chair, inches from where he'd been shot through the chest.

"Brace yourselves," Vitaly ordered as he secured himself in the mounted helmsman's seat with a seatbelt across his lap and shoulder. Without further warning, he dumped the starboard ballast tank. The submarine suddenly lurched to the right like it'd just had a leg kicked out from underneath it. Alexis, Jonah, and Dr. Nassiri all fell to their knees, crawling over the jagged surfaces of the bulkhead mounted consoles that had once been on the right wall as the submarine turned over on her side.

Vitaly swore, pounding away at the command console, adjusting the depth planes and trim with furious speed, his fingers dancing over the controls as if conducting an eighty-piece symphony orchestra.

"Brace, brace," he chanted. "We must show belly!"

The submarine lurched forward, propelled by emergency power that he had dredged from god-knows-where, her depth planes cutting through the water, forcing her upside down. Every metallic member of the submarine shuddered and rattled, every unsecured bunk, computer monitor, manual, loose change, everything came tumbling out of its place, spilling across the ceiling of the submarine as she showed her underside to the distant surface.

And for one perfect moment, there was stillness as the submarine plunged into the depths like a tucked-wing bird of prey, upside-down, passing 2500 feet. With one last scraping groan, the twisted wreckage of the *Fool's Errand* peeled from the submarine and fell away into the darkness.

Vitaly hung from the ceiling in his mounted chair, arms and legs dangling like a dead deer ready to be trussed.

"He's unconscious again!" shouted Alexis. Without prompting, she stood up and slapped him across the face, hard.

Vitaly snapped to consciousness, shaking his head and regaining control of the computer console.

"*Da, da, da!*" he shouted with such conviction that Dr. Nassiri actually found himself wondering if this was not the strangest position the young Russian had found himself waking to.

Vitaly's fingers jabbed at the controls, plunging the bow further down, adjusting the depths planes—and then it happened. The submarine twisted, slowly regaining her equilibrium as the depth gauge nearly touched three thousand feet. Both ballasts blew simultaneously, rocking the vessel back upright, stopping the depth gauge cold and sending the unburdened vessel shooting upwards.

"No way that should have worked," breathed Jonah. Alexis looked at Dr. Nassiri. She was more shell-shocked than happy, the sheer magnitude of the past hour weighing heavily on her shoulders.

Twenty-eight-hundred feet, read the gauge. Twenty-seven fifty. They'd break through the surface in minutes. Dr. Nassiri unbuckled Vitaly's seat belt and carried him to the nearest bunk, laid him on the mattress, and set the IV drip to work. He injected Vitaly with a sedative and watched as the Russian's eyes fluttered, then closed. It would be a rough couple of days, but the young man should survive his initial gunshot wounds. Whether or not he could survive this expedition—if any of them could—was another matter entirely.

CHAPTER 10

Dr. Nassiri sat alone in the command compartment of the submarine, eyes fixed on the radar screen. It was quite a different sensation to be on the surface again. The submarine rocked and bobbed in the gentle waves like any other midsized vessel, but there were no windows to anchor one to the horizon. A little nauseating, if one was completely honest with oneself.

None of them spoke during the interminable ascent through the water column, no cheers when they'd finally broken through the surface or opened the hatch. Battle fatigue set in, a kind of stillness in the soul made up of equal parts physical exhaustion and spiritual reflection. Dr. Nassiri found himself playing the day back like a movie reel, pointing out moments where he should have been faster, should have been cleverer, should have been killed but wasn't.

He brushed his fingers across the name placard of the submarine.

Scorpion, it read.

Appropriate. Named for an arachnid that lies in wait for its prey, stinging when least expected. Perhaps this ship should not be renamed as was the *Conqueror*. What would be the point? There was no slipping this weapon through a shipping channel or canal with little more than a paint job, fake papers, and a forced smile.

Alexis worked alone in the engine room, trying to repair the batteries or at least isolate the damage. Dr. Nassiri found her technical explanations difficult to understand at best. At least he understood enough to get that the *Scorpion* was kind of like a hybrid car, using conventional diesel fuel on the surface, battery electricity while submerged.

Finding himself useless to her or Jonah, he occupied himself with the logs of the latest series of drone surveillance flights. Apparently Charles Bettencourt took his pirate neighbors to the west very seriously, taking great care to spy on each pirate harbor in turn.

One of the high-resolution aerial spy photos caught the doctor's attention. At first, the harbor looked like all the rest—a single cut-out deep harbor guarded by two tall stone towers. Two rusting mother ships were nestled within, surrounded by a dozen fiberglass skiffs tied up by the bows. The compound was walled off with a corrugated steel fence. Apparently the pirates feared attack by land just as much as assault by sea. Several broken-down trucks dotted the interior of the wall. Whether they drove or not—in fact, whether anything in the compound worked—couldn't be ascertained by the photograph alone.

Then he realized what had caught his surgeon's eye.

One of these is not like the others, he thought. A dark shape in the far corner of the harbor couldn't be ignored. It was somewhere between the size of a skiff and a mothership. Unlike the rusting white steel ships, this one was matte black.

Dr. Nassiri zoomed in with his fingers on the tablet computer. His first instinct was correct, this was no pirate ship. From the high-resolution surveillance photo he could make out the build of the ship, a futuristic ultra-lightweight trimaran carbon-fiber racing yacht. The name *Horizon* was painted on the side, but not recently. More interestingly, he recognized the distinctive crimson and gray logo of MIT, the Massachusetts Institute of Technology. The name and the ship seemed familiar somehow, like he'd read about it in a newspaper or a magazine some long time ago. But then again, anything before about two weeks ago felt like it'd happened to a different man.

Dr. Nassiri realized he could see two shadowy figures on the back deck. They didn't look like pirates, but then again, what did a pirate look like?

He zoomed in closer. Then closer again.

He could see now—the two figures were women, one young and one older, both with dark hair. The young one wore hers in a close-cropped, androgynous style. He scrolled over to the other woman … and then he saw her.

Dr. Nassiri climbed the boarding ladder and exited through the open hatch in the top of the conning tower. Jonah sat at a fold-out seat at the top, binoculars strung loosely around his neck, massive deli sandwich in hand he'd made himself, watching the African sun settle low over the horizon in a spectacular sunset. He nodded at Dr. Nassiri in acknowledgement, a friendlier gesture than the doctor had expected.

"Hey Doc," said Jonah. The American split the sandwich in half and tried to hand it to Dr. Nassiri.

"No thank you," the doctor said. "But that is very kind."

"Take it," said Jonah. "It's what Americans do when somebody we care about dies. We feed each other. I'd give you a casserole, but all I have is this sandwich."

"What type is it?" said Dr. Nassiri.

"It's turkey," said Jonah. "I don't know if that's your thing or not, but there's no ham in it or whatever."

Dr. Nassiri looked at Jonah quizzically for a moment, realizing the offer was completely genuine. He almost felt a little foolish for not taking it to start, especially once he realized how hungry he actually was.

"Why not?" said Dr. Nassiri. He smiled and accepted the sandwich. Both men ate in silence.

Jonah spoke first. "I'm sorry about your cousin," he said. "I didn't know him all that well, but he seemed like a decent enough guy."

"Sometimes he was, sometimes he wasn't," admitted Dr. Nassiri. "Technically speaking, he was killed in the commission of a crime."

"Nobody back home needs to know that."

"There's only so much of the truth that one can sanitize," said Dr. Nassiri with a shrug.

"Doc, I know the timing sucks," said Jonah. "But I have more bad news."

"More than usual?" asked Dr. Nassiri.

The doctor had met cocky Jonah and warrior Jonah, but not this Jonah. Not sympathetic Jonah.

"Probably not by comparison to the last couple of days," continued Jonah. "But I really need you to listen to me on this. I shouldn't have yelled at you when all that shit was going down. I had no idea what you were doing—I thought you froze up."

"It would have taken me too long to explain," said Dr. Nassiri.

"Nice job, by the way. Hell, it was a masterful job. I thought he was fucking dead, bam-bam, done for. You stick your hands in him; get a needle in his vein and he's up and walking around like fucking Lazarus. And you did it with me yelling in your ear the whole time. Couldn't have made it any easier. Think we can trust him?"

"No. And he's not your admirer right now."

"Well, I'm not a big fan of his either. How's he doing?"

"As good as to be expected. I have him on a full course of antibiotics. He'll be getting all of his fluids and nutrition intravenously for some time, and as much supplemental oxygen as we can spare. It probably doesn't help that we have him handcuffed him to the bunk, but I suppose that's necessary."

"He'd better be happy he's alive. He and his crew put the hurt on us in a big way."

"He is."

They both took another bite of their shared sandwich at more or less the same time, leading to an awkward bout of synchronized chewing before anyone could speak.

"You're not going to want to hear this," said Jonah. "But we can't go to the crash site, not now. Charles Bettencourt will have the area staked out; they probably already have drones on it, maybe even a ship. They're going to want this submarine back."

"You think they know we've taken the *Scorpion*?"

Jonah looked up, surprised the doctor didn't challenge him on the decision to scrub the mission.

"The submarine chirped its coordinates and status back to Anconia Island seconds after we resurfaced," said Jonah.

"I cut it off, but not in time. They probably don't have the full picture, but they know the *Scorpion* is on the water and not under their command."

"And this limits our options to simply running," said Dr. Nassiri.

"It does. But at least we have that Russian kid. He seems to know his way around the controls. I'm decent with a ship, but Jesus, I can't make sense out of half of these systems. Same for Alexis, I'm sure. Submarine training's not something you generally get in marine engineering school."

Dr. Nassiri nodded. Even the yacht had been a total mystery to him, the idea of piloting a submarine seemed absurd at best, suicidal at worst. More silence, more eating. Jonah passed Dr. Nassiri a cold beer, something imported from Italy. When the cool amber liquid touched his lips, Dr. Nassiri almost felt human again.

"Where are we going?" asked Dr. Nassiri.

"Right now? Doesn't matter, we're just running. Just trying to get the fuck out of here without getting sunk or captured."

"And after?"

"Hell, I don't know. I feel like we're sitting on a potential jackpot with this submarine. Even beat to shit, she's probably worth, twenty, maybe thirty million to a motivated buyer. I don't mind cutting you and Alexis in on it, couldn't have done it without you. I can promise we'd get your family out of hock at the very least."

"I'm not certain I have a home to go back to," said Dr. Nassiri. "Not if any word of this gets out. Charles Bettencourt has deep pockets and a great deal of influence with the government of my country."

"If we sell the sub to the Columbians, you could probably buy your way into whatever country you want. That being said, I'm not sure of a way to arrange it where we don't all get cartel neckties in the process."

"I'm not familiar with that aphorism."

"Slit throats."

"Ah," said Dr. Nassiri. He took another drink.

"Maybe one of the smaller, unpopular militaries," said Jonah. "Libya. Burma. I can put some feelers out. But one thing is certain—we can't stay here."

"Burma had a change in government," said Dr. Nassiri. "As did Libya."

"No shit?" Jonah looked up from his sandwich. "Did not know that. But what I do know is this—Anconia Island will be fully mobilized and looking for the *Scorpion*. We may be a needle in a haystack, but there's going to be a lot of firepower looking for that needle."

"I suppose it is incumbent upon us to make their efforts fruitless," said Dr. Nassiri.

"Sure," said Jonah, taking a sip of his beer. "It's simple, but sometimes the old tricks are the best ones. We'll steam south, close to the coast as we can, skirt Madagascar. Between the devil and the deep blue sea, best as we can. Surface all night, submerge all day. At least until we are far, far away from here."

"I'm not certain there is any place in the world far enough from the influence of a man like Mr. Bettencourt," mused Dr. Nassiri. He leaned back against the railing for a moment and grimaced. He felt the weight of the tablet computer in his hands. "Mr. Black—Jonah," he began. "I'd like to show you something."

"As long as it isn't more bad news," said Jonah, choosing to ignore his change in status from Mr. Blackwell to Jonah.

He finished his sandwich and clapped the last of the crumbs off his hands.

Dr. Nassiri pressed the tablet into the American's hands, showing him the bird's eye image of the older woman he'd discovered in the reconnaissance photos.

"Who's this?"

"It's my mother," said Dr. Nassiri, tears welling up in his eyes. "She's alive."

Jonah scowled as he zoomed out, discovering for himself her predicament in the midst of a pirate compound.

"When was this taken?"

"Two days ago."

"Jesus, Doc …" Jonah shook his head.

"I don't expect this to change anything," said Dr. Nassiri. "Not after the way Youssef died. And I wouldn't even entertain the notion of using any leverage on you to force a rescue. You've kept us alive, Jonah. And for that alone, your debt to me is more than repaid. I will fulfill as much of my obligation to you as I am able."

"I don't need you to cut on my face or tuck in my ears or whatever," said Jonah, still scowling at the tablet computer. Dr. Nassiri saw something flickering across Jonah's face, recognizing it for what it was—could the American actually be formulating a plan?

"Jonah—" began Dr. Nassiri again.

"I'm going to stop you there, Doc," said Jonah. "I've been giving this a lot of thought. I'm reasonably certain they tried to kill us because of your mother's research. They wouldn't have tried to sink the *Fool's Errand* like that if the issue was over the stolen yacht."

"It's been bothering me as well. Why not simply detain us at Anconia Island?"

"Because we could still talk if we were detained. Tell the world what we were after. Killing us would close the loop permanently. We would have simply disappeared. They would have blamed it on Somali pirates and everyone would've believed them."

"There's no reason to suspect they won't try again."

"I'm assuming they will try again. But next time, I'm going to know why. Let's just say they've aroused my curiosity."

"You—you would do this? Assist me in rescuing my mother?"

"Let's not get ahead of ourselves," said Jonah. "Losing Buzz hurt us. I know he was an idiot, but he was a reliable idiot. I'm in, but I need Alexis as engineer. If she's not in, it's *no-can-do*, full stop. We can't risk an engine problem leaving us dead in the water."

"Fair. More than fair."

"I'd like to say I'm doing it for you." Jonah tipped his head back and finished his beer. He chucked the empty over the side and into the ocean.

But he's not, the doctor thought to himself, mentally finishing Jonah's sentence. Finding my mother might provide the only leverage we'll ever get.

As if summoned, Alexis popped her head out of the conning tower hatch, just in time to see the last rays of the sun dip beneath the horizon, rewarding the three observers with a thin flash of soft green as it disappeared.

"Got the autopilot workin'," she said in a sing-song voice, laying on the Texan accent as thick as she could. "Soon we will be mother-fucking-fuck the *fuck* out of here."

Dr. Nassiri and Jonah looked at each other.

"Uh oh," she said. "What now?"

CHAPTER 11

Sunset descended over the pirate outpost, an intense paint-streaked display of light filtering through third-world dust and smoke. Two large stone towers guarded the concrete and stone walls of the small harbor, vestiges of a decaying public works project of some long-ago Marxist regime. Much of the stonework and concrete underpinnings of the jetty were gone, as were dreams of a better future for the nearby city. The unnamed patch of settlements were little more than a loose collection of dusty tower blocks and tin shacks.

The guard towers overlooked a sheen of oil, plastic, and sewage coating the harbor water as it lazily seeped into the ocean. As poor as it was for the aesthetics of the harbor, it couldn't have been better cover for the *Scorpion*.

Temporarily roused from his medical sedation, Vitaly had done a masterful job of steering the *Scorpion* into position just outside the harbor. The Russian helmsman set the submarine down on the shallow, sandy seafloor, deep enough to remain undetected. Even the largest pirate ships could pass overhead without colliding. More importantly, they were shallow enough to use the periscope to spy on the harbor.

"Raising periscope," said Jonah, more to himself than anyone else.

Vitaly was back in his bunk, but he didn't seem to mind the handcuffs. In fact, he didn't act like he minded much of anything—except Jonah. He never missed an opportunity to flash Jonah a scowl thick with a millennia of Russian indignation. It was as if he believed receiving two gunshot wounds from point blank range—while unarmed, no less— was a cosmic imbalance in need of eventual rectification.

Earlier, Jonah had tried to ask him why the *Scorpion* had been deployed against the *Fool's Errand*.

"Sometimes goat eat wolf," was his only reply.

Jonah suspected that particular folk saying may have lost something in the translation. And that was that, as much as anyone could get out of him. Even Alexis took a flirty soft-touch run at him to the Russian's complete disinterest and total lack of cooperation.

He'd been compliant, but Jonah resolved not to leave his back turned to him, not if it could be prevented. People were funny about revenge, especially Russians coming down from a healthy dosage of opiate painkillers.

Jonah reached down and unlocked the periscope, leaving the device hanging from the ceiling. He felt a sense of satisfaction that the *Scorpion* had one of the old-school types with actual mirrors and lenses instead of a video screen. An old-school periscope couldn't fail if the power was ever knocked offline, and no pixel-smoothing algorithm could match a well-trained human eye.

The American started with a full 360-degree swivel to check if the pirates had noticed the periscope pierce through the sheen of oily water to spy on the harbor. For a moment, a small collection of plastic garbage washed by, obscuring his vision. With any luck, even if spotted, the periscope would be mistaken for trash.

He checked on the two stone guard towers first, adjusting the angle upwards to see the bored guards within. In the taller of the two towers, the single guard was dimly illuminated by the screen of his cell phone. In the other tower, two guards played an endless card game by lamplight.

At first, Alexis, Dr. Nassiri, and Jonah had tried to divvy up the spying duties equitably, each taking a few hours at a time. As time wore on, Jonah took up longer and longer shifts until the other two found it best to simply leave him in peace. Jonah kept elaborate notes on the comings and goings of the pirates—shift changes, food delivery, prayers, even visits by girlfriends. In Prison 14, the only timekeeping was the movement of men, and Jonah had developed a seemingly inexhaustible patience for the practice.

Jonah twisted the periscope, allowing his vision to fall on the *Horizon*. The hijacked racing trimaran yacht gently rocked in protected waters of the harbor. She looked like a long-since broken wild stallion, grime and dust coating her matte-black carbon fiber skin, poorly patched bullet holes across her hull. She'd been at dock nearly four years and looked like every day of it.

I don't belong here, the yacht whispered. Set me free.

For the seventeenth time that day, Jonah decided he'd rather see this beautiful vessel on the bottom than tied up in a pirate harbor, crumbling away. She was a mechanical work of art, pure function over form. She'd been captured long ago, so long that Jonah had actually remembered a bit about the incident.

It seemed the pirates more or less left the two female occupants of the *Horizon* to their own devices. They were not free to come or go, but they had reign of the imprisoned ship, spending long periods of time sitting on the rear fantail, sometimes in silence, sometimes in conversation. A guard was always watching from shore. When they eventually went below decks, the pirates did bed checks every four hours, their timing just random enough to make Jonah nervous.

The older of the two women was Fatima, Dr. Nassiri's mother. She came out less than the other one and spent too much of her time pacing. She'd clearly never been confined for any significant period of time.

"She's very beautiful," Alexis remarked when first seeing her two days ago during her shift.

Darkness fell and Jonah switched over to night vision. The *Scorpion* had a decent third-generation system, capable of taking starlight alone and rendering it into green tones.

The second woman stepped onto the fantail. Jonah found himself breathing a little faster. She was young; maybe mid-twenties, but the youth he assumed could have been just her utilitarian pixie haircut. Like Fatima, she had dark hair and a small stature. Unlike the scientist, her skin was pale and fair.

Dr. Nassiri sat down next to Jonah and set a plate of food on his lap. The incredible richness of the smell pushed Jonah from his prisoner's concentration, forcing him to take notice. It smelled so good he could have almost cried, it smelled better than he remembered food could ever smell.

"*De Laa* lamb," said Dr. Nassiri. "Grilled chops with dates, mint, and orange sauce."

Jonah dug in with his hands and shoveled it into his mouth. Amazingly, it tasted even better than it smelled.

"The larder is surprisingly well stocked with Moroccan staples," said Dr. Nassiri.

"Thanks. Are all Moroccan surgeons this good at cooking?"

"I certainly hope not," said Dr. Nassiri. "This was always my secret weapon when courting a woman."

"Well, I'm not going to let you seduce me," said Jonah. "But this is still crazy good."

Alexis walked into the command compartment holding her own plate of food.

"I hate to be a bother," said Alexis, "but we're going to have to deal with this eventually. The bodies in the forward compartment? They've been in there for, like, three days."

Dr. Nassiri sighed. "I can do it," he said. "I imagine I've dealt with worse in the past. The deceased hold little mystery to me."

"No," said Jonah, his mouth full of food. "Don't worry about it, I'm already on it."

"On it?" asked Alexis. "That door hasn't budged in three days! I wake up thinking I can hear them in there! Seriously, it just … freaks me out."

"No worries," said Jonah, still chewing. "I reconnected the HVAC system and hacked the environmental controls. I've been blowing 110-degree humidity-free air in there for the last thirty-six hours."

Dr. Nassiri considered this, and seemed a little taken aback. "That's actually a very clever idea."

"I don't understand," said Alexis.

"Let me put this into Texan," said Jonah. "I'm making beef jerky. That should make the whole clean-up process a lot less of a hassle."

"Oh God," said Alexis, holding her stomach and turning a distinct shade of green. She slammed the plate of food onto the nearest console and ran out of the room towards the bathroom.

"Must you play the psychopath?" asked Dr. Nassiri.

"Hey, free food," said Jonah, taking Alexis's plate and scooping the contents onto his own with his fingers. "You know what would go really well with this?"

"A piss-flavored American beer?" volunteered a thoroughly unimpressed Dr. Nassiri, scowling at him for both the treatment of Alexis and the meal.

"I was going to say a nice mint tea, would really compliment the lamb. I'm not a total barbarian."

"I prefer a glass of Sangiovese myself," said Dr. Nassiri, getting up from his seat.

"Is that a red or a white?"

Dr. Nassiri rolled his eyes, not rising to Jonah's obvious bait.

"Hold up, Doc," said Jonah. "Tonight's the night."

"You believe so?"

"Yeah, I do." Jonah licked his fingers. "Come with me."

Dr. Nassiri followed Jonah up the boarding ladder and into the claustrophobic interior of the conning tower. Jonah twisted the large wheel of a hatch built into the side of the vertical passageway. The hatch released, opening into a tight chamber where Jonah had stacked diving gear from the *Scorpion*'s ample armory.

"It's a diver's lockout chamber," said Jonah. "We don't even have to surface. We flood this chamber, I swim out, get your mother, bring her back here."

"What's this?" asked Dr. Nassiri, picking up a large pack with straps on it. It looked almost like a backpack with a hard skin, albeit with two regulators and an inflatable buoyancy-control vest.

"Don't touch that," said Jonah. "That's a rebreather. Very finicky, dangerous as hell. You can just be swimming along, tra-la-la-la-la, one moment you take a breath and everything is groovy, the next moment you take a breath and die. It's the CO_2 mix … the body doesn't have a mechanism to tell you that the air mixture is off besides passing out and dying. Incredibly, incredibly dangerous."

"Then why use it? Why not use a traditional scuba tank? I know there must be some back there—"

"The rebreather system doesn't leave any bubbles. Recycles every breath, very stealthy. And who knows? Maybe the technology has improved over the past few years."

"You think so?"

"Probably not. Engineers have been working on it for more than a hundred years."

"Oh," said Dr. Nassiri.

It wasn't Jonah's intention, but he could tell he made the doctor feel a little foolish. Foolish and worried, to be exact.

"Let Alexis know tonight's the night and then meet me back here in a half hour. I'm going to need your help getting all this shit on."

Thirty minutes later, Dr. Nassiri watched with a surgeon's impassive face as Jonah stripped down to his skin. Next came the wetsuit, the same one Jonah had worn when the *Fool's Errand* came under attack. Jonah had patched the worst of the holes with silicone, giving the pricy wetsuit a ragged, secondhand look.

"I assume you're taking more than a knife," said the doctor, nodding at the blade stuck in Jonah's belt.

Jonah held up a plastic dry bag with a polymer pistol. "Sixteen rounds, one in the chamber, and a spare mag."

"Of course," the doctor murmured. "I'm sure the pirates only outnumber your bullets three or four to one."

"Maybe they'll come at me in single file."

"One can only hope they won't come at you at all."

"OK, I'm all set. Close the hatch behind you," Jonah said, waving the doctor away and busying himself with the dive computer. On paper, this was going to be the simplest dive he'd done since his Basic Open Water certification at the age of fourteen. In real life … well, it was Somalia. Anything could happen.

"Jonah?" asked the doctor before closing the hatch. Jonah turned around, a little annoyed that the Moroccan hadn't left yet.

"What?"

"Thank you," said Dr. Nassiri, his arms open, a strange mixture of irritation and earnestness written all over his face. "You're an arrogant, insufferable bastard … but thank you."

Jonah smiled a sly kind of half smile. It took a lot to get that kind of acknowledgement out of the uptight doctor.

Dr. Nassiri exited the dive chamber, clanging the massive steel door shut behind him.

Here goes nothin'. After all, what was the worst that could happen? Besides being spit-roasted by pirates or dying of a faulty rebreather, of course.

Jonah pulled the lever, flooding the dive chamber. Cold water swirled around his ankles as he pulled the dive fins on, and in moments, the water was up to his waist, then chest.

Remember to breathe, he thought to himself as he cleared his ears. The first breath was always the hardest. A diver had to fight the small primal voice in his own mind that told him he was about to drown.

The seawater wasn't as cold as he'd been expecting. A lowering tide had pulled beach-warmed water away from the shores, making the experience not altogether unpleasant. A rush of intense memories hit him almost at once. Floating through the ghostly halls of the *Costa Concordia*. Hiding from sharks in the massive steel pillars of an offshore oil platform. Seeing the first glint of silver buried deep within the ancient wreckage of Roman caravel. He'd never realized how much he loved diving, he'd never allowed himself to think about it during his time in prison.

Jonah opened the outer door to the chamber and floated out, adjusting his buoyancy to gently float on the bottom of the sea floor, the massive bulky form of the *Scorpion* protecting him from the current.

Navigation was going to prove a challenge. The sunlight was fading quickly and the *Scorpion* disappeared from sight after just three strong kicks as he entered the dark waters of the harbor. No matter, blackout conditions were no mystery to him. Hands stretched in front of him, Jonah drifted forwards under the inertia of the kicks for just a moment. Contact—he'd found the jetty wall. Jonah cracked and dropped a chem-light, watching it as it tumbled down and landed on the sea floor. When he returned, he'd know just where to push off from the jetty to find the submarine. Now it was just a matter of following the jetty into the harbor.

Seconds turned into minutes and the minutes into more than an hour. Finally, Jonah found his target—a long, dark trimaran shape in the water above him, a streamlined racing hull saddled with a large pontoon on either side. Jonah pushed up from the sea floor and allowed himself to slowly rise to the surface. He emerged from the water between the main body and the starboard pontoon, just as he'd intended. Stashing the flippers, he pulled himself and the lightweight rebreather apparatus up a small boarding ladder on the side of the racing yacht.

Stepping onto the moonlit deck, Jonah found a dark corner and drew his pistol. It was a last-ditch option at best, possibly only buying seconds when considering the kind of ordnance the pirates had at their disposal. For instance, the long tubular weapon mounted to one of the nearer Toyotas looked like anti-tank artillery. Christ.

Jonah pulled the small radio from his vest and pulled it out of the plastic bag.

"On board," he whispered, no louder than he dared. As far as he could tell, the pirates only stopped by once an hour or so, but it wouldn't have been terribly difficult to spot him from the nearby dock.

Shit. The radio was ruined. Seawater had seeped inside, destroying the sensitive electronics. Triple-bagging the device and wrapping it all up with duct tape hadn't been enough. The screw up, minor as it was, made him feel rusty, off his game.

Jonah ducked through the main entranceway to the cabin of the yacht and crept inside. As beautiful as the ship was from the outside, it was ugly on the inside. Just a few bunks, an open galley and a marine toilet with a curtain for the door. Everything smelled strongly of paint, salt and disinfectant. At least the cockpit was something to brag about, twin lightweight seats facing consoles that would have been at home in a fighter jet. The controls were all inert, with a thin layer of dust covering them. The *Horizon* hadn't sailed an inch since first arriving in the harbor as a pirate trophy.

The American pulled back the curtain of the nearest bunk. A single beam of starlight fell on the pale face of the young woman he'd seen through the periscope. She wasn't conventionally attractive, not with the boyish haircut and small frame, but something about her struck Jonah deeply. Pity he couldn't help a second hostage escape.

He carefully replaced the curtain and went to the next bunk. Pulling back it's curtain, he saw the sleeping form of Professor Fatima Nassiri. Though easily over sixty years in age, she still retained the features of an exceptionally beautiful woman, black hair, dark skin, but the facial lines of someone who laughed too little. She wore a loose button shirt and shorts, revealing endless rows of cuts and bruises. She'd been through hell.

Before waking her, Jonah produced her son's passport from a plastic baggie. With one hand, he held it out in front of him, opened to the doctor's picture. With the other, he firmly placed his hand over Fatima's mouth.

The doctor awoke suddenly, struggling and clawing at his wet, neoprene-clad arms, her eyes flashing. She caught sight of the passport photo and her eyes locked on the image of her son. She froze, unable to tear herself away from the photo. Jonah slowly loosened the pressure of her mouth. Once satisfied she wouldn't scream, he removed his hand.

"Do not speak," said Jonah. "Do you recognize this picture?"

Fatima nodded.

"Good. Your son sent me to get you out of here. I came in using SCUBA gear. We will leave using SCUBA gear. You will cling to my back and use my spare regulator. You will not open your eyes. It took me an hour to infiltrate the harbor; it could take twice that leaving. You must mentally prepare yourself for what's to come."

Fatima nodded again, but with a hint of defiance this time. The more she gained her faculties back, the more Jonah could see that she had her own ideas about how this would go down.

"You're an experienced diver, right?"

Fatima shook her head. "Once only," she whispered. "At a resort."

"Seriously? I thought you were an oceanographer or some shit—look, nevermind. Just hold on, control your breathing and keep your eyes closed. We have a sub—I mean a ship waiting just outside the harbor."

"How many men are with you?" asked Fatima.

"No time for questions," said Jonah, turning around. "Let's get moving."

"But what about Klea?" demanded Fatima, dangerously loud.

"Jesus! Lower your voice!" said Jonah. "She's not my problem. I have one spare regulator, and it's yours. Time to go."

"I will not leave without Klea," insisted Fatima. She rose to her feet. Though a foot shorter than Jonah, the professor stood toe to toe with him as if she were a titan facing a mere mortal. Un-fucking-believable.

"Fatima, it is theoretically possible to evacuate you unconscious," threatened Jonah.

"We're watched during the night," she hissed.

"We don't have time!" Jonah said. Then hearing footsteps behind him, he whipped around, pistol in hand, only to see the bright glint of the steel blade flash just below his chin, millimeters from his exposed throat.

The young woman from the first bunk stood before him, chef's knife in hand. Jonah's hand instinctively went to protect his throat, his fingertips brushing the tangled, severed lines of his regulator tubes. She'd slashed them in half, both his main and his spare. Air rushed out unimpeded with a hoarse roar, expending the reserve oxygen tank in seconds. Repairing them wouldn't do a goddamn thing; the entire system was useless without the reserves.

Rage rushed through him like a flash flood in a bottleneck canyon. Reaching forward with his left hand, he grabbed Klea around her neck, his massive hand constricting her airflow as the other hand tightened his grip on his pistol.

She didn't move, didn't flinch, didn't beg for her life. She just looked at him. His surveillance from the submarine hadn't done her justice, not her smooth, pale skin or dark Audrey Hepburn eyes, glassy under the moonlit sky.

"What in the actual fuck?!" demanded Jonah, shaking her.

Still she didn't react, didn't even fucking blink. Through his grip, Jonah felt the slightest muscle movement, the faintest twitch. He looked down to see her adjusting her grip on the weapon. His prison instincts told him she was intently considering stabbing him. With a knife that size and her obvious commitment, she had a good chance of grievously injuring him before he ended things. Not a good situation for either of them—she'd be dead and he'd be gutted.

He loosened his grip. Klea didn't need another sign; she wriggled herself loose and stepped back. Fatima stood frozen, looking at both as they faced each other down, Jonah with pistol drawn, Klea with her fierce, dark eyes and sharpened blade.

"Talk," said Jonah.

"I have a plan to get us out of here," she said, her voice hoarse from his grip. "All of us. So drop the frogman gear and come with me."

CHAPTER 12

"Fatima," said Klea as she flipped the knife around to hold it by the handle. "Take this. Cut the mooring ropes down to a thread. They must appear normal but break with the slightest pull."

Jonah grimaced. The plan was to wake up Fatima and only Fatima, stick an air regulator in her mouth, jump overboard, and *sayonara*, suckers. If Klea woke up, Jonah had planned to say some bullshit about a second diver coming just for her. Or a helicopter. Or a goddamn aircraft carrier group. It didn't matter. A lie was a lie.

Fatima took the knife from Klea, pulled a black *hijab* over her head and disappeared out of the main hatchway.

"What are you?" demanded Klea. "US Navy? Special Forces? Private contractor?"

"Escaped convict," answered Jonah. "And if your plan is to use this boat to outrun the pirates, your plan sucks."

"You know nothing of my plans," said Klea. "And at least I intend to get us all out of here together."

"This shit-box has been shot to pieces. Look at this!" said Jonah, waving his hand past a particularly ugly streak of stitched-up bullet holes in the fiberglass upper works.

"I fixed it," she spat back.

"Let's see if you can follow my train of thought," he said, hissing out every word as he holstered the pistol into his dive suit, took off his goggles and dropped them to the deck. "This ship, fast as she may be, was captured by pirates. Therefore, this ship is *not fast enough* to outrun pirates."

"She doesn't run," said Klea. "She flies. Follow me."

Klea lead Jonah into the engine room at the extreme rear of the ship, accessible below the main hatchway. The amount of damage was shocking, even to an experienced salvage diver like Jonah. Thick black marks streaked the interior walls, evidence of a vicious fire. Exposed wires dripped melted silicon insulation. Crudely patched bullet holes polka-dotted most of the compartment. The pirates had directed most of their fire at the engine room in order to disable the ship and capture it intact.

"She was scrap when I started," said Klea. "Even the biodiesel tank was shot up and mixed with seawater. Our captors kept it all around anyway. They don't really throw anything away here. They mostly wait for it to fall apart or sink on its own."

Jonah looked closer at the bullet-scarred metal, his eyes straining under the dim solar lighting. Something was wrong about this damage …

Ah, clever girl.

The scarred-over engine compartment was all for show, an illusion. The massive twin biodiesel engine blocks certainly looked shot to pieces—but when Jonah ran a finger over a particularly nasty hole in the intercooler, he felt a perfectly welded patch. The "leak" was painted on. Same for the valve guides, cylinder liner, and the oil pump.

The damage had been long since repaired, as awful as it'd look to the untrained eye. She'd done a similar job to the battery bank, repairing the ones that weren't too badly damaged and bypassing the ones that were. Maybe the *Horizon* could still fly after all.

"Seawater in the fuel lines still is a problem," said Jonah, not yet ready to fully acquiesce to her suicidal plan.

"Well, duh," said Klea. "That's why I distilled it. It's now completely pure. Probably better than when we first bought it. They know I work on the ship once in a while, but I've been charging the batteries off of the excess juice from one of the shore generators. Reprogrammed the arrays to work more efficiently, and I managed to boost their capacity by twenty percent."

"I'm still waiting to be impressed," said Jonah, crossing his arms. She had his attention, but they were still a long way from an effective escape plan.

"I re-engineered the engine to run diesel and electric simultaneously," she continued. "It will give us a significant extra boost of power before the pirates can completely mobilize, easily pushing her past thirty knots."

"Bullshit," said Jonah. "I saw the propellers when I swam in. They're built for efficiency, not speed. How are you going to deal with the supercavitation issue? Those props spin fast enough, they're just going to chop the water into foam and leave you stranded."

"This is a hybrid," explained Klea with no small measure of irritation.

"So?"

"So I programmed the engines to pulse."

Jonah stood back for a minute to consider this. He'd read about this technology in a journal a lifetime ago. How could one engineer, a prisoner on her own ship no less, duplicate it with zero resources in Somalia?

Jonah nodded. "That's some next-level shit," he said. "I mean, we're dead the moment we approach those two guard towers at the mouth of the bay, but I'm genuinely impressed. How much range have you sacrificed?"

"We'll have enough electricity and fuel to get us to Oman."

Jonah did the math in his head. Oman was optimistic, even foolhardy. The plan was reckless, overly complicated, and relied entirely on a series of untested assumptions.

"I'm more worried about getting out of this harbor. But if we do, Mombasa is probably a better choice."

"Mombasa then."

"Any weapons to speak of?"

"You'll like this, frogman," said Klea. Reaching up, she grimaced and slid open an aluminum wall panel. The panel resonated with a scraping sound as light spilled upon her creations.

This is some serious Mad Max shit, thought Jonah. The young woman had spent just as much time creating weapons as she'd spent fixing the engine compartment and patching the hull. His eyes scanned over several single-shot harpoon guns made with welded metal, thick bands of surgical tubing and sharpened steel rebar shafts for bolts. Nasty stuff, the steel bars were usually used to reinforce concrete. Probably not as useful or accurate as his 9mm, but they'd certainly make a statement.

She'd also assembled a set of floating mines. Klea had spent the most time on these, bringing the total to more than ten devices, mostly created from steel bottles of propane and other cooking fuels. Jonah could assume that once thrown, they'd explode when hit by one of the low, open-topped lightweight fiberglass hulls with powerful engines that were favored by pirates.

Next were two small handmade radio transmitters. Maybe to set off previously hidden explosives? All he knew is that they made him nervous; open-frequency detonators were finicky. His mind flashed back to an old news story about a terrorist who exploded himself in his apartment after getting a spam text over the mobile phone he'd rigged to his bomb.

Discount dick-enlargement pills available now, he thought. *Boom*.

"What's this for?" asked Jonah, pointing to a particularly mysterious duel-ended crossbow weapon. Rather than firing one bolt forward, it simultaneously fired one metal arrow to the right and one to the left at ninety-degree angles. The two bolts were linked by some type of ultra-lightweight, high-tensile fiber wire.

"Prop fouler," said Klea. "We use that at the mouth of the harbor, cut off the exit point. It's neutrally buoyant, almost invisible when in the water. When they run over it, the high-strength line will get wound up into their propellers. At the very least, it'll stop them dead in the water and force them to spend hours cutting it out of the propeller shaft. At best, they'll burn out engines trying to chop their way through it."

"I'm game," said Jonah, resigning himself. "Let's do this."

It suddenly occurred to him that she didn't even ask his name. This fact made him deeply concerned as to whether or not her plan included his survival.

"Fatima should be done with the mooring lines," said Klea as she and Jonah exited the engine room.

Jonah and Klea froze, hearing the signs of a struggle, two sets of footsteps banging on the carbon fiber deck of the fantail, a loud voice yelling. Drawing his pistol, Jonah pushed Klea behind him, instinctually protecting her.

Fatima stood on the fantail, still clutching the knife with white knuckles while a pirate pointed an ancient AK-47 rifle at her head.

The pirate screamed at her in a language Jonah could not understand. All around them, the sleepy compound began to rouse. Lights flicked on in rusting corrugated tin shacks as humming generators struggled to keep up with the increased power load.

Drop the knife, thought Jonah, wishing, hoping, willing Fatima to get smart and just drop the knife.

The pirate screamed again, jabbing the rifle towards her aggressively.

Jonah wanted the rifle.

The diver stepped out of the hatchway onto the fantail, pistol already raised to eye level, drawing a bead on the pirate. He waited just long enough for the pirate to see him, to turn. But it was too late, and Jonah brought the butt of the pistol down on the pirate's forehead.

The pirate's head lolled and his body collapsed. Shabby, heavily armed men flooded out from shacks around the harbor and crowded against the deck railing of the mothership, pointing and shouting. Jonah grabbed the assault rifle from the deck and slung the strap around his shoulder.

"I—I didn't finish!" said Fatima, pointing at the nearest mooring line, only half way cut.

Jonah risked a glance around the harbor as he kicked the unconscious pirate's body off the fantail. It fell into the filthy water with a loud splash.

"You did good," Jonah lied. "Fatima, go below decks. Go help Klea."

Klea must had heard the thump because the engines of the *Horizon* suddenly roared to life and surged forward, almost knocking Jonah off his feet and sending the kitchen knife dancing across the deck and into the ocean. One of the two mooring lines snapped instantly, but the second refused to budge. Shit, he had his dive knife at his side, but it was designed for fishing lines, not entire mooring ropes.

The engines surged again, pulling at the mooring line. Jonah watched as the entire mooring post shifted, imperceptibly at first, then sharply as the pylon snapped. The *Horizon* leapt forward like a horse from the starting gates, gathering speed as it charged into the harbor. Shots rang out, disorganized, none impacting the ship.

Jonah ran into the cockpit, which was now lit up like a Christmas tree. Klea had done her job keeping everything in working order. She sat in the command chair, feeding power to the throttle and steering directly for the harbor entrance. Two stone sentry towers looming before them.

"You are straight-up ballsy," said Jonah, putting a hand on the top of her chair, which was taller than she was. It felt like years since he'd talked to a woman, most of the ones he'd known before that had been ex-military or hard-core sat divers. Alexis didn't count; she had too much of a sisterly vibe for Jonah.

But Klea didn't react. She stared forward, impassive, then started giving orders. "Engine room," she said. "Get the two radio transmitters."

Jonah bolted out of the cockpit and into the engine room. Now lit up with a single halogen bulb, the transmitters were easy to spot. He grabbed both and ran back to the bridge.

"We're getting some heat spikes in the engine," said Fatima, her voice thick with concern.

"To be expected," said Klea. "They'll cool off once we're underway. Just tell me if they start redlining."

The two towers loomed closer and closer. Dark shadows shifted as the guards inside scrambled to load their light machine guns and rocket-propelled grenades, muzzles resting against the bulwarks of the towers.

"What's the plan?" asked Jonah, fingering the triggers on the two radio transmitters. "Pirates don't do warning shots."

"Wait," said Klea. "We're still out of their range."

Jonah knew this wasn't true, but didn't want to argue. Then the first tower opened up, sending a long stream of tracer bullets into the harbor water ahead of them. The pirate adjusted aim midfire, sending the stream dancing across their bow and into the port pontoon.

"Still think we're out of range?" exclaimed Jonah, ducking as the bullets narrowly missed the cockpit.

"Now!" said Klea.

Jonah jammed the triggers of both transmitters simultaneously. Nothing happened. The second guard tower opened up, hitting a patch of water dangerously close to the engine room. Jonah knew they'd find the sweet spot within seconds. He jammed the transmitters again, again nothing happened.

"There it is," said Klea, pointing to the base of the tower to the right.

Artificial smoke billowed out of some hidden emitter, just wisps at first, but then massive, roiling billows that obscured the guard towers and the exit to the harbor.

Behind them, the pirates assembled men and weapons, jumping into the fast skiffs tied to the motherships. Jonah wished he'd counted them before the action had started. Jesus, there were so many—ten? A dozen? Every one of them mounted with high-performance marine engines, every one of them a fast, lightweight hull more than capable of running down the *Horizon*. At least they weren't shooting yet, unlike the guard towers.

The *Horizon* plunged into the gathering cloud, reducing their visibility to mere inches. Klea increased power, navigating by memory alone. Looking into her eyes, Jonah could tell she'd practiced this a hundred thousand times in her mind, driven by pure focus. He hoped her mind was half as sharp as she clearly thought it was.

Jonah had been hoping for an explosion, a fiery detonation that would bring the guard towers tumbling down. He coughed, the acrid smoke entering his lungs. Even so, he was impressed. Any MIT freshman could make a decent smoke bomb. But it took a truly brilliant mind to make a radio-controlled smoke bomb trigger that would still work after being buried in mud for months, even years.

Bullets whipped past, but with more uneven frequency due to the smoke. One impacted right next to Jonah's feet, making him jump back as a spot in the deck exploded into splinters.

"Engine room," said Klea, wasting no words. "Prop fouler."

Jonah needed no more instruction. He ducked into the engine room and snatched the twin-crossbow prop fouler line. Exiting the compartment, he quickly took a position on the fantail, waiting for just the right moment.

The machine gun fire stopped. Jonah guessed they were afraid of hitting their own men. That meant the skiffs would be in close pursuit.

The *Horizon* slipped past the smaller guard tower. This was it, the narrowest section of the harbor entrance. Jonah snapped the catch from the twin crossbows. The two bolts disappeared in opposite directions, dragging the prop-fouling line behind them. He played out the last of the line with his hand and dropped the crossbow in the water.

Tracer fire lit up from the closest guard tower, dancing across the starboard pontoon and the fantail. They'd seen the shadow of the *Horizon* through the cloud. Jonah dove for cover and fired back at the source with his 9mm, no idea if he'd even come close to hitting anyone.

A buzzing whine sounded from behind the *Horizon*, the unmistakable engine note of an approaching skiff. The yacht burst through the far side of the cloud and into open ocean. A pirate skiff appeared close behind, but the prop fouler bit deep before the crew could react, bringing the boat to a sudden, jolting halt. A second pirate skiff impacted the first and flipped, dumping her crew into the ocean. Jonah watched as the injured pirates disappeared into the darkness behind them. He smiled. The pile of broken fiberglass would serve a much better barrier than a thin strand of high-tensile fiber. Another impact rang out as a third skiff slammed into the growing pileup at the narrow entrance to the harbor.

Now in open water, Jonah desperately scanned the surface of the ocean for the *Scorpion*'s periscope. He waved wildly, hoping someone, anyone, was watching the unfolding scene.

"Follow us!" he shouted to empty ocean.

Looking at the shoreline, Jonah realized Klea had turned to the North, towards Oman. So much for taking his opinion into account. Apparently it was her production and he was just a bit character. But by the time Jonah reached the cockpit, he'd decided it was a non-issue.

"Are we being chased?"

"Not as far as I can see," he said as he took a pair of binoculars off the console. "Big pileup at the mouth of the harbor. Nice work with the filament, I didn't think that little trick would work."

Klea smirked, a victory over both the pirates and her surly visitor.

Jonah returned to the fantail, binoculars in hand. He scanned the waters behind them. No *Scorpion*, not yet. Either the submarine hadn't yet surfaced or the *Horizon* was a great deal faster than he'd given Klea credit for. He swiveled back towards the mouth of the harbor, watching as pirates surrounded the three crushed skiffs, trying to untangle wounded men from the shattered fiberglass hulls.

Good, thought Jonah. If the whole pileup could suddenly burst into flames too, well, that would be super.

His next thought was *uh-oh*. He stepped back into the cabin and tapped on the back of the captain's chair until Klea turned around.

"What?" she demanded.

"We may have a problem," he said, pressing the binoculars into her hands and leading her to the fantail.

Back at the harbor, the pirates had worked out a solution to the invisible filament. The entrance to the harbor was still an unmitigated disaster, so they simply carried their skiffs over the jetty wall and splashed them into open water.

And there were still a lot of boats, at least seven or eight.

"I really hope your people can give us some backup," said Klea.

"And I hope you know this will turn into a straight-up fight," said Jonah. "I'm going to need a body back here helping me."

"My place is at the helm. I'll give you Fatima."

The pirates hung back behind the *Horizon*, keeping pace but waiting until the last of their skiffs made the journey over the jetty wall. They'd start gaining ground soon, and in full force.

Still no *Scorpion*. Turning around would be suicidal. Jonah couldn't fathom whether or not the *Horizon* could outrun the pirates or not, but his guess was that it would come down to combat.

Jonah removed the clip from the assault rifle slung around his neck and looked at the bullets within. Ten, maybe eleven rounds. Not much. He really should have checked the body of the pirate he'd shot for more bullets before kicking him overboard. Too late now. The pistol wasn't in much better shape for ammo.

Fatima joined him on the deck, her arms overflowing with mines and extra rebar spears.

"Easy there," said Jonah, carefully removing the mines from her uncertain grip. "These … these you bring up one at a time, okay?"

Fatima tried to mumble out an okay in return but couldn't quite form the syllables.

Jonah took a position in the rear hatchway. It was open to the fantail, but still provided him a little cover, not that it would matter much. The last of the pirates spilled over the jetty walls like army ants on the march. The metastasizing collection of pirate skiffs surging forward, gaining ground on the *Horizon*.

Stashing the rebar spears in the wall, Jonah found a

place for the mines at his feet. Fatima crouched behind him.

"Fatima," said Jonah. "Here's what I'm going to need from you. I'm going to use the pistol and rifle as best as I can, but there's going to come a time when I get down to the spear guns."

"Do you want me to use any of these weapons?"

"Only if I'm hit. Whenever I shoot the spear gun, I'm going to hand it to you for reloading and you hand me one with a spear in it, okay?"

"Understood."

Fatima prepared for her job by rearranging the spear guns. She brought the nearest one, loaded, right past Jonah's face, the sharp metal spear almost brushing his cheek. Jonah sighed. Not a good sign.

"If it has a pointy end," he said, "do not aim it at me."

"Sorry," Fatima replied.

Two guns, two crossbows, ten mines and my swingin' dick, thought Jonah. Some cloudy part of his brain remembered being in a worse position at some point in his life but couldn't quite place it. Where the fuck was the *Scorpion*?

The collection of ten pirate skiffs danced across the water, just out of firing range. Unlike the *Conqueror*, the *Horizon* was a marathoner, not a sprinter. One of the skiffs on the edge of the main pack broke ranks, charging forward. Shit, it was fast. Klea laid on more power but the pirates gained visible ground with every second. The skiff used the smooth wake behind the *Horizon* as drag strip, charging towards the fantail.

Wait for it, thought Jonah.

Close now, the pirates on the bow of the skiff stood up, preparing to leap onto the *Horizon* the moment the two vessels touched.

Wait for it, he told himself.

The pirate skiff reached the stern of the *Horizon* and the first pirate, Kalashnikov in hand, leapt over onto the fantail. Jonah caught him with two shots to his legs. He stumbled backwards, falling into the narrow gap between the yacht and the skiff, disappearing with his weapon into the foamy wake.

The wounded man didn't dissuade the other attackers. Jonah exposed his position, standing up to empty round after round into the crew of the attacking skiff. A lucky shot—the last one in the magazine—caught the pilot in the shoulder, spinning him around and knocking the tiller of the skiff hard starboard. The skiff, now full of bloodied, bruised men, jerked to the left, impacting the starboard pontoon with enough force to rattle the entire yacht. The skiff flipped, spilling men and weaponry into the frothing sea. The head start hadn't been nearly enough to outrun the pirates.

The pirates didn't stop for the swimming men. Instead, every single skiff advanced towards the *Horizon* simultaneously. Jonah heard the fierce crack of rifles firing as pirates on multiple skiffs opened up simultaneously, forcing him to take cover as bullets snapped past. Chunks of carbon fiber exploded from the hull.

Ten rounds, thought Jonah as he snuck a glance towards a crouching Fatima.

The professor was holding up, at least as far as he could tell. Her son would have reason to be proud—assuming they survived long enough to arrange a reunion.

Jonah took aim with the assault rifle, carefully squeezing out one single shot at a time, rationing fire into the massing cluster of skiffs. It was too far away to tell if he actually did any damage or not, but the shots seemed to hold the skiff fleet back, even if for a few moments. His rifle clicked empty and useless. At least with the pistol he had two or three bullets left, the Kalashnikov held nothing.

"Time for the mines," Jonah called to Fatima. "I'm going to start chucking them over the back. I need you to hand them to me, one after another."

Fatima nodded and handed him the first. Jonah clicked on the crude switch and threw it, arcing it over the back of the fantail and into the wake. Fatima handed him a second, third, and fourth, each disappearing into the foamy seawater in turn.

Shit. Nothing happened.

Then in the far back of the pack, one of the skiffs erupted into blistering smoke and fire, tearing apart the thin fiberglass hull of the vessel and dumping her crew into the sea. At least one of the mines had struck true.

No longer content to hang back and suffer whatever Jonah could shoot, launch, or throw their way, the pirates surged forward, firing, intent to end the engagement. All Jonah could do was duck as bullets whizzed overhead.

Jonah grabbed for the nearest of the two spear guns and fired. The rebar spear flew true at first, then spun, lost aerodynamics and dropped into the water.

Not good, thought Jonah. He would have liked to see a pirate kabob. He wished Klea really had had the opportunity to test the spear guns, work out the kinks. He handed it to Fatima for a reload but the surgical tubing was already shredded from the single shot.

Fearing ricochets, the pirates stopped firing and massed around the rear of the *Horizon*, dangerously close. They were about to be overrun.

Out of the darkness, the *Scorpion* burst into view, a dark shape charging from behind at flank speed. The massive conning tower slammed into a skiff, tossing it aside like a toy. The other pirate skiffs bounced and knocked into each other trying to get away as the *Scorpion* smashed into the center of the pack like Moby Dick, scattering their numbers.

The submarine slid up next to the *Horizon*, just off the port side of the yacht. If they were two tall ships three hundred years ago, they'd be trading broadsides and musket fire. Dr. Nassiri climbed out of the hatch at the top of the conning tower and signaled to Jonah. Behind them, the pirates attempted to regroup, falling back as they assessed the unexpected threat. Vitaly had put on a masterful performance of navigation.

Dr. Nassiri threw a sling rope over to Jonah.

My mother, he mouthed, unheard over the din of engines and waves.

"Fatima, get over here!" shouted Jonah as bullets cracked and whizzed past him, sling in his hand.

The professor crawled out of the rear hatchway and froze, not trusting her balance against the rolling waves.

"Now, goddamn it!" screamed Jonah. "We're running out of time!"

"I ... I can't!" shouted Fatima, her knuckles white as she crouched as the edge of the fantail.

"Get your ass over here!" shouted Jonah, too distracted in his anger to see the stitch of automatic weapons fire dance up the deck towards him. Fatima sprang forward, crossing the deck with incredible speed. She struck Jonah just below his waist, driving him to the ground as three rounds whistled inches above his prone body. Glaring at the professor, Jonah lassoed her with the sling, putting it underneath her backside like a painter's seat. He instructed her to hold onto the rope as tightly as she could.

Behind them, the pirates watched the transfer and recognized it for what it was—vulnerability. Their reduced fleet surged forward just as *Horizon* hit the submarine's bow wake.

Fatima lost her balance, almost dropping into the ocean as Dr. Nassiri and Alexis strained at the rope to pull her up. She swung across the gap between the speeding vessels, slamming into the side of the submarine's conning tower with hands outstretched as the doctor and Alexis braced against the weighted rope.

Two enterprising skiffs beached themselves at the back end of the *Scorpion*, disgorging nearly a dozen pirates. They ran forward, trying to reach Fatima and the conning tower. Alexis and Dr. Nassiri made one last pull, yanking Fatima over the lip of the conning tower. The hatch slammed shut just as the pirates scaled the exterior boarding ladder. The *Scorpion* was a superior potential prize to the recapture of the wounded *Horizon*.

Klea ran out to the fantail, just in time to see the *Scorpion* crash-dive into the water, shaking off the few pirates still clinging to the conning tower and leaving them to tumble into the foamy wake. The *Scorpion* was gone.

"Should have seen that coming," said Jonah. The *Scorpion* wouldn't be able to surface again, not now. Jonah and Klea were on their own. There were too many pirates, too close. And Dr. Nassiri had already gotten everything he wanted.

"I've put the *Horizon* on autopilot," said Klea. "But we don't have much of this speed left in us and we won't be able to maneuver."

"We'll be overrun soon," said Jonah, his gaze faraway.

As if his declaration carried with it the weight of providence, the pirates massed again, ready for their final assault. They wouldn't be after a prize now. They'd be after revenge.

Enjoy the show, you self-serving fuck, thought Jonah. Dr. Nassiri and everyone else aboard the *Scorpion* could probably see everything from their periscope. That goddamn, rat-bastard doctor.

Klea looked at Jonah, angry tears streaming down her cheeks. She wasn't ready to give up, not yet. Jonah watched as she grabbed mine after mine, flicking each switch in turn and throwing them overboard. Only one hit, splintering the entire side of a pirate skiff and throwing the crew into the water. But the rest kept coming.

The young woman pulled out the last mine, a large bottle of propane with a volatile primer charge. She prepared to throw it over, but Jonah caught her arm and took it from her.

"I'm sorry," said Jonah. "There's just too many of them."

Without warning, Jonah threw the mine into the main cabin of the *Horizon*. The interior of the experimental yacht exploded, sending fragments of carbon fiber, metal shrapnel and burning fuel arcing through the air. Jonah held Klea in his arms, protecting her with his body against the searing wave of heat as she fought him, kicking, elbowing, punching, and screaming.

The blast transformed the *Horizon* into a flaming torch, a single tall pillar of fire licking upwards with blistering temperature. It was all the distraction Jonah needed. He kicked a plastic self-inflating raft overboard, held Klea in his arms, and dropped into the narrow space between the external pontoon and the main body of the yacht.

The two tumbled in a whirlwind of ocean foam, black, moonlight sky, motion and intense cold. Jonah didn't let go of Klea, didn't relax his grip for a moment. A propeller slashed against his arm, leaving a deep, clean cut as it churned past. Klea tried to swim up, tried to reach the surface, but Jonah pushed her deeper as multiple pirate skiffs cut through the water above their heads, still chasing the burning yacht.

Klea bucked and twitched, her body forcing her to suck seawater into her lungs as the last skiff flew by overhead. Jonah finally dragged her to the surface just before the last flicker of life left her body.

She popped her head out of the ocean, choking and spitting. Jonah wordlessly pointed to the inflated life raft. She followed and they both swam towards it. In front of them, the tailing pirate skiff slowed and broke formation, returning to inspect the raft.

Jonah willed the pirates to investigate the raft rather than just shooting it up. With luck, it'd look like one more piece of debris thrown free by the explosion. Jonah and Klea hid behind the raft as the pirate skiff slowly circled. Both ducked under the water as it slowly passed by. Moments later, the engine roared up to full pitch and the skiff sped away, satisfied the raft was empty.

Klea clambered in first, assisted by Jonah's steady hand. Now alone in an unforgiving sea, Jonah and Klea watched wordlessly as the flaming hulk of the *Horizon* disappeared into the night.

CHAPTER 13

Dr. Nassiri watched from the periscope as the burning *Horizon* vanished into the distance like a Viking funeral pyre, remaining pirate skiffs chasing closely behind. It was fitting, in a way. The doctor tried to rationalize the probable outcome of events as an honorable death, but suspected Jonah would have preferred not to die at all.

His mother stood behind him, silently clutching her wrist. The doctor felt cheated; there was no laughter, no tears of joy, no grateful embrace. Just a lonely ship vanished into the night, chased by murderous outlaws.

Dr. Nassiri shook his head and stepped away from the periscope. The *Scorpion* couldn't catch up, not while running submerged on battery power. The hit-from-behind trick was a card they could only play once.

The doctor looked at the assembled refugees standing in the cramped command compartment. His mother to his left, leaning up against the interior boarding ladder to the conning tower. Vitaly at the pilot's console, his drugged eyes sunken with pain. Alexis, standing at the hatchway between the engine room and the command compartment.

He realized with immense discomfort that they were looking to him for orders. The idea bothered him. Jonah was a natural, albeit reluctant leader. Dr. Nassiri didn't want the role or the weight of command.

"They're gone," said Dr. Nassiri. Vitaly nodded gravely and Alexis buried her face in her hands. Fatima looked down and away, her face heavy with shame.

It wasn't your fault, thought the doctor. There would be time to comfort her later.

"What happened?" asked Alexis.

"I don't know," said Dr. Nassiri. "There was a massive explosion aboard the *Horizon*. I doubt it was survivable. Complicating matters, the pirates are still in pursuit and we can't match their speed without exposing ourselves."

"The pirates told us they'd kill us if we tried to escape," said Fatima.

"They could have been just threatening, bluffing—" began Alexis.

"And what exactly would you know about that?" interrupted Fatima. "It wasn't just a threat. They only kept us alive because they believed Islam forbade the murder of Muslim women."

"Klea deserved a better end to her sufferings."

"So did Jonah Blackwell," said Dr. Nassiri. "Your erstwhile rescuer."

"If nobody ask," said Vitaly. "I ask. Now what?"

Dr. Nassiri set his hand on Vitaly's shoulder and glanced down. A large, angry splotch of red seeped from the Russian's chest. He'd broken his stiches.

"Back to your bunk," ordered Dr. Nassiri. "Now."

"*Chto za huy!*" swore Vitaly, looking down at the spreading stain. "New shirt *ruined*."

"Let's find another one," said Dr. Nassiri, helping him to his feet.

The doctor walked the Russian to the bunk beds in the compartment just forward of command and helped him lie down. Taking a pair of scissors from a side table, the doctor cut off the shirt, exposing the two wounds. Several of the stiches had indeed separated, but it wasn't as bad as he'd feared. Vitaly was healing quite well, all things considered. The mere fact that he was no longer in danger of slipping into shock at any moment represented significant progress.

"We still do bracelets?" asked Vitaly, motioning towards the handcuffs on the side of the bunk.

"I'm sorry," said Dr. Nassiri. "But you must wear the manacles when you're in your bunk."

Vitaly was getting stronger every day; the cuffs were no longer an unnoticed nuisance in the dreamlike twilight of medicated sleep.

They must be maddening to wear, thought Dr. Nassiri.

Time to give Vitaly his shot of painkillers. The doctor hoped they didn't need a skilled navigator, at least not for the next four or five hours. Alexis was passable, but of course didn't know the complicated array of systems to the same degree as Vitaly. It was just like medical school. Some used a scalpel like an artist's brush, others like a child's crayon. During her first few tries, Alexis "porpoised" the *Scorpion*, diving, pulling up, diving again, up, down, up, down until Jonah had finally relieved her of duty.

Dr. Nassiri filled his syringe from a tiny bottle of refrigerated painkiller. He tapped it and squeezed a little, freeing two tiny air pocket from the body of the instrument. He went to administer the shot but Vitaly caught his wrist to stop him.

"You must know," he said. "I am in your debt. This very important for Russians."

"And I'm in your debt," said Dr. Nassiri in the same soft voice he reserved for all his patients. "You single-handedly saved this vessel."

"Not same," said Vitaly. "My comrades of the *Scorpion*. And myself. We came to kill you. I could lie, I could say Vitaly protest, Vitaly never know real mission. But none of this true. I must tell truth. We came to give you no chance to fight, no chance for life. You and your crew, you fight, you win. And you still save me."

Dr. Nassiri didn't know what to say. He let the silence hang over both men.

"I treated you because I needed you," began Dr. Nassiri. "I needed you to pilot this vessel. Many men died that day. You almost died that day."

"No!" Vitaly's eyes were bright. "You save me because you save people. You save your mother. You save me. And I think you will save Jonah."

"From prison?" asked Dr. Nassiri. "Because I helped him escape from prison?"

"No," said Vitaly. "I think you save Jonah *now*."

"He's gone, Vitaly," said Dr. Nassiri. "And I don't understand why you'd say that. He nearly killed you."

Vitaly scowled, growing frustrated with the doctor, trying to communicate a point that was simply not received.

"Shot now please," Vitaly finally said. "Very much pain."

Dr. Nassiri nodded and stuck him with the syringe, delivering the powerful painkillers deep into the Russian's arm. Vitaly's eyes fluttered and closed. The doctor sighed and placed his palm on the young man's chest, willing healing energy into the Russian's broken body.

Hearing a noise from behind, Dr. Nassiri turned away from the bunk to see his mother standing behind him, still holding her wrist. He vaguely remembered her reaching out with the same hand to brace herself as she slammed into the conning tower.

"I … I didn't mean to interrupt," she said.

"Nonsense, let me take a look," said Dr. Nassiri. He took his mother's hand in his, and gently probed with his fingers. "Does this hurt?"

"Very badly," said Fatima through gritted teeth.

"You have a fractured wrist," he said. "Normally I would order an x-ray to make certain there are no misalignments. I'm afraid we do not have that luxury."

Dr. Nassiri directed his mother to sit in a nearby chair as he dug through the medical kit to find an adjustable splint and bandages. It wouldn't be a proper cast, but it'd have to serve as one for the foreseeable future.

"What have you uncovered?" asked Fatima. "What do you know about the red tide?"

"Too little," admitted Dr. Nassiri. "We've been forced to react to circumstances as they arise. I thought you dead—we were attacked by this very submarine and forced to capture it to survive. It was only then I discovered your incarceration in the pirate encampment."

"Charles Bettencourt is the key to everything," said Fatima. "Who else could deploy an anti-aircraft missile in the middle of the ocean such as that? Too sophisticated for pirates, that much was certain. I believe I know why he wanted to silence me, wanted to kill us all."

"You speak of your research?"

"I do," said Fatima. "I have a theory on the Horn of Africa red tide, the de-oxygenated waters that have decimated sea life in this ocean. The spectrometer readings left little doubt. It's such a shame that all that beautiful data is now rotting on the bottom of the ocean. I saw … *something* … before we were hit."

"What did you see?"

"I don't know for certain. But I think it was the first concrete evidence of the Dead Hand."

"The what?"

The professor sighed. "A thing too terrible to exist," she finally said.

Dr. Nassiri formed the metal and foam splint and carefully arranged it around his mother's wrist, wrapping it with bandages. He finished his work by gently pinching the tips of her fingers, ensuring that he hadn't inadvertently cut off any capillary blood flow.

"This is unfortunate," said Dr. Nassiri. "But I believe your research is irretrievable at this time, perhaps forever. The transponder has stopped communicating and we have reason to believe the submerged crash site is guarded. To attempt to reach it would invite ambush. We are in no position to defend ourselves with Jonah gone."

Crestfallen, Dr. Nassiri realized he'd almost said *with Jonah dead.* He cleared his throat.

"Tell me what you found," he continued. "Tell me what you know definitively, and what you surmise."

"I believe my research represented the final piece of the puzzle," said Fatima. "I'd suspected dumping of biological and radiological waste from medical facilities throughout Europe. It's known that elements of organized crime control this practice, and have so for nearly thirty years. Even if legitimate institutions are paid to deal with the waste, it's cheaper to subcontract the task to criminals and take the difference in straight profit. After all, Somalia is the last coastal region on earth without some type of navy."

"So this is it? The dumping of medical waste? All of this death, all of this destruction—over that?"

Fatima shook her head. "Hardly," she answered. "That would only explain a fraction of what I saw."

"I'm afraid I don't understand."

"Ten years ago, a rumor began circulating throughout the halls of oceanographers and marine biologists. It still chills me to think about, a nightmare one hoped some small pang of conscious would have prevented its conception or smothered it at birth." Fatima sighed and stretched out her fingers, touching her simple cast. "In the mid-1980s, the Soviet Union had a dilemma," she continued. "American president Ronald Reagan introduced his plan for a missile shield, terrestrial and space-based technologies that would render Soviet missiles useless. It would give the Americans the ability strike first then swat any Soviet retaliation from the sky. Unable to compete with the sudden advancement in American nuclear and missile technology, Soviet strategists discussed other means of ensuring the survival of the communist experiment."

"What did they do?" asked Dr. Nassiri in a hushed tone.

"They created the Dead Hand," said Fatima with a wry, sad smile. "The Kremlin called it *Mertvaya Ruka*, the hand from the grave. It ensured that even upon total destruction of the Soviet state, the military would retain the fully automated ability to strike back with the most virulent plagues and poisons, borne not by missiles, but by sleeper agents and unmanned drones. This was the game, to find some way to rebalance the powers, perhaps even give the Soviets some distinctive edge."

"Were there not treaties? Something to prevent such horrors?"

"There are always treaties," said Fatima. "But treaties were broken. Post-collapse, this program became a massive liability. The plagues and poisons necessitated disposal, and it is extraordinarily difficult to dispose of such virulent materials. I believe the waters off Somalia have been designated as a sacrifice zone. By whom, I do not know. When I saw the readings of this region, I felt I saw the fingerprint of the Dead Hand. Evidence indicates this is done under the direct supervision, protection, and profit of Charles Bettencourt and his mercenaries. The entire purpose of Anconia Island may well be to secure, facilitate, and conceal this disposal effort. He will stop at nothing to ensure our silence."

With Vitaly asleep, his mother cooking in the galley, and Alexis at the tiller, it might be time for a job he'd been putting off, a job he'd been dreading. Jonah's little science project in the forward compartment had to be nearing its inevitable outcome. Dr. Nassiri shuddered a little just thinking about it. He'd already stacked up a rough equivalent to biohazard gear, mostly amounting to a painter's mask, gloves, and a pair of slick plastic coveralls. He'd also found a discarded axe, an implement he desperately hoped he wouldn't need. At least the *Scorpion* had a few body bags on hand; otherwise the job would be wholly unmanageable.

Sighing, Dr. Nassiri put on his gloves but stopped when he heard footsteps behind him.

"Hey," said Alexis, leaning up against the wall, hands in the pockets of her cutoff jeans.

"Hello," said Dr. Nassiri. "Just about to begin the ... unpleasantness."

"Can I help?" she asked.

"It's no job for a woman," he stammered. Dr. Nassiri instantly regretted the sexist remark, what little he knew about Alexis should have told him she'd hate hearing that.

"So I'll just go back to painting my nails," said Alexis irritably, waving her engine-grease-stained fingers in his face.

"I'm sorry," he said. He leaned against the wall, took off his gloves and let them fall to the floor. He crossed his arms. "I've been really dreading this task. The very thought of what lies beyond this threshold turns my stomach."

"And you're trying to spare me from it," she said. "Thoughtful, but still super sexist and kinda dumb to boot."

"I don't want you to help me," said Dr. Nassiri. "Disposing of burned bodies is a horrible task. If I allow you to help, you'll look at me differently."

"How do I look at you now?" she asked.

Was she ... blushing? Dr. Nassiri smiled and looked away. He tried to come up with some answer, any answer, but couldn't. To him each glance they shared, however fleeting, held immense meaning.

"What would you be doing right now if you were home?" asked Alexis, changing the subject and sparing the doctor the painful silence.

"My life in Morocco is very ordinary," he answered. "I live in one of the smaller cities near the coast. Very beautiful. My flat had a very pleasing sea view. And I have a cat. *Had* a cat."

"Girlfriend?"

"No," laughed Dr. Nassiri. "Despite the best efforts of my extended family. Although I've dated some, most women I know are interested in immediate marriage and family life. I suppose I wasn't ready for that."

"I hear you there," said Alexis. "Pretty much all the girls from my high school and college are married and pregnant. My Facebook feed is babies, babies, babies."

"Truth be told, most of my friends are unattached and incorrigible bachelors. They like the finer things in life—good food, expensive drinks, beautiful cars."

Alexis absentmindedly tapped her wrench against the bulkhead, thinking.

"I don't think I'd fit in with your friends," she finally said. "And your mom already hates me."

"Perhaps I must find new friends," said Dr. Nassiri. "And I believe mother will eventually come around."

Dr. Nassiri coughed and gagged as he scrubbed at the last long, angry tendril of smoke damage. He glanced over at the two bagged bodies, little more than blackened skeletons covered with dry, crepe-paper like fragments of skin.

A burial at sea would have to do; the freezer was already full of dead men from the command compartment. They'd run out of shelving space for the engineer, his clear-plastic unwrapped corpse lay on the freezer floor. The forward compartment was more or less wrecked, but the doctor had cleared it of all the burned-up equipment. At the very least, it could serve for storage at some point in the future. He couldn't image anyone sleeping here, not after what had happened.

"Doc!" called Alexis from the command compartment, her voice echoing as it came up through the main passageway.

He and Alexis didn't know how to use the intercom system, and it wasn't worth waking up Vitaly for something so minor.

Dr. Nassiri glanced around the forward compartment. It was probably good enough; the bodies and the worst of the damage more or less mitigated. Still he closed the heavy hatchway between compartments before stripping off his gloves and making his way back.

"What is it?" he asked, stepping into the command compartment.

"Check out the periscope," she said.

Dr. Nassiri dropped the periscope and stepped up to it. He was surprised to see the sun in the sky. Daylight already and he hadn't slept. Fortunately Fatima had found a quiet place to get some rest; he supposed she needed it more than he did.

Alexis yawned, mirroring his exhaustion. Dr. Nassiri felt terrible, his eyes sunken, face unshaven, complete exhaustion anchoring every sigh and footstep.

Visible through the periscope, a single wispy column of smoke rose from the horizon. Alexis kept the submarine on course, advancing on the mysterious target. Before them, the smoking hulk of a ship lay dead in the water.

"It's the *Horizon*," announced Dr. Nassiri. "Continue forward, dead slow."

"Dead slow," confirmed Alexis as she piloted the submarine ahead.

The *Scorpion* edged closer to the hulk as Dr. Nassiri scanned the area for any remaining pirates. None appeared on the radar screen or through the periscope. They'd either given up the chase or decided the smoking wreck was not worth retrieving.

"Surface," he ordered. The *Scorpion* rose through the water, her conning tower slicing through a dissipating biodiesel slick.

"What should we do?" asked Alexis.

"I'm going to take a look," said the doctor.

He left the command compartment, made his way through the engine compartment and stepped into the bunk room. Vitaly could continue sleeping but he'd need Fatima. He gently touched his mother's shoulder, allowing her to gradually wake.

"What is it?" she asked, rubbing the sleep from her eyes.

"We've found the *Horizon*. She's dead in the water."

"Any sign of Klea? Or the pirates?"

"No pirates," said Dr. Nassiri. "And no signs of life. I'm going to take a look; I'd like you to accompany me."

"Of course," said Fatima. "Give me a moment to dress."

Fatima followed him up the interior ladder of the conning tower. Dr. Nassiri wrestled with the hatch until it came free and squeaked open. He lifted himself outside, feeling better for a moment as sunshine and fresh air washed over him. For the first time, he could see the true extent of the damage inflicted when the *Fool's Errand* rammed the *Scorpion*. Much of the steel plating behind the conning tower was torn away down to the pressure hull. Chunks of carbon fiber and aluminum were still stuck in the submarine's skin like shrapnel. Thick gouges and scars covered much of the rear of the submarine.

The still-smoldering hulk of the *Horizon* bobbed in the water. Dr. Nassiri descended the conning tower, paused for a moment, then jumped onto the nearest pontoon of the experimental yacht. Hand over hand, he made his way to the main body, to the cockpit, and the fantail. The entire cockpit of the ship had been completely torn open by a single explosion, laying the interior bare to the hot sun beating down from overhead.

The yacht was an unsalvageable mess. She was completely holed; the only thing keeping her afloat was her half-empty pontoon fuel tanks. Seawater washed over the deck, more with each passing wave. Fatima leapt onto the fantail, awkwardly clambering up to join her son.

"Any bodies?" she asked.

"No," said Dr. Nassiri. "No bodies."

"The pirates could have taken them. Or just dumped them at sea."

Dr. Nassiri said nothing. Fatima tapped a nearby railing.

"There was a lifeboat here," she said. "Maybe they escaped in that."

"Doubtful," said Dr. Nassiri.

"What do you want to do? They're not here."

Dr. Nassiri stood for a moment, watching the *Horizon* toss in the waves, flexing and groaning with each movement. Jonah must be dead. The alternatives were worse—captured or floating alone in an unforgiving ocean, far from shore. Every professional instinct in his body insisted to him the hopelessness of the situation.

"We stay," said Dr. Nassiri. "Jonah is not a man to give up. Neither shall we. We will search until we find him."

CHAPTER 14

Jonah slowly stirred awake, sunlight easily penetrating the thin safety-orange ceiling to the ten-man inflatable raft. His gaze fell across Klea, who stared at him cross-armed as if she were trapped in the raft with a tiger.

"How can you sleep?" she demanded, her fierce eyes flashing.

Jonah gave her a pained smile but didn't answer.

"I'm actually asking you how you can sleep right now," she said. "It's not a rhetorical question."

"It's a trick every sat diver picks up eventually," Jonah answered. "Learn to sleep anywhere. You don't know when or where your next snooze is coming, so you have to get 'em in as you can."

"What's a sat diver?"

"Saturation diver," said Jonah. "Like recreational SCUBA divers, but much deeper and for industrial projects. Oil and gas industry, shipwrecks, that sort of thing. We stay underwater or in a pressurized environment for days, sometimes weeks at a time. Atmospheric gasses dissolve into our tissues to the point of saturation."

"Tell me how you do it. How do you sleep like that?"

"I don't know. Try forcing yourself to stay awake."

"That's stupid," she said.

Jonah pulled himself up against one of the bumpers of the circular raft, using the wall for support. The raft was relatively well stocked. A side pocket held bottles of water amounting to about three gallons, fishing gear, a small knife, medical kit, and flashlight. He reached up and checked his slashed arm, finding it not as bad as he'd feared. It'd long since stopped bleeding, probably wouldn't even need stitches. Good. He wasn't looking forward to sewing himself up with repurposed fishing gear.

"What about you? How did you sleep when you were a prisoner on your ship?"

"Routine," said Klea. "My captors gave me small electronics projects to work on, mostly from their outboard motors. Sometimes televisions or radios. I think they were running a little side electronics repair business for the locals. I'd work on those for most of the day. I'd make myself meals from whatever they'd bring me. I worked on the *Horizon* and made weapons all night. And then I'd do exercises until my arms and legs couldn't move. I'd get maybe three or four hours of sleep if I was lucky."

"Three hours a night? That sucks."

"So what's your secret?"

"My first rotation on a research ship was pretty rough. I was part of a base crew for a saturation expedition to a sunken turn-of-the-century ocean liner. Spent more time dodging hurricanes than we spent actually getting any work done. I barely slept. Every night was the same. We'd ride these waves like a roller coaster; bow in, one after another. Eventually I would get used to the rhythm and fall sleep. But then we'd have to turn around so that we weren't so far off station when the storm ended. The ship would start to change course and we'd take a massive three, four story wave almost completely broadside. The entire ship would heel over nearly forty-five degrees. Anything not strapped down would go flying across the entire breadth of the ship. Terrifying. I'd get jolted completely awake. For a moment, I'd be absolutely convinced that the ship was going to turn turtle and I was about to drown."

"How long did this last?"

"Weeks. Eventually, I realized I could catch a few minutes here and again if I slept in my full uniform and steel-toed boots. Maybe part of my brain figured it was safe to sleep if I could wake up at a moment's notice and make a run for it. Eventually I didn't need the boots anymore."

"What's your name?" asked Klea out of the blue.

"Jonah. Jonah Blackwell."

"Your last name sounds familiar."

"It's usually attached to 'disgraced CIA section chief'," said Jonah.

"Can't be you. You're much too young."

"My father."

"Do you know my name?"

"Klea something."

"Klea Ymeri."

"Slovakian?"

She shook her head. "Kosovar. From what used to be Yugoslavia. By birth, anyway."

Silence fell between them. At least she'd stopped looking at him like he was some evil, treacherous bastard that would throw her overboard at any moment.

"I'm really sorry about wrecking your dive equipment," she finally said. "It's my fault we're stuck out here."

Jonah nodded, considered the apology. It seemed heartfelt enough.

"I probably would have done the same thing," he said. "So I'll get over it."

"Seriously? Just like that? You're what, over it now?"

"Seriously. It was pretty shitty of me to come in with no intent of saving you. You saw your opportunity and took it. It wasn't like you weren't prepared, you certainly weren't being vindictive. I mean, your plan to escape kinda sucked, but we made a decent go of it."

"I spent years working it out," she said. "I was so certain. I visualized every detail, mapped out as many outcomes as I possibly could."

"By the look of things, you may have missed a scenario or two."

"No need to be a dick about it."

"That's not what I meant."

"What other way could I possibly take it?"

"Let me put it this way. Fatima's son didn't exactly hire me. He sprung me from a prison where'd I'd spent three years. I'd spent that time trying to dream up a way to escape. Lots of ideas came to me, but no real way to carry them out."

Klea remained silent.

"So Doc Nassiri comes along," continued Jonah. "And he offers me a way out. A real, bona-fide release from prison in exchange for some basic diving work. Basic for me, anyway. I got the sense he probably couldn't pay anybody else enough to do it given the proximity to Somalia. But you know what I did?"

"What did you do?"

"I came within one second of taking his gun and trying

to shoot my way out of the prison. And you know why? Because I only really knew of one way out. Death. I didn't have a life to go back to outside those walls. Family is all gone; all my friends think I'm dead or holed up in Thailand with a needle in my arm. They'd said their goodbyes years ago. It was the one certainty I could find, the one absolute I could still control. Maybe I'd take a few assholes with me, maybe not."

Klea shook her head, refusing to look up, refusing to make eye contact.

"I'm sorry I destroyed your ship," he said. "I truly am. I know you can relate to what I'm saying. Your elaborate plan? All that Mad Max shit? Harpoons, spears, explosives, smoke clouds? I think you wanted to put yourself in a position where the only choice the pirates had was to kill you. I think you wanted to die on the *Horizon*."

She was too strong to sob, but Jonah could feel her heart breaking with every word.

"I should have died four years ago," she finally said. "I should have died with my friends."

"Why does the *Horizon* mean so much to you?"

Klea sat back in the raft, her eyes open, and her cheeks dry.

"I was born in Kosovo," she said. "This has a point to it, I promise. I was still pretty young during the troubles, but old enough to remember hiding in the woods and the six months I spent in a refugee camp. It's the sort of thing that college admissions officers swoon over. That was great, because I was good at school. Like, really good. Especially math, physics, anything with numbers, formulas or computer programming. My family stayed observant, we drifted apart when I lost my religion.

"And then I met Colin. He was two years ahead of me at MIT. He was brilliant, an actual certifiable genius. Always smiling, always laughing. Friends with a lot of the girls in his classes but didn't get many dates. He was kind of awkward and a little overweight. But he was so brilliant and so kind. He showed me a world of phenomenal creativity and passion. Passion for me, a type of intense infatuation I'd never experienced before. It was so pure, so painfully earnest. Maybe other girls found it smothering. One of his exes even tried to warn me off. But I thought it was wonderful. He became my best friend. And then he became more, much more.

"The *Horizon* was his masterpiece, the culmination of every moment he spent at MIT. He didn't just want to build a ship that could go around the entire world using less fuel than any other ship before it; he wanted one that was fast and beautiful as well. Every line on this ship was an expression of his brilliant mind and open heart.

"He wasn't quite what you'd expect of a globe-trotting record-setting maritime explorer. Colin could be a little ridiculous. He wore sandals with tube socks pulled up to his knees, and khaki shorts. Squared-off glasses, even though I went out of my way to get him fitted for contacts. He wouldn't even go outside unless he was dripping with sunscreen. But I didn't care about any of that. If you'd met him, you'd understand why.

"So there we are, sailing in the Indian Ocean. Colin thinks he's planned for everything. We're more than a hundred miles off the coast of Somalia coming out of the Gulf of Aden. Colin thinks there is no possible way the pirates are going to detect a vessel as small as ours."

"But they still came," said Jonah.

"Yeah, they still came. We had no idea how hungry these men were. How could we? Given my childhood, I thought I was wise to the world. We even laughed about the threat, can you believe that? Colin made jokes about joining them, said it'd make for a better career choice than trying to enter a down economy as a mechanical engineering major."

Jonah allowed himself a tiny chuckle. Klea fell silent for a few moments, but Jonah didn't mind. She'd finish her story at her own pace.

Finally he spoke up. "You must have gotten along well. The two of you, alone on the ship for all those weeks. Not many couples can do that. Most of the divers I know spend their rotations wishing they were home with their wives and most of the time home with their wives wishing they were out on rotation."

"Oh no," said Klea. "It wasn't just the two of us. Colin's best friend came along too. Kyle. He programmed a lot of the electronics. That was his ticket onboard. I think he was really just there for the adventure. He brought his girlfriend, Molly-Anne. She was a nurse; we figured she would be really useful in case any of us got hurt or sick, especially in some of those more remote regions. She was there because Kyle was there. I don't think she really cared for the ocean or boats or anything. Molly loved Kyle, but I don't think she trusted him very much by himself in foreign cities. More specifically, she didn't trust him around foreign girls."

"Girls liked him?"

"Girls *loved* him," said Klea, laughing. "Kyle was one of those friendly, handsome guys that thought the world was just a really great place because of how nice everybody was to him. Super trusting. Smart, but not smart enough to realize how uniquely he was treated. The trust fund didn't hurt either. If Colin would have let him, we probably wouldn't have needed a single sponsor. Kyle could have personally funded the expedition without breaking a sweat."

Jonah smiled and watched as Klea relaxed a little, sinking deeper against the inflated side of the raft.

"Kyle drove some old muscle car," mused Klea, almost more to herself than Jonah. "Hadn't thought about that ridiculous thing in a long time. I adored him and Molly. They had been together for a long time. I think Kyle was under some pressure to get on with it, if you know what I mean. He would have proposed eventually, I'm certain of that. Colin and Kyle would have been the best men at each other's weddings.

"The four of us were about as close as friends could be. Molly was so jealous when Colin proposed to me the day we departed. He got down on one knee on the fantail of the *Horizon* in Bordeaux as the sun set behind us, gave me a ring he'd forged himself in the metallics laboratory."

Jonah found himself gulping, trying to square his unconscious attraction to Klea with the specter of her martyred fiancé. He tried to look away but his eyes stayed locked with hers. Then, glancing away in discomfort, he found himself looking for a ring on Klea's left hand. Klea caught him and waved the ringless hand in his face.

"It was stolen," said Klea. "Ripped it right off my finger while others ran their hands through my pockets. Probably on the hand of some … pirate wench."

Both Klea and Jonah simultaneously broke out in stifled laughter.

"A very lucky pirate wench."

"The bitch had better appreciate it," said Klea, still

smiling. "So there we are, we're making good time—not as good as Colin had hoped, but we were still on track to make the record, especially if we gained time during a spate of good weather we had anticipated over the following weeks. We'd already passed the point where we were closest to the Somali coast; we figured we were more or less in the clear. Still pretty stressful, but the worst should have been over. Colin was piloting, Kyle was in his bunk with Molly. I was on the fantail doing the fuel consumption calculations.

"That's when I saw this glint in the distance, a single speedboat approaching us. We were out in the middle of nowhere, there should have been nobody and nothing around. I got curious and grabbed my binoculars. When I got a good look, it dawned on me that we were being stalked by a pirate ship. We heard this foreign language over the radio; I realize they'd called in other skiffs. They had a mothership on a scouting expedition in the area and were trying to box us in. We changed course, increased speed to maximum but they gained on us. Soon, there were two other boats chasing us.

"Everybody was up at this point. Molly was freaking out, Colin was more scared than I'd ever seen him, he and Kyle were yelling at each other while trying to squeeze just a few extra knots out of the engines. I was on the fantail, watching. The pirates started falling back, losing ground. Kyle and Colin got excited, they started whooping and hollering. They were already rehearsing the war stories they'd tell at the Miracle."

"The what?"

"The Miracle of Science," said Klea. "It's an MIT bar. Our hangout spot. They've got a drink menu that looks like the periodic table of elements."

"Ah," said Jonah.

"Suddenly, I realized that we were not outrunning the speedboats. They were hanging back, getting into position. Getting ready to take a run at us. Molly stormed out of the cockpit, started yelling at me to come inside. The speedboats came towards us at full speed, firing guns at the *Horizon*. Molly just stood there, mouth hanging open and got hit twice in the chest. I'd never seen someone get shot before, not even in Kosovo. I was on my stomach, trying to find somewhere to hide. Kyle came running out, trying to drag Molly inside. He got her inside the cockpit but was shot in the back. He made this long, awful sound and dropped to all fours. I saw him crawling away and I never saw him again.

"I realized the pirates weren't aiming at me because they thought I was already dead, I was just lying there on the deck doing nothing. They pulled back. What was really frustrating was how arbitrary it all was. They decided everything, when to attack, when to stop. We couldn't fight back; we were just a bunch of college students. I couldn't even tell what the pirates were trying to do. Were they trying to disable the ship? If so, why fire at us? Were they just trying to kill us? Then why were they shooting at the ship, too?

"At this point, I was too scared to move. Colin stepped over Molly to get to me, almost tripped over her body. He was trying to get me to move, to come inside. I wouldn't do it. And then I saw his shirt, he'd been shot twice through the abdomen. He was white as a sheet, losing blood. He got woozy, went down to his knees. Then he was out, eyes rolling back into his head, breathing fast and shallow. I tried to remember what Molly told me to do, find the entrance and exit wounds, stop the bleeding. I stripped off part of his shirt but couldn't make sense of anything. The *Horizon* was bouncing off waves, going *way* too fast, the engines were howling, there was blood everywhere, and I couldn't even find out where it was coming from."

"Jesus."

"Then I took out my cell phone," said Klea. "I still have no idea why I did this. Maybe the idea of leaving no record was unbearable. I was certain Colin was dead. Molly definitely was and Kyle had crawled off somewhere to die."

"But you were alive."

Klea pulled her shirt up to reveal one long, ugly scar against the left side of her toned abdomen.

"I didn't even notice it," she said. "Worst scar I have, and I don't even know how it happened. So I had my cell phone. I recorded this ridiculous message on video. No memory whatsoever of what I actually said. I ran below decks. I didn't see Kyle, but I saw a long blood trail where he'd dragged himself away. I found an empty mayo jar. I popped the cell phone in the jar and chucked it overboard. By the time I made it back up on the fantail, the pirates had boarded."

"What did they do?"

"They did what pirates have done for centuries. Went through my pockets, beat me, stripped away my clothes. I started screaming out every prayer I knew from childhood, screaming in Arabic as loud as I could. They stopped beating me, stopped ripping my clothes. After that, they really didn't know what to do with me. There wasn't much of a plan. They gave me a veil and stuck me in a shipping container for a few weeks, then moved me back on the *Horizon* in the middle of their harbor."

"You've been out here a long time," said Jonah.

"But it didn't end there," she said. "I spent years living in Colin's mausoleum. It was like being buried in his grave, him dead next to me and me clawing at the lid of the coffin. Every morning I would wake up in the bed we once shared. Every day, I would walk past the chair where he'd piloted the *Horizon*. I would sit for hours in the same spot he took his last breath. I saw Colin everywhere. You ever love someone like that?"

"No," he lied.

Klea turned away, refusing to allow Jonah to see her cry. And for just a moment, the briefest of moments, Jonah wished he'd told her the truth.

"What happens next?" she asked. "How long can we hold out?"

"I'll spare you the list of potential sufferings," said Jonah. "At least we have water for a few days, maybe longer if we ration it wisely."

"Food?"

"Don't worry about food," said Jonah. "Given our shared histories, I think we're well-suited for some temporary starvation."

"Not much to eat in a pirate compound. I suppose the same rings true for a Moroccan prison."

"Yeah. There's going to come a time—maybe soon—when we don't want to carry on the struggle. When that time comes …"

Jonah trailed off. He drew the pistol from his belt with one hand, the two remaining bullets with the other. The implication was clear. There was no need to unnecessarily prolong their ordeal.

Angry, Klea tried to snatch the weapon away from him.

"What are you doing?" he demanded.

"I'm throwing it overboard," she said. "I'm not finished yet."

"I'm not goddamn finished either," said Jonah. "But there's no sense in limiting our options. If we're out here for too long, there will come a time when you want the merry-go-round to stop."

"Fine," said Klea. She watched angrily as Jonah replaced the weapon and bullets into his wetsuit.

For a few moments, they simply stared at each other until Jonah felt uncomfortable and looked away.

"You got any tattoos from prison?" asked Klea.

"Muslim country," said Jonah. "Not big on prison ink."

"Any scars?"

"Sure. Got a good one pretty recently. Still sewn up."

"Lemme see," she said.

He shrugged, and then decided to oblige. He reached back behind his back and pulled at the zipper cord, then stripped down to his waist. Jonah looked down at the knife wound in his abdomen from where the Rabat gangster had stabbed him. The ugly wound was still held together with Dr. Nassiri's perfectly spaced stiches.

They'll be ready to come out soon, he thought. He always healed fast, ever since he was a kid.

When he looked up, Klea was already halfway across the small raft, steadying herself on all fours as she made her way to him. She wasn't looking at the wound; she was looking at him, staring intently into his eyes.

Oh, thought Jonah. This was unexpected. Klea crawled on top of him, straddling him, pressing her body into his. She pushed her face towards his, kissing him deeply, biting his lower lip.

"Why?" he whispered as she ran her fingers through his salt-encrusted hair.

"Because I'm not finished yet," she whispered back.

CHAPTER 15

Dr. Nassiri stood on the fantail of the *Horizon* and stared off into the distance. It wouldn't be long now; the experimental yacht had already begun to break apart in the gentle swell. One of the pontoons was nearly separated from the body of the ship and the flooding in the main cabin increased with every wave. She'd soon be on the bottom of the ocean, joining the *Fool's Errand* and centuries of ill-fated ships. He released the mooring line, separating the *Horizon* and the *Scorpion*. The physical exertion felt good, especially in the fresh sea air and the still-cool early morning.

Fatima stepped up beside him, love and pride welling up into a powerful mixture of emotions she was not well-equipped to demonstrate. Her son had risked everything to save her—no, not her; he thought she was dead—but her legacy. He had willingly set his life aside to finish what she had started. How does one thank a son for that?

She looked up at him. Dark, unruly hair ruffled in the wind as he squinted into the vast emptiness, searching for any sign Jonah and Klea had survived the explosion. He was as handsome as his father had been. No wonder the

American girl watched his every move. The girl tried to hide it, of course, but a mother could always sense a woman's interest in her son. But a Texan? Not what she'd imagined for Hassan, but she wouldn't interfere. Not after all this. Without thinking, she licked the palm of her hand and went to work trying to pack down an errant clump of hair.

"Mother!"

Alexis stuck her head over the lip of the conning tower, just as Dr. Nassiri batted his mother's hand away from his head.

Alexis laughed and Dr. Nassiri turned and held his hand to his forehead, blocking the sunlight to get a better look. The morning light did the Texan more than justice, she was radiant. He swallowed hard and ignored his mother's ministrations.

"Thought you should know—we're getting incoming radar contacts," shouted Alexis. "Looked like a flock of birds at first but they're flying too straight and much too fast. Vitaly says they're drones bearing in from Anconia Island. They're fifteen minutes out on a direct intercept course."

Dr. Nassiri frowned. A cluster of drones wasn't a good sign. Just one might have been surveillance or on some unrelated mission. A cluster meant they were potentially armed and maybe even accompanied by a surface vessel. He held the mooring line fast as his mother gingerly stepped from the smoldering yacht to the submarine. She ascended the ladder to the conning tower and disappeared inside.

"Are they weaponized?" he shouted.

"Vitaly says yes. Air-to-ground missiles."

Dr. Nassiri ably hopped from the yacht to the submarine and deftly untied the mooring line. Knots came easily to his surgeon's muscle memory, even unfamiliar designs. It was his guess that a surveillance drone had picked up on the smoke column from the *Horizon*. Whether any of the drone operators had seen the *Scorpion* or not, he couldn't guess. But he knew he didn't want to be around when they arrived. Dr. Nassiri climbed the boarding ladder and joined Alexis on the top of the conning tower.

"We have another problem," said Alexis. Wrench in hand, she pointed towards the snorkel pipe rising behind them as it hummed along, gently exhaling a steady stream of diesel exhaust.

"What is it?"

"Batteries are charged off of the diesel engines," she said. "And they're only about twenty percent of capacity. We're not going to have much juice to play with if we submerge now."

"That does sound like a problem," he mused.

Alexis stepped onto the interior boarding ladder. He followed, slamming the hatch shut behind them, twisting the wheel until it sealed tightly.

Dr. Nassiri dropped into the command compartment, right next to where Vitaly manned the pilot's console. Vitaly shot him a pain-tinged smile—it made Dr. Nassiri just a touch uncomfortable, but he couldn't place why. Fatima found a seat in the corner, close enough to listen in, but far enough away to keep out of the action. Dr. Nassiri got the sense that she needed a job on board, something to keep her busy and useful.

"Submerge the *Scorpion*," ordered Dr. Nassiri. "Head towards the coast. Let's get a little distance between us and those drones. Appreciate the warning, Vitaly."

"Is not problem," said Vitaly. "Vitaly does not want to

die. Making depth one-zero-zero feet." He pressed forward on the controls, and the *Scorpion* almost imperceptibly leaned forward as she slipped underneath the waves. The side-to-side motion of wave action ceased, replaced by a sense of momentum and calm.

"Set to cruising speed," continued Dr. Nassiri. "No need to use any more electricity than necessary."

"What's the decision about Jonah?" asked Alexis.

"We will stay and find him," said Dr. Nassiri. "We will search as long as possible. He deserves that much."

Fatima nodded at him with a look of approval. "As does Klea."

"We save?" asked Vitaly, not completely convinced.

"We save," confirmed Dr. Nassiri. "My working theory is that Jonah escaped on the missing life raft at some point after we rescued my mother. Perhaps Jonah set the explosion off himself as a distraction. It would certainly be his style."

"I do not understand—why blow up own boat?" asked Vitaly.

"They couldn't outrun the pirates, not without a greater head start. From my examination, it appeared the explosion came from within the main cabin. That's interesting to me for two reasons. First, I don't think the pirates could have hit the cabin interior with a rocket-propelled grenade. It's just too lucky of a shot. Second, why the cabin? Why not the engines? I think the goal was to make a big explosion without immediately sacrificing speed. To me, it appears deliberate and purposeful. A desperate plan, but a plan nonetheless. There was plenty of debris for them to hold on to … overturned skiffs, parts of the hull, maybe even a life raft. We can't be out here indefinitely, but I imagine we can search for a least a few days. After that, it wouldn't matter either way. What do you think?"

"If Jonah alive, he know Vitaly stay and save him," said Vitaly "If Jonah dead, Vitaly will know for sure. Either way, Vitaly sleep better at night."

"So we need a plan," said Fatima.

"I have not only plan. I have solution," said Vitaly. "You know search theory Bayesian?"

"No," Fatima admitted.

"I learn this some time ago," said Vitaly. "Is mathematical equation for finding lost man at sea. We start with the voyage of the … what is the name of Batman's yacht?"

"The Batboat?" said Dr. Nassiri, a little incredulous.

"No! The ship we chase! Look like Batmobile."

"Ah," said Alexis. "The *Horizon*."

"Yes, yes," said Vitaly. The Russian pulled up a regional map on his console and inputted a series of coordinates.

"So we know coordinates where beautiful Fatima rescued," said Vitaly, pointing at a blinking cursor.

Vitaly flashed a very genuine smile towards Dr. Nassiri's mother. She visibly blushed despite herself. Alexis rolled her eyes just a little too obviously.

"And we know speed of *Horizon*," said Vitaly. "And we know point where we find her drifting. According to calculation, she is under power for seventy-three minutes after rescue then stop and drift. This seventy-three minutes is window where big man Jonah escape with lady friend of Fatima."

Vitaly added in a second set of coordinates to his map, the location where the *Horizon* would have lost power. Dr. Nassiri noticed that the coordinates were a little off from where the *Horizon* currently drifted. Vitaly had already compensated for the hours the stricken ship spent in the current.

"What if he abandoned the *Horizon* after she lost power?" asked Alexis.

"If he abandoned ship after lost power," said Vitaly. "Then they would drift together. Same current, same drift. We would have found already."

"Yes, that makes sense," said Fatima.

"Okay, no more stupid question," said Vitaly. "Let Vitaly do Vitaly magic." Vitaly punched in additional variables, creating a search grid, showing the potential area over six, twelve, and twenty-four hours.

"Given sight distance of periscope and range of radar," he said, "we have eighteen hours to find Jonah."

"And Klea," added Fatima.

"Why eighteen?" asked Dr. Nassiri.

"After eighteen hours, every hour we search represent exponentially greater search area," said Vitaly, with a confident facial expression that indicated he expected everyone assembled to be impressed. "After this, odds of finding big guy very small."

"Impressive. How do you know all this?" asked Fatima.

"Learned in Russian Navy while looking for lost sailor," said Vitaly. "He took piss off back of aircraft carrier. Lost balance, fell in ocean."

"Did you rescue him?" asked Alexis.

"We find him!" announced Vitaly with no small amount of pride.

"That's good—why, that's fantastic!" said Dr. Nassiri. For the first time, the doctor felt a warm surge of optimism flow through his body. Maybe it was possible to find Jonah after all.

"Not so good," said Vitaly. "Lost sailor drowned. But we find him!"

At least they found him, thought Dr. Nassiri.

Despite Alexis's protests, Dr. Nassiri insisted they run the batteries down to less than seven-and-a-half percent before the *Scorpion* surfaced to charge batteries. As near as anyone could guess, seven and a half seemed to be the magic number, any lower and vital systems were compromised or rendered inoperable. It was a gamble. They'd be dead in the water if they were caught, but surfacing earlier or at intervals would leave a trail of breadcrumbs leading the Bettencorps mercenaries directly to their location.

"Preparing to surface," said Vitaly, slowly bringing the *Scorpion* up for air.

It wasn't night yet, not quite, but it should be close. Dr. Nassiri raised the periscope. Through the lens, he could see the perfect reds and purples of yet another brilliant African sunset.

Alexis started the engines, and the entire command compartment was instantly filled with the soothing, familiar hum of the massive twin-diesel engines. A few hours like this and they'd be at full battery power and ready to tackle anything. Vitaly had smartly piloted the massive submarine to one of the far corners of their computer-modeled search area. The course was intended as just random enough to throw off any pursuers while still making effective ground in the search for Jonah.

Dr. Nassiri slowly swiveled the periscope in a full circle. Once clear, he'd have Fatima join him on the conning tower with a pair of high-powered binoculars.

Suddenly, the view out of the periscope fell on a pair of incoming rigid-inflatable zodiacs, the type favored by commandos and pirates alike. They were gaining ground on the *Scorpion* with every second, and both vessels bristled with heavily-armored mercenaries and weaponry.

"They found us!" shouted Dr. Nassiri. "Dive, dive, dive!"

"The batteries—they're too low!" said Alexis, almost shouting, intense distress in her voice.

Fatima just stared ahead, wide-eyed and terrified.

"How close?" demanded Vitaly.

"Close," said Dr. Nassiri. "Dive, dive now!"

"How close to reaching us?" demanded Vitaly again.

"I don't know," said Dr. Nassiri. "Fifteen seconds. Maybe less."

"How did they find us?" said Fatima, breaking her silence.

"Engines to full power," said Vitaly. He pressed the throttle forward and was rewarded with a rapidly increasing pitch from the engine room as the *Scorpion* surged to flank speed.

"I ordered a dive," shouted Dr. Nassiri, clapping a hand on the Russian's back. "So dive, Vitaly! *Dive now!*"

"Please trust," said Vitaly. "Give me countdown."

I suppose the betrayal was inevitable, thought the doctor. Vitaly actually wanted him to count down to his own capture and probable execution.

The next few seconds played out in his mind. The Bettencorps mercenaries were going to beach their boats on the back of the *Scorpion* and rush the conning tower. They'd blast open the hatch and—

In fact, they wouldn't even need to blast it open. They had Vitaly. The Russian could simply toggle some unseen switch and the hatch would fly open. *Please make yourself at home. Remember to wipe your feet.*

Dr. Nassiri drew his pistol.

"Fine, no countdown for Vitaly," said the Russian.

Vitaly abruptly threw the submarine in reverse. Time froze for a moment as anything not bolted down flew forward—computer monitors, operational manuals and human bodies alike. Dr. Nassiri barely braced himself on the periscope as the entire submarine rattled and groaned with a symphony of a mechanical torture, gears grinding, propeller shaft shrieking under the strain. Fatima tumbled forward as if blindsided by an errant rugby tackle, falling through the hatchway, protecting her broken wrist while trying to brace herself with the other, landing hard. A loud, Texas-accented *goddammit* echoed out of the engine compartment, accompanied by a loud clattering.

Dr. Nassiri grabbed the periscope and brought it to bear at their attackers. One of the two inflatable boats had overshot the *Scorpion* completely and was circling back for another pass. The second had been sucked into the reversed propellers, leaving chopped-up rubber, screaming men and an oil slick in the *Scorpion*'s wake. One out of two wasn't bad—and maybe they'd gotten both if he'd given a Vitaly a proper count-down. But they couldn't count on trying the same trick twice. Worse, the remaining inflatable boat wasn't alone. Her mothership, a massive, battleship-grey converted transport, fell into the submarine's long wake, throwing out rescue lines for the survivors.

"Brilliant work," said Dr. Nassiri as he re-holstered his pistol.

"So maybe you don't shoot me?" asked Vitaly as he increased to flank speed again.

"So maybe next time you tell me the plan."

"Learn Russian," Vitaly grumbled. "To explain English take longer than just do plan."

Fatima rose to her feet and found a seat in the communications console next to Vitaly. "Is there any way we can charge the batteries without exposing the *Scorpion*?"

"Is tricky," said Vitaly, squinting as he spoke. "I think we bring *Scorpion* to snorkel depth. We then use diesel engines to charge batteries. Takes *excellent* pilot to do correctly."

"Please be our excellent pilot," said Fatima.

"Okay," Vitaly said with a boyish grin.

The Russian released some of the ballast air from the tanks, allowing the submarine to glide beneath the waves with only the periscope, diesel engine intake, and exhaust snorkel still exposed.

Dr. Nassiri knew they wouldn't escape this way—all the mercenaries needed to do was follow the trail of diesel fumes—but it might give them the time they needed to charge the batteries, submerge the submarine, and slip away.

The militarized transport ship caught up with the *Scorpion*, coming alongside. The mercenary mothership paced the submarine, maintaining a standoff distance of less than a hundred feet. Mercenaries crowded the railing, heavy assault weapons slung across their backs. Men manned a series of three heavy machine guns, none of which scared Dr. Nassiri. Even if surfaced, nothing less than a howitzer could put a dent in the *Scorpion*'s thick steel hull, and the mercenaries knew it.

Without warning, the mothership broke her course, swinging hard towards the *Scorpion*.

"They're going to ram us!" shouted Dr. Nassiri.

Vitaly swore in Russian as he reversed the engines and

pushed the tiller hard to port, but not fast enough. With unexpected speed and maneuverability, the mothership cut across their bow. The mothership impacted the snorkel structure, narrowly missing the periscope. The intake and exhaust sheared off instantly. Dr. Nassiri's ears popped with a sudden vacuum pressure as the emergency valves in the snorkel clapped shut, forcing the engine to suck in air directly from the internal compartments of the submarine. Emergency sirens wailed as the suffering diesel engines belched exhaust into the engine compartment.

"Now we dive!" shouted Vitaly over the din of impact and siren.

The diesel engines choked to a stop as the *Scorpion* plunged beneath the surface, her metal skeleton groaning under the increasing pressure.

The depth gauge barely registered two hundred feet when the bow of the *Scorpion* dug into the soft sedimentary seabed, scraping to a halt atop an ancient layer of mud and seashells. And then all was silent, save for the *chu-chu-chu* of the mothership's propellers cutting through the waters above.

Alexis stumbled out of the engine compartment, coughing. She'd caught the worst of the exhaust. Dr. Nassiri hoped the ventilators were up to the task, the air was so filled with sulfuric diesel fumes it was barely breathable.

"How in the hell did they find us so fast?" asked Alexis.

Before anyone could answer, the main communications relay crackled to life, the *Scorpion*'s external hydrophone automatically receiving an acoustic transmission.

"Calling the hijackers of the *Scorpion*," sounded a booming voice over the radio. "Come in, *Scorpion*."

Dr. Nassiri saw Vitaly shudder with recognition. Over the hydrophone, the voice was tinny, distant, echoing as it transmitted through the thermoclines of the water column.

"Who is that?" whispered Dr. Nassiri.

"Colonel Westmoreland," said Vitaly. "Commander of all Bettencorps forces."

Dr. Nassiri thought for a moment, then clicked the transmit button.

"This is the *Scorpion*," he said.

"Very happy to hear your voice," continued Colonel Westmoreland. "Everybody okay down there? Our multibeam sonar indicates you are set down on the bottom. That's good, just stay there. You good for batteries? Air? No leaks, I hope? You guys took a pretty nasty hit."

"What should we do?" said Fatima.

"Just listen for now," said Dr. Nassiri.

"Even listening very dangerous," protested Vitaly. "Colonel Westmoreland is liar."

"We're at about ten percent for batteries," added Alexis. "But every system—air circulation, lighting, everything—is sucking juice. We've only got a couple of hours before we're dead on the bottom."

"How much air do we have?" asked Fatima.

"I think we'll circulate out most of the fumes out in the next few minutes," said Alexis. "The CO_2 scrubbers don't need any power for the lithium hydroxide to do its job. Breathable air could last for days, maybe even a week or more. We'll freeze to death first."

"You want me to be impressed?" continued the colonel over the hydrophone system. "I'm impressed. You've had a great run. Charles Bettencourt is not interested in drawing this out. You have our vessel; we want it back. No need for further messiness or hurt feelings. Let's just get you to the surface and we'll figure things out from there."

"He's bullshitting," announced Alexis.

"Agreed," said Dr. Nassiri. "But given our situation, I'm not certain if there is anything to do but play along."

"Guys, I hate to do this, but there's always a stick to go with the carrot," continued Colonel Westmoreland. "I've got nothing but time and resources. How charged are your batteries? Forty percent? Thirty?"

Ten, thought Dr. Nassiri.

"You cannot outrun us. You cannot outlast us. Every time you surface, we will be waiting. I'm giving you a one-time offer of a negotiated surrender—"

Vitaly clicked off the hydrophone systems. He'd heard enough. It went without saying that any surrender would end with the abrupt execution of all aboard.

"Vitaly, give me a solution," demanded Dr. Nassiri. "Something other than listening to this man talk us into our own murder."

"I have theory," said Vitaly. "I believe there may be hidden transponder on this ship."

"How would you not know?" asked Fatima.

"Is only for hijack scenario, hidden even from crew," said Vitaly. "I believe it broadcast our location."

"Can we find it?" asked Dr. Nassiri. "Turn it off somehow?"

Vitaly shook his head. "Whole purpose is so hijackers cannot find, cannot deactivate!"

"There's got to be a way," said Fatima. "Think!"

"Cannot be done!"

Dr. Nassiri slammed his fist into the console with anger as Vitaly shouted at him in Russian. Commando divers were probably already on their way, secretly mobilizing to board the *Scorpion* and kill everyone—

"I can do it," whispered Alexis, her volume almost imperceptible.

Everyone stopped dead and stared at her.

"What?" said Dr. Nassiri.

"I can do it. I can find the transponder."

"How?" demanded Fatima.

"It's going to be powered, right? It has to be powered in order to transmit."

"How would we possibly find it? There are active electronics everywhere."

"We shut it all down," said Alexis. "Every console, computer, light, oxygen supply, anything with an electromagnetic signature. And then we scan every millimeter of the submarine. The transponder should be the only system still active."

"Is possible," mused Vitaly. "I never consider this."

"I saw an EMF detection meter earlier. I'm not going to pretend the transponder will be easy to find, but I don't know what else we can do."

"How do we begin?" asked Dr. Nassiri. "Time is of the essence. Obviously."

"I can't do it," said Fatima. "Crawling around in the dark, feeling for who knows what? I'm sorry Hassan, but after the crash, being underwater is—"

"That's fine." The doctor put an arm around his mother's shoulders and earnestly hoped he wouldn't be forced to search the forward compartment alone. Too many bad memories made all the more vivid by the dark, to say nothing of the smell of antiseptic and burned skin. "Find a bunk and close your eyes. It will be over soon, one way or the other."

"Beginning system-wide electronic shutdown," Vitaly

said as he powered down the computer systems to the command compartment.

"Vitaly, I think we have to put you back in your bunk. I don't want you crawling around in the dark; the risk to your stitches is too great."

"I get handcuffs?" asked Vitaly glumly.

"No handcuffs. I trust you."

The doctor was impressed with the speed of Vitaly's recovery and had been slowly weaning him off a series of powerful painkillers. Even so, the Russian was still not very mobile and struggled to get in and out of his chairs and bunk.

"Two days," said Vitaly exuberantly, his mood now entirely improved by the proposition. "In two days, I will be recovered. I will wrestle you, Doctor! Russia versus … Egypt?"

"Morocco."

"Russia versus Morocco! One night only! Crowd is very excited!"

Fatima followed closely behind as the trio made their way into the bunk compartment. After Vitaly was settled, she found an unoccupied bed, climbed in without taking off her shoes, closed the curtain and rolled a blanket over her head. Maybe she could convince herself she wasn't marooned in a steel tube on the bottom of the sea.

Dr. Nassiri joined Alexis in the engine compartment. The Texan experimentally held the EMF meter up to a light bulb. It chirped, the needle dancing. She hoped it'd be sensitive enough to discover the source of their tracker, concealed somewhere in the length of the submarine. Alexis nodded, satisfied. With a final grunt, she tripped the series of main circuit breakers for the battery bank.

Compartment by compartment, the lights flickered and died.

The doctor felt as though he'd just fallen into an ocean of darkness in the center of the earth, a vast emptiness of starless space. The darkness surrounding him was so deep, so intense, that the effort of his eyes and mind adjusting to the sudden blackness resulted in dull, flickering hallucinations, flashes of imaginary light.

He heard Alexis's footsteps beside him, heard her breath. In the stillness, he almost thought he could hear her heartbeat over his own.

"Shall we?" he asked.

"Might as well," she said. "Can't dance, can't sing, and it's too wet to plow."

He didn't know what this meant, but could sense her fear matching his own. Alexis's hand brushed against his chest, feeling down his arm. He allowed her to grasp his hand, their fingers intertwining. With his limited perception, the heat of her fingers and the electricity of her touch became his entire world.

"Let's start with the weapons locker," said Alexis.

Dr. Nassiri allowed her to lead him, taking cautious steps towards the stern of the submarine while he reached forward with his free hand, trying to anticipate when he'd reach the hatchway. Alexis was a good guide, she found the hatchway in moments. She released his hand, and a twinge of loss ricocheted through his body.

Sounds—Dr. Nassiri heard Alexis running the silent EMF meter over the walls, along the deck. She bumped the device against rifles and ammunition boxes. The detector made not so much as a burble.

"Maybe it's not working," whispered Alexis.

"May I?" replied Dr. Nassiri in his own hushed tone.

The doctor gingerly walked towards her voice, making little gentle sweeps with outstretched fingertips to find her. He touched something firm, her shoulder, and ran his hand down her upper arm. He reached her wrist, fingers softly running over the barely-there peach fuzz of her forearm. The doctor felt goosebumps, felt her shiver. Strange—it was not cold in this compartment. He felt around the outside of her hands, coming across the plastic construction of the EMF reader and slipped it from her grasp.

The doctor placed his free hand into the small of Alexis's back and brought the EMF reader up underneath her left breast, gradually increasing pressure until it was firmly against her chest. He felt the muscles in the small of her back tense up for just a moment, then release.

The EMF reader gently chirped, reading a faint signature.

"It's your heart," he whispered, holding the device in place. "The EMF reader is detecting the electrical charge in your skin from each beat."

"It works," whispered Alexis, breathlessly.

She fumbled against his hands, taking the device back as his hand fell away from her lower back. No guiding her fingers this time, he was forced to follow the sounds of her footsteps as she exited the weapons locker for the engine room.

Dr. Nassiri followed, trying to keep up with her. She stopped dead and swiveled and the doctor collided with her. He'd just opened his mouth to utter a profound apology when he felt her arms reach around his torso, running up and down the length of his abdomen, pulling away at his shirt. His body reacted before his mind could issue a single command. He found himself lifting her entire body onto his, her legs wrapped around his waist as he held her in his arms, hands sliding across her back and up to the nape of her neck.

Her mouth found his. The EMF reader dropped on the ground and clattered across the metal deck as Dr. Nassiri pressed Alexis into the wall, her nails digging into his skin, days of tension and attraction between them culminating in a singular moment. She ripped open his shirt, buttons bouncing off the engine block as she pressed herself against his bare chest.

The EMF reader sat unnoticed a few feet away, as if content to chirp away merrily and without attention.

"Wait! Did you hear that?" Alexis pushed Dr. Nassiri's face away from the tiny dimple just above her clavicle.

"What?" he asked as he held Alexis suspended, her legs still wrapped around his waist.

"I ... I think it's beeping," said Alexis.

The Texan wriggled her hips, lowering herself to the ground. Both she and the doctor dropped to all fours, feeling around for the reader.

"Found it," Dr. Nassiri said, his fingers brushing against the undamaged plastic casing of the device. Alexis took it from him and began running slow sweeping patterns across the floor and wall. The beeping strengthened as Alexis found the source of the signal behind a panel just a few degrees off the apex of the rounded ceiling.

"Clever putting it in here," said Alexis. "The electromagnetic signature from the batteries could have made it impossible to find. I guess we're lucky they're so low right now."

"Lucky," mused Dr. Nassiri. He could still taste her lips on his.

"I think it's just behind this panel," said Alexis. She grabbed Dr. Nassiri's hand, a little more forcefully this time, forcing him to mark the location.

"Got it," said Dr. Nassiri.

"Don't move," she said. "I'm going to turn all the lights back on."

With that, the Texan walked away, the sound of her footsteps disappearing into the far end of the compartment. A few moments later, the lights flickered back on. Dr. Nassiri winced, covering his eyes with his free hands as the blinding illumination forced its way through the gaps between his fingers.

Looking down, he saw his pants askew, and the entire front of his shirt was open, buttons missing. Alexis reappeared, grinning at him as she adjusted her tank top and shorts. One of her shoes had fallen off, it lay not far from Dr. Nassiri's feet.

They both turned as Fatima entered the compartment, rubbing her eyes against the light. Embarrassed, Alexis ducked behind a console and busied herself in a toolbox.

"Did you find it?" Fatima asked, her glance shooting between her son and the American girl. "What happened to your shirt?"

"I … caught it on something in the dark," gulped Dr. Nassiri. "It ripped."

Alexis stifled a snicker which she tried to mask by clattering around in a drawer. Fatima frowned and crossed her arms.

"But I think we found what we were looking for. How's Vitaly?"

"He's asleep," said Fatima, scowling. "Whatever you gave him really knocked him out this time."

"I didn't give him anything."

"Maybe he finally understands we won't murder him in his sleep," Alexis said, brandishing a particularly menacing-looking crowbar. She stood on her tip-toes and stuck the edge of the crowbar underneath the panel, carefully prying it away from the wall.

Rivets strained then popped and the panel fell free, still suspended in the air by electrical cording.

"Um," said Alexis, emerging from behind the hanging panel. "There isn't anything back here."

"That's not good," mumbled Dr. Nassiri. He looked, and didn't see anything either.

"What do we do?" asked Fatima. "Are you sure about the reading?"

"A hundred percent," said Alexis. "A transmission is coming from that location, it couldn't be anything else."

Dr. Nassiri looked Alexis squarely in the eye and realized they were both thinking the same thing.

"It's on the outside of the vessel's hull," he said. "So it cannot be accessed while submerged."

"Can we surface?" asked Fatima.

"There's just no way," said Alexis. "Even if we surface, we can't dive again, not until we've charged the batteries to at least twenty percent. The mercenaries will be on us like a tornado on a trailer park."

"Charming," interjected Fatima.

"I'll do it," said Dr. Nassiri.

"Do what exactly?" demanded Fatima. "What are you going to do? You said it cannot be accessed while submerged!"

"It's obvious what has to be done. Someone has to swim out of the lockout chamber, find the transponder and deactivate it."

"Certainly you cannot—" began Fatima.

"Your mom's right," said Alexis. "It's suicide, and we—we *need* you."

"Who would you have me send?" he demanded, his voice raising. "Mother, look around you. Shall I send the only man who can pilot the ship, a man who can barely get in and out of his bed? The woman who runs the engines we'll need to escape? Or perhaps you'd have me send my own mother out with her broken wrist?"

Fatima fell silent.

"I'll go," said Alexis.

"You will not," said Dr. Nassiri. "I will not further imperil your life."

Alexis too fell silent.

"I don't know how to dive," he admitted, "but I paid attention when Jonah was preparing for our dive in Malta—"

"Malta?" Fatima interrupted.

"It's a long story." He turned back to Alexis. Just one air bottle would probably be safest. I do not intend to be outside the submarine for long. Alexis, please use a hammer and rap it against the hull loud enough for me to hear it. Mother, please go attend to the lockout chamber. It will just be matter of pressurizing the chamber until it matches the pressure of the sea outside.

"Once flooded, I can simply open the door and swim out. I will change into a wetsuit and join you shortly."

Fatima nodded, and left the engine room without another word. Wrestling with his own fear, Dr. Nassiri stormed into the weapons locker. He found a small bottle of air—he believed he'd heard Jonah refer to it as a "pony bottle"—and a marine flashlight. He grabbed a wetsuit that appeared to be more or less his size and stripped off his shirt. He noticed that he seemed leaner somehow, tauter than he'd remembered. While this dangerous life did not suit him, his body had already begun to adapt.

"Hey," came a voice from behind him.

Shirtless, the doctor turned towards the voice. Alexis stood in the hatchway, blocking his path. She raised one long, graceful leg and braced it against the bulkhead.

"Hello to you as well," said Dr. Nassiri, giving her the benefit of a small smile despite his overwhelming sense of impending doom.

"I want to finish what we started," she said. "So come back in one piece."

Alexis turned around and with that she was gone. Her promise lingered, if in no other place than Dr. Nassiri's vivid imagination.

Fatima was still familiarizing herself with the controls of the lockout chamber when her son climbed up the ladder to meet her.

"Lock chamber," she whispered to herself, reading the manual, her fingers pretending to press the buttons. "Pressurize interior at a rate of no more than one atmosphere per every ten seconds. Check interior pressure against exterior pressure. When equalized, flood chamber. Open outer doors."

"You understand what you'll need to do?" her son asked.

"I woke Vitaly up. He gave me a brief overview," said Fatima. "He says he has to stay in the command compartment."

"I don't think he can stand for any prolonged period of time yet," said Dr. Nassiri.

Fatima nodded, opened her mouth to speak then closed it again.

"It will be okay, mother."

"I made this for you," said Fatima, breaking eye contact and nodding, trying to reassure herself as well. The professor reached into her pocket and drew out a small glow stick on a long shoelace. She tied it around his neck and cracked it, illuminating mother and son with a gentle yellow.

"Thank you."

"It's like a lamb's bell," she said, her eyes welling up with tears. "Please come back safe, little lamb."

"I will."

The doctor wasn't certain whether to be deeply touched or mortally embarrassed. He gave his mother a light kiss on the top of her head and entered the diver's chamber, a small compartment no larger than a shower stall. Fatima closed the door behind him. When it shut with the loud sound of bolting locks, he realized all he could hear was the sound of his own breathing.

Swim out. Get the transmitter. Swim back.

Do it, he mouthed to his mother through the tiny four-inch portal window separating them. Vents hissed loudly as tanks released air into the chamber. The compartment pressurized quickly, too quickly, forcing Dr. Nassiri to gulp air, plug his nose and violently squeeze it into his ear canals before the increasing pressure burst them. Everything hurt, his teeth, his eyes, every joint protested with pain at the rapid pressurization.

The hissing stopped. With a click, water rapidly rose through the gaps in the steel deck. He shivered from the moment it touched his toes, the cold water of this depth was only a few degrees above freezing, more than a match for his thick neoprene suit. With his last few seconds, Dr. Nassiri adjusted his swimming goggles and took two experimental breaths out of the pony bottle.

Water flowed over his face and head. For a moment, Dr. Nassiri wondered why he wasn't floating. Between the air in his lungs and the neoprene suit; he thought he'd need to practically peel himself off the ceiling. Not at this depth, he recalled. The air in his lungs, the bubbles in the neoprene, all would be compressed by the surrounding pressure. At least that was good news, the idea of stepping out of the chamber and rocketing to the surface for crippling decompression sickness and immediate capture wasn't appealing.

The door to the lockout chamber clicked open and swung wide, revealing the bow deck of the submarine. He could only see what little was illuminated by the light streaming out of the chamber; the rest disappeared into impenetrable darkness.

He clicked the flashlight on and swam out of the lockout chamber and around the back of the conning tower. A sudden wave of contentment and ease washed over him, strengthening with each muscled exertion.

Nitrogen narcosis, he lazily thought to himself. Why didn't I think of that before?

He knew the hazards of surface air breathed under so much pressure—tranquility, loss of reasoning, calculation errors, poor choices and over-confidence, not entirely unlike the benzodiazepine family of pharmaceuticals. He did the math. If every thirty feet below sixty was about the same as drinking a martini, that would put him at what, six martinis? Seven? Part of him felt like maybe all the concern was unnecessary. This was going to be easy.

As he swam along the length of the deck to the immediate rear of the conning tower, Dr. Nassiri realized he could hear the tinny clanging of a hammer against steel over the sound of his own hissing, ragged breath. Somewhere inside, Alexis was doing her job. Time to do his. He played his flashlight around the area where the clanging emanated but saw only bare hull. The device, wherever it was, had to be between the pressure hull and the outer hull.

Dr. Nassiri swam down into the massive gash left by the *Fool's Errand* where it had stripped away the gun emplacement and large chunk of the outer hull. The clanging now seemed to be coming from everywhere, every direction. He felt for the vibration of the hammer with his fingers, lazily allowing them to crawl over the cold metal skin of the submarine and lead him to the source. The doctor wriggled between the cross-members between the inner and outer hulls.

He sucked at the regulator and felt resistance. Terror flooded over him. He managed one more half-breath, then let the pony bottle fall away from his mouth and disappear into the darkness, empty and useless. At six atmospheres of pressure, he'd sucked through the bottle six times faster than he'd intended. In his shock, he tried to turn around and smashed the face of his flashlight against one of the crossbeams. With a distinct pop, the plastic front imploded and the light vanished.

The clanging grew louder and louder, almost matching the ferocious volume of his heart in his ears. At least the cold water would slow his metabolism, buying him a few precious seconds to try to make it back to the lockout chamber. Dr. Nassiri tried to back his way out. His wetsuit caught on something blocky and plastic.

Clang, clang, clang, clang, the hammer banging on steel just wouldn't stop. He could feel Alexis on the other side; she was there, right below him, inches away. She was banging with the hammer and he was drowning. Dr.

Nassiri pulled at the blocky shape, snapping plastic rivets and freeing it from its mount on the pressure hull. He saw two now-severed wire leads hanging and realized he'd been caught on the transmitter. He yanked hard and it came free.

Boxy transmitter in hand, Dr. Nassiri wriggled free of the tight compartment, losing precious seconds and oxygen as he did. His chest pounded, his vision swam, his lungs involuntarily spasmed, trying to force him to *just breathe*!

The electronic transmitter dropped from his hand, knocking once against the side of the submarine and vanishing into the all-encompassing darkness. He desperately kicked towards the light of the lockout chamber, hand outstretched, trying to reach for something, anything to pull himself inside. He caught the rim of the outer hatchway and forced himself into the chamber, squeezing it shut behind him. Just as the last of his consciousness slipped away, he sucked in a massive lungful of freezing sea water and his entire world vanished into white.

CHAPTER 16

Klea slept in Jonah's arms as if she'd hadn't slept for a thousand years. He held her tight, her body pressed into his, cradling her head against his shoulder, running his hand through her short, dark hair, around the curve of her ear, against the nape of her neck. He kissed the crown of her head like a whisper.

"Colin, it's too early," she moaned, so quietly Jonah could barely make out the words. Then she nuzzled closer, sheltering herself against him in the quickening heat of the early afternoon, their third day at sea.

They hadn't spoken much, not since her little ruse on the morning of the first day. Jonah appreciated her ease with silence.

Sometimes they'd sit far from each other with hands outstretched, barely brushing the very tips of their fingers against each other, as if anything but the slightest contact would overwhelm the senses.

Other times, mostly in the cool evenings, she would crawl over and curl up on top of him, so much so that her much smaller body would be completely suspended upon his, not one stray toe touching the inflatable raft.

With no speaking came no complaining. Jonah understood three days without eating was simply an immutable fact, no more changeable than the sun in the sky.

They'd gone through significantly more water than he'd had anticipated. The orange tent over the raft turned the small inflatable vessel into a floating greenhouse. Try as they might to catch the wind with the tent flaps, the exercise was futile. Jonah couldn't risk repositioning the raft by paddling with his hands. His hands would accumulate salt and sores would soon follow, to say nothing of passing sharks.

Eyes closed, Jonah first felt a gentle, almost imperceptible nudge against the side of the raft. Then a shadow fell across nearly half of the tented canopy. He shook Klea awake. She startled at first, but Jonah held a single finger to his lips, and pointed for her to hide in the far corner, as far from the open tent flaps as possible. It wouldn't be good to reveal a woman on board the raft, not until he knew what he was dealing with.

Jonah struggled towards the entrance. He hadn't realized how weak he'd become, every movement felt like a battle against gravity and his own tired, wasting body.

He threw open the flap and shielded his face against the morning sun with his hand. The bow of a sixty-foot wooden fishing vessel curved over him as it nudged the raft like a collie herding a lamb. The vessel was local to the region, with an assortment of garish whites, blues, yellows, and reds painted over the wheelhouse and curved glassless windows.

An older man leaned over the side of the bow, staring down at Jonah, his dark face framed by day-glow-orange hair and beard. Two middle-school-age boys stood beside him, resembling him in the way that only sons resemble their father. They looked a little young for pirates, a good sign.

"*Assalamu alaikum*," said Jonah, using the traditional Islamic greeting.

"*Subah wanaagsan*," said the father, smiling to reveal a jack-o-lantern grin and pink gums.

"English?" asked Jonah. The father shook his head. Jonah smiled back, stuck an index finger in the air signaling for the man to wait, and briefly ducked into the tented raft again.

"I think we've got a ride," Jonah said to Klea. "But they don't speak English."

"That won't be a problem," she said, pushing her way past him to reach the tent flap.

Jonah realized he shouldn't have been surprised when Klea stuck her head out of the tent and spoke to the father in rapid-fire dialect. He wasn't able to see what was happening, but Klea seemed to be holding her own in the very animated conversation. While he'd been in prison, he didn't pick up much more than the essentials of Moroccan-accented Darija Arabic; Klea's fluency was more evidence that she was a quicker study than he was. Within moments, she ducked her head back inside.

"So?" asked Jonah.

"So he'll help us. I told him my husband accidentally set our ship on fire, and we were forced to abandon it. He says he'll bring us to his home, but he can't guarantee his village is safe for westerners."

"Thanks for making me look like a moron," Jonah said with a laugh.

"My pleasure," said Klea with a sly smile. "Thanks for playing the part so ably."

The fisherman navigated his boat to the side of the raft, using its mass to shadow against the intermittent ocean breeze. Jonah grabbed a waterproof bag, stuffed his pistol inside, and climbed up first, standing to reach the scuppers, then pulled himself up like a rock climber. It felt good, wonderful even, to stretch and use his muscles after three days of virtually no movement.

Fighting off a wave of hunger and dizziness, he brought himself up to his full height on the deck, easily dwarfing the father and two boys. The sons laughed and poked at his neoprene wetsuit with their fingers, amused at the sponginess of the futuristic material.

Jonah wondered what he was supposed to do now. Shake hands? Bow? Hell, he'd dance an Irish jig for the fisherman if thought that would help. The father just smiled at him, offering no clues. Jonah pressed his hands together like a prayerful child and bent slightly. "Thank you," he said with every ounce of earnestness he could muster. He hoped his appreciation translated, but couldn't tell for certain. The father, still smiling, waved Jonah away. It's nothing, the gesture seemed to say.

"Here," Klea called, stretching to hand over the remaining water bottles to Jonah, who took them and handed them to the boys. The two boys scampered away to secure the bottles in some unseen corner of the painted wheelhouse.

Plumbing his last reserves of energy, Jonah reached down and lifted Klea out of the raft, pulling her light frame to the safety of the wooden deck. The father clicked the wheezing engine into gear and the life raft slowly fell by the wayside, bobbing in the waves, as the fishing boat pulled away. Jonah knew the life raft would someday wash up on shore of some distant coastline, be it days or months. It'd be pushed against some sharp rock or branch and puncture, deflating like a cast-off skin. The bright orange would fade to a gentle pink and eventually to a dirty white. Sun damaged, it would slowly disintegrate into strips. And then there'd be nothing left of the proud *Horizon*.

The father, still smiling his wide nearly toothless smile, slapped himself on the chest gently and said, "Burhaan." He pointed at Jonah and Klea.

With a glance at Klea, Jonah patted his own chest and said, "Jonah."

Klea repeated the process and then pointed at the boys. Burhaan beamed as he introduced his sons, Qaasin and Madar, and then he took Jonah by the hand and led the two Americans into the wheelhouse. It was then that Jonah noticed the man had only one arm—the other, which Jonah initially thought was hidden behind the man's back, was missing from the shoulder joint, without so much as a stump to indicate where it should have been. Still, with deft movements, he opened a clean wooden box to reveal a slab of thick, doughy *lahoh* bread covered in lamb and onions and swimming in a dark red sauce that smelled of basil and sweet tomatoes. Jonah's mouth started watering, and he couldn't tear his eyes away. Burhaan spoke to Klea, pointing at the food.

"He's asking us to eat," she said.

Jonah didn't need to be told twice. He and Klea dug in with their bare hands polishing off half the contents, but making sure to leave enough for their rescuers.

Soon the food settled and Klea nodded off, her body fatigued with the effort of digesting an unexpected meal. Jonah lifted her into a hammock in the wheel house just as she was about to fall out of her chair, and then joined Burhaan and sons on the rear deck.

The fishermen cast their nets overboard with a skillful twist. Jonah watched as the nets spun open and sank into the light blue waters. With another twist, the fishermen drew the nets back, empty more often than not, but occasionally with a host of wriggling, flopping fish. There was a casualness to the affair, a simplicity. The brothers each pointed out their larger catches and laughed when the other brought up an embarrassingly small catch or drifting plastic from a far-away land.

Qaasin, the older of the two boys, saw Jonah watching and gestured for him to take his net. His father scolded at first, but then allowed to attempt to duplicate the elegant twisting, flinging motion. With his first try, Jonah managed to dump most of the net directly overboard. When he drew it back, it was a hopeless, tangled mess without so much as an errant piece of seaweed trapped within. Jonah aped helplessness and sent the boys into peals of laughter.

The next two casts were minor improvements, until the fourth, when Jonah mastered the exact twist of the wrist and the angle of the cast. The net flew out beautifully and dropped into the water. He retrieved it with the reverse motion. A single panicked fish flopped within. Jonah removed it and tossed it in the bed of the boat, the fish landing on a small but growing pile. His rescuers nodded in approval.

The manual labor allowed the stress of the past few days to slough off Jonah's shoulders. He practiced the precise motion of casting the net, enjoying the reward of a successful retrieval. In what felt like minutes, Jonah noticed the sun was now low in the sky. The father retreated to the wheelhouse, steering the fishing vessel towards the distant Somaliland shoreline, drawn in by a restless sea breeze. They were going home. The fact that it was not Jonah's home didn't seem to matter.

Sitting in a hammered-copper tub with his bare knees nearly touching his chin, Jonah let Qaasin and Madar gleefully pour an entire bucket of fire-warmed water over his body. He ascertained he was in the men's side of the fisherman's family compound. The home itself was some Soviet bureaucrat's vague notion of a coastal dwelling. What was left of the mummified structure with its crumbling façade, broken windows, and peeling paint stood surrounded by traditional-style huts and a timber wall ringing the perimeter.

The two boys scrubbed at his scalp and face with fierce thoroughness. Their small hands were better than the high-pressure shower nozzles on the *Fool's Errand*. His thoughts briefly drifted to Klea, to the gaggle of smiling young women that had taken her by the hand and lead her away. To the sly smile she shot at him as she disappeared. To her dark brown eyes and smooth pale skin. To her mouth on his, hot with desperation, with the need to feel alive.

Behind Jonah, Burhaan prepared a pan of mysterious, sweet-smelling oil. Orange hair blazing in the cool courtyard, he poured a small amount into his palm from a repurposed bottle of engine coolant. He rubbed his lone hand against his own bare chest, warming the oil. Suddenly, his hand was on Jonah's neck, shoulders, and back, nimbly finding each tight muscle, each bundled cluster of nerves.

Jonah slumped in the tub, eyes closed, air leaving his

lungs in a long, relaxed sigh. Finished, Burhaan motioned for Jonah to stand up. He shooed his two sons away, and they ran off, laughing and pushing each other.

"Okay," said Jonah, shrugging. He stood up, dirty water flowing off his naked body and into the copper tub.

Burhaan held two small white ceramic bowls in his hand, each with a hinged ceramic cap. He flipped opened the first, revealing a foul-smelling yellow liquid. Before the American could react, the father dabbed two fingers in the bowl, quickly covering Jonah's slashed shoulder and stitched abdomen with a thick layer of yellow animal fat.

Setting the first aside, Burhaan then did the same with the second, this time with a thinner, lighter shade of the same yellow. He treated Jonah's developing salt sores, to the American's profound relief.

I never want to see that wetsuit again, thought Jonah. Not after those three days of suffering in it. He hoped he wasn't expected to squeeze himself back into it once his wonderful bath was over.

Burhaan placed the ceramic bowls back in their hiding place in a small nook built into the side of the nearest hut, and returned to Jonah's side with a tin can full of a deep brown powder, offering it to Jonah.

"What is this?" asked Jonah, taking the offering. He pointed at his mouth. "Is this food?"

Burhaan shook his head and gestured to his own orange hair. It wasn't food; it was henna hair dye, the same he'd used for himself. Jonah briefly considered taking him up on the offer. It'd certainly get a rise out of Klea, might be worth it for that reason alone, but Jonah politely declined.

The two boys returned, carrying with them a kilt-like man's dress. Jonah stepped out of the tub into a pair of waiting sandals, and allowed the boys to secure the dress around his waist. It was made of clean, soft cotton and dyed with a beautiful red pattern.

The kilt was joined by an open-necked cotton shirt with short sleeves and an intricate abstract sun pattern embroidered on the chest. Burhaan, Qaasin, and Madar wore their versions loose, but the shirt stretched tight across Jonah's chest, shoulders, and biceps.

A bell rang in the courtyard, and Burhaan ushered Jonah and the two boys inside the main building. The main room had been stripped of walls and converted into a large family gathering area, bedrolls piled in the corner and a low wooden table surrounded by sitting mats. Jonah sat on the father's left, and the two boys on his right. Three women walked in carrying hot dishes of bony silver fish, yellow rice and minced goat, each with unique and distinctly aromatic chutney, tamarind, and green pepper sauces. The women wore a Somali version of traditional Islamic dress, ornate robes and skirts with sashes and embroidered cloth.

He's a polygamist, thought Jonah; flashing the father a knowing smile as the women busied themselves with preparing the meal. Not just a polygamist, but probably a village elder as well, maybe even the leader of a small clan.

The beaded entranceway between the women's side of the compound and the main building parted, and Klea entered with a Somali woman on each arm. She'd been scrubbed clean and clothed in an immaculate wrap-around dress cinched at the waist with an embroidered belt, and her hair shone as it peeked from underneath an ornate purple hijab, complementing her fair skin and dark eyes. She flashed Jonah a little smile and proudly showed him her hands as if showing off a new manicure. The women had been busy—both of Klea's hands were adorned with an elaborate henna pattern, crossing her palms and the back of her hands before disappearing up her forearms and toward parts unknown.

Klea sat directly opposite Jonah, maddeningly out of reach. He wanted to be close to her again, even if that closeness meant only the soft brush of his fingertips against hers.

"You're very beautiful," he said.

"I think this is a wedding dress," said Klea, blushing as she acknowledged the complement. "It's all they had in my size."

Jonah laughed. "As you can see, I'm tough to fit in this part of the world."

"I'm liking your skirt," teased Klea right before Burhaan motioned for all in attendance to begin. Klea and Jonah obliged, and after a few minutes of uninterrupted eating, Jonah looked at Klea until she caught his gaze.

"I need you to translate," he said.

"M'kay," she answered, her mouth still full.

Jonah reached for the waterproof pack he'd taken from the raft and slowly withdrew his polymer pistol. He'd already disposed of the bullets, casting them into the ocean from the deck of the fishing vessel. Everyone in the room stopped to stare. Jonah carefully showed everyone the slide was back, the chamber empty. He laid the pistol flat in the palms of his hands and, with head slightly bowed, presented it to Burhaan.

"Tell him this is a gift," said Jonah. Klea gulped loudly and translated.

Burhaan accepted the pistol, nodding wisely, testing the weight in his hand. He said something and handed it to Qaasin. The boy ran the weapon into another room and returned unarmed. Burhaan spoke in rapid-fire dialect to Klea.

"He says he could not possibly accept such a fine gift," she translated. "It's a tribal platitude. He completely intends to keep it."

"Tell him the gift is barely worth a mention in comparison to his kindness and hospitality."

"I don't know the word for *hospitality*," mused Klea, before choppily translating the message.

Burhaan smiled and clapped Jonah across the back like an old friend, then said something to Klea. She answered him without translating for Jonah.

"Yeah, he definitely liked it," she said to Jonah. "Rifles in this area represent power, but pistols convey status. He asked the construction, I told him it was German. I think he was happy with that fact—said Germans make the best firearms."

Everyone began talking at once and soon the plates were empty and the wives cleared the low table with the same order and efficiency with which they'd served the meal. The father gestured for Jonah and Klea to get up and join him as he exited the main building and the compound.

Jonah's kilt hung just above his sandals, but Klea's dress brushed against the sandy ground, forcing her to hold the hem up to the amusement of the other villagers gathered along the beach. Though the sun had set, the moon was nearly full, and several gas lanterns and other fires kept the small village illuminated with a low flickering light.

Jonah acknowledged the villagers as they passed, some of them reaching out to touch the tanned skin of his hands, others pulling at his short, blonde facial hair.

Despite the earnest warmth of the assembled villagers, Jonah felt something was wrong. A small cough here, a rattling exhalation there, a woman unsteady on her feet, a strange smell of sickness. Jonah realized his elaborate meal may have been more than many of the villagers had seen in some time.

"Come on," said Klea, pulling at Jonah's hand.

"What is it?" asked Jonah.

"He wants to show us something."

Breaking away from the group of villagers, Burhaan stepped onto the beach, his bare feet sinking into the soft, immaculate white sand. He said something to Klea, but she shrugged, not understanding. He repeated himself, a little frustrated, pointing at his arm. Jonah caught a word—Bettencourt.

"He says Bettencorps is responsible for his missing arm," said Klea, looking up at Jonah. "This is a great dishonor to him—forced to eat and wipe ... well, you know. There is no dignity in this."

"How?" asked Jonah, examining the stump. It looked like a clean amputation competently stitched closed. Maybe not surgical, but certainly performed by an able hand and a sharp implement. Burhaan spoke quickly, forcing Klea to interrupt to translate.

"He was fishing," said Klea. "And he found a round metal object. He thought it might be worth something, so he looked at it closely. It was leaking a yellow liquid, which ran down his arm when he held it up to the light. It smelled terrible, like peppers—peppers? I don't know this word. But he threw it back in the ocean. His skin began to swell with terrible blisters that covered his entire arm. Very painful. Eventually a local doctor was forced to remove the arm. I think he's describing an infection."

"Probably a mustard gas grenade," said Jonah. "I've heard similar stories coming out of Italy, the Baltic Sea, even the American eastern seaboard. Fishermen find some strange artifact and they have a reaction like he described. Turns out it's an old piece of chemical munitions."

Burhaan waited for Jonah and Klea to finish talking and then went on with his story. Klea listened closely, asking him to slow down so she could follow.

"He says it got worse,"

"His arm got worse?" Jonah asked.

"No—the situation became worse, not for him, but for his village. Over the past three years, many people have become sick with strange symptoms, many have died. He says it is the fault of Bettencorp, Anconia Island. But he's not calling it Anconia Island. He's calling it ... I have no idea what he's saying. Sun-killer? The moon of death? I'm at a loss."

"Death Star?"

Kleah translated and Burhaan nodded and repeated the words in English. "Death Star."

Jonah drew in a long breath. "If anything could earn the name Death Star, Anconia Island would be it."

Burhaan continued and Klea translated. "He says they've been piling what they find over here," said Klea, pointing to the far end of the beach.

As Burhaan and Klea followed, Jonah led the way across the beach towards a distant dark pile. The villagers didn't follow. Soon it became clear that the pile was a large collection of rusting barrels and tanks, all washed up from the sea and leaking.

"Apparently this is just some of it," Klea said.

Jonah studied the pile. Collecting for years, it'd easily

take four or five semis to even attempt to remove it all. He leaned as close as he dared, coughing as toxic fumes poured off the pile. He recognized multiple warning labels and military designations in Italian and Cyrillic Russian. Jonah guessed it was a collection long-obsolete munitions. Hell, a couple of the larger barrels looked like Cold War-era submarine depth charges.

"They've got to get rid of this stuff," said Jonah, more to himself than anyone else. If even one of the explosives nestled in the pile cooked off—

"How?" asked Klea.

"I have no goddamn idea. Can't burn it. Can't bury it. Hell, stick it on a raft and mail it back to sender. Makes sense that the rest of the world would send their shit out here. Nobody's going to be looking for it, not in this godforsaken corner of the ocean."

"Everybody in the village seems affected," said Klea. "When I was being dressed, I noticed most of the women had sores and burns. I didn't know what to make of them at first."

"Ask him about the children," said Jonah, his voice catching on a lump in his throat. Klea nodded, and passed the message along. Burhaan responded animatedly as they backed away from the toxic pile.

"He says Qaasin and Madar are not growing as they should and that he's worried for them. He's already lost a son and two daughters to disease. And the same ailments have struck many of the village children. Many stillborn babies, too many to be by chance. He says he feels sometimes that his village is cursed by Allah."

"It's no curse," Jonah said through gritted teeth. "This was done intentionally."

Klea didn't catch up to Jonah until he was already nearly two full miles down the beach, walking alone in the moonlight. He hadn't said much since seeing the pile, disappearing soon afterwards. Old habits die hard—and for him, solitude was a familiar respite.

"Don't leave me like that," said Klea, half-running, half-walking to match his pace.

Jonah nodded, slowed his step and came to a stop. He sat down on the sand, looking towards the moonlit waves. Klea sat down next to him and slipped her hand around the back of his arm.

"Burhaan says we can hitch a ride on a truck," said Klea. "His brother-in-law is on his way down to Mozambique with a load of sheep and he always stops by the village for a meal. They're expecting him soon, maybe even tomorrow. There's a US consulate there. We may have to hide in the back through some of the militia checkpoints, but that will be a cakewalk compared to what we've already done."

"It's a good plan," said Jonah.

"We could go home."

"Home for you," he said. "Not for me."

"You're an American," said Klea. "Why can't you go back? What did you do?"

"Not me. I didn't do anything. It was my father."

"What could your father have possibly done?"

"It's a long story."

"It's a long night."

Jonah squinted at Klea. She wasn't going to give up, they both knew it. He begrudgingly set aside his resistance and started to speak about things he'd long held inside.

"Growing up, it was just my father and I," he said. "On paper, he was a mid-level functionary that specialized in security requisitions for American consulates and embassies in hot spots, areas with sudden political or social upheaval."

"But off paper ... he was what? CIA?"

"Yeah, CIA. By the time I was in the picture, his boots-on-the-ground days were long over. He was a section chief, ran all intelligence and covert operations in whatever region they'd placed him, usually to clean up someone else's mess."

"And your mother?'

"No memories of her. I've spent a lot of time thinking about it, and I'm fairly certain she was one of his intelligence assets. I think she was killed not long after I was born. My father rarely spoke of her.

"I was left with my grandparents when I was very young, but that couldn't last forever. Pops eventually took me with him. I spent a few months at a time in DC getting dropped into upper-crust private schools. We didn't have the money—government salary, after all—but my father certainly had the right connections. Then we'd spend the rest of our time at whatever embassy he'd been assigned. If the CIA needed him there, it usually meant that most of the other kids had already left for home due to safety concerns. I got pretty good at sneaking out and hanging with local kids, when that was too dangerous, I'd hang with the marine guards."

"Seriously?"

"Sure. Once they got over the fear of my hard-ass dad coming down on them for letting me follow them around, they were usually pretty cool. Treated me like a mascot. Dressed me up in oversize battle-rattle, took me down to the weapons range, let me pop off some rounds. They'd have me play hostage sometimes, and when I got older I got to be the 'hostile'."

"You liked being the bad guy," Klea said with a smile.

"Loved it," said Jonah. "Speaking of which, have to tell you this one story. So we get a new squad into the embassy, right? They think they're tough shit. Commander says he's putting them through the 'kill house'—the standard urban combat room-clearing exercise on base. They're talking among themselves; they say they're going to set a new course record.

"Commander laughs, says they're going to be up against one guy. And then he trots me out. I'm fourteen at the time. All the Marines can do is stare; they think it's some kind of a joke or something. Eight tough-as-shit Marines against a fourteen-year-old Foreign Service brat.

"Suspecting a set-up, they take no chances. I find a hiding spot in the kill house and they come in *hard*. They figure the commander is lying to them and they're going to face off against a whole squad. After all, Marines have turned fucking with each other into an honored art form."

"But it was just you."

"Just me. And I'm hiding in the ceiling, wearing my fake haji clothes. They clear the place, then they're all just standing around, baffled. Wondering what they're doing, why they're all just standing around with nobody to shoot at. Some of them start saying they got the time wrong, they're not supposed to be there for another hour or two. One of the Marines separates from the others; I drop out of the ceiling and pop a paintball into his facemask."

"Was he pissed?"

"Hell no. He got it instantly. You ever play sardines as a kid? It's the type of hide-and-go-seek with a bunch of people. They all break apart, whenever someone finds the hiding person they have to squeeze in with them. So sure, I pop him in the face, but now he's on my side. He can barely keep from laughing out loud as I steal his helmet, vest, and rifle, put it on myself. Now I'm looking like a mini-marine."

Klea laughed, trying to picture the ridiculous scene.

"So I stalk from room to room, shooting these guys one at a time. None of them know what's going on, they just know that they started with eight, now there are five, then three, the bodies are stacking up. And once these guys are down, they say nothing. They're in on it too. Comes down to the last guy—the squad leader. I walk right up to him and stick a rubber shock-knife up against his nutsack. Never saw it coming. They called him electro-nuts for the next six months."

"And your father didn't care that you were running around, electrocuting Marines?"

"At the time, I thought he didn't know. Eventually, I realized he knew everything. Hanging with Marines, dating local girls, all the other shit I got up to."

"He didn't care?"

"I think ... I think he just knew me well enough to let me explore the world. Growing up in embassies was tough, especially when your dad was up to his eyeballs in secret-agent shit. He knew I needed to find my own way."

"He sounds like a hero," said Klea. "Not a traitor."

"Maybe both. Maybe neither. All I know is that one day he just disappeared. Happened just before my eighteenth birthday. Everybody was freaking out, thinking he was captured or killed. I wasn't too worried at first. But then, well, it was different this time. I actually got delivered back to the states under armed guard, supposedly for my protection. I started college not long after, studied marine engineering. About a year and a half after his disappearance, the story went wide. Apparently a lot of classified files went missing at about the same time he did. I didn't know what to do, but it wasn't looking good for dear old Dad, so I got out of the country. I think leaving pretty much confirmed what everybody already thought of me."

"That he was a traitor, and you were in it as well."

"Yeah, as if I knew what my father was up to and missed the chance to jump ship with him. I tried college overseas at first but the fact I was no longer in the US meant the gloves could come off as far as the intelligence services were concerned. I'd catch cars following me and the stuff in my apartment wasn't always where I'd left it. They hacked my computer. Eventually, a couple of my remaining backchannel connections got in touch and warned me that my name was being floated as a potential grab target. So I left again, hooked myself up with a pretty decent set of fake papers, and went underground.

"I'd always been interested in diving, so I completed my saturation certification in Norway. Really took to it. Spent the next few years bouncing from one salvage or energy sector dive job to the next. Some of it was legal, the better-paying jobs weren't. So that was that, until I ended up in prison for an illegal salvage mission off Morocco."

Klea nodded and sighed. "You think we'll see Fatima and Hassan again?"

"The good doctor got what he wanted. Maybe not the way he wanted it, but I don't think they're looking for us." He stretched out his legs, tipped his head back and looked up at the star-spangled sky. "I think getting to Mozambique's a good start. Maybe I can jump a cargo ship towards the South Pacific. Seems like one of the few places a wanted American can still make a go of it."

"I don't have a life to go back to either," Klea said. "Not sure I'd want to go back to MIT after Colin … and things were very bad with my parents when I left."

"Make up with them. Let bygones be bygones."

Jonah leaned back and laid on the sand, his hands behind his head.

"So that'll be it? I go my way, you go yours?" She turned to look at him.

"Was there ever another plan?" He met her eyes, dark, moonlit. "I've got nothing, Klea. If not for Dr. Nassiri, I would have eventually died in prison. Maybe I'll find somewhere to land, maybe I won't—but I know for certain I'll be running for the rest of my life."

She laid back next to him and looked up. The constellations, familiar friends all those endless nights of captivity, seemed cold and soulless.

"You, on the other hand, will be a returning hero," Jonah whispered, his voice soft, rough. "A survivor."

"I don't feel like a hero. Just a survivor."

"What will you do?"

"I guess finish grad school. Get a job. Get on with life."

"Write a book and do all the morning shows," he said. "Just don't make me look like some reckless asshole."

"I do have an obligation to the truth to consider," she laughed and rolled onto her side. "What about you? You have to have thought about it. Dreamed about what would happen if you ever escaped."

"I'll get on with life, too. In my own way, at least. Maybe I'll be a salvage diver or SCUBA instructor in Thailand, Vietnam. Somewhere beautiful and very, very far away from here."

"Is there a woman in this vision for the future?"

"There are lots of women in this vision," joked Jonah. "But none like you."

"There could be," she said as she laid back and deftly unraveled a single central knot in her robes. Her headscarf slipped back, revealing her short, dark hair, shimmering in the moonlight. She slipped off her embroidered belt and opened her dress, revealing her full naked form, her freshly-scrubbed skin nearly glowing.

Jonah raised himself to his elbow and drank in the sight, marveling at the way her fresh henna tattoos danced their way up her arms, down her clavicles, collecting like a teardrop in her solar plexus, emphasizing the curves of her small breasts. He crept onto her laid-out robes, pausing for one last look before he kissed her. And for the first time, he felt she was actually making love to him, not to the ghost of her lost fiancé, not some long-ago memory fading on a burning funeral pyre, and not some desperate stranger in a life raft, but to him, Jonah Blackwell, and him alone.

Jonah and Klea walked slowly back to the compound, fingers intertwined, every step soft and measured, as if together they could float across the surface of the moonlit sand without leaving so much as a footprint. Jonah gave Klea one last deep, silent kiss and opened the front gate to the sleeping compound, the wooden panel gently sliding opening as chickens and goats stirred from their slumber.

Multiple lights flashed, blinding him. He held a hand up to his face to shield himself when a rifle butt caught him in the side of the head at the same time the back of his legs were kicked out from underneath him, forcing him to his knees. With harsh, white light still overwhelming his vision, he felt a dozen rough hands feeling over his arms, his legs, inside his kilt, searching for hidden weapons. Several voices barked out orders in English. Finding nothing, the unseen men threw him forward. Jonah landed face-first on the concrete slab, his arms held behind him as a rope wound around and between his wrists. Eyes adjusting, he caught a glimpse of the orange-haired father, his two boys held back by his single arm, wives holding up their hands in surrender as several mercenaries held them at gunpoint.

A hulking, mammoth man leaned over him, muscles slithering underneath a too-tight synthetic shirt, twisted face squinting as his eyes darted over Jonah's prone form. The colonel, the man who'd stumbled drunk onto the *Fool's Errand* a lifetime ago. The mercenary stank like sour sweat.

"I should have gunned you down in the bar of your stolen boat," drawled Colonel Westmoreland. "I saw you itching to pull on me—should have given you the bullet you deserved right then and there."

Jonah raised his head and opened his mouth to issue a smarmy response, but the wind left his lungs as the massive soldier kicked him in the back of the head, slamming him back into the concrete. Klea screamed from beside him, her wail piercing the stillness of the night.

The colonel lifted Jonah a second time, pulling him to his feet as his knees buckled beneath him. Jonah tried to make sense of his blurry vision, the bitter, metallic taste in his mouth, his pulse ringing in his ears like a gong. He caught a single glimpse of Klea's dark eyes staring at him in horror and for he realized that for one infinitesimally small moment he was Colin, staring back at her as he was torn away, bottomless loss welling up in her eyes.

"You just made one of these skinny-ass sand niggers a rich man," bellowed the colonel. "They couldn't fucking *wait* to drop a dime on your ass."

The colonel pulled back a single fist, ramming it like a piston into Jonah's left kidney. Jonah collapsed, blacking out just long enough to wake up to the sound of his own gasping breath. Mercenaries grabbed fistfuls of his borrowed clothing, dragging him bodily out of the compound—and into a hail of stones and chanting.

The village had awoken. Men and women—from young, tall sons to hunched grandmothers—surrounded the mercenaries, massing and indistinct in their flashing lights. Eyes and teeth glinted white in the glare, fists waved in the air with righteous fury. A cascade of unintelligible shouting and chanting was accompanied by an irregular rain of arcing rocks, pummeling the men from all directions.

Panicking, one of the mercenaries jerked his rifle to his shoulder, eye already at the custom scope as he yanked back the plunger back to chamber a live round.

"Did I say you were cleared to engage?" barked the colonel, slapping the twitching man's barrel to the ground before he could loose a bullet. "Push your way through!"

The mercenaries shoved back at the building crowd, Jonah wriggled free of the colonel's grip for just long enough to shove Klea free of her captor. She spun, her light frame launched sideways. In an instant, she tripped on the hem of her beautiful dress, stumbled and fell, disappearing into the mass of villagers.

Swearing, three mercenaries rushed into the spot where she'd fallen, beating the crowd back with kicks and rifle butts. But she was gone, vanished into the mob as if she'd never been anything more than a figment of Jonah's imagination.

"Leave her!" shouted the colonel as the churning body of villagers pushed against the mercenaries, threatening to envelope them as well. Furious, the three soldiers retreated to the colonel's side.

Having taken a prize from the mercenaries, the crowd grew ugly, daring, bravely advancing on the them, grabbing at their leveled weapons.

"You're going to regret that," whispered the colonel to Jonah, his lips pulled back to reveal gold-capped molars and a cruel sneer.

Jonah met the sneer with a smirk, watching as the colonel drew his pistol, cocked it, and aimed it at Jonah's head, oblivious to the crowd. Reconsidering, he thumbed the safety back on, drew his hand back and slammed the butt of the gun into the side of Jonah's face once, twice, three times, each with a sickening sound of metal on bone.

Jonah lapsed into forced unconsciousness with a sick feeling of total satisfaction seeping into his very soul.

You go your way, he thought, holding Klea's dimming image in his mind. *I'll go mine.*

CHAPTER 17

The convoy wound its way through the scrublands of Somalia, a mismatched collection of rusting Land Cruisers following the faint ruts of a long-forgotten trail. Perhaps a hundred thousand years ago the area was lush jungle and fertile savannah wetlands. Now it was little more than motley drab brown underbrush with the odd patchy tree defending any ground where moisture briefly accumulated. A handful of tiny white clouds spread across the radiant blue sky, too slight to even cast a shadow as they passed across the rippling sun.

Jonah bounced in the open bed of a Regan-era Toyota truck. He'd been tied to a machine-gun emplacement in the tailgate, hands bound behind his back. The SUV behind him was missing its front windshield. Jonah could see the squinting mercenary within. He had a single new bandage wrapped around his head and over one eye to add to a collection of scarred-over facial wounds.

The one-eyed driver caught Jonah making eye contact and scowled back, drawing a callused finger across his throat.

Jonah briefly wondered what motherless shitbird had

sold him and Klea out. He doubted it was the orange-haired village elder, his rescuer. Then again, Jonah doubted much happened among the clan of fishermen that wasn't under the man's direct instruction and supervision.

Still, Jonah preferred to think of his rescuer as a friend. Besides, a bullet was still a step up from a slow death by dehydration.

In the distance, Jonah caught sight of a single spec hanging in the clear blue sky. He recognized it as a Bettencorps corporate helicopter from Anconia Island, approaching from the sea. The shiny white craft hung low, rotors slicing through the oppressively hot morning air as it passed the convoy with a roar of engines and airfoil blades. Ahead now, the helicopter flared and landed behind a hill in a cloud of blinding dust and sand.

The convoy crossed the crest of the hill, winding down to a landing zone inside a dry lake bed. Wind and dust drifted by in clouds, propelled by the still-oscillating helicopter blades. Four bodyguards spilled from the helicopters and set up a perimeter. The heavily armed men ushered the convoy into the lake bed, waving in one vehicle at a time.

The one-eyed mercenary got out of his truck to cut Jonah's hands free. Jonah tried to stretch his arms, but the mercenary yanked him off the back of the truck and shoved him up against the side. A second, baby-faced soldier searched him again for hidden weapons while the other kept watch. The men zip tied Jonah's hands behind his back again and forced him to kneel in front of a small motor pool. The collected vehicles appeared for the most part to be of the same drab, rusting collection, but one truck stuck out in particular. Jonah recognized it as a high-performance Ford Raptor, a pickup with bulked-up wheels and suspension, massive engine, designed for the rigors of desert racing.

The zip-ties hurt; they dug into his wrists as the two mercenaries lifted him to his feet and led him to a canvas tent on the far side of the lake bed. They walked him past the center of the group, past fuel tanks, ammunition, medical supplies and finally three late-model Toyota Land Cruisers. This was no ordinary mobilization; this was a staging area for a large contingent of private soldiers. Somebody in the region—be it a pirate compound or terrorist cell—was about to have a very bad day.

One-Eye and Babyface pushed Jonah into the tent, and back onto his knees. The colonel stood behind a folding standing desk, typing on a ruggedized laptop. He was dressed in the same stinking blood-flecked armor he wore in the village the previous night. The colonel grabbed Jonah by his shirt, towering over him. The man wound his fist back, almost to his right ear, closing his eyes with a look of intense, nearly sexual pleasure on his face.

At least we got straight to the point, thought Jonah.

Behind Jonah, the main entrance to the tent rustled with the sound of two men entering.

"Really, Colonel Westmoreland?" came a droll, almost bored voice as a handsome, tall, and very tanned man stepped behind the colonel and clapped a single, friendly hand on the armored back of the still-scowling mercenary.

It took Jonah a moment to recognize Charles Bettencourt. The CEO wore an obnoxious desert-chic outfit, white Egyptian-cotton dress shirt open two buttons down, and a pair of khaki dungarees with tan leather boots. It was as if everything he knew about the desert came from a glossy fashion editorial.

"Nice shirt," said Jonah. "Louis Vuitton?"

"Hugo Boss," said Bettencourt dismissively. "Nobody wears Vuitton anymore."

"Hate to break it to you," said Jonah. "But the real high-fashion out here is an oversize T-shirt from last years' losing Superbowl team."

Bettencourt chuckled, if for no other reason to assure Jonah that the insult landed without effect. The front tent flap rustled and another figure stepped out from behind Jonah, a smaller, glasses-wearing man in an expensive suit wholly inappropriate for the setting. The man—an accountant or a lawyer, maybe?—moved with the sort of nervous energy of someone clearly uncomfortable with military operations and prisoners. He walked around Jonah with a smartphone in hand, taking pictures of Jonah's face from every angle.

"Somebody didn't get the memo about the dress code," said Jonah, nodding towards the lawyer's expensive suit.

"He was born wearing it," said the colonel, smirking.

"It's definitely Jonah Blackwell," said the lawyer, ignoring the jibes at his expense. "Computer says 94.7% match."

Jonah found himself wondering about the five-point-three percent discrepancy. He supposed there were any number of violent face-mashings that could have accounted for the mismatch.

"Jonah … Blackwell …" Bettencourt said, considering him. At first, Jonah registered a little surprise that the CEO knew his name. He supposed it would have been easy enough to pull his face from the security cameras around the Anconia docks and run it through any number of facial identification algorithms.

"Now what?" asked Jonah.

"Now what? Good place to start, because that would largely be up to you," said Bettencourt, cocking his head. "Jonah—buddy—I don't even know where to begin. The Somali rumor mill is spinning off its axis. Word is that the local pirates think you're some kind of Navy Seal or some shit. I am genuinely fucking impressed. You come here on some half-assed salvage mission on a hijacked yacht. The next thing I know, my submarine is missing and the *entire goddamn crew* presumed dead. Fucking incredible. Just to keep matters interesting, you and your friends don't just leave like anybody in their right mind would, you turn around and hit my closest allies in the region. From all accounts, you seriously fucked their shit up. Half of the locals have got it in their heads that you're the guy that killed bin Laden, like you're some kind of a one-man Rambo wrecking ball. They want your oversized nutsack on the end of a rusty machete, my friend."

"We're more of a wrecking *crew*," explained Jonah with sarcastic earnestness.

"That you are indeed. So what's next? You're going to break your zip ties, knock out the guards, grab a couple of machine guns and take on my whole army?"

"Sure, but I'd settle for some granola bars and a thirty-minute head start," suggested Jonah with a smirk. "At least it'd be sporting."

"Bear with me," said Bettencourt, ignoring Jonah's sarcasm. "I'm making a larger point here. You know what made me such a good hedge fund manager back when I actually thought that was a challenge?"

"Cocaine and a lack of accountability?" asked Jonah, determined to needle the executive.

"No ... emotional ... attachment." Bettencourt sounded out each word as if it were the gospel itself. Behind him, the lawyer nodded in sycophantic agreement as his boss resumed his ridiculous, self-serving speech.

"If you're bleeding money," continued Bettencourt. "You stop the bleeding. And you, my friend, are bleeding the *fuck* out of me. So here's the deal. I want my goddamn submarine back. She was extraordinarily difficult to obtain. The general I bought it from was recently shot for treason, so I'm not likely to get another. How you and your crew of amateurs even know how to operate it is beyond me. Seriously, what do you even plan on doing with it once this is all over?"

"Good question," mused Jonah. "Maybe offer deep sea tours of Anconia Island's submerged ruins?"

"Don't be passé," said Bettencourt, an air of disappointment in his voice. "Revenge is an outdated concept. Former adversaries are often well-suited collaborators. I want you to think about how much chaos you've caused over the last couple weeks, and with zero support. What did you have at your disposal, some Middle Eastern doctor and his simpleton cousin? A Texas farm girl? Am I missing anybody?"

Bettencourt sighed and broke eye contact with Jonah for a moment while the captive remained silent.

"You're a startup, Jonah Blackwell," continued the CEO. "A startup with incredible potential. But you're green and you've got no backing. Without a grounded partner, guys like you spin right out of orbit and never make anything of themselves. You know what we could do with you if I gave you a couple of hard-ass blood-and-guts mercs and some walking-around money? Jesus Christ, it'd be fucking beautiful. You could go on happily fucking shit up—and get paid to boot. Why are we even at odds? For Christ's sake, I don't even know what I did to offend you."

You tried to kill me, thought Jonah. And goddamn near succeeded.

"He wants to eat a bullet," interjected Westmoreland. "Look at him—he doesn't want your fucking money."

Ignoring his subordinate, Bettencourt continued his pitch. "Hell," said the CEO, "I could use your help now. Believe me, this whole production isn't for your benefit. You've been a short-term problem, sure, but I've got a long-term problem that is in serious, overdue need of some attention. You ever hear of the pirate Dalmar Abdi?"

Jonah shook his head.

"That's probably a good thing. He's a pain in my ass."

"And he's fucking dead," added the colonel. "If he thinks he can park his operations outside of our tactical range, he is sorely fucking mistaken."

"So what do you say?" said Bettencourt. "How about we bring this messiness to a close, gunslinger?"

"What about Klea?" blurted out Jonah. He kicked himself for the obvious question. Shit, if they weren't looking for her before, they sure as hell would be now.

Bettencourt frowned, looking from Jonah to Westmoreland and then back to Jonah. He suddenly broke out in a massive smile.

"Oh shit," said Bettencourt, laughing out loud. "You mean that MIT girl, the pirate hostage? This is too perfect! I should have seen it coming. You've been fucking each other. That is … that is just too good. I guess you had that whole white knight, damsel in distress thing going on. So what about her? First things first, let's get her home to her parents. They've been begging me to find her for years."

Jonah forced himself to impassively stare forward, refusing to flinch. "I can be persuaded to let bygones be bygones," he lied. "And there's no need for Klea or her family to know anything. Given the circumstances, she just might hold her dead fiancé and best friends against you."

"Forgive me if I don't immediately trust your intentions," said Bettencourt with a thin smile. "So I'm going to need an act of good faith. I'm done dicking around—I want the *Scorpion* back. And you're going to help me get it."

"How?" asked Jonah.

"Let's get you in touch with your ... what did you call them? That's right, your wrecking crew," said Bettencourt. The CEO motioned for his lawyer to approach. The lawyer set a small bag on the folding desk and drew out a complex hand-held radio. It looked like one of the old-school brick cell phones, but with a long, looping antenna.

"Satellite phone," explained the lawyer. "We've already got the *Scorpion* dialed in. If the submarine is within three thousand miles, they'll get the transmission."

"So we're doing this?" asked Bettencourt, slapping a hand on Jonah's shoulder.

"You see another way out of this for me?" asked Jonah. "Not the toughest decision I've made recently."

"I imagine not," admitted Bettencourt. "Let's get this call done; we'll work out the details later. Medical, dental, 401k, all that jazz."

"Can't thumb the company employee manual with my fuckin' hands tied," joked Jonah, nudging his zip-tied wrists toward Westmoreland. "You mind?"

"Not happening," said the colonel, crossing his arms.

"We have a deficit of trust to overcome," said

Bettencourt. "But Jonah—believe me when I say this phone call is the first step towards a beautiful friendship."

"Just bring the phone over here," said Jonah.

The lawyer stepped forward, pressing a green button on the interface as he held the phone to the captive's face. It clicked and the line went live. Jonah listened but didn't hear any sound from the other end. Bettencourt motioned for him to start talking.

"This is Jonah Blackwell," he said. "Is anyone there?"

The silence on the other end of the phone turned into a shuffling sound, then was replaced by a voice on the other end.

"Jonah!" exclaimed Dr. Nassiri, his aristocratic accent unmistakable despite the crackling interference. "We've been looking for you everywhere! Are you safe?"

Shit, thought Jonah. The *Scorpion* should have been long gone. He hadn't expected the doctor to stick around, not after he got what he came for. A dead line or a fleeing submarine would have left him with some time to bluff— the doctor's newfound loyalty had manifested itself at a highly inconvenient time.

"You're looking for me?" said Jonah, incredulous. "You're still in the area?"

"Of course we're still in the area—" began Dr. Nassiri.

Jonah cut him off before he could continue.

"Are you *kidding me?*" shouted Jonah. "Get the fuck out, fucking now, *run!*"

Too slow, the lawyer yanked the phone away from Jonah, but the damage was already done. The line went dead.

"Now that was really annoying," shouted Bettencourt, pinching the bridge over the top of his nose.

"I almost respect him," Westmoreland said with a laugh as he unfolded his arms. "His friends wouldn't have lived through the recapture of our asset."

"They still won't," mused Bettencourt. "This is more of a shame than a setback; it really is. We've recently received some supplies from some … associates. Anti-submarine warfare detection equipment and munitions, to be exact. Sonar, depth charges, acoustic torpedoes, fun stuff. We'll get her back or put her on the bottom trying. Colonel Westmoreland—we're done here."

With that, Charles sat at the folding desk and flipped up the laptop screen, blocking his view of his prisoner. Jonah no longer mattered to him, any utility he might have had now expended.

Colonel Westmoreland grinned as he reached for Jonah with his two beefsteak hands. He motioned for One-Eye and Babyface to assist him.

"Take this fucking nuisance behind a sand berm," Westmoreland ordered. "If you put less than a magazine into him each, don't bother coming back. The fucking hyenas that find his body will be picking lead out of their teeth for days."

The two men nodded. One-Eye grabbed Jonah, dragging him out of the tent and towards a long wall of sand.

They'll sing songs of my deeds for a thousand years, laughed Jonah to himself. But now there were no more jokes, no more schemes. Just him, the two mercenaries, a few steps over a sand berm, and a bullet to the skull. A shallow grave in a shit part of the world—an inevitability when one stopped to think about it. Pleading for his life would have been embarrassing, the supposed job offer reeked of bullshit. At least he could pretend Klea and Alexis and Dr. Nassiri and his mother made their way home, long as their odds still remained.

Jonah briefly wondered what Klea would think of him now. She'd probably still think he was an asshole.

"Can I at least bum a smoke?" asked Jonah as Babyface shoved him over the top of the sand berm at the edge of the dry lakebed.

Babyface responded by kicking Jonah's legs out from underneath him. Jonah crashed face-first into the sand, tumbling to the base of the berm and out of the sight of the camp.

"Stupid question," mumbled Jonah, pulling his knees up to his chin as he sat at the bottom of the hill shaking sand out of his hair and ears. "Nobody smokes anymore."

Hell, Jonah didn't even smoke, never did and never wanted to. He just didn't want the ride to end, wanted any excuse to hang on to life for a few moments longer.

"Stick of gum maybe?" asked Jonah, wincing as he rose to his feet. "I'd go for pretty much anything but Big League Chew."

Babyface sneered as he drew back the butt of his assault rifle for a vicious blow.

ZZZZZZZip.

Jonah braced for the impact, but instead watched in total surprise as the back of the man's head erupted in a puff of pink mist. Babyface toppled backwards to the sand, eyes wide and unseeing, both front teeth missing where a sniper's bullet had passed into his open mouth and through his skull.

Jonah sprang forward towards One-Eye, propelled by fear and rage and hate and adrenaline, slamming the second man to the ground with a shoulder tackle. Hands still zip-tied behind his back, he flipped around and slipped the plastic binding around One-Eye's throat. Jonah squeezed the back of the man's head against his tailbone as he fought and kicked, slapping his hands at Jonah's feet.

Eyes darting for the source of the sniper's bullet, Jonah strangled the mercenary until he felt the windpipe collapse. For good measure, he snapped One-Eye's head to the side, enjoying the sickening sound of the cervical column breaking.

There it was—the glint of a sniper's scope, a hundred and fifty yards distant under the shade of a scrubby tree on top of a small hill. The sniper had picked his spot well; it gave him total oversight of the entire military encampment.

Hands still behind his back, Jonah fished a sheathed Ka-Bar knife out of One-eye's vest and sawed through his zip-ties. They released with a snap, and Jonah closed his eyes and sighed as he rubbed his wrists, blood flowing back into his fingers. He felt comfortable, relaxed even, like he could briefly enjoy a moment of contemplation as his unknown guardian angel kept watch. The mercenaries probably wouldn't be back to check on the missing men, at least not for a while. The single shot had been well silenced, no cause for alarm.

Unembarrassed, Jonah theatrically saluted the sniper-scope glint in the distance as he slipped out of his sarong and tribal shirt. Babyface's outfit may have fit him better, but the body lay face-up in a pool of blood which had now soaked into most of the clothing. Jonah opted to strip One-eye instead, taking boots and pants and silently hoping the dead man hadn't shit himself when he'd expired. Smoothing out the legs to his new pants, Jonah snapped the clasp to the pants shut and reached for the assault rifle.

ZZZZZZip.

The weapon spun out of his hands, torn away by the snap of an unseen force as Jonah jerked back like he'd been hit with a cattle prod. Jonah stood frozen, allowing his eyes alone to drift to the cast-off rifle. A single smoking bullet hole stood out in the center of the weapon's receiver, rendering it useless.

No guns allowed, thought Jonah. That was fair enough, they'd only just met. Jonah smiled and raised his hands.

"You got me," he said to the glint in the far distance, knowing he wouldn't be heard. "Your rescue, your rules. I'm going to go ahead and find my own way from here, if that's alright with you."

Seeing no movement, Jonah slowly leaned down to snag a half-filled canteen from One-Eye's corpse and took no more than two steps away from the encampment and towards the open desert.

ZZZZZZZip. ZZZZZZZip. ZZZZZZZip.

Jonah stopped cold as three puffs of sand and dust kicked up inches in front of his feet.

"You son of a bitch!" Jonah swore, impotently kicking sand towards the distant glint. Walking into the desert apparently wasn't allowed either, and the sniper hadn't made a move to establish contact. The chances of this being a rescue were diminishing rapidly. By all appearances Mr. Sniper had something else entirely in mind. And then it hit him: Jonah was to walk back into the encampment as bait.

Not only was he being set up—probably by the same man who'd called Bettencorps forces on his location in the fishing village—he suspected that the sniper's plan probably did not require his long-term survival.

Begrudgingly, Jonah realized he admired the plan. The goal must be to draw Bettencourt or Westmoreland out into the open. The sniper was certainly good enough to eliminate both men before anyone could figure out what'd happened.

Approaching the rim of the sand berm, a shirtless Jonah raised his hands and grimaced as he stepped down the hill and into the midst of the encampment. Mercenaries rushed towards him, aiming rifles, shouting conflicting orders. Jonah ignored them and sauntered towards the command tent, just knowing the unknown sniper would put a bullet in him the moment he stopped.

Colonel Westmoreland burst from the tent, eyes wide, nostrils flaring, Bettencourt following close behind.

"What in the mother-fucking-*fuck* does it take to kill you?" demanded Westmoreland.

"Why is he back?" shouted Bettencourt, gesturing futility around for anyone to answer him. "What is he doing back here?"

"Don't ask me," responded Jonah. "Ask your friendly neighborhood sni—"

Westmoreland leapt to the side and tackled his boss to the ground before Jonah could get the entire word *sniper* out of his mouth, throwing the executive out of the way milliseconds before the *zzzzip* of a silenced bullet sliced through the empty space and buried itself into the thick dry mud of the empty lake bed.

Bullets rained down on the company as the mercenaries scattered. With two more zips, two men were down, bleeding and rolling and screaming as the sniper attack continued.

The nearest soldier grabbed Jonah by the collar. "Where is the shooter?!" he screamed, shaking Jonah and waving an ugly, squared-off pistol. The man suddenly winced, dropping to the ground with a bullet in his back.

Bettencourt's white helicopter rose from the lakebed with a roar, gaining altitude with every second.

One enterprising fighter threw open the door to the Ford Raptor and dove behind the wheel, using the bulk of the engine block as cover as he started the engine and advanced the massive truck towards the berm and the sniper's nest. Four mercenaries huddled behind the tailgate, following the truck as it clawed its way up the berm, sand spitting out in a rooster-tail from behind the oversize tires. Sniper shots rang out against the truck, and one sliced through the shin of a soldier, who tumbled from formation to writhe on the ground, screaming.

Jonah felt like the eye of a hurricane, the spindle on a record-player—calm as the chaos of the universe spun around him. And then he slipped the squat, ugly pistol from the still-twitching grasp of the paralyzed mercenary.

Jonah began walking, calm and deliberate at first, slowly picking up the pace to a sprint as he ran up the side of the sand berm towards the hunched mercenaries. The attackers broke off from the truck, spreading out and flanking the sniper's position, mercilessly pouring fire into the bushes. Jonah caught up with a straggler and fired a single shot into his knee from behind, felling him amidst the din of automatic weapons.

The sniper risked one final shot, catching the leader squarely through the eye but betraying his position in the process. The final soldier drew a bead, only interrupted when Jonah shot him three times through the back. Shocked, the driver of the truck turned to see Jonah just in time to get a pistol butt against the side of his hand and his limp body thrown out of the truck.

Jonah stuck the pistol in his waistband, put his hands

up and walked towards the sniper's nest, pushing aside bushes. Disarming himself had been a useless gesture—the sniper lay shaking under white robes, trying to stanch a neck wound with his turban and slippery, blood-soaked fingers, his Russian Dragunov sniper rifle lying inert beside him.

The white robe fell away, revealing a dark, handsome face and a glinting white smile.

"'Sup?" asked Jonah. The sniper didn't answer. It'd be a pity to let such a devious bastard bleed out on the sand. Gunshots echoed from the dry lake bed—the mercenaries were regrouping. Jonah grabbed the sniper by his bloody hand and dragged him into the truck, practically throwing the man's massive body into the passenger seat. He turned the ignition and the engine roared back to life.

I can flee across the desert, thought Jonah through red-tinted vision. But the adrenaline in his system had crested the levies that held back the tidal force of nature and Jonah became the God of War, the Lord of Chaos, an invincible force of nature, enslaved to the power of destruction.

He slammed the vehicle into gear and floored the accelerator. The Raptor responded instantly, throwing the truck forward like a cannon, all four wheels off the ground as it did a tight U-turn and launched off the sand berm. Landing in the dry lake bed, the massive shocks absorbed the violent impact. As hiding soldiers fired potshots at the truck, Jonah aimed at the tent, hoping Bettencourt might still be inside.

The lawyer stepped out of the tent, dumbfounded at the chaos. Jonah stared him down and yanked the wheel of the truck towards him, the accelerator pegged against the rubberized floor. The lawyer froze, took one awkward step to his right as the truck hit him square on, his flinching body disappearing underneath the tires with a sickening sound of bone against the metal suspension. The truck bounced, the steering wheel yanking to one side.

"No way I should still be alive," said Jonah, staring at the eye-level bullet-craters in the glass windshield. No way the truck should have been able to absorb that much fucking gunfire and keep running.

"Armored," gurgled the sniper dying in the passenger seat. "Hennessy Motors of Texas. Very satisfactory for Somalia."

"In that case …" Jonah yanked the wheel to the side, throwing the truck into a massive slide back into the heart of the lake bed, nearly up against the command tent. He threw open the door, jumped out, and ran into the tent looking for the radio transmitter. He spied it still sitting on the folding desk, grabbed it, and ran back towards the Raptor.

Jonah threw the massive truck in gear just as two mercenaries appeared, weapons drawn and trained on the vehicle. They paused just long enough for Jonah to speed off, two massive rooster tails of dirt behind him. The Raptor impacted the berm at the far side of the dry lake and jumped again, all four wheels off the ground, again landing with a massive *whump* absorbed by the beefed-up suspension. Rifle fire pounded against the truck, rattling the interior like a vicious hailstorm.

Beside him, the wounded man coughed and spit up more blood.

"Shit, man—" said Jonah, reaching over to put pressure on the man's neck. "Glad you're still breathing."

"'Tis but a scratch," said the sniper. "Only a flesh wound."

"Are you seriously quoting *Monty* fucking *Python*?"

demanded Jonah. He was far from sold on taking the sniper with him, but the Monty Python quote didn't make for a bad start. And the man had saved his life, so he owed him. For now. Besides, he didn't have any better plan. He wrapped his fingers in the tail end of the turban and redoubled the pressure on the wound.

Using his knee to steer, Jonah pulled up the satellite navigation system. Good—only about ten miles to the shoreline. The Raptor could make that in minutes and could handle the rough trail like a Baja trophy truck. He spotted a small nearby town with a big central avenue that stretched out to what looked like a long dock extending far out to sea.

One hand on the sniper's neck, Jonah thumbed the redial on the sat phone as he kept the accelerator nearly floored.

The line clicked live again, but no voice came from the other side. He checked the rearview mirrors, the Raptor's massive dust cloud obscuring any vehicles pursuing them. "This is Jonah," he shouted over the roar of the truck's engines and desert passing beneath them. "*Scorpion*, come in."

"*Scorpion* here," came Dr. Nassiri's voice.

"Change of plans. I need a rendezvous."

"Where?" To the point—Jonah liked that.

"City called Dishu. At the end of the long dock."

"Vitaly is checking it on the map," said Dr. Nassiri. "Okay, we see where you are. We can be there in less than thirty minutes," said Dr. Nassiri.

"Not fast enough," replied Jonah. "Need you there in ten or less."

Three Land Cruisers rippled in the rearview mirror

beyond the dust cloud, struggling to keep up with the more powerful Ford. Only silence came from the other end of the phone.

"We can do it," said Alexis, her voice tinny and distant. "We'll have to surface, and run the electrics and diesels simultaneously—"

"Great," said Jonah. "Don't care how, just do it."

"Got it," said Alexis.

"Oh, and keep a decent distance from the end of the dock," said Jonah.

"Why?" asked Dr. Nassiri.

"Because I'm going to jump a truck off it." The Raptor bounced over a brutal set of bumps in the trail and the sniper tried to brace himself, momentarily airborne. "And Doc, prepare your surgical gear. I've got a man with a neck wound, and I can't stop the bleeding."

Fingers still pressed into the man's spurting neck, Jonah looked in the rearview windshield. The Land Cruisers were losing ground, but not by much.

"Start talking," ordered Jonah to the wounded man. "Or you're out the door."

"We share an enemy," said the man with a gurgle.

"That don't make us friends," retorted Jonah.

In response, the sniper issued a massive, coughing belly laugh that filled the entire cab of the Raptor. Jonah looked down at the flowing pool of blood—if he didn't get the sniper to Nassiri, like *right now*, he was going to bleed out in the passenger's seat.

Jonah whipped the 4x4 onto a rutted two-lane road, the city coming into view just ahead. Within seconds, the speedometer mashed up against the governor-regulated top speed of a hundred and ten miles an hour. With the smoother road, it wouldn't take long for the Land Cruisers to start gaining ground.

"Where are we going?" gurgled the sniper.

"Making a run for a long dock in Dishu," said Jonah. "Our ride will meet us there. Maybe even provide some covering fire so we're not cut to pieces."

"*Dishu*?" the sniper croaked, suddenly perking back to life and struggling against Jonah's grasp.

"Hold … still!" Jonah yelled. The front cab of the truck looked like a triage center in the aftermath of a train wreck.

"Dishu is not a good place," hissed the sniper. "One of Bettencourt's men was kidnapped by their mayor."

"I'm not stopping at City Hall to ask for a kabob stand permit."

"Bettencorps' mercenaries retaliated by driving through Dishu and firing on militia buildings and private residences," continued Dalmar. "Recently. From this truck."

Shit.

The outer city gates approached at incredible speed. It was too late to turn around. Even from the distance, Jonah could see the city populace scrambling out of the way and mobilizing arms. Cars and delivery trucks of all types fled the main street, trying to escape the incoming convoy.

The Raptor burst into the city at top speed, engine howling, the three pursuers inches from its rear bumper. At first, all was good—a smooth road and no obstructions between them and the long dock out to sea.

Then the trap snapped shut.

Militiamen popped up on the roofline of every building on main street. They opened up with AK-47 fire, clattering against the armored doors and roof like a tornado-fueled hailstorm. The front windshield clouded with bullet-fragments and broken glass. The armor wouldn't hold forever, bullets would start finding their way through in moments. Jonah took his bloody hand off the sniper's neck and held them to his ears, eyes half closed, trying to shut out the incredible noise as the pirate slumped in the seat, unconscious.

Jonah caught just a glimpse of the three pursuers behind him. Shot to pieces, tires blown out, the first Toyota wobbled, lost control, and slammed into a pillar on the side of the road, while the second disintegrated in a barrage of small-arms and RPG fire. Unarmored, the vehicles didn't stand a chance. The third slowed and rolled to gentle stop, the driver and passengers shot dead.

The Raptor took a three-foot drop from the road and onto the dock. Glinting in the sunlight, the *Scorpion* plowed through the water at flank speed, racing to intercept. Jonah watched as the end of the dock approached with incredible speed until the Raptor soared off the end, arcing in a balletic leap, then dropping nose down, slamming into the whitecaps hard. Water rushed into the cab through twisted metal and bullet holes.

Jonah kicked the door open against the pressure of the rushing water, grabbed the sniper by the collar and pulled, taking one last breath as the Raptor slipped beneath the waves, sinking to the bottom of the bay. The sniper came free of the cab and Jonah kicked twice, propelling both men to the surface. Swimming backwards, the sniper's head on his chest, he reached the external boarding ladder for the *Scorpion*'s conning tower as the submarine slowed to a stop, engines in full reverse.

With one final look towards the city of Dishu, Jonah hefted the sniper's muscled bulk over one shoulder; the Somali's mass dwarfing his own. He climbed the ladder, one rung at a time, and then passed the man to Dr. Nassiri and Fatima at the top of the boarding ladder. Between the two, they somehow lowered him down into the command compartment, wrestling the sniper's limp form to the deck. It was an awkward, chaotic affair leaving streaks of blood throughout the interior boarding ladder as the man's neck bled unstaunched. Jonah dropped down behind them as soon as they'd moved him out of the way.

"Who is that?" Vitaly said, turning to stare as Dr. Nassiri threw open his triage kit and went to work on his unconscious patient.

"The man who used me as bait to draw out Bettencourt and almost got me killed in the process."

"He's lost a lot of blood," Dr. Nassiri said without looking up.

"Will he live?" Vitaly asked.

"Vitaly, stop staring!" Jonah ordered. "Reinforcements could show up at any moment—so move your ass and get us out of here!"

Vitaly turned back to his control panels, and Jonah put his hand on the doctor's back. "What's the prognosis?"

"I don't know yet," Dr. Nassiri motioned to his mother to grab the man's legs. "I'm going to get him into a bunk. He needs a transfusion."

"Do me a favor, Doc," Jonah said. "Save his fucking life."

"Getting contact," shouted Vitaly, glancing up from his station. Jonah nodded in acknowledgement, climbed back onto the conning tower, and turned seaward. In the distance, Bettencorp's mercenary mothership, the battle-ship-grey transport, bore down on them, rapidly closing the gap between the two vessels. Soon mercenaries would be within range to pick off anyone stupid enough to stick their head out of the main hatch. Charles Bettencourt had no intention of letting his submarine slip away again.

CHAPTER 18

Jonah ducked into the interior of the conning tower and closed the hatch behind him, sealing himself and all aboard into the *Scorpion*.

"Make our course due east," Jonah barked to Vitaly and anyone else within earshot. "Hard out to sea, full power. We're being pursued."

"Set for silent running, Captain?"

Captain, thought Jonah. He wasn't sure how he felt about that.

"No," ordered Jonah. "Not yet. We have to get into deeper water first. As soon as the bottom allows, bring us to 300 feet. But if you find a thermocline, hide in it. Bettencourt says the mothership has upgraded anti-submarine warfare capabilities."

Vitaly nodded, Jonah didn't need to explain his plan. A thermocline—an invisible oceanic border between waters of different temperature and salinities—would be an ideal place to shelter, capable of masking or reflecting their sonar signature and auditory trail.

"Alexis!" Jonah shouted towards the engine compartment. Alexis popped her head out of the hatchway, one ear of her protective headphones pulled back to hear him.

"Diesels are five by five," she said, anticipating his request. "But batteries got bled pretty good chasing you down."

"Charge?"

"Still two-thirds."

"Excellent."

Alexis glanced up at the interior boarding ladder to the main hatch in the top of the conning tower. She didn't need to say anything for Jonah to know exactly what she was thinking. He knew she was looking at the hatch, trying to imagine the massive volume of water between herself and the surface. He always imagined the same thing.

"Alexis, I need you out of the engine room for a moment," said Jonah, handing her a chunky plastic headset. "Put on these hydrophones and get a feel for the noises of this submarine, the *Scorpion*. If you hear any noises that aren't us, you need to report them to me."

"How will I tell?"

"You'll be able to tell," assured Jonah.

Now well beneath the surface, the *Scorpion* sped forward, unencumbered by the waves and wind of the surface. Once deep, everything changed, her wobbly, top-heavy form shifted into beautiful, efficient forward movement, every line guiding her through the dark waters.

After he was satisfied they were on their way to safety, Jonah stepped away from the command compartment and walked forward into the sleeping compartment, the bunks just forward of command. The sniper lay in a lower rack as Dr. Nassiri carefully wrapped a clean, white bandage around his neck. Fatima sat in the next bunk, her eyes closed, her face a little pale. A single long, red plastic tube joined the radial vein of her inner elbow to the same in the patient's arm as the scientist gave a battlefield blood transfusion.

"Status?" Jonah asked.

"The damage to your rescuer's neck was severe but localized," Dr. Nassiri.

"To set the record straight, I rescued *him*," said Jonah, knowing full well he wouldn't have been in any position to rescue anybody if the sniper hadn't saved his own ass first.

"Indeed. He looks like the kind of man who would dispute you on that point. In any case, I've disinfected and sewn up the wound. He's going to be fine. I've given him a light sedative and a dose of painkillers. My mother is giving him a transfusion to stabilize his blood pressure. You have no idea who he is?"

"Based on what Bettencourt said, I've got a notion his name is Dalmar Abdi."

Fatima sat up with a start. "Wait a minute. Did you say *Dalmar Abdi*?"

"That name mean something to you?" asked Jonah.

"Dalmar Abdi," Fatima leaned forward and continued in a whisper, "is the pirate *other pirates* fear. And you brought him back with us? I'm giving him a blood transfusion to keep him alive?"

"Not to worry, Mother," interjected Dr. Nassiri. "He's not going to be able to harm anyone, not in this state. Besides, he's alone. How much damage could he possibly cause?"

"Let's see if it's even him," Jonah said. He leaned down and touched the man's shoulder, gently shaking him awake. "Dalmar, hey. How're we doing?"

The sniper's eyes flew open. "Glorious!" he said, trying to sit up, twisting around to see Fatima. "I have the blood of a beautiful woman running through my veins!" The medicated look returned, and Dalmar's features softened and then went slack as he sank back into unconsciousness.

"This man is dangerous," Fatima hissed, standing and moving as far away from Dalmar as her blood-filled tether would allow.

"He's the enemy of our enemy," said Jonah. "Whether that makes him a friend or not, I don't know. But what I do know is this—we both would have been dinner for the vultures if we hadn't crossed paths. I would have been shot if he hadn't attacked the Bettencorps encampment, and he would've bled out in the sand if I hadn't dragged him back to the *Scorpion* for your son's expert care."

"I don't understand." Fatima's brow wrinkled in confusion. "What does Bettencorps have to do with this?"

Shit, thought Jonah. She doesn't know. He took a deep breath to continue. "I'm pretty sure the pirates that held you and Klea were working for Bettencorps the whole time. It was likely a Bettencorps missile that shot your plane out of the sky."

Fatima and her son exchanged glances. "We had already guessed it was his forces that shot down my plane."

"Klea and I were rescued yesterday by a fisherman, but someone in his village—I don't think it was him—sold us out. Bettencorp's head of security paid the fisherman a visit, and I was captured. Klea escaped, and with a little luck, is on her way to a US consulate as we speak."

Fatima wavered on her feet, forcing Hassan to wrap a supportive arm around her waist.

"But why? If Charles Bettencourt wanted us dead, why would the pirates who worked for him keep us alive?"

"I don't know," admitted Jonah. "Maybe because you and Klea are Muslim. Maybe because they wanted dirt on

Bettencorps in case the alliance ever went down in flames. Maybe they didn't even have a reason at all and would've gotten around to killing you eventually. But what we do know is that they were not in the business of ransoming you or Klea. As far as the world is concerned you're both dead. And by Bettencort's own admission, this man, Dalmar Abdi, is a big thorn in his side. That puts him on our side, at least for now."

Fatima sat back down on the bunk, her eyes frozen with a far-away stare as she processed the new information. Hassan leaned over to disconnect the blood transfusion. Dalmar would have to do with what he'd received, Fatima had given enough already.

Jonah knew he was needed back in command, but paused to address one last lingering doubt. "Doc," he began with uncharacteristic hesitation. "Can we trust Vitaly?"

"Yes," Dr. Nassiri answered with an emphatic nod. "Unequivocally."

Jonah frowned. "I'm not ready to make that leap," he said finally.

"We'd be dead without him."

"He saved himself," rebutted Jonah.

"No. It's more than that. He believes he has a debt to all of us for his role in ambushing the *Fool's Errand*. After you vanished, Bettencorp's mercenaries followed a secret transmitter and caught up to us. We were able to disable the transmitter, but Vitaly fought courageously against his former comrades when he could just as easily have rendered our ship helpless."

Jonah considered this. Maybe Vitaly didn't have to convince him. Maybe convincing Dr. Nassiri was good enough. "I still need proof, but I'm willing to consider him your responsibility for the time being. Okay?"

"Okay."

Jonah turned to leave when the doctor stopped him. "Jonah?"

"Yes?"

"You may call me Hassan."

Jonah smiled and clasped the doctor's arm. "Sure thing, Doc."

Back in the command compartment, Jonah rejoined Vitaly and Alexis.

"Status?" asked Jonah.

"Crossing three hundred feet in depth," said Vitaly. "Still driving hard to sea at eighteen knots."

"The mercenaries are right on top of us," said Alexis, pressing both headphones tight against her ears. "I hear propeller sounds from everywhere."

"Not surprising," said Jonah, listening to the churning of the propellers overhead though the thick steel hull of the submarine. "We're running noisy."

At this rate, the mercenaries could pursue them indefinitely. He feared they had a computer-assisted listening array capable of directionally tracking the *Scorpion* at any depth. Even crossing through a thermocline might not throw this pursuer.

Jonah hit the all-call button on the bulkhead and prepared to address the crew.

"We're rigging for silent running," he ordered. "Cancel the horseshoes and hammer throws. Please remain at your station—no unnecessary movement or sound."

Vitaly nodded, and his fingers danced across the console. The cadence of the engines changed, the vibrations lessening as the *Scorpion* slowed, but only slightly. Throughout the length of the massive submarine, all went quiet. A silent predator, the submarine slipped through the waves. The *thump-thump-thump* of the mercenary ship's propellers filled the compartment from above.

"On my mark," said Jonah, "turn us hard to starboard and drop to four hundred and fifty feet."

"Aye," said Vitaly.

"Keep the rudder pegged over. We'll corkscrew around two hundred and seventy degrees, exit the turn to the north. They should lose track of us as we change depth and course. Alexis, report?"

"I think I hear dolphins!" whispered Alexis, leaning over her console. "They're singing!"

Jonah smiled. He wished he could hear them, too.

Vitaly ably worked his console, struggling to keep the *Scorpion* from heeling over as she corkscrewed through the tight turn. Reaching the end of her plotted path and depth, her surface planes and rudder snapped into place, guiding her out of the spin and onto a deep, northward course.

"Propeller noises fading," said Alexis. "I still hear them above us, but the noises are disorganized now. I think they're searching for us, trying to track our path."

Jonah realized he'd been holding his breath. He allowed himself to exhale, releasing some of the pressure from his chest and stomach. They weren't free yet, not by a long shot, but maybe this was the first—

PIIIIIIIIING. The sound rippled throughout the *Scorpion* as the submarine was assaulted with a massive sonar noise. Alexis ripped off her headphones, throwing them against the console, holding her ears with both hands to block out the noise. The mercenaries had deployed a massive, amplified underwater sound wave to discover the location of the submarine. *PIIIIIING, PIIIIING, PIIIIIIING,* rang the sound again and again, reverberating and echoing throughout the submarine and against the seafloor. With just as much warning as they'd started, the pings ceased.

"Pick up those headphones, Alexis," ordered Jonah. He took no pleasure in the command, the pinging had hurt his ears through the hull alone, he couldn't imagine what they would have sounded like through amplified hydrophones.

Without protesting, Alexis picked them up and slid them right back over her ears, wincing in slight pain as she did so.

"We're still being pursued," said Alexis. "Propeller noises are moving … if my readings are correct, I think they're moving ahead of us."

"Hold course," said Jonah to Vitaly. "Hold it—"

"I hear …" began Alexis. "I hear splashes. Wait—make that three splashes."

Dawning realization hit Jonah like a hammer. "Hard to port!" he yelled at Vitaly. "Belay silent running! Engines full! Make depth five hundred fifty feet!"

Swearing, Vitaly punched a series of commands into the navigation console, forcing the entire submarine to suddenly roll to the side as it completed a rattling, tight left-hand turn. Jonah's hand punched the alarm button on the wall next to the intercom, then the all-call to the speakers strung in every compartment.

"Brace for incoming!" he shouted into the microphone.

Silence fell. For just a moment Jonah felt himself believing that perhaps, just perhaps, the splashing sound was nothing, his orders an overreaction. The *Scorpion* descended to the ordered depth, silently slipping through the darkness.

The detonation came suddenly and without warning, deafening Jonah and violently twisting the entire bow end of the *Scorpion*, throwing everyone in the command compartment to the deck as lights popped and electrical boxes arced. Like being caught between Thor's hammer and anvil, concussive force ripped the breath out of Jonah's lungs, leaving him gasping on the floor, ears ringing as the submarine moaned and shook off the force of the blast. Before he could drag himself to his feet, a second concussion hit the submarine amidships just above the conning tower, jerking the entire body of the submarine to the starboard as everything in the galley and engine rooms threw themselves out of their drawers and across the compartments, crashing across the deck and into the bulkheads.

Fatima screamed loud and shrill as the third violent concussion hit the engine room, knocking the steady *whump-whump-whump* of the propeller shaft into a squealing mechanical nightmare of sound. Sparks showered down around them as the lights died a second time.

"Holy fuck!" Jonah gasped, as he tried to regain his ragged breath and unsteady footing. He could barely hear his own voice over the ringing in his ears. Hydraulic oil streamed out of the snaking command and control valves, collecting on the deck and turning it into a slippery mess.

Vitaly pounded his fists against his computer console, then leapt up to the bulkhead. Hydraulic fluid flowed over his face and hands as he manually attempted to override the malfunctioning steering mechanisms. "Planes and rudders not responding!" he shouted, spitting out fluid. "Attempting to compensate!"

Alexis had taken cover underneath the communications console, still clutching the hydrophones in her hand. The concussion had knocked the entire system offline—either that or she'd been deafened by the blast.

"What was that?" Hassan yelled.

"Depth charges," Jonah yelled back. "Barrels of explosives dropped off the side of a ship to detonate when they reach a set depth. Crude, but they'll do us in if we don't lose our pursuers."

Out of balance, the *Scorpion* wobbled forward, misaligned diving planes in the conning tower threatening to pull her on her side. The struggling engines squealed, metal against metal, trying to maintain momentum. Acrid smoke wafted into the command compartment from some unseen source, collecting against the low ceiling.

Jonah ripped oxygen masks out of a bulkhead compartment and slipped one over his own face. The effect was immediate claustrophobia and Jonah forced himself to be calm and breathe normally as he tossed a second mask to Alexis. She let it hit the floor then yanked it underneath her console. Vitaly allowed his to hit him in the back of the head. Swearing in Russian, he picked it up and put it on.

Smoke drifted from the engine compartment, accompanied by a brutal, metallic grinding sound. All Jonah had to do was point and Alexis jumped out from underneath the communications console and sprinted down the corridor. With his mask in place, Jonah grabbed three more and ran them into the bunk compartment.

Fatima had curled up in the same bunk as Dalmar, wrapping herself around his sleeping form, whether to protect him or comfort herself, Jonah had no idea. Hassan stood against one bulkhead, halfway crouching, his hands over his head as if the ceiling could collapse at any moment.

"Doc, I need you," said Jonah, pressing the oxygen masks into his hands. "Get these on your mother and Dalmar, and get in the command compartment now. Fatima, go to the engine room, I need someone in there if Alexis needs help."

The doctor nodded and instantly responded. So he wasn't locked up or frozen with fear—he just needed to be told what to do. Fatima unwound herself from the pirate, put her mask on and followed.

As Jonah sprinted back to the command compartment, he realized he didn't need a pair of hydrophones to detect a new set of splashes from the surface above. The sound penetrated the depths and the thick steel skin of the submarine. Behind him, Hassan looked up. The doctor had heard it, too.

"We're no longer rigged for silent running," said Vitaly as he struggled with the manual systems. "Diving planes are knocked out of alignment. Can only be fixed from outside."

"Can we send a diver?" Hassan asked.

"The shock wave from a depth charge would liquefy a diver."

"Belay that," said Vitaly, squeezing a valve. "I think I've got—"

BOOM! BOOM! BOOM! BOOM!

Four depth charges went off in quick succession, every detonation in close proximity to the *Scorpion*. Half the bulbs in the command compartment exploded in a cascade of sparks and broken glass, spilling across the deck. Pipes burst, spraying greywater and oil into the compartment as the emergency lighting flickered. Wooden and particle-board cabinets in the galley exploded, showering the interior with splinters. Between the tight quarters, the smell, and perfect chaos, Jonah felt as if he were riding out a tornado in an outhouse.

"We can't take much more of this!" Vitaly screamed through the smoke and darkness, his voice muffled by the oxygen mask.

Alexis ran out of the engine room wearing a full oxygen hood and welder's gloves, a strange combination with her tank top and cutoff shorts. A massive cloud of ugly black smoke followed her. Without speaking a word, she yanked a fire extinguisher off the wall of the command compartment and rushed back into the engine room with equal speed.

Hassan stepped towards Alexis, instinctively trying to follow her. Jonah caught him by the shoulder.

"Doc, I need you here," whispered Jonah.

"But my mother is in there!" protested the doctor.

Suddenly, despite the chaos, the noise, the flickering lights and raging fire in the engine compartment, Jonah stopped and stared. On one small console screen, a small blip indicated the position of the submarine on a map. A strange sense of familiarity washed over him. Could it be…?

"Surface the ship," ordered Jonah.

"Are we surrendering?" asked Vitaly.

"Hell no," said Jonah. "I have to make a phone call. Doc is in charge until I come back."

"Phone call, *da, da*, of course he wants to make phone call now," grumbled Vitaly as he adjusted the manual controls. The *Scorpion* lurched, careening towards the surface. Jonah yanked open the drawer underneath the communications console, finding a thick, black satellite telephone.

"Vitaly—tell Alexis to put all power to the engines when we surface," ordered Jonah. "I know we can't outrun our pursuers, but we can at least keep the distance as best we can."

Vitaly relayed the instructions as he and Jonah watched as the depth meter climbed from 300 feet below to 250. More depth charges detonated, rumbling through the bones of the submarine, but far away from *Scorpion* and too deep to have any effect.

Jonah tossed the hydrophones at Hassan and clambered up the interior boarding ladder, right up against the hatch. He wanted to be ready when *Scorpion* reached the surface. Dialing the phone number, his fingers floated over the send button, ready to press.

The *Scorpion* broke free of the waves at the crest of a massive swell. The submarine leapt from the surface of the ocean and crashed down with enough force to nearly knock Jonah off the ladder. He twisted the massive circular lock to the main hatch, swinging it open to the stern of the ship as collected seawater rained down the interior conning tower. His one dared glance around the side of the hatch confirmed his fears—the mothership bore down at flank speed, already launching her inflatable boats.

Jonah pressed send. The phone buzzed to life. Within seconds, the signal bounced off three separate orbiting satellites and a thousand miles of fiber-optic cable to a hard line on the far side of the world. He yanked down his oxygen mask, letting it dangle around his neck.

"Hello?" came a sleepy voice from the incredible distance. Despite the grainy connection, Jonah was relatively certain he could hear the soft patter of a Seattle drizzle.

"Hey beautiful," he said, trying to adopt his best calming voice. She was going to be pissed receiving this phone call. What time was it in Seattle, anyway?

"What the hell?" demanded the voice from the other end. "Is this Jonah?!"

"Marissa," said Jonah. "I am so happy to hear your voice."

"Jonah fucking Blackwell?" shouted Marissa, anger overriding the sleepy tones of her voice. "I thought you were dead! You say you're going to Spain for a week and then you fucking vanish!"

"Who is that?" demanded a male voice from the other end of the line.

"It's my ex," said Marissa, just as much to Jonah as the man sleeping in bed next to her. "For Christ's sake, Jonah! You let me think you were on the bottom of the ocean or buried in a shallow grave somewhere. What the hell happened to you?!"

Half-listening, Jonah watched as the mercenary mothership disgorged two small boats into the water. Behind him, the broken-off snorkel in the rear of the conning tower belched out black smoke as the engines drove beyond full capacity. At least Alexis seemed to have knocked the misaligned propeller shaft back into place.

"Marissa, I'm really, truly sorry," said Jonah. "And I can explain, but that's not why I—"

"Fine!" yelled Marissa. "What do you want? It's two in the goddamn morning! Are you in jail? A car accident? And how many people did you call before you called me?"

Jonah stomped at the diving plane, trying to drive it back into alignment. "Marissa," said Jonah, taking a break from stomping to get some air. "This is literally the first phone call I've made in years."

Gunfire ripped around him, pinging off the conning tower and open hatch, sending Jonah flying back behind the hatch for cover.

"What the fuck was that?" yelled Marissa.

"Somebody's shooting at me," said Jonah. "I hate to cut this short, but I'm kind of on the clock here. Remember that silver wreck we worked off the Horn of Africa?"

"I don't understand—the SS *Richard Thompson James*?"

Jonah remembered the name now. The SS *Richard Thompson James*, an Allied Victory-class ship transporting silver coins to the Saudis in the closing days of World War II. An American ship pursuing American strategic interests but under British protection, the British allowed it to wander alone into the hunting grounds of a particularly prolific German U-boat. It was torpedoed and sank in nearly six hundred feet of water, abandoned until Jonah and a small team of salvagers ripped it apart for the silver within.

Another burst of gunfire rattled around him, interrupting his thoughts.

"What about it?" she demanded. "And why is someone shooting at you?"

"Pretty sure they're trying to kill me. Look, I need the coordinates to that shipwreck, Marissa. I need them right now. I don't have time to get into the details."

"Fine, whatever," said Marissa. He heard the sounds of her climbing out of bed, walking to her office around the corner of her bedroom, booting up her computer. Part of him missed her, missed her smell, her warmth, and the normalcy in which she conducted herself and all her affairs. That was to say, all her affairs outside of the one she shared with him.

"Thank you," he said. "Seriously, thank you. You're saving my life here."

Marissa started rattling off a series of numbers, the

coordinates to the silver shipwreck. Jonah memorized the numbers and aimed one final kick at the depth plane, forcing it back into alignment with a snap of metal against metal. A fresh salvo of gunfire clattered off the hatchway and conning tower, the ringing ricochets narrowly missing him.

"I don't even want to know what you need this for," Marissa asked. "Can I go back to bed now?"

"That's all I needed," said Jonah. "Thank you. Let's, uh, do lunch sometime."

"Lose my number, asshole." Marissa slammed down the phone with the fury of a woman who'd probably be on the next flight out if Jonah would only ask. But he didn't. Instead, he ducked back inside the conning tower and slammed the hatch shut behind him. He raced down the interior boarding ladder and re-secured his oxygen mask.

"Helm, dive now!" ordered Jonah.

Vitaly nodded and sent the *Scorpion* into a tight, stomach-churning dive at a speed and angle Jonah thought impossible.

"Make our depth five-five-oh feet," said Jonah as he plugged the new coordinates into the navigational computer. Good news—they were less than fifteen minutes away, maybe less if Alexis drew the batteries hard and pushed the electric engine beyond spec. He stole a suspicious glance at Vitaly, who maintained his stoic vigil at the helm. Vitaly turned and glared back through the clouded plastic of his oxygen mask.

"That's still within range of the depth charges," protested Vitaly.

"Doesn't matter," said Jonah. "We can't out-dive the explosives."

"Rig for silent running?" asked Vitaly.

"No," said Jonah, pressing the intercom to the engine room. "Stay noisy. Alexis, full power to the engines. I don't care about range or endurance, just speed. Vitaly—follow my course, but be unpredictable. Run like a rabbit. I want them wasting depth charges. Doctor—report!"

"Fire in the engine room has been contained," Hassan said. "We lost a few batteries, nothing crippling. Hydrophones are working again. Vitaly rerouted the systems past the damaged circuits. They're still following us—and they've made no attempt at communications."

"Do we still have those bodies in the freezer?"

"We do," said the doctor, confused. "But why—?"

"Hand the headphones to Vitaly and follow me," said Jonah, walking towards the bunkroom-adjacent galley. "I want those frozen bodies in the diver lockout chamber along with any trash from the galley."

"Splashes!" came Vitaly's tinny voice from the command compartment. The submarine abruptly changed course, speed and depth, sending the *Scorpion* jolting in a new direction, almost dropping Jonah and the doctor to their knees with the abruptness of the course change. They righted themselves and opened the small walk-in freezer where five lumpy bodybags were stacked against one wall.

"Two should be enough," said Jonah over the distant popping sound of three underwater explosions. The mercenaries had missed again. Vitaly was a talented navigator, especially under such pressure. Whether or not he could keep it up for the next critical minutes was another question entirely.

"Let's get the burned ones from the front compartment," Hassan said. "They're in pieces, should be lighter."

"I like the way you think," said Jonah, chucking one bag of body parts towards Hassan and grabbing the other for himself. They exited the freezer, each grabbing a stacked bag of kitchen waste as they did so.

"What's happening?" asked Fatima as they both passed.

"I wish I knew," Hassan said, closely following Jonah.

The mercenaries stopped dropping charges, not wanting to waste them on the seemingly panicked, fleeing crew of the *Scorpion*. Jonah and Hassan opened the body bags, gagging as they dropped the burned, chopped-up, frozen ,and tattooed body parts into the lockout chamber along with two massive bags of galley waste.

"Go ahead and throw up if you need to," said Jonah, dry heaving. "It'll just add to the effect."

"You never told me what we're doing," Hassan said, covering his face and mouth with one hand, unable to tear his eyes away from the horrific scene.

"Garbage shot," said Jonah. "We blast this out of the lockout chamber. The bodies and trash float to the surface. They'll think we're dead."

"Ah, clever."

"Not really. It's an old trick from World War II. Problem is nobody'll buy it without a massive oil slick."

"How do we do that?" asked the doctor. "Can we vent from the fuel tanks?"

"Not enough to sell it." Jonah slammed the hatch to the lockout chamber shut.

"So what—"

Jonah cut him off. "You're not going to like it." Fingers punching the controls, Jonah programmed the chamber to over-pressurize.

"What do you need me to do?"

"Stay here," said Jonah. "When my signal comes, press the green button. The outer hatch to the chamber will open automatically and the air pressure will evacuate the contents."

Hassan stole a look through the small portal window into the chamber. "I'm about to evacuate my contents," he said.

"And hold on," said Jonah. "The ride is going to get bumpy."

"Captain!" shouted a voice from command compartment below. "Come quickly!"

Jonah slid down the ladder, joining Vitaly at his helm console. The Russian brought up a passive acoustic reading to the main screen, rendering the underwater terrain as a crude, shifting 3-D model.

"What is it?" said Jonah.

"This," said Vitaly, pointing at the screen. "I following your coordinates, but I believe there is obstruction."

The screen depicted the forward-looking sensor reading of the *Scorpion* as it steamed towards a large, blocky object.

"It's not an obstruction," said Jonah. "It's a shipwreck, the SS *Richard Thompson James*. I dove her during a salvage mission a few years ago."

Vitaly looked up at Jonah, eyes wide with understanding. "This is suicide."

"We have to create an oil slick. Our pursuers won't believe the possum act without floating bodies and lots of oil. That wreck is chock full of seventy-year-old bunker fuel. The tanks are amidship, right in the center of the ship. Aim for them."

"I do not like this plan," said Vitaly, as he bore the bow of the *Scorpion* down on the increasingly clear acoustic image of the hulking war transport. The *Scorpion* zeroed in on the image at frightening speed. Jonah realized the window to change his mind was approaching quickly. He swallowed and allowed it to pass.

One final time, Jonah punched the all-call button. "All hands, brace for impact!"

Vitaly ducked underneath his console and Jonah slid underneath the communications console. Jonah slipped his oxygen mask once more over his face. He didn't want to suffocate while unconscious, if it came to that.

The submarine slammed into the fuel tanks of the shipwreck, driving deep into the hulk like a spear, bucking and throwing her crew across compartments like toys. Emergency klaxons rang as pipes burst, flooding the compartment with rushing water and white, foamy spray. Fires burst from consoles. Vitaly leapt to his feet, grabbed the remaining extinguisher and hosed down the sensitive electronics. Water rushed down from the damaged forward compartment, frothing as it ran across the deck and over his feet. From above, Jonah heard the familiar *whoosh* of a diver's lockout chamber as Hassan obeyed the order to activate the outer door, sending burnt body parts spinning into the rising column of debris and fuel oil.

Ignoring the fires and the spraying hydraulic lines of the command compartment, Jonah rushed into the burned, blackened forward compartment. The nose of the submarine had absorbed the worst of the impact. Several of the seawater circulation pipes had sheered, spilling their high-pressure, foamy contents into the compartment. The submarine's stern sank until it hit the ocean floor, seawater rushing downwards like a newly-formed river of oil and debris.

Behind him, Vitaly scrambled from console to electrical box, trying to keep ahead of the dancing flames. Jonah used all of his strength against the feeder valves, trying to stanch the powerful flow of water. He dug deep, reliving every betrayal, heartache, prison whipping, gunshot, stabbing, dead friend, and ruined life. Joints popping, muscles straining, the valve squeezed close, choking off the flood.

An immense, overwhelming *PIIIIIIIING* rang through the submarine, fraying already-shattered nerves as Jonah made his way back to the command compartment. He put his hands over his ears. *PIIIIIING, PIIIING, PIIIIIIING,* rang the assaulting sound three more times, reverberating in the submarine and against the speared shipwreck. With just as much warning as they'd begun, the noises ceased.

Jonah crawled to the communications console, one hand holding the earphones to the side of his head, listening intently. He held up a single finger, forbidding anyone from saying a word. Hassan paused on his way down the interior boarding ladder, careful not to move or make a sound.

They waited in silence.

"They're leaving," he said, at first with a mumble, then louder. "They're leaving!"

Surely enough, the soft *swish-swish-swish* of propeller screws slowly faded into the distance, replaced with the still-settling metal of the wartime shipwreck's hull against their own.

"Don't get comfortable," he warned. "Probably intend to return with a salvage crew, pick through our bones."

"Let's not be here when they return," Hassan said, dropping down next to Jonah.

"Agreed," said Jonah. "This bought us time, but it won't take long before they they figure it out."

In the dim emergency lighting, they surveyed the remnants of battle, the filthy, sewage-ridden floodwater swirling around their ankles, burn-marks and extinguisher foam on the bulkheads and electrical boxes, flickering lights and the vicious cuts and bruises worn like medals of valor by all of those aboard. Around them, the shipwreck settled, steel members moaning as they found new forms after the vicious impact. From the engine room, Alexis emerged, holding both welding gloves in one hand, oxygen hood in the other. Dirt, grime, blood, and tears streaked her face. Shaking, she opened her mouth to speak, but made barely a noise before she closed it.

"I ... tried—" she began again.

"What?" asked Jonah.

"She won't breathe."

"Where is she?" Hassan's face contorted with horror. "*Where is my mother?*"

Alexis shook her head and looked up at him, eyes glistening with tears. Hassan shoved her aside and charged into the engine room, Jonah, Alexis, and Vitaly at his heels.

Fatima lay face-up in a collecting pool of water, skin pale and white, eyes open but unseeing, muscles bound, small flecks of white foam in the corner of her mouth. Hassan dropped to his knees beside her and picked up her hand. Her fingers were charred to the second knuckle. He glanced up at a blackened, smoldering electrical panel and tore open his mother's shirt, revealing a white spiderweb of electrical burns encircling her heart.

"I tried to resuscitate her," Alexis said, barely audible over Hassan's hoarse, ragged breathing.

"You wouldn't have been able to," he said, "She was dead"—his voice warbling with grief—"the moment she touched the panel."

Alexis choked back a sob. "I'm so sorry."

Hassan leaned down and kissed his mother on the cheek, using his fingertips to close her eyes for the last time.

"Goddammit!" Jonah yanked the oxygen mask from around his neck, rubber straps snapping, and hurled it against a bulkhead. It clanged off the hatch, dropped into the water and bobbed face-down like a drowning victim.

Vitaly crouched in the filthy water and wrapped both arms around Hassan's sagging shoulders.

"These motherfuckers are not going to stop," Jonah growled. "We've taken everything, *everything* they've thrown at us. We've been shot at, shot down, beaten up, blown up, tortured. We've spilled blood, theirs and ours. If we don't fight back, they're going to keep coming until we're done for."

"What can we do?" Alexis asked. Behind her, Dalmar emerged from the bunk room, disoriented and unsteady. Seeing Fatima, he shook his head, drew in a long breath, and turned away. Vitaly stood and drew Hassan back to his feet.

The muscles in Jonah's jaw clenched and unclenched as he surveyed his traumatized crew. "I'll tell you what *I'm* going to do." His face twisted with rage. "I'm going to walk into Bettencourt's playground and knock his fucking sandcastle down."

Hassan simply shook his head, unable to even bring tears to his eyes.

Jonah cleared his throat to continue, suddenly wishing he wasn't still wearing a pair of dead man's pants. "Charles Bettencourt deserves what's coming to him, but I can't ask you to risk your lives again, not now that we finally have a real, solid window to escape. We can make for Oman so everyone who wants to leave can leave. We'll run dead silent and submerged as far as we can to the north, then recharge the batteries with the snorkel as needed."

"Boss, no snorkel," said Vitaly.

"That's right," said Jonah, recalling the sheered-off snorkel. "What happened?"

"Collision with ship," said Vitaly. "You missed much excitement when you on little vacation."

"Fine, we'll charge surfaced," Jonah fixed his gaze on the engineer. "Alexis, you have your parents and a life back in Texas. What are you still doing here with us pirates, deserters, and outlaws, anyway? It's time to go back to the land of big hair, big trucks, and barbeque. What do you say?"

Alexis glanced down at Fatima and then let her eyes rest a moment on Hassan. "I'll follow you on down the road apiece," she said with an exaggerated drawl. Then she crossed her arms and stared at Jonah. She didn't need to say another word for everyone to know she fully intended to stay.

Jonah nodded and turned to the doctor. "Hassan, take your mother home, give her a proper burial. You can still go back to your medical practice."

Hassan frowned. "There is nothing for me in Morocco," he whispered. "Besides, Bettencourt will not let me live in peace. You know that."

"Vitaly?" said Jonah, turning his attention to the Russian helmsman.

"You shoot Vitaly if he leave?" Vitaly said with a grim smile. "Again?"

"Hell, I might shoot you for staying," said Jonah.

"You are terrible captain." Vitaly shook his head as if

Jonah was a great disappointment. "But I take my chances with *Scorpion*. She good ship. I stay."

"Good," cracked Jonah. "Because I know fuck-all about sailing this thing."

Jonah started to speak again, but Dalmar interrupted, his solemn baritone filling the engine room. "I am with you in this. We will rain destruction upon him. Blood for blood, for the doctor's beautiful mother, for my people. My men and I will provide whatever support we can whenever you need it."

Hassan spoke up, his voice barely a whisper. "Charles Bettencourt has no right to do what he's doing. He thinks everybody is too stupid, too poor, or too weak to oppose him. I've lost my cousin and my mother … and for"—his voice broke—"for what?"

"We can't bring back what was lost," said Jonah. "But we can show the world who Charles Bettencourt really is."

CHAPTER 19

Vitaly increased the tempo of the *Scorpion*'s engines, slowly throttling up to one-quarter reverse. The submarine reverberated and shook, a spear vibrating deep within the belly of the sunken World War II transport ship. The *Scorpion* shifted but didn't retreat, structural members of the broken shipwreck moaning as they chafed against the steel skin of the submarine. Hassan shivered, it sounded like the pipes of a discordant church organ.

"Mother-*fucker*!" yelled Jonah, slapping the back of Vitaly's chair in frustration. "Rudder! Rudder! Vector that engine thrust!"

"*Nyet!*" protested Vitaly. "We come out with least resistance with direct reverse! Your plan will wedge us, kill us all!"

"Listen, you Ruskie fuck," said Jonah. "This isn't my first time stuck in the *Richard Thompson*. We need to wriggle our way out. A straight reverse thrust will create too much friction."

"I disagree," said Vitaly. "You make worst captain."

"I'm not asking you, I'm fucking telling you," retorted Jonah. "Start shaking the *Scorpion*'s ass until we pull our nose out of this goddamn wreck. If we run the batteries to zero with your bullshit, I am going to use my last moments in this glorified sewer pipe beating the ever-loving shit out of you with a fucking wrench. I'll just keep *beating* and *beating* and *beating* until I fucking asphyxiate."

"*Yob tvoyiu mat,*" grumbled Vitaly. He complied with the order, harshly jamming the rudders back and forth as the engines roared to full power. The *Scorpion* shifted back and forth by the stern, unable to pull herself free.

Jonah and Vitaly's exchange barely registered as Hassan sat behind them on the deck of the command compartment. He leaned against the bulkhead, knees pulled nearly to his chin, alone in his thoughts.

Maybe it wouldn't matter if they freed themselves. Maybe it'd be better to take his chances in the lockout chamber, make one last push for the surface as nitrogen narcosis numbed his mind and quelled the grief. The doctor fixated on the image of his mother splayed out in ankle-deep wastewater, eyes open, heart slammed to a sudden stop by electrocution. He had lost her, then found her, only to lose her again, and the grief the second time around was infinitely worse.

Everyone had left him alone as he prepared her body, removing her wet, filthy clothing, washing her face and hands as best as he could. He wrapped her from head to toe in the last of the clean white sheets. The first layer he arranged like a wedding dress from a long-forgotten picture. The second he bound up like a funeral shroud. Sewing her into the sheets with one careful stitch after another, the doctor kissed her forehead for the last time. Finishing his work, he'd realized he couldn't bear to place her in the freezer with the other bodies. He instead placed her in her bunk, closing the curtains behind as he left.

Hassan's attention snapped back to the present. With a scraping, metallic groan, the *Scorpion* pulled loose, shuddering as she reversed out of the shifting wreckage. Beams and deck plates rained down from the SS *Richard Thompson James*, slamming against the steel hull one after another, until, with one last wobble, the *Scorpion* slipped free and retreated into unobstructed waters.

"Straight back," commanded Jonah. "Maintain full power to rear thrust. Leave the rudders alone."

"So we live," said Vitaly, frowning. "Hooray for us."

"Aren't you glad I'm not beating the shit out of you right now?" asked Jonah.

"Yes, yes. Very glad."

"Nicely done," congratulated Hassan. Despite his admiration, the doctor's budding trust in the American was not without its reservations. Jonah still had a disconcerting habit of presenting a plan with unassailable confidence, then behaving with just as much surprise as everybody else when it actually worked.

"Vitaly, seriously, good work," said Jonah. "I couldn't be more pleased. I'm going forward to check the rest of our motley crew."

"Who is number one helmsman? Who is best of best?"

"You are," answered Jonah, pretending to kowtow as he backed his way out of the compartment. "I bow before the skills of the master. Now there is a certain pirate I'm trying to keep an eye on—I'll be back in a moment. Set a westerly course towards the coast, silent running."

"You still worst captain," said Vitaly, smiling as he punched in helm instructions. "Now go check on our pet pirate while I steer submarine."

Yes, go check on the pirate, thought Hassan, pulling himself to his feet. While Hassan had no idea how to approach Alexis or what to say to her after his mother's accident, he didn't relish the idea of Jonah giving her too much attention. He would have to talk to her sometime, but hoped to put it off for as long as possible. It was all just too confusing … too painful. In the meantime, he was confident Jonah would keep an eye on Dalmar.

Hassan wasn't quite sure what to make of the massive Somali yet. The ready-to-kill, ready-to-die attitude was perhaps heroic on some level, but Hassan sensed there was something deeper, more complicated at play. He waited until Jonah was well out of hearing range before taking a seat next to Vitaly at the pilot's console.

"Don't worry about Jonah," said Hassan. "He's … he's an asshole."

"Yeah, asshole. But *our* asshole. So maybe I don't mind so much. And he right this one time."

"But that doesn't mean your idea wouldn't have worked."

"Maybe," said Vitaly. "Maybe not. I more happy to be alive than correct, no?"

Alexis walked into the command compartment, wiping sweat off her forehead. Hassan glanced in her direction, then riveted his gaze firmly at the deck, unwilling to make eye contact. *Maybe she needs to see Vitaly. Maybe she will go back to the engine room.* Uncomfortable, Vitaly rose from his seat and busied himself on the far side of the compartment with his back to the pair.

The tank-top-wearing engineer stood for a moment, one hand playing with the stiff fingertips of the welder's glove on the other hand, waiting for the doctor to acknowledge her. When he didn't, she sat next to him in

Vitaly's seat, staring at him until he looked up at her.

"I need to talk to you." Her voice was serious, halting. "About Fatima."

"You needn't say anything. Everyone's been very kind."

"It's important."

"Alexis, there's nothing—"

"Could you shut up for a minute?" She leaned forward cupped his chin, forcing him to look at her.

Hassan nodded, silenced by her outburst.

"I know your mother didn't exactly take to me during the short time we knew each other," she began. "She knew somehow that I ... I could feel her watching me. Knew she didn't approve. But she was your mother. When we were being hit with those depth charges, there was smoke and fire and electrical discharge. Things were going very wrong in the engine room. Worse than you knew. Your mother came in to help. She said Jonah sent her. Hassan, she was incredibly brave, did everything I asked, but then, we got hit hard and lost computer control. I needed to bypass the control system to switch to manual mode. I thought the electrical panel was dead. I told her to open it for me."

Hassan squeezed his eyes shut and shook his head. If couldn't see her talking, maybe the words wouldn't matter.

"I should have known it was still electrified." Alexis looked down at her lap. "I didn't check first. She didn't know what she was doing. She wouldn't have known the risks. I'm just so sorry." She put her face in her hands and sobbed quietly.

After a moment, Hassan put his hand on her knee. "She was a scientist. She was not inexperienced with dangerous equipment."

Alexis wiped the tears from her cheek and choked back another sob. "But … I can't stop thinking about it, can't stop seeing her face. Hassan, it's my fault. It should have been—"

"Don't you dare say it," he whispered, his voice rough-edged with grief and anger and … and he didn't know what else. "Don't you dare say it should have been you."

She looked up at him, her eyes brimming with tears.

"But it's my fault—"

Overwhelmed with conflicting emotions, he sprang to his feet and towered over her, his face crimson with rage. "Why are you even still here?" he demanded.

Alexis stared up at him, eyes wide.

"I all but kidnapped you!" His voice got louder with every word. "Every second you are in my presence, your life is at risk. You have no business here. None! Go home, go back to your real life."

Without thinking, Alexis jumped up, whipped off the welder's glove, and slapped him hard across the face.

"Nobody talks to me like that!" She gripped the glove like a vise in one hand and pointed at his chest with the other. "You don't get to yell at me. *Ever.* Or make decisions on my behalf. I got left on the *Conqueror* by accident. So what? You were just as surprised as I was. You're not a mystery, Hassan. I could tell instantly that you were doing the wrong thing for the right reasons. So maybe I wanted to tag along at first, have myself a little adventure. Run away with a beautiful doctor on a stolen yacht, and go home with, I don't know, a story none of my friends could beat when we talked shit at the hometown bars. But I'm not fucking stupid, no matter what you think."

"I don't think you're stupid." His voice dropped as his

hand unconsciously touched the bright red mark on his face.

"But that was before Charles Bettencourt nearly succeeded in murdering all of us. And you want me to leave? Now?"

"I don't want you to end up like—"

"You know the second I get off this submarine he's going to come looking for me. None of us are safe while he's still out there. You just don't want me to be your fucking burden anymore."

Hassan threw his hands up in frustration and turned his back to Alexis, unwilling to trust himself to say anything more.

"Fine," she said. "Screw you, too. I'm sorry about your mother, whether or not she thought much of me. But next time you talk to me like that, we are done."

The doctor didn't sit back down again until the sounds of Alexis stomping away long since subsided.

"Ouch," said Vitaly, interrupting the silence. "That was brutal."

"Don't pile on," Hassan mumbled.

"She care about you," said Vitaly, ignoring the doctor's command.

"She's just trying to stay alive like the rest of us." Hassan's whole body felt hollowed out, arms and legs like empty appendages. Despite Jonah's courageous words, everything seemed so doomed. Maybe it was a fool's errand after all, and he the fool. People like him and Alexis didn't get happy endings, not with a man like Bettencourt chomping at their heels.

Avoiding Alexis would be difficult given the small size of the submarine, but becoming further entangled was not a good idea. He shook his head and started to walk away.

"Wait," said Vitaly. "Don't leave. I must show you important thing. Dive chamber has video feed, recorded to central computer. I think you should see this."

"There's a video recording of my swim outside of the sub?" asked Hassan. "When I disabled the transmitter?"

"No, no," said Vitaly. "There is video of when you return to diver chamber. Is very important you see."

Hassan didn't want to see and said so. He was still acutely aware of the aftereffects—sore rib cage, lingering cough, the awful sensation that he hadn't quite expelled the last of the seawater from his lungs. Regardless of his feelings, Vitaly cued up the video feed on his terminal screen.

The single screen held two feeds. Fatima swayed from side to side, staring at the flooded, open lockout chamber. Bright white inside, it was open to the complete darkness of the abyss. Hassan registered a pang of shock and hurt seeing the images of his mother.

Out of the darkness, he saw himself swimming towards the light, convulsing, the autonomic response of his lungs forcing his abdomen to violently contract and spasm. The doctor wasn't swimming so much as he was crawling through the water, ineffectually flailing his hands, reaching for anything to drag himself inside. The lack of sound in the video served only to make the events more horrifying. He wanted to look away but couldn't. He watched the tears stream down his mother's face. She'd seen the convulsions, the missing pony bottle, the broken flashlight dangling from his wrist.

In the video, the doctor found a handhold on the outer rim of the chamber, dragged himself inside and struggled to close the outer door. He watched himself take a massive lungful of air, his mouth sucking in seawater, eyes rolling back into his head as he seized up. The exterior slammed shut but did not lock. His mother struggled to reverse the sequence, failing. She tried again and again, hands shaking, tears flowing like a burst pipe.

Then Fatima screamed, silent over the pre-recorded video feed.

Alexis scrambled up the interior boarding ladder to the chamber behind Fatima and shoved the older woman out of her way. The engineer ran through the same sequence. When it failed, Alexis ripped off the panel cover. Sparking wires dangling, she touched leads against each other until water expelled from the chamber, draining into unseen vents in a massive, foamy whirlpool. On the screen, Hassan lay dead on the deck.

So this is what it's like to have an out-of-body experience, he thought as he stared at his own drowned corpse.

Alexis pulled open the heavy interior door the chamber and squeezed in. There was barely enough room for her and the collapsed doctor. The young woman listened for breath but found none. She checked for a pulse and shook her head in frustration. Fatima buried her head in her hands.

The young Texan straddled the doctor's body and pounded on his chest with both hands, trying to restart his heart, force the seawater from his lungs. She leaned over his cold, motionless body and her lips met his. Air rushed into his lungs, his chest rising.

Watching the video, Hassan unconsciously touched his lips, as if he could detect some tiny residual sensation of her lifesaving breath. On screen, his entire body contracted with enough force to throw Alexis into a bulkhead. The doctor continued convulsing, pink-flecked foam gathering at his lips.

Decompression sickness, he thought, diagnosing the symptoms with clinical precision. Systemic pain, pink-flecked foam from the lungs, it couldn't be anything else. To reach him, Alexis had been forced to initiate a rapid, dangerous decompression. All of the gasses that had saturated into his blood and tissues were now expanding inside the doctor's body like a shaken soda can, gathering in his joints, bloodstream and spine.

On the video, Alexis sealed the inner door and ordered Fatima to re-engage the pressurization sequence. Alexis winced, her ears popping as the pressure inside rapidly built, slowing the doctor's unconscious convulsing. Fatima tried to ease the pressure build-up, but Alexis urgently waved for her to speed it up, faster, fast enough to save the doctor's life.

The pressure leveled off and Alexis held the breathing doctor in her arms like a limp rag doll. His skin was still blue from the cold and lack of oxygen but he did not shiver. She zipped down half of his wetsuit and felt inside his armpits.

She's checking core temperature, he realized. She knows I'm hypothermic.

He watched as Alexis unzipped the rest of the wetsuit, slipping his naked body out of the neoprene. Vitaly looked slightly away from the screen, preserving some modicum of modesty. Alexis stripped off her wet tank top to a sports bra. Pulling off her cutoff shorts, she rolled the doctor's inert body onto her own, holding him in her arms, rubbing his skin, warming him with her own body heat.

Mercifully, Vitaly killed the video feed. It presumably

continued for hours as Fatima and Alexis fought the hypothermia and pressure sickness. All Hassan remembered was waking up in his own bunk.

"I show you this," said Vitaly, turning to look at Hassan, "because if someone feel this way about me, I would want to know."

Hassan opened the door to the armory in the far stern of the submarine. He'd hoped it was empty; somewhere he could spend a few hours sorting medical kits alone with his thoughts.

"It's the butcher come to see me again," Dalmar said, looking up. The pirate sat cross-legged on a towel he'd draped over the deck, a disassembled assault rifle laid in front of him.

"I see you're making yourself at home."

"Indeed," said Dalmar as he reassembled the freshly cleaned and oiled rifle. "Home is in the company of my friends and brother."

"Aren't your friends and brothers back home? In Somalia?"

"My men are in Somalia," said Dalmar. "My brother is here, with me."

"I don't follow."

"It's simple, very simple," said Dalmar. "Your Captain Jonah saved me at the risk of his own life. This makes him my friend."

"He's saved all of us," said the doctor.

"But you," said Dalmar. "I do not particularly like you. You are not my friend, but you are my brother. Your mother's blood flows through my veins, just as it flows through yours. We are family now. You are brother Doctor Hassan Nassiri. I am brother Dread Pirate Dalmar Abdi. Our mother has been killed by our sworn enemy."

"I've never had a brother before." The pirate's statement was so bold, so genuine, Hassan could do little but accept it at face value.

"I have spoken with Jonah," announced Dalmar, reaching across the assault rifle to clasp Hassan's hands in his own. "He has agreed to bring me home to my soldiers. There is much to do, much planning to be prepared if my friend needs me in the battle of Bettencourt."

"I will be sad to see you go," Hassan said, his hands bound by the pirate's. *"Asalaam alaykum* ... and safe journeys."

"I wish peace upon you as well," said Dalmar. "But there is little peace in my country. My friend is taking me to the fishing grounds of another dear and trusted friend. I will find my men there. But as my time with my friend and brother draws short, I find myself troubled."

"Troubled? How?"

"Brother Hassan the Butcher, I have come to a crossroads. I am a man who has outlived his purpose. I am not a revolutionary, I am a fox. I love to play this ancient game of hide and seek—deadly as it may be. But the game's rules are always set by the hyena. When the fox becomes too much trouble, the fox is called jihadist, terrorist. Illegitimate for rule, even after victory on the battlefield. For even if the fox expels or defeats the hyena, the world will shun the fox."

"What should the fox do?"

"The fox should die honorably. I vowed I would never outlive what little good I have done with my life."

"And what of Jonah? And myself? How do we fit into this ancient game of fox and hyena?"

"This I do not know," admitted Dalmar. "I think Jonah is a man who will only play a game by his own rules. But he is no hyena. And this changes everything."

"Indeed."

"Enough with this idleness." Dalmar released Hassan's hands and slapped his thighs, abruptly ending the musings. "We are speaking like two old women. The Russian—find out if he likes me. Will you do that for me, brother?"

"Vitaly?" Hassan asked, taken aback. "I guess I can ask," he said, despite having absolutely no idea how to broker such a request.

"Good!" The pirate smiled mischievously. "He is very beautiful, you think so? Maybe he would make the fox happy."

A pirate who asks before the taking, thought Hassan. Hardly a blood-thirsty brigand. Perhaps they weren't so different after all.

"Everyone assemble in the command compartment," crackled Jonah's voice over the intercom.

Hassan sat up in his bunk, but an overwhelming pall of grief prevented him from moving any further. Passing by, Dalmar extended his hand, pointing at the doctor with a single extended index finger.

"Come with me, my brother," he ordered.

The pair made their way into the command compartment, joined by Alexis from the engine room. Vitaly sat down at a central computer console and the others crowded around him. Jonah pushed his way to the center of the pack.

"This," Jonah began, pointing to plans of Anconia Island on the screen, "is the Bettencorps fortress."

Dalmar snickered. "And the thermal exhaust port is the key to the fortress."

"Thermal exhaust port? I don't get it," said Hassan.

"It's a Star Wars joke," Alexis said without looking at the doctor.

"Anconia Island is a massive, heavily fortified, heavily reinforced target," Jonah went on. "She's built off the same underpinnings as North Sea oil platforms, designed to take typhoons and tsunami alike. We could ram her with the *Scorpion* at full speed and it wouldn't so much as knock a pen off Charles Bettencourt's desk."

"Please say ramming Anconia is not plan," said Vitaly.

"It's not the plan," said Jonah. "In fact, I'd like everybody to hear *your* plan."

Vitaly looked around and cleared his throat. "This based on talk with captain," he said. "We think Bettencorps jettison chemical weapons in water, this is source of red tide. Source of problem Fatima find. Problem she die for."

"He's turned the Arabian Sea into a sacrifice zone," said Hassan. "Killing nearly all multicellular sea life in the dumping grounds and harming coastal peoples, as you witnessed."

"My mother came to believe Bettencorp was dumping illegal germs and chemicals from a long-defunct Soviet weapons program. Something she called the Dead Hand."

"Somebody's certainly dumping seriously bad shit in the area," said Jonah. "Not run of the mill industrial waste. The leaky barrels on the beach and sick people I heard about from Burhaan, the fisherman who rescued Klea and me, also seem to confirm it." He gestured toward the computer screen. "Vitaly and I have been analyzing the *Scorpion*'s computer systems And while they don't directly confirm the dumping activities, it turns out the computers reveal a lot more about Anconia Island and her operations than would first appear."

"Like what?" asked Alexis.

"You look now." The Russian flicked open a menu, displaying a rotating 3D display of Anconia Island. He zoomed in on a massive support pillar at the end of the floating runway. The virtual camera broke through the pillar's skin, revealing a massive high-security server farm within.

"If dumping records anywhere, it here," said Vitaly.

"So we need to steal the records. Without that data, anything we say will be unfounded," Hassan mumbled.

"How does this work?" asked Alexis. "How do we even find what we're looking for? What are we supposed to do when we find it, carry the servers out by hand? There must be two hundred!"

"You think analog," said Vitaly with a smile. "We live in digital world. This is clever bit. In examination, I come across many orphan algorithms. I believe *Scorpion* software basically same as Anconia Island."

"So we have a stripped down version of the same operational software," said Jonah. "Rather than taking the useless code out, the original designers just disabled the unused sections."

"That's where I find heel of Achilles." Vitaly looked up, beaming.

"The thermal exhaust port," Dalmar boomed again. "Key to destroying the Death Star."

Vitaly nodded at Dalmar and went on. "Key to everything is catastrophic power loss event," continued Vitaly.

"Or if computer system think Anconia Island has catastrophic power loss event. All of island will shut off computer terminals and switch to emergency battery backup. Then island uses dedicated satellite system to copy all data to remote server farm."

"For backup and safekeeping," added Jonah.

"So?" said Alexis.

"Weak point!" Vitaly exclaimed. "I know all confusing—all talk of thermal port, heels of Achilles."

"Jonah, spell it out for us," Hassan said.

"Okay." Jonah took a deep breath. "I sneak aboard Anconia Island. I break into the server room. I tell the computer system that there is a catastrophic power loss. But when the servers back themselves up at the remote site, we will divert the data stream to servers of our choosing."

"We have servers?" asked Hassan.

"We don't need servers of our own," said Jonah, grinning. "This is where it gets good. Activist and environmental organizations have established drop-box servers for corporate and governmental whistleblowers. Anyone can dump data into these, but nobody can access the information but the recipient. Not all of them will be able to process a high-speed mega-data-dump like this, but all it takes is one. So a bunch of Greenpeace types pick through the data, find the disposal records, and the secret goes worldwide. We can provide a little hand holding if necessary, but believe me—the data dump will arouse curiosity. I'm sure many have their suspicions about Anconia Island already."

"I'm stuck on the part where we go back to Anconia Island," said Alexis. "Aren't we running from those guys?"

"That's the easy part," said Jonah. "We follow a resupply

ship straight in. It will completely mask our signature. Vitaly, you think you can handle that?"

"Is no problem," said Vitaly with a smirk. "Easy peasy for number one pilot Vitaly."

"Good, I like easy peasy," said Jonah. "We'll briefly surface next to the jetway a couple of hours before sunrise. I'll wear mercenary clothes and use our dead sub captain's security badge to let myself into the server farm. With a little luck, it'll just be a matter of walking in, loading Vitaly's hack and walking right back out again."

"You won't be alone," Hassan said. "I'm coming with you."

"I hate to be the one who keeps pointing out all the obvious flaws in this amazing plan," said Alexis. "But what if the security badge doesn't work? Or if Vitaly's code doesn't work?"

"I don't know," said Jonah with a shrug. "We'll probably end up getting shot."

"Great back-up plan." She looked at Hassan and back to Jonah. "Okay, let's go expose this bastard," said Alexis. "Or get Jonah and Hassan shot."

"Or both," Vitaly said with a grim laugh. "Both always possibility. Doctor save my life, but Jonah worst captain ever."

Jonah stood on the deck of the surfaced *Scorpion* with Dalmar and his crew, watching as a rusted-out pirate mothership drifted closer. The approaching vessel was in bad shape. Maybe a lifetime ago it was a pleasure yacht, but now it was a chopped-down, welded-over Frankenstein with years of rust running down every scupper. How the pirates even kept it running was beyond Jonah's imagination.

The maroon waters around them stank of death. Pools of blood-red algae bloomed, discoloring the sea itself. Poisons had leached into the schools of fish, suffocating them. Their silvery, bloated corpses dotted the water like stars in an endless sky. Jonah coughed and his eyes watered—the smell was unbearable.

Beside him lay three black body bags filled with frozen corpses and the sheet-wrapped body of Professor Fatima Nassiri. Hassan knelt down beside the cotton-encased body, placing a hand on his mother's shrouded shoulder.

"I'm impressed you didn't need a radio to find your fighters," Jonah said to Dalmar as he pointed towards the fishing boat.

"A radio is not necessary," replied Dalmar. "Not when you know the ways of the sea and the ways of men."

The pirate ship gently bumped against the hull of the submarine as dozens of unsmiling men leaned over the railings, ancient rifles and RPG's sloppily slung over shoulders.

Dalmar waved and greeted them in the local language, then pointed to the stitched up wound on his neck. Several men nodded and then tossed bow and stern mooring lines to Alexis and Vitaly, who secured the pirate vessel alongside.

"I regret I will not accompany you on your infiltration," said Dalmar, watching as a boy rolled a boarding ladder over the side.

"Me too," said Jonah. "What do you think of our odds of survival?"

Dalmar's eyes flickered over Jonah's crew and landed on Vitaly, locking their gazes long enough for the Russian to blush and answer with a sly smile.

Did I miss something between those two? Jonah thought.

The pirate turned his gaze back to Jonah. "When you fight such men, you must welcome death."

Shit. He's not giving us even odds. Jonah sighed and nodded, acknowledging the grim appraisal.

Two pirates dropped down the boarding ladder, shirtless men holding the aluminum-and-wood frame in place with their own body weight. One of the men against the railing waved his arms and started speaking the rapid-fire local dialect. Dalmar responded in kind, and for the first time, the pirates at the railing broke out into smiles and uneasy chuckles.

"He said they missed me!" exclaimed Dalmar as he stepped onto the ladder. "They thought I was dead. But nothing can kill Dread Pirate Dalmar Abdi!"

"Any news of Klea?" asked Jonah.

Dalmar looked up and asked his men. Several shook their heads. Dalmar shrugged. There was no message to translate.

"Tell your men we wish we could show them more hospitality," said Jonah, gesturing to the four bodies on the deck. "But they've arrived just in time for a funeral detail."

"We understand," said Dalmar. "We have seen much death as well."

Beside them, Hassan busied himself by attaching roping chains and other weights to the feet of the body bags. Finishing, he stood up.

"I believe we're ready to bury the bodies of the mercenaries," said Hassan. "Anyone want to say anything?"

"Good riddance," said Alexis.

"I say something," said Vitaly, stepping forward. He bowed his head and cleared his throat, hands folded in front of him.

"Go ahead," said Jonah, nodding as everyone circled around the three black body bags. When Vitaly began to speak, Dalmar stepped off the ladder to stand beside him.

"You have died," began Vitaly. "Captain Jonah killed you. But that does not mean he think you bad men. Some of you my friends and I am very sad you dead. There many reason for soldiers to come to far side of world. Together we did bad things, but some of us did bad things because we know nothing else. And for many soldiers, war never stop, even if fighting stop. May you find peace in death you not find in life."

With that, Vitaly and Hassan slid the three bodies off the submarine's deck, one after another. They each splashed into the water and disappeared into the depths in a cloud of expunging bubbles. The act felt sacrilegious, cruel, a debasement of the human body to consign it to such foul waters.

"I don't know if that was a eulogy or an exorcism," Alexis mumbled.

Hassan looked at his mother's body, then to Jonah.

"I know I'm supposed to say something," he said, loud enough for the entire crew to hear. "But I can't. And I can't bury her with them. Not in these waters—they represent everything she lost her life fighting."

"Brother Hassan," said Dalmar, stepping forward and wrapping a massive arm around the doctor' shoulders. "Allow me to take our mother's body. I will bury her to the customs of my tribe. She will be placed in consecrated ground forever facing the Holy City. I swear to you she will be honored as a beautiful Moroccan princess. My people will protect her grave and they will always welcome you as a clan elder."

"I'd … I'd like that," whispered Hassan.

The crew of the *Scorpion* surrounded Fatima's body and slipped their hands underneath her wrapped form, raising her up. They silently carried her to the pirate vessel. Solemn pirates reached down and lifted Fatima the final few feet, laying her body on a low interior bench in the cool shade.

Away from the others, Dalmar looked Jonah in the eyes and placed a hand on the American's arm.

"I must leave now, my friend," said Dalmar. "May you be victorious in your quest. May you find success or die honorable deaths. And when you need your army, you will have it."

CHAPTER 20

Anconia Island rose tall and proud into the moonlit night, skyscrapers jutting against the pinpricked fabric of the heavens. Far below the glass and steel buildings and their massive rising columns of supporting concrete and steel lurked the submarine *Scorpion*. Thirty feet beneath the surface and masked by the man-made island, Jonah felt nothing but confidence in their hiding place as he marched into the command compartment.

"Captain's naked," said Vitaly, shielding his eyes as Jonah Blackwell strode in wearing nothing more than a tan and a large waterproof bag slung over one shoulder.

"Again?" blurted Alexis.

"What do you mean, *again*?" said Jonah.

"Ha!" shouted Vitaly. "Alexis is Peeping Tina."

Jonah plopped the waterproof bag onto the deck and sighed.

"Fine!" said Vitaly, exasperated. "If nobody ask, Vitaly ask. Captain, why must you be naked?"

"My Russian friend, I assure you there is a perfectly logical reason for being naked," said Jonah, gesturing towards himself. "Our mission demands it. Indeed, this is tactical nudity."

Hassan stuck his head through the hatch, and glanced at the assembled crew.

"What are you waiting for?" asked Jonah. "Come on in!"

"Jonah, I genuinely do not understand your orders." Hassan stepped gingerly over the hatch threshold and into the command compartment, wearing nothing but a tea towel over his privates and a flush on his face.

Alexis whistled and then looked behind her as if it wasn't her.

"Vitaly should get naked, too?" The helmsman pretended to begin unbuttoning his shirt. "Maybe this Vitaly-kind-of-party."

"Please don't," said Hassan with a groan.

"Here's the deal." Jonah hefted the waterproof bag again and prepared to climb up to the lockout chamber. "We're not going to surface the *Scorpion*. We'll exit the lockout chamber, swim up through the water and sneak onto Anconia. Once we're out of the water, we crack open this dry-bag and dress in mercenary clothing. Just like crossing the Rio Grande."

"I'm Moroccan," said Hassan, playing indignant. "Not Mexican. And another thing—I understand the concept, but wearing nothing, not even a pair of underwear? What difference could a pair of underwear possibly make?"

"I ... didn't think of that," admitted Jonah.

"Too late now!" Vitaly laughed. "We have seen *yelda* already."

"Guys!" said Jonah. "You're thinking about this all wrong. Imagine you're telling this story at a ritzy country club someday. Would you rather say you broke into a high-security facility, or that you broke into a high-security facility while buck-ass nekkid?"

"It does have certain ring," admitted Vitaly. "But what is club of country?"

"Just be safe," said Alexis. "Vitaly got us into the systems—I'll be watching over Anconia's internal security feed the whole time."

"Our guardian angels," said Hassan. He risked a glance at Alexis.

"Sure," said Alexis. "But a guardian angel that won't be able to do a damned thing if you get caught."

"Not planning on getting caught," said Jonah.

"Name one thing you've done that ever went according to plan," said Hassan.

Ignoring Hassan's crack, Jonah stepped onto the ladder to begin the climb towards the lockout chamber in the conning tower. "Onwards and upwards," he said. "Alexis, you're in command until I'm back."

"Holding station thirty feet below surface," said Vitaly. "You clear to exit."

Hassan followed behind Jonah, glancing up as he put a hand on a rung of the ladder. He grimaced and looked away.

Jonah opened the door to the lockout chamber and climbed into the closet-sized space. Hassan squeezed himself in next to the American and sealed the hatch behind him. Alexis followed up the ladder, finding her station at the controls, watching them through a narrow portal.

"This is going to be a cinch," said Jonah. "We flood the lockout chamber, open the exterior door, and swim out. There's a lot of air in the waterproof bag, it's going to rocket us straight to the surface. Just hold on."

"I'll have you know I nearly died the last time I attempted this," said Hassan.

"Just remember to slowly exhale as you ascend."

Hassan combed through his brain for a moment to come up with an answer. "The air in our lungs will be expanding as we rise to the surface. Unless we release that pressure, we risk pulmonary embolism and death."

"Bingo," said Jonah. "Let's not pop a lung if we don't have to."

Outside the chamber, Alexis shot a twitchy thumbs-up through the portal window, her reservations painted across her face.

"I suppose we should just get this over with," said Hassan.

"Unless you want to stick around and snap each other with gym towels."

Ignoring Jonah, Hassan gave the thumbs-up to Alexis. Air hissed and cold seawater rushed up from vents in the deck, flooding the chamber. Jonah and the doctor floated up to the top of the chamber and filled their lungs with one final breath.

Jonah ducked underneath the surface and released the outer hatch door. Both he and Hassan took hold of the waterproof bag and pushed themselves out of the chamber. The massive jetway floated above them, shadowing the submarine from the moonlight of the predawn hour. Jonah and Hassan rose through the thirty feet of water separating themselves from the surface, drawn upward by the buoyant bag, each exhaling a tiny trail of silver bubbles.

The bag broke the surface at the foot of a massive concrete pillar next to the floating aircraft runway. Jonah hefted the bag over his shoulder and dragged himself up a ladder onto the runway, Hassan close behind. The two dressed themselves in fatigues and pulled ballcaps low over their eyes and wet hair. Jonah drew two pistols from the bag—his pearl-handled .45 and Hassan's Moroccan military-issue 9mm—checked them and handed the smaller to the doctor. They stood up and straightened their disguises. Jonah nodded, stuck a small radio into his ear and kicked the empty waterproof bag off the side of the runway and into the ocean. It quietly burbled and slipped beneath the surface with a trail of bubbles.

The two men casually walked towards a massive reinforced hangar door built into one the circular pylon holding the superstructure aloft. Jonah scanned the stolen security badge against a reader. The hangar doors slid open, revealing an immaculately clean white vault filled with rows of warm, humming computer servers.

"Security pass worked," whispered Jonah, holding a finger to his earpiece. "Entering the vault."

"Good," crackled Alexis's voice from the other end of the connection. "Vitaly has control of the hacked security feed. I'm watching your every move, anybody else is going to see a pre-recorded loop. Find the command and control terminal at the far end of the room."

Jonah led the way to a computer console at the opposite side of the circular room, the doctor following closely behind. He sat down at the console and booted up the computer while Hassan stood guard, pistol in hand.

"We're there," said Jonah. "What now?"

"Take the memory drive out and plug it into the command terminal," ordered Alexis. "Vitaly says it will mimic a scheduled software update and bypass the lockout protocols. When the island experiences the power-loss event, the updated programming will have Anconia's servers dump to the whistleblower drop-box servers instead of the corporate remote site."

Jonah drew a solid-state memory drive out of his pocket and plugged it into the terminal. The screen flashed, loading Vitaly's hacked software update. Completing the process, the terminal automatically shut down and restarted with the new programming.

"Done," said Jonah.

"Now we crash the power management server," said Alexis. "Remember to get out before the barn doors fly off."

"Easy enough," said Jonah, getting up from his chair. "Hell, we could be in Oman by breakfast, catch the fallout on CNN from a swanky hotel room."

"Don't get cocky," said Alexis. "But I'm definitely up for room service—if you're buying. From a separate room. In a different hotel."

"Which server are we looking for?" asked Jonah.

"I'm watching you over the cameras," said Alexis. "I want you to go one row to your left—strike that, your right. Then down three servers. Yes, that's the one."

Jonah and Hassan looked at the blinking black server, then at each other. It seemed indistinguishable from every other identical unit.

"Are you certain?" said Hassan into the radio. "They may not have noticed the software update, but they will *definitely* notice this."

"Plug in the second memory drive I gave you," said Alexis over the radio.

Hassan and Jonah looked over the server, pushing and prodding at it.

"I don't see a place to plug this in," said Jonah.

"An off-switch would probably work just as well," said Alexis. "Keep looking. Hold on—I'm getting activity. I see security personnel and mercenaries mobilizing. It's disorganized, but something is definitely happening. They may be on to you."

"How much time do we have?" demanded Hassan.

"I don't know," said Alexis. "Just hurry."

The doctor frantically circled the matte-black server, feeling over the sides, the top, circling it trying to find a switch or a port, anything that would allow him access into the computer itself.

Hassan looked up, just in time to see Jonah run towards him with a fire axe raised high over his head. The doctor tripped over his own feet and fell back as Jonah yelled a war cry, swung the axe and buried the metal head into the server. Yanking the blade out of the blinking machine, Jonah swung again into the now-smoking face of the computer, smashing glass and sending plastic and metal shavings scattering across the clean white floor.

The doctor hopped to his feet, yanked a fire extinguisher off the wall and joined Jonah, bashing the computer server over and over again as the metal casing crumpled underneath the assault.

"Seriously?" shouted Alexis over the radio. "This is the solution? You guys are a couple of Neanderthals."

"Did she … say something?" said Hassan, short of breath.

"She called us cave men."

"I'll have … you both … know," wheezed Hassan between blows with the butt of the fire extinguisher. "I'm a … highly skilled … surgeon!"

The server made one last long, sorrowful grinding sound and expired. The floodlights around the clean room flickered and died. Dull, lifeless emergency lighting faded to life. The axe and fire extinguisher clattered as Jonah and

Hassan dropped their blunt instruments onto the dark floor. The two men ran over to the main terminal computer just in time to see the download bar budge, the first few percentage points of progress as the massive data stream shot up into the dedicated satellite overhead. Vitaly's software update was working—Anconia Island's computer servers began to spill their secrets to activist organizations across the world.

"Shit, just lost video feed," said Alexis over the radio. "Probably due to the power interruption. Nothing more you guys can do. Get out of there!"

Jonah and Hassan drew their pistols and sprinted towards the hangar door. As they drew close, the door opened on its own, the first rays of the dawn spilling through. Dark shapes moved on the other side—mercenaries. A hulking man stepped out from behind the door with an automatic rifle in hand. The massive figure fired, sending bullets ricocheting into the floor, inches from Jonah's feet, driving him back into the room.

"Go to the backup escape. The ventilation shaft," shouted Alexis through the radio. "Far side of the room! *Now!*"

Jonah fired his pearl-handled pistol twice over his shoulder as he and the doctor retreated, neither shot striking true. Behind them, Colonel Westmoreland's bulky form stepped into the emergency interior lighting, radiant in his sadistic glory. He shot just below Jonah and Hassan's ankles, ricocheting bullets off the deck and pushing the retreating intruders further into the server farm.

Jonah caught Hassan by the collar, dragging him behind a server, forcing the pair to bob and weave through the forest of computers as the colonel and his heavily-armed mercenaries stacked up at the hangar-door entrance, ready to move in.

"Go to the main terminal!" hissed Jonah. "Run!"

Hassan followed Jonah as both men sprinted the last length of the room, throwing themselves to the ground and sliding to a stop underneath the desk. Jonah risked a quick glance at the progress bar. The download had been interrupted less than ten percent into the process. It wasn't enough, not nearly enough.

Hassan ripped the vent-cover off the wall to reveal an opening that wouldn't fit a five year old.

"Now this is a proper cock-up," said the doctor.

"We're not getting out this way," Jonah said into the radio. "Alexis—you know what to do."

Alexis started to speak, but Jonah ripped out his earphone and stomped it to bits before she had a chance to say anything.

"The vent looked big enough according to the building plans," said Hassan.

"But it's not," said Jonah. "We'd probably just get shot in the ass while crawling away anyway."

"This is bad."

"It gets worse," agreed Jonah. "They've got us cornered and they know it. We should be dead already—they're trying to take us alive."

Hassan grimaced and pointed to his gun and then to Jonah. "We could … you know … each other …" said the doctor.

"Are you shitting me?" said Jonah. "No, I'm not going to let you shoot me. Let's play this out. Jesus, man."

Footsteps approached, combat boots clicking on the white plastic floor.

"Jonah fucking Blackwell, I presume," boomed Colonel Westmoreland's voice. "No doubt joined by your tagalong doctor. You're a couple of tenacious bastards, I'll give you that. What was that old ruse you pulled with the submarine? The junk shot?"

"Thought you'd want your men back," shouted Jonah at the unseen mercenary as he played for time. "Sorry they were in so many little pieces."

Colonel Westmoreland laughed. "That's the problem with using a seventy-year-old trick," he boomed. "Body parts and a fake oil slick. I knew I'd been had when I inspected a severed arm you sent floating to the surface. But by then it was too late. I've only seen one tattoo that reads 'Rats get fat while bastards die'. Nice coloration, really great fucking artwork with the death's head. Of course, I liked it a lot better when it was attached to a friend of mine. Begs the question—are you a rat or a bastard? Because right now, you're hiding like a fucking rat."

Jonah shook his head and didn't answer. In the cover of darkness under the desk, his body pressed up to Hassan, his pistol covered the room, searching for a target. The colonel's voice seemed to come from everywhere and nowhere.

"I want to make sure your situation is perfectly fucking clear," continued the colonel. "First—whatever you were trying to accomplish, my nerds have already stopped it. Second—I can shoot the left nut off a cat's ballsack at a hundred yards. That means I had to go far out of my fucking way to avoid shooting you as you ran off like a couple of little fucking *schoolgirls*."

"Much obliged," shouted Jonah back to him.

"So here's the deal," said the colonel. "If I give the order, my men are going to come in shooting and put you both the fuck down. It will be for keeps this time, that much I promise. Or—toss the peashooters and we'll settle this like fucking *men*. Fight it out hand-to-hand. In fact, I'm feeling so generous this fine morning, I'll let you both take me on. If you tap out, I'm throwing you in zip-cuffs and hauling you upstairs to meet the boss. And let me tell you—he's pissed. But if I tap out … you're free to leave."

"Utter nonsense!" exclaimed Hassan. "What will Charles Bettencourt have to say about that?"

"This is between us," said the colonel. "He can blow it right out his fancy ass. This is the fairest deal you'll ever get."

"The two of us against him," Hassan whispered. "How hard could it be?"

"Hard," answered Jonah, taking Hassan's handgun from him. "Assuming the deal is legit to begin with. But I don't see another fucking option at this point. You ever do any fighting?"

"Not since primary school," admitted Hassan.

"This won't be a schoolyard throw-down," said Jonah. "Aim for soft points. Don't bother playing fair. And for Christ's sake, keep your thumbs on the outside of your fists."

Jonah took his pearl-handled 1911 and Hassan's military pistol and threw them across the floor, sliding them to the other side of the long white room. Colonel Westmoreland emerged from the shadows, stepping on the 1911 to stop it. The colonel picked the weapon up and inspected it, nodding in approval before handing it to an associate along with his personal assault rifle and customized H&K pistol. With a sinister grin, he stepped forward, massive in his body armor, arms wide open and inviting Jonah and Hassan to attack. The other mercenaries backed out of the server room, holding Jonah and the doctor in their iron sights until the hangar doors slid shut, locking the three men in the impromptu gladiatorial arena.

"End it fast," whispered Jonah. "Go for the legs. I go left, you go right. Take him off his feet. I'll hold him, you kick his face in."

Jonah and Hassan crossed each other, picking up speed as they ran to intercept. Their adversary hunched down and charged like a linebacker. Colonel Westmoreland grunted in surprise as both legs were knocked out from underneath him. He slammed against the ground chest first, arms splaying. Before he could flip himself over, Jonah jumped on his back and wound an arm around his neck with a vicious chokehold.

But before the doctor could strike, Colonel Westmoreland jumped to his feet, Jonah hanging onto his back like a rodeo cowboy. Hassan stood in stunned silence, the mercenary towering over him.

Westmoreland raised his right leg and kicked Hassan square in the solar plexus, sending him flying back into a server, knocking both over with the brutal, crashing impact and the tinkle of broken glass. Reaching behind his head, he smashed Jonah in the face with a fist and threw him to the ground with both hands. Jonah rolled away just as the man stomped the ground where his face had just been.

Hassan drew himself to his feet, moaning and clutching his chest. Grimacing, he adopted a fighting stance, unwilling to let the pain slow him down.

"Motherfucker, you are *fast* for a drunk," said Jonah, whipping a fleck of blood off his lower lip.

"And you've got a smart fucking mouth for a dead

man," came the retort. "And you, Doc Haji—what are you so pissed about?"

"You killed my mother and my cousin," said Hassan, jutting his chin out in anger. "And I promise you this—you're not leaving this room alive."

On their feet, Hassan and Jonah circled Westmoreland like a pair of hyenas, flanking the colonel on either side. Jonah snapped a nod to Hassan and both men prepared to charge.

"You two are off to a *shitty* start," barked Westmoreland, cracking his neck and his knuckles. "I've had better fights from women."

The colonel absorbed the full force of the doctor's flying tackle as he simultaneously caught Jonah by the throat. Using Jonah like a battering ram, the colonel pinned Hassan against a server, repeatedly punching Jonah in the face with a free hand, sending the back of Jonah's head smashing into Hassan's unprotected face.

Jonah managed to wiggle free and jumped on Colonel Westmoreland's back a second time. The mercenary grabbed Jonah's wrist, wrenching it as he flipped Jonah over his shoulder and to the ground. Before Jonah could react, the mercenary thrust a shinbone into his face.

Jonah stumbled to his feet, allowing one glance over to Hassan's unconscious, crumpled form.

Shit, thought Jonah. The doctor wouldn't be much help going forward. Without a third man in the fight, it would turn into a straight-up boxing match.

"Well, now I'm fucking bored," said the colonel.

Face and hands a mess of cuts and blood, the mercenary swung at Jonah, easily breaking through the block and catching him on the chin. Jonah felt the fight leave him as he hit the blood-splattered floor, stars dancing in his blurry vision. Westmoreland violently kicked him in the side of the head, the final coup de grâce knocking Jonah into the sweet release of unconsciousness. Somewhere deep in his battered mind, Jonah felt a small spark of happiness. He hadn't won the fight—but stalling Charles Bettencourt was the next best thing.

Jonah stirred to life just as the cloudy glass panels to the penthouse elevator faded to clear. The elevator soared like a gondola over Anconia Island, rising high above the oceanic city. Jonah pushed himself to his knees, blood draining from his mouth. Beside him, Hassan had managed to push his battered body against the corner of the elevator, staring at him with empty eyes. Jonah looked back at him with a glance that said more than a thousand empty words. Their victorious captor stood above them, bulky arms crossed, tapping a steel-toed combat boot in impatience.

Colonel Westmoreland smirked as the elevator doors opened, revealing an angled, glass-roofed penthouse. The massive exterior helicopter pad clung from the side of the building, completing the architectural opulence. Charles Bettencourt's gleaming white personal helicopter idled, rotors lazily spinning, ready to depart at a moment's notice.

The colonel grabbed Jonah and Hassan by their zip-tied wrists and dragged them across the marble floor towards Bettencourt's mahogany desk.

"You're leaking," mumbled Hassan to Jonah, glancing towards Jonah's bleeding leg. The wound left a long trail of smeared blood as Jonah slid along the floor.

"Shit," Jonah groaned. "I hadn't noticed."

Silence reigned for a moment as the pair considered their fate.

"I was going to say this earlier," murmured Jonah. "But now is a good of a time as any. Doc, I've been abandoned by a lot of people in my life. You are the first one who chose to come back. I'm sorry it didn't work out like you planned."

"Maybe in another life," whispered the doctor. "We could have been friends."

"Doc," laughed Jonah, coughing up blood as he spoke, "in this life, you're the only friend I got."

The pair of wounded men passed free-standing glass panels holding parchments of colorful and ancient dragons, kraken, samurai, and geishas.

"Nice digs," commented Jonah through a mouthful of blood. "The artwork looks expensive."

"It's human skin," said Hassan, chuckling with pained, mournful snorting.

"Charming," said Jonah. "Very *Martha Stewart Living*." His face twisted with pain and amusement, joining the doctor in the absurdist giggling. Before long, the two were howling in pathetic, insane laughter at the sheer hopelessness of their situation.

Rolling his eyes, Colonel Westmoreland stopped at the foot of the desk and spun them around to face the corporate cutthroat. Hassan and Jonah drew themselves up to their knees. Charles Bettencourt stood behind the desk, arms crossed, a deep scowl on his face. His lawyer sat beside him in a wheelchair, unshaven, wearing a loose sweatshirt, and with both legs in casts.

"I don't even know where to begin." Bettencourt, shook his head in bewilderment. "The very fact that you both are alive is a testament to the *total incompetence* of my security forces."

"Nice to see you too, Chuck," said Jonah, a smile still on his bloody, swollen face. "You know—I never actually caught the name of your lapdog attorney. Nevermind that, I'm just going to call him Wheels."

"You son of a bitch!" shouted the lawyer from the wheelchair. "*You* did this to me, you fuck!"

Bettencourt scowled and held a hand to silence the man. "He knows he did it to you," said the CEO with a tone usually reserved for dealing with exceptionally stupid children. "That's why he said it."

"Boss, I brought you a gift," said Colonel Westmoreland, drawing Jonah's pearl-handled 1911 pistol out of his waistband and setting it on Bettencourt's desk. "Figured it would look good in the ol' trophy case."

"This is one classy hand-cannon," mused the CEO. "He doesn't seem the type. Vintage?"

"Look at the serial number," said Colonel Westmoreland. "Built in 1928. Beautifully restored with modern internal components. A fine weapon. I'm keeping the doctor's military-issue nine-millimeter for myself."

Bettencourt nodded and set the weapon on the desk with a click of metal against glass.

"So Wheels," said Bettencourt, putting a hand on the back of his lawyer's shoulders, "what's our exposure here?"

The colonel laughed.

"Don't you start," said the lawyer. "I'm coming off some serious painkillers, and I'm not in the fucking mood."

"Just answer the question," barked Bettencourt.

"Fine," said the lawyer. "So there's no question that we have data in the wind. The good news is that we managed to shut down the satellite uplink before more than about fifteen percent of total server capacity reached any remote servers."

"Who do they belong to?" demanded the CEO. "Competitors?"

"That's the bad news," said the lawyer. "They're whistleblower drop-boxes. Activists, NGOs, and political organizations, many of which have it in for us. So whatever they did get, they're going to be able weaponize with the help of the media. We're going to have to assume they know everything about our disposal program. The Conglomerate … well, I can't speak for how they will react."

"They speak the language of money," Bettencourt said. "And they need me. We could be on the ropes for a while, but it's far from game over. I've prepared contingency plans for just such an event. Get our legal and public relations folks mobilized. Get them everything they need to start shoring up public perception. Our Investor Relations guys know what to do to keep share prices from plummeting. I'll call our Russian friends; try to smooth things over there. Hell, Tony Hayward at BP convinced the public he gave a shit about estuaries. This should be a walk in the park by comparison. Nobody gives a flying fuck about Somalia, and *nobody* plays this game better than we do."

"And the prisoners?" asked Colonel Westmoreland.

"What prisoners?" Bettencourt said. "As far as I'm concerned, they're already dead. Don't fuck it up this time."

Colonel Westmoreland nodded and put his H&K pistol to Hassan's head, cocking the hammer with his thumb.

"Jesus!" Bettencourt shouted. "*Not* in my fucking office."

"I got to know just one thing," said Jonah as Colonel Westmoreland reached for his zip tied hands to drag him away. "Was the job offer real?"

Bettencourt sighed and put a hand on his hip. The colonel stood, waiting for the answer.

"It wasn't supposed to be this way," said the CEO. "I wanted to create a stable, secure, permanent installation off the Horn of Africa. A place that would provide economic opportunity free of national interests. But instead I was met with suspicion and violence."

"What self-serving rubbish," said Hassan, interrupting him.

"You're wrong! It's not bullshit. I was trying to *help* them, goddammit. But they're slaves. Slaves to their tradition, to their nonsensical fundamentalism, to poverty and ignorance. I wanted to set them *free*."

"By poisoning them," Hassan added.

"Well, I do admit that is truly unfortunate," murmured Bettencourt. "But new nations are expensive. As are new ideas. I came to realize these people are beyond help, they're the one nation on earth too fucking backward to even form some *semblance* of self-government. I was overextended financially, risking not just Anconia Island, but the whole of the Bettencorps empire. And then the Conglomerate came to me with a proposal that could save everything, a problem for which they required the utmost discretion. They had in their possession dangerous relics of a forgotten war—weapons so dangerous they were more valuable destroyed than sold."

"And you took these weapons," snarled Hassan, "and you buried them in the deep waters of the Indian Ocean."

"Of course I did! I was forced, *forced* to agree that the best place to hide weapons that shouldn't exist was among people who didn't matter. It was such an easy choice to make. What they wanted was so simple—their interests protected, a blind eye turned, and for that I got my bottom line secured."

"Round of applause for the despondent plutocrat," said Hassan, his voice dripping with sarcasm. "For he can never fail the world, the world can only fail him."

"Chuck, here's what I find truly amazing," said Jonah. "It's amazing that you're still failing to ask yourself a series of very simple questions. I'm disappointed, I really thought you knew us better than that."

"I'm listening."

"What do you think our objective was? To expose you to the world, only to watch you bribe and manipulate your way out of infamy? See you pay an army of lawyers and spin doctors and put a fucking smiley face on an empire of poison? Do you really think our war against you will come down to dueling interviews on *Larry King Live*?"

"Larry King went off the air in 2010, you ignorant dipshit."

"What you've failed to consider is that we do not play by your fucking rules," continued Jonah. "You cannot hide behind a rigged system. Not from us."

"Charles, what you've failed to consider," said Hassan with a smile, "is that we are just the distraction."

Bettencourt frowned, considering this new information.

"They're bluffing—" Westmoreland snapped derisively.

The CEO cut him off with a wave of a hand. "We can't take that chance." He turned to the lawyer. "Check on the status of every ship within a hundred miles. Look for anything out of the ordinary; I don't care how small it seems."

The lawyer wheeled himself over to the desk and activated the built-in screen. The mahogany surface disappeared, replaced by a computer display.

"Maybe the colonel is right, maybe you're full of shit,"

said Bettencourt, turning back to Jonah and Hassan. "But I'm not. Believe me when I say we're going to hunt and sink your submarine and kill your friends."

"How you use your little remaining time is your own business," said Hassan.

"'Cause it is *on* like motherfucking Donkey Kong," added Jonah, waggling his head.

"Found something," interrupted the lawyer. "There's a note in the file of the SS *Erno Rubik*. Cargo container supercarrier, on route from India to South Africa. They reported a fire in the generator room less than an hour ago and are currently communicating by telex only."

"Have they asked for assistance?" asked Colonel Westmoreland.

"No—we've offered several times and they've refused. Could be nothing. What should we do?"

"Contact our security team on that ship," said Colonel Westmoreland.

"Hold on," said the lawyer, squinting his eyes at the map. "The radar feed is updating. They're turning and increasing speed. I ... I think they're turning towards Anconia Island."

"Tonnage?" demanded the CEO.

"One-hundred-and-eighty-six thousand tons," said the lawyer, the blood draining from his face. "Four times the size of the *Titanic*. She's more than a thousand feet in length, one of the largest cargo ships ever put to sea. And she's on a collision course."

CHAPTER 21

Bettencourt paced behind his desk as his lawyer unsuccessfully hailed the cargo container supercarrier SS *Erno Rubik* for the fourth time. Still too far away to see from the penthouse, the massive container ship had broken away from course and increased speed to eighteen knots, bearing down on Anconia Island on a high-speed collision course.

"Come in, *Erno Rubik*," said the lawyer into the marine radio, his voice betraying fear and urgency. "SS *Erno Rubik*, please state your intentions."

From the other end, the radio crackled to life.

"Anconia Island, Anconia Island," boomed a silky baritone voice. "This is Dalmar Abdi, dread pirate captain of the SS *Erno Rubik*."

"Colonel," said Bettencourt, holding his clenched fist in front of his mouth. "I thought you told me that the pirates couldn't fucking hijack the supercarriers."

"We have a security team on that ship," protested the colonel. "We've never had a problem before—"

"I think you're having a problem now," Jonah said.

"As my first act as pirate captain," continued Dalmar. "I am renaming this fine ship the SS *Fuck Your Mother*."

There was a brief silence in the glass-roofed office penthouse, wasting precious seconds as the gargantuan ship slowly closed the gap between itself and the immobile island. Bettencourt fished a pair of binoculars out of the desk drawer and handed them to Colonel Westmoreland. The mercenary took station by the window, scanning the distance.

"I'd answer them if I were you," said Jonah, smirking. "Sounds like it might be important."

Charles bent over the desk and pressed the transmit button. "SS *Erno Rubik*," he began. "This is Anconia Island, Charles Bettencourt speaking."

Silence greeted him.

"Why won't he answer?" demanded the CEO.

"I believe he was quite clear about the name of his ship," said Hassan.

"Goddamn it," said Bettencourt, stabbing the transmit button again. "SS... *Fuck Your Mother*... this is Anconia Island, Charles Bettencourt speaking."

"Hello Charles," said Dalmar through the radio. "I've long admired your shining city upon the sea."

"I've got Jonah Blackwell and Hassan Nassiri with me. At gunpoint. Change course or we'll kill your friends."

"Hello Jonah and Hassan!" exclaimed Dalmar. "Is it true you have been captured?"

"Unfortunately yes," said Jonah, loud enough for the microphone to pick up his voice.

"Glorious!" said Dalmar. "I am so pleased you will die a good death at the hands of our sworn adversary!"

"Whoops," Jonah said, shaking his head. "We'd be a better bargaining chip if he cared about keeping us alive."

The colonel slapped Bettencourt's hand away from the transmit button.

"How well did our last chat with Dalmar go? Pirates don't bargain for their own," he hissed as he shoved the binoculars into the CEO's hands. "Look—the container ship is within visual range."

Bettencourt hit the transmit button again. "Can we talk to our security team?" he asked.

"Only if you can commune with the dead," responded Dalmar. "Your five men laid down their arms the moment they were surrounded! I was certain you would be very disappointed at their cowardice, so I executed them on your behalf."

The lawyer shuddered.

"Mr. Charles Bettencourt," continued the pirate, "I've found our rivalry thrilling, but I'm afraid the game is nearing the end. While you have earned yourself an honorable death by my hand, I have no quarrel with your people. Heed my warning. I give you a chance to evacuate Anconia Island before I strike. You have twelve minutes."

"Dalmar, buddy, this isn't a ship," countered Bettencourt. "This is a city, a city in a really nasty part of the world. You can't just tell everybody to leave. Where the hell are they going to go?"

He released the transmit button and resumed pacing, while the radio crackled silent, Dalmar unwilling to respond.

"You talk to him," demanded Bettencourt, pointing at Jonah. "Tell him to divert course, give us more time, anything!"

"Why of course," shouted Jonah, spitting flecks of blood as he spoke, filled with sudden anger. "Take a mulligan with Dalmar's 180,000-ton battering ram. He'll just stuff that ship up your ass on your schedule. How's your Tuesday? Actually, strike that—I just looked and mine's terrible."

"Order a general evacuation." the CEO said, pointing at his lawyer. "Get everyone out of the buildings and onto anything that floats—do it now!"

Around them, lights flashed and instructions appeared on wall-mounted screens. A public-address system calmly issued pre-programmed evacuation instructions.

"I'm not kidding around, Dalmar," Bettencourt said, making one last-ditch effort to speak with the pirate. "I'm sorry about the attempts on your life and that of your men. Really, I am. I've clearly underestimated you. That's my mistake. I own that. But you're making a mistake here, too. Nobody's done anything yet that we can't walk away from. I can make this right. But if you do this—if you threaten the lives of my people, your actions will follow you for the rest of your short life. I'm not leaving. I will defend this city with my life."

"Pish-posh," interrupted Hassan. "You have no intention of dying on anyone's behalf, not even your own."

"I will throw everything, *everything* I have at you," shouted Bettencourt into the radio, losing control. "And I swear by everything holy that I will end you this time."

"You have eleven minutes to try," said Dalmar. "Good luck. Dread Pirate Dalmar Abdi, Captain of the SS *Fuck Your Mother* out."

"He makes a good pirate captain," said Hassan.

"That he does," mused Jonah. "He has style. Style is very important for a pirate captain."

"He needs an eye patch though, don't you think?"

"And a parrot," Jonah nodded and squinted out the window, catching his first glimpse of the supertransport through the floor-to-ceiling penthouse windows as the massive ship bore down on Anconia Island.

"Mobilize everything!" Bettencourt shouted at the colonel. "Get all non-combatants to lifeboats and the jetway! Attack that ship!"

Face red and boiling with anger, Bettencourt picked the pearl-handled 1911 from his desk, strode up to Hassan and whipped the doctor across the face with the loaded weapon.

"Stop wasting time," Colonel Westmoreland barked. "My men will launch drones and our helicopters will assault."

No sooner had he spoken than a pack of eight triangular drones launched from underneath the island, correcting their trim and altitude with eerie synchronicity as they formed up for an attack run. The gleaming white drones were larger than Jonah had expected, each with wingspans of nearly thirty feet, jet engines whistling as they passed the penthouse at eye level.

Approaching the *Erno Rubik* fast and low, they simultaneously disgorged their missile bays into the ten-story bridge castle with a ticker-tape of white contrails. The barrage of missiles flew towards the container ship at impossible speed, tumbling out of formation as they impacted the massive bridge castle in a disorganized spread.

Flashes from the bridge castle—small arms fired at the now-retreating drones. The jet engine of a single drone puffed with white smoke and fell from the sky like a wounded bird.

"Out of missiles," reported the colonel.

"Are you fucking kidding me?" demanded Bettencourt. "That didn't do shit. Do they have time to rearm?"

"No time," Westmoreland said. "But we can order the pilots to remotely ram the ship."

"Do it." Bettencourt, breathing heavily, wiped sweat off his forehead. A disorganized patch of hair fell over his face.

Orders received, the formation of drones whipped around and lined up for a final kamikaze run at the bridge castle. One after another, they threw themselves into the tombstone-shaped bridge castle from all sides. First burst out of the structure, consuming it in black, billowing clouds of smoke.

"It's still coming!" shouted the lawyer.

"We're not done yet," said the colonel. "Just wait until my trigger-pullers get on board the *Erno Rubik*. They're a pack of heartbreakers and life-takers. If I were Dalmar Abdi, I'd be shitting my pants right about now."

"Certainly," added Hassan. "It's not as if your mercenaries have ever gotten their arses handed to them by a few pirates before."

Three Blackhawk attack helicopters swooped in after the expended drones, preparing to board and take the container ship. Two of the helicopters came in low over the bow, dropping fast-ropes onto the deck. A dozen men slid out of the aircraft, distant and oblivious to the pirate's intermittent fire into their ranks.

The third helicopter broke off from providing overwatch cover and charged the bridge. The Blackhawk turned to the side, exposing the side door gunner to strafe. The gunner fired a long staccato salvo into the bridge until the tail rotor caught a strand of nearly invisible high-tensile steel monofilament strung between bridge and the midship crane. The rear rotor blades sheared off, sending the out-of-control helicopter spinning downwards, knocking a tall stack of containers off the side of the *Erno* as it tumbled into the sea.

"Ouch," said Jonah. "That looked expensive."

"It's insured," replied Bettencourt, with a far-away look in his eyes.

"Your premiums might be going up in the near future," cracked Jonah.

The remaining two helicopters retreated from the bridge of the *Erno Rubik*, firing continuously as they strafed, hanging back and away from the wires. Heavy gunship rounds impacted the structure until the helicopters broke off the attack, out of ammunition.

The SS *Erno Rubik* was now close, too close to stop the impact.

Far below the bird's-eye view of the penthouse, the mercenary mothership made a desperate attempt to ram the cargo ship against the port side bow, frantically trying to push the cargo supertransport off course. It hit with a crushing blow, sinking her angular bow deep into the hull of the *Erno* like a prison shank. Hopelessly outclassed and disabled, the damaged ship scraped and bashed along the entire length of the *Erno Rubik* without so much as nudging the massive cargo ship an inch.

"Brace for impact!" Colonel Westmoreland shouted.

The SS *Erno Rubik* slammed into Anconia Island with the deafening impact of a tsunami. The penthouse rocked, knocking Charles Bettencourt to his knees while Colonel Westmoreland fell off his feet and onto the marble floor, glass shattering and raining down around them.

With the sound of a thousand diesel locomotives dropped into a chasm, the *Erno Rubik* drove deep into the heart of the city, splitting the fault line between platforms.

The smaller office buildings on either side crumbled, joined by an avalanche of shipping containers. From the high vantage point, Jonah watched as the *Erno Rubik* cleaved the entire artificial island in half. The container ship wallowed, covered by collapsed stacks of shipping containers and demolished buildings, weighing down on the supporting structure of Anconia itself. On the jetway far below, dazed and disoriented masses stared up, forced to witness the destruction as the very ground buckled beneath their island.

"Well," said Charles Bettencourt as he surveyed the chaos from the penthouse windows, arms crossed. "I really don't see what else I can do here. Colonel, it's been a pleasure."

With a curt nod, the spry executive walked towards the sliding glass doors to the helicopter landing pad.

"Where do you think you're going?" demanded Colonel Westmoreland, resting his bloody palm on a holstered pistol. "You are going to stay and defend this fucking position."

"Am I?" shouted the CEO, waving Jonah's pearl-handled pistol in the air. "Because I thought that's what I've been paying you for."

The colonel didn't respond, and simply flicked the leather catch off his holster, ready to draw.

Without waiting, Charles thrust his pistol towards the colonel and fired three times. The mercenary grunted and stepped back as the bullets hit him in the unprotected abdomen just below his body armor, his customized pistol slipping from his slashed palm. Wobbling on his feet, the massive soldier slowly tipped forward like a felled tree, landing face-first on the ground with a bone-rattling crash. Blood flowed out of his stomach wound, collecting in the seams between the marble tiles.

"I think I'll be leaving now," said the CEO, throwing the now-empty 1911 to the ground.

"What about me?" asked the lawyer. "Take me to the helicopter, goddammit!"

"What about you?" mimicked the CEO as he walked towards the glass doors. "I don't see a handicapped ramp."

Colonel Westmoreland rose to his knees, animated by pure rage alone. The hulking man lurched forward towards his employer, blood gushing out of his belly unstaunched and dripping down to his crotch, teeth gritted in pain and fury, fists clenched and muscles bulging. He stood transfixed as Charles Bettencourt boarded the helicopter without so much as a wayward look back to his ruined island, his betrayed men.

Screaming, the lawyer pulled himself out of the chair, dragging two cast-encased legs behind him as he pulled himself up the stairs towards the landing pad. The blades of the executive helicopter spun faster, cutting through the air, until the entire vehicle lifted off the pad and soared through the air, away from Anconia Island for the last time.

The blood-soaked colonel fixed his pain-deadened, glazed-over eyes on Jonah and Hassan. He drew a knife out of the front of his chest armor and crawled towards them. Too beaten and exhausted to fight, Jonah grimaced and thrust his zip tied hands out in a desperate act of self-protection, all the while waiting for the mercenary's knife to sink into his chest. He felt a fumbling on his zip ties, heard a snap, and the pressure around his wrists came free. Having cut him loose, Colonel Westmoreland turned his attention to the doctor to do the same.

Incredulous, Jonah and Hassan stared, rubbing their raw, bruised wrists as the colonel wobbled on his feet, face pale from blood loss. He collapsed forward onto his knees.

"Help me carry him to the elevator!" shouted Hassan.

"Give me a minute," protested Jonah as he dragged himself to his feet. Picking up his pearl-handled pistol from the ground, he half-limped, half-crawled over to the mahogany desk. Jonah threw open the top drawer, pocketing a pair of Tibaldi fountain pens, a single Mont Blanc, and a Patek Philippe wristwatch.

"What the hell are you doing?" demanded Hassan.

"I'm stealing shit, goddammit!" Jonah shouted. "Just give me just one fucking minute!"

Grunting as he carried himself over to the nearest free-standing glass slab display, Jonah kick it free of the mountings. The display tilted over, slowly at first, but then picked up speed as it fell and shattered against the marble floor. Jonah leaned over and brushed the glass off an ornately tattooed yakuza skin, rolled up the human leather and tucked it under an armpit.

"Now we can go," said Jonah. "These are worth a shit-load on the black market."

Jonah shoved himself underneath the mercenary's other massive arm. Between the two of them, they managed to drag the colonel to the elevator. Westmoreland's head lolled as he struggled to move his feet, to somehow assist with his own evacuation.

Jonah and Hassan collapsed, dropping Westmoreland to the elevator floor. The doctor stripped away the colonel's shirt, revealing an ugly pattern of blood and bullet wounds, trying to find a place to apply pressure as Jonah punched the button for the lobby before slumping beside him.

"Don't leave me here!" screamed the lawyer as the door slid shut.

"Is he going to make it?" asked Jonah, turning his attention to the colonel.

"The big man will outlive us all," said Hassan, patting the man on the chest. The doctor then shook his head at Jonah—comforting words aside, the wounded soldier had little time.

"This island's going to fall," Westmoreland whispered with a wistful, far-away baritone. "You can hear the metal fatigue. It's all snapping like so many twigs. Her spine is severed—nothing is holding her together."

"If you don't make it, do you have anybody we should talk to on your behalf?" asked Jonah, reaching underneath the mercenary's shaved head with a hand to support his thick neck.

"Not anymore." Blood dripped out of the corner of his mouth. "Any man worth seeing, I'll meet again in the next few minutes." The bleeding man coughed, his breath ragged and rattling. "Maybe I'll see my wife," he wheezed. "She was a good woman, so maybe not. It's okay; I got women in the other place, too."

"I can get him to the *Scorpion*," offered Hassan, desperately trying to think of a solution. "My facilities there are rudimentary—but he might have a chance."

"Don't bother," rasped the colonel. "This is as good a place to die as any."

With that, his eyes rolled back into his massive head and his ragged breath grew short and stopped. Hassan rolled the mercenary's eyelids shut as the elevator doors opened. Jonah and the doctor exited the elevator, leaving the inert body abandoned behind them.

The pair wove their way into the grassy courtyard, taking cover as the remaining few soldiers dashed across the field, trying to find some way off Anconia before it slipped beneath the waves. The island moaned a deep, pain-filled rumble. Driven into the fissure between the platforms, the superstructure of the SS *Erno Rubik* slipped from view, the behemoth slowly sinking into the ocean.

"We don't have long," said Jonah, surveying the destruction as an empty office building crumbled in a cloud of concrete, steel members and dust.

"What do we do?" asked the doctor as he shielded his face from the sudden blast of wind and debris.

Without a word, Jonah lead the way over to the edge of the island, a simple glass railing overlooking a three-hundred foot drop into the ocean below.

"We jump," said Jonah. He swung both legs over the side of the railing, surveying the stomach-churning drop below. Hassan mirrored his movements, and the two men sat at the edge of the precipice.

"On three?" asked Hassan.

"Maybe next time," said Jonah, pushing the doctor off the railing. The surgeon screamed, wheeling his arms and legs through the air as he fell, ending with a massive splash into the waves far below.

Jonah leapt into space. The water rushed up to meet him with incredible speed, air swooshing past his ears, while holding onto the rolled-up human leather as tightly as he could.

Clinch those buttcheeks shut, thought Jonah a split second before impact. Tumbling through the frothy water, he stared up at the surface nearly fifteen feet above him, white foam and dark sediment surrounding him. Everything was dark and cloudy, he couldn't see, couldn't think, couldn't breathe. Despite his twisted ankles, he managed two hard kicks to the surface, popping up beside the doctor. Too stunned to be angry, the doctor treaded water beside him.

A lone lifeboat from the *Erno Rubik* approached from the side, slowing as it reached them. Inside, Dalmar Abdi stood at the bow, bare-chested with a rocket-propelled grenade strapped to his back. Behind him, several more lifeboats fled towards the distant shores of Somalia, abandoning the fight.

"My friend Jonah Blackwell!" Dalmar reached down to pluck both men out of the water. "And my brother Hassan the Butcher! I am so pleased you have lived. Jonah—I believe this makes three times I have saved your life."

"But who's counting?" said Jonah as he slumped into the bottom of the fiberglass boat.

"I am counting!" said Dalmar. "You shall name your firstborn child after me!"

"What if it's a girl?" asked Hassan, collapsing next to Jonah.

"Ha!" shouted Dalmar with a frighteningly gregarious laugh. "Then Jonah must name her Dread Pirate Dalmar Abdi! A good name for a woman, she will bear many grandsons!"

With that, the pirate commander kicked the lifeboat into gear, speeding towards the *Scorpion* as she lay surfaced several hundred yards away from the mortally wounded island. Behind them, the smallest of the three platforms collapsed into the sea, sending out a massive tidal wave through the floating debris and oil. Fires broke out in the other abandoned platforms, sending columns of inky-black smoke skyward as thousands of survivors watched from the still-floating runway.

Alexis waited on the forward deck of the submarine,

weapon slung behind her back, waving the lifeboat in. Dalmar beached the craft against the deck and helped Jonah and Hassan out, one after another.

"I knew you were alive!" Alexis shouted, throwing her arms around the doctor. Hassan smiled and embraced her back despite the pain in his battered body.

"Let's get you inside," said Alexis. "Vitaly says a US Navy carrier group is inbound to rescue survivors."

"I should not be here when they arrive," said Dalmar. "My men are returning home, but—" he turned to Jonah. "May I join your crew, Captain Jonah?"

"Welcome aboard," said Jonah. "I could always use another potato-peeler. Doc—let's go. We have to move."

Arm encircling Alexis's waist, Hassan ignored him, staring at the stricken city like Lot's wife lamenting the destruction of Sodom. "I'm going to watch," he said, his voice far away. "I believe I've earned the right."

Jonah turned to see Anconia Island, still gleaming in the morning sun. The remaining two platforms failed in sequence, both halves of the city collapsing into the water with the roar of an earthquake, spilling into the sea as the floating runway detached with the sound of snapping steel cables, setting the crowded platform adrift. The debris settled, slipping beneath the waves. And within moments, it was as if the glittering island had never graced the face of the earth.

EPILOGUE

THREE WEEKS LATER ...

The *Scorpion* slipped through the luminescent fog of a cool Puget Sound morning, the sky and the surface of the ocean blending together in a seamless gradient. Silently navigating a hidden cove, the sub slowed as it approached the massive concrete dock of a long-abandoned shipyard. Jonah opened the top hatch to the conning tower, squinting against the glare. The submarine bumped up against the dock and he scrambled down the exterior boarding ladder onto the deck, pulling long mooring lines out of hidden compartments and roping the bulky length of the vessel against the concrete wall.

Hassan brought a heavy leather briefcase out of the conning tower as Jonah inspected the ropes at the docking cleats. Satisfied with his work, Jonah took the briefcase from the doctor and hopped onto the dock, walking up the length towards shore.

Frizzy brown hair blowing in the sea breeze, Marissa Jenkins purposefully strode out to meet Jonah, anger building with every step. Her eyes stared daggers and were matched by the pursed scowl of a scorned ex. Jonah suddenly found himself remembering that he'd never technically broken things off.

"Hey Issa," said Jonah, trying to break the ice with a broad smile.

Marissa stopped dead and slapped him squarely across the face, hard enough to leave a bright red handprint.

"Ow!" protested Jonah. "What was that—?"

"You said you were bringing a *ship* in for repairs," said Marissa with an accusatory tone. "That is a *submarine*. Do you have any idea how much trouble I could get in?"

"So we'll throw a tarp over it," said Jonah, rubbing his stinging face as he set the briefcase down. "And it's nice to see you, too."

Hassan and Alexis walked down deck of the submarine. The engineer slipped her hand into the doctor's as the two jumped onto the dock to join Jonah.

"Hey," said Jonah to the pair. "Where's Dalmar and Vitaly?"

Hassan gave a pained look. "They're … uh … still …" he began.

"I think the technical term is *banging*," added Alexis, squeezing Hassan's hand.

"Banging?" asked Jonah.

"Like a screen door in a tornado, Cap'n," said Alexis.

Marissa shook her head in irritation at the whole situation even as she gestured to a collection of shipping containers and bulky equipment crates on the shore next to the concrete dock. "So everything you wanted is here—air lifters, winches, arc welders, plasma cutter, gantry cranes, newly rolled high-strength steel plating, and all manner of electronics. It's everything you'll need to repair your … ship. We'll bring in a diesel barge in a couple of days to top off your tanks."

"Much obliged," said Jonah. "I'm very impressed."

"Well, you'd better not fuck me on payment," said Marissa. "Because I'm out serious money on this, especially the rental deposits. Keep in mind you already disappeared on me once."

"It's covered," said Jonah, snapping open the briefcase and swiveling it around to show the contents to Marissa.

Her eyebrows shot up. "Those are … gold bars. Lots of gold bars."

"Ninety-nine point ninety-nine percent pure," said Jonah. "Had them assayed myself."

"What in holy hell am I supposed to do with gold bars?"

"It was either this or Indonesian rupiahs," said Hassan. "Or Burmese kyats—"

"This will be fine, thank you," interrupted Marissa, taking the suitcase from Jonah and closing it. "So how did you get this much gold?"

"You'd be very surprised what collectors pay for black market human skin these days," said Jonah.

"Ugh! I shouldn't have even asked," said Marissa, putting her index finger and thumb on the bridge of her nose and squeezing. Jonah recognized it as a symptom of an early-onset tension headache.

Sweaty and still buttoning their shirts, Dalmar and Vitaly emerged from the conning tower, waving at the rest of the party.

"That reminds me," added Marissa, pulling half a dozen folded-up loose leaf pages of printer paper from her back jeans pocket. "Jonah told me to run your names, see what the authorities have on you."

"I've been kinda dreading this moment," said Alexis.

"It will be fine," said Hassan, giving Alexis's hand a reassuring squeeze. "You've not done anything wrong."

"Jonah—we'll start with you," said Marissa. "Looks like INTERPOL wants you for questioning over what happened at Anconia Island. I'd also keep away from any US cities for … well, forever. And most major western countries as well."

"No surprises there," said Jonah.

"Dr. Hassan Nassiri," continued Marissa, reading off the page. "You've been formally charged with desertion and facilitating the escape of a prisoner. You're also wanted in Malta in connection with a stolen yacht—wait, you guys were the ones that stole the *Conqueror*?"

"Yeah, and kidnapped me while they were at it," said Alexis.

"Good," said Marissa. "Well, the kidnapping part isn't good. But the owner of the *Conqueror* was a real asshole."

"And then they sank it," added Alexis. "Can you believe that?"

"Seriously?" Marissa shook her head. "Jonah, this is why you can't have nice things."

Dalmar and Vitaly stepped up to the group at the dock, a ruddy flush on both their faces.

"I assume you're Dalmar Abdi?" asked Marissa, pointing at the massive pirate.

"I am Dread Pirate Dalmar Abdi," he answered in his booming voice. "And you are very beautiful woman."

"My computer almost crashed when I Googled your name because you, my friend, are an internationally wanted terrorist. I could probably go to Gitmo just for talking to you."

"I am finally famous!" shouted Dalmar, waving his fists at the heavens.

"Congratulations. And you are … Vitaly Kuznetsov?" asked Marissa, nodding towards the Russian pilot.

"That is me," said Vitaly.

"Vitaly, I can't find anything about you anywhere. Frankly, I'm not convinced you even exist."

"Even so," said Vitaly, "Russia not so safe for me right now. Some people not so happy with Vitaly. I stay with submarine."

"Alexis Andrews," said Marissa with an apologetic tone. "I hate to say this, but you may want to lay low for a while. There are no warrants out, but there are a lot of angry people who want to ask you some really serious questions."

Alexis nodded and looked at the ground. "I have letters," she finally said. "Can you get them to my family?"

"Of course," said Marissa. "Which brings me to Charles Bettencourt. You guys catch the news?"

"We put up a satellite dish, but it keeps getting washed off," complained Jonah.

"Well, then you'll like this. Bettencorps CEO Charles Bettencourt is officially missing and presumed dead. His helicopter was found abandoned near a small fishing village on the coast of Somali. His helicopter pilot was found nearby."

"Alive?" asked Vitaly quizzically.

"Not so much," said Marissa. "Body was mutilated. And he'd been forced to drink so much toxic waste that authorities had to take his body to a chemical weapons disposal furnace in Belarus for cremation."

"Ouch," said Jonah.

"Yeah," said Marissa with a wry smile. "Ouch is right. The Anconia data dump wasn't complete, but Jesus, what a mess. Environmental groups and NGOs from around the world jumped on it. The red tide off Somalia is still bad, but there are early indications that it's starting to fade.

An American carrier group is in the area, their deep-dive program already pulling up barrels. Nobody knows what to call the stuff, much less what to do with it. Inside sources say it's going to be a full-scale cleanup effort, especially for anything that washed up onshore."

"Fatima would be pleased," whispered Hassan. Beside him, Alexis nodded.

"So … you've got yourself a goddamn submarine. What the hell are you going to do with it?" Marissa surveyed them.

"Seek adventure!" Dalmar spread his arms wide.

"Probably more crime," admitted Vitaly.

"Babysit these guys." Alexis rolled her eyes.

"I'm of the hope that they will need my services as little as possible," said Hassan.

"It's a big ocean," mused Jonah. "We'll just have to see what comes our way."

"I've got a job for you and your crew in Japan if you're looking for work. Yours if you want it," said Marissa, hoisting up the suitcase and preparing to leave. "I'll give you the details in a couple of days. Jonah, I hope you're a better captain than you were a boyfriend."

"Same here," admitted Jonah. "And thanks for everything. I know you're risking a lot to help us."

"Not done yet," said Marissa. "You know that certain someone you asked me to keep an eye out for?"

"Yeah?" said Jonah, just barely daring to hope.

"Klea," shouted Marissa as she waved back to her car. "You can make your dramatic entrance now. We're all good—everybody is cool and no helicopters swooping in. Yet."

A slight, pale, dark-haired young woman exited the car, cautiously at first. But when she caught sight of Jonah, she broke out into a full run. Jonah caught her in his arms as she embraced him and buried her face in his chest. For the briefest of moments, Jonah's mind flashed back to their long journey in the inflatable life raft.

"I—I thought—" began Klea.

"It's okay." Jonah held her close, running his hands up and down her back. "We made it. What happened?"

"Burhaan's family hid me," said Klea. "Took me south, just like they said they would. I showed up at an American embassy and told them to take me home. I thought you were dead until Marissa called me."

"I'm so happy to see you," admitted Jonah. "I can't even find the words—"

"I can come with you," said Klea. "I can help, I know things—engines, electronics, navigation—"

"We'll manage," said Jonah, holding her tightly. "Klea, I'm just happy at least one of us is allowed back in the world. It should be you."

Klea threw her arms around Jonah's neck. And for one perfect moment, he felt her smile as she kissed him.

"Everybody, this is Klea," said Jonah, introducing her to his wrecking crew. She smiled and waved.

"Nicely done, Captain," said Vitaly. "She very pretty."

"You want a tour?" Jonah offered Marissa and Klea.

"Pass," Marissa said.

"Maybe starting with the captain's cabin?" Klea cocked her head and raised an eyebrow.

Jonah grinned and took her under his arm.

"Oh, and one last thing," Jonah said, digging into his pocket. "I got a present for you, Marissa."

"More gold I can't unload? Or did you save some black market human skin just for me?"

"Better." He tossed her a small silver voice recorder. Marissa caught it one-handed, frowned, and held it to her ear as she pressed the play button.

"I was over-extended financially, risking not just Anconia Island, but the whole of the Bettencorps empire," began the recording of Charles Bettencourt, arrogance dripping from his voice. "And then the Conglomerate came to me with a proposal that could save everything, a problem for which they required the utmost discretion."

The tape dropped out for a moment, returning when Hassan's cool aristocratic voice broke in. "And you took these weapons," said the doctor over the recording. "And you buried them in the deep waters of the Indian Ocean."

"Of course I did!" the CEO shouted, his voice tinny over the recording. "I was forced, *forced* to agree that the best place to hide weapons that shouldn't exist was among people who didn't matter. It was such an easy choice to make, what they wanted was so simple—their interests protected, a blind eye turned, and for that I got my bottom line secured."

Marissa clicked the recorder off and smiled.

"Dead or alive, the world is going to know the truth about Charles Bettencourt," said Jonah, turning back toward the *Scorpion*, his fingers entwined with Klea's.

"Is the world going to find out the truth about Jonah Blackwell, too?" shouted Marissa after him.

"We'll see, won't we?" said Jonah.

~ THE END ~

COMING NEXT
Red Sun Rogue

CHAPTER 1

May 6, 1945, 2315 Hours
Kriegsmarine Type XXI Underseeboot U-3531
Grid Position KR86, Approximately 450 Miles
SW of Madagascar
Silent Running at 30 Meters Depth

The German submarine U-3531 slipped invisible through the bottomless depths of the Indian Ocean, masking her acoustic signature as she skipped like a stone across pooling thermoclines. The long steel craft stalked the waters thirty meters below a raging monsoon storm, beneath her the vast, crushing emptiness of the deep abyss. A silent hunter, her cutting-edge design represented an uncommon marriage of triumph and desperation—sleek, hybrid-electric engines a generation beyond her time, faster, quiet, deadlier than her enemies. Yet despite her recent christening, she already bore the jagged scars of a battle-tempered weapon.

Fifty-seven. Fifty-seven haggard, unshaven boys, fifty-seven Jonahs within the dimly lit belly of a dank metal whale, never knowing when fate would vomit them to the surface or send them to watery internment among the serrated metal bones of their artificial cetacean. To exist in the gut of this beast was to live in a purgatorial netherworld of dim, flickering light and the sickening, omnipresent odor of sweat, diesel, and human shit.

Doctor Oskar Goering frowned as he probed a midshipman's tongue with a warped balsa-wood depressor. Mentally attempting to extinguish the maddening, pervasive hum of the engines, he glowered at the thin wooden walls of the closet-sized medical quarters that doubled as his berth. Thin trails of blood flowed from his patient's gums, pooling in the back of young sailor's blotchy, swollen throat, angry and bright under the harsh yellow glare of his dangling ceiling lamp.

The doctor frowned again, releasing the lamp to swing free and returning the room to the dim illumination of the single yellow bulb. Despite the tomfoolery and gallows' mirth of his pimple-faced shipmates, he couldn't recall the last time he had lifted a corner of his mouth for even a tiny, rueful smile. The medical quarters were a place of pain and sorrows only, a place of crude battlefield surgery, and he both the reigning king and reluctant torturer.

Here he was to take appendixes, probe infections, treat sexual disease and nutrient deficiencies. Here recently died a man, a suicide, an officer too old for his rank and too timid for wartime service, a man who gurgled his final breath through a half jaw after misaiming a 9mm Parabellum Luger inside of his own mouth. Here Doctor Goering repaired the afflicted bodies of men and boys and returned them to the insatiable appetite of the Fatherland. Though the role of ship's surgeon was a specialized job for a trained medical mind, the only skill truly necessary aboard the Fuhrer's submarine was the capacity for endurance. As not every torpedo-man can sleep beside his primed warhead, not every doctor can sleep upon his own surgical table. When his thoughts were quiet, Doctor Goering sipped a brandy blotted with three drops of morphine until his body relaxed and his vision faded to a white dreamless sleep. When the idea of any slumber seemed as distant as his family's pastoral home in Rostock, he retained a small stash of Temmler methamphetamine pills; and with each pill seventy-two jittery hours without fatigue.

The open-mouthed, bleeding midshipman before him stunk. Not distinctively or overwhelmingly, but slightly more than the stink of every other unwashed sailor aboard the submarine. As the doctor bent down over his patient, he couldn't help but breathe in particles of sweat-impregnated wool and cotton, matted hair, and dandruff. Grimacing, the doctor felt the sticky texture of his patient's arm. It was revolting—he could scarcely stand his own touch, much less the skin of this frail and doleful boy.

More than twice the age of the second-oldest man on the submarine, the doctor felt only weariness of the damnable war, exhaust of uncertainty, annoyed at the youth of his shipmates and the endless dreary months. Any sympathy he could muster he reserved for his own lot, leaving nothing but irritability for his young comrades. He'd already fought his war as a young man in the trenches of western Germany. His fight wasn't against the French, English, or Americans—as medic he battled chemical poisoning, burns, perforated limbs, shock, and disease, meeting blood with scalpel and bandage in a perfect hell of flesh, steel, and sickly yellow gas. Rank mattered little on the stretcher or in his medical tent, every soldier before him was an identical hollow-eyed, useless husk. But when the Fatherland demanded, perhaps it was better to accept service and retain the illusion of choice and honor than suffer the indignity of involuntary conscription. The doctor tried not to think of the desperation of a military machine that demanded the services of an old country physician, a man now more suited for delivering the infants to farmhands and milkmaids than safeguarding the health of an elite submariner crew. Perhaps this was the true problem with young men— that their numbers were not infinite. But what difference could a paunchy, cynical old physician now make against the swelling tide of a dozen Allied nations?

The doctor hated the U-3531. To him, it was no more than a perpetually dim, humid, metal tube, the electronic shadows of hostile planes and foreign ships dogging their every heading. No sooner would the undersea craft surface to recharge the batteries or recycle stagnant air than the radar detector would squawk in urgent warning. The very ether of the universe was thick with waves of penetrating radar, the skies black with hostile planes, the seas swirling with enemy destroyers. At least the undersea was their own—they'd survived depth charges off Ushant, twisting and rolling under the barrage of explosions. Destroyers hunted them for a thousand miles as they made their way south. A seaplane attack off Capetown forced the submarine to crash-dive as enemy retro-rockets fell from the skies and shook them to their bones. Now far off the coast of East Africa, perhaps they'd slipped their pursuers—but he doubted it.

The physician adjusted the tongue depressor and sighed, staring at the growing sheen of black mold on his wall. Claiming a larger stake of his wall with every passing day, the aggressive mold threatened to claim his only real treasure aboard the ship, a single smudged, fading photograph of his wife and grown daughter. He could never quite kill the invader, not even after scrubbing it with bitter lye and metallic chlorine until the beds of his fingernails cracked and bled. It was as if the mold had infected the very bones of the vessel and was now so deep in the marrow that any efforts to expunge it would compromise the backbone of the submarine itself. Turning his attention back to his fidgeting patient, the doctor hunched over in the claustrophobic examination room that doubled as his berth. The young midshipman stretched and sat up on the surgical table that doubled as the doctor's bed.

"You have not been ingesting your vitamins," declared the doctor. It wasn't a question.

"I 'ave," protested the sailor, his swollen tongue squirming against the depressor in a futile effort to form proper consonants. "E'ery 'ay."

"Every day?" confirmed the doctor. "Without fail?"

"E'ery 'ay," insisted the sailor.

"I cannot cure your ailment if you lie to me."

"E'ery 'ay, 'oc!" the sailor emphatically repeated.

The doctor issued a wheezing, skeptical *harrumph* through pursed lips as he further probed the bloody mouth. The wooden depressor easily bruised the irritated, spongy gums. A single hair drifted from the midshipman's scalp and slowly pinwheeled onto the examination table.

"And your excrement?" asked the doctor, withdrawing the tongue depressor.

"Loose, I think," said the midshipman. "But I don't look at it after."

"Check it," said the doctor. "Tell me what you see. Better still, leave it in the bowl and summon me."

"Yes, Herr Doctor," said the midshipman, knowing full well the action would announce his difficulties to the rest of the tightly-quartered crew and invite open ridicule. Life on board a Kriegsmarine *underseebooten* was difficult, the misery of others often the only entertainment, anything to distract from the ever-present specter of death.

The doctor shook his head. The boy must be lying or confused; the cause scurvy, or some other nutritional deficit. Maybe the vitamins they took on in Norway were contaminated or otherwise lacking—perhaps even sabotage. Even the most determined propaganda couldn't mask the havoc American and British advances wreaked with German supply chains and the increasingly inconsistent and slipshod quality of German manufacture, to say nothing about the darkening disposition of the conquered races on which the war effort relied.

"Very well," sighed the doctor, scribbling a short note to check in on the young man in a few hours' time. It wouldn't do to keep him longer; the cause of the strange ailment remained elusive for now. Best to find him after his duty shift and probe further. "Where is your bunk?"

"I'm not supposed to say," said the sailor.

The doctor gritted his teeth. More foolishness, maddeningly expected.

"Midshipman," said Doctor Goering, "do *not* be a horse's ass."

"I bunk in the aft torpedo room," said the young man, then stole a look back and forth, as though anyone larger than a footstool could have stowed away in the tiny compartment. He continued his statement with a whisper: "*On top of the ray gun.*"

"The *what?*" asked the doctor, genuinely baffled by this new nonsense.

"You know we have *no torpedoes* in the torpedo room," said the sailor. "Left 'em back in Trondheim before our departure for Japan. Couldn't take them, see? We needed space for all the … um … *special* crates."

Doctor Goering nodded. He'd seen the boxes—radar detectors, prototype rifles, aviation turbine engines, technical plans, and similar marvels. The cargos were the best technologies that Reich scientists could offer, only to be born away from Fatherland soil for use by the Asiatics. It was all *luftschloss* to the doctor, castles in the sky, the idea that the massing mongrel hordes of America and Australia could be turned back by a single yellow race armed with German-made x-ray guns and jet-planes.

"So?" asked the doctor.

"I'm sleeping on top of a *ray gun*," said midshipman. "It has to be the cause of everything! What else could cause my sickness? No one else is afflicted! Marvelous, no? If this happens when one merely *sleeps* upon the weapon, just imagine it discharged upon the Americans! We could *roast* entire divisions where they stand!"

Carried away by his own mirth, the midshipman made a few imbecilic 'zapping' noises towards imagined enemy troops until he was silenced by the doctor's profound lack of corresponding amusement.

"You're dismissed," said the doctor. "I will call on you in a few hours. Do you remember what I said?"

"Continue taking my vitamins," said the sailor glumly, unhappy that his pet theory had not gained traction with the doctor.

"And?"

"Keep my *scheisse* in the bowl until you inspect it."

"Dismissed," said the doctor, shepherding the sailor out of the medical cabin. For a moment, he stood leaning out into the main corridor, the hollow spine of the submarine connecting every compartment. Diesel and grease-stained men shuffled their way through net-hung fruits and breads, passing each other in the cramped quarters with silent familiarity, moving with the eerie synchronicity of scavenging ants.

The doctor adjusted his uniform and walked the three meters to the captain's quarters, doffing his hat as he knocked at the door to the cabin that doubled as the armory.

"*Kommen,*" came a familiar voice from the other side of the thing wooden door. Captain Duckwitz needed not request the identity of the knocker—only one of the top lieutenants, chief engineer or the doctor himself would ever consider interrupting the captain in his private quarters.

Doctor Goering pressed open the door, stepped inside, and latched it behind him. The captain looked up from a handwritten letter, his weary grey eyes meeting the gaze of the ship's doctor, rows of Mauser pistols and rifles, signal guns, hand grenades and several matte-black MP40 sub-machine guns racked behind him. Two Japanese *katana* swords hung from the rack as well, conspicuous and out-of-place amongst the futuristic weapons.

Captain Duckwitz was just twenty-eight, too young for his authoritative mannerisms and steely bearing, too young for the weight of responsibility or the wrinkles around the corners of his unusual eyes. The doctor's daughter had expressed genuine horror upon finding the captain's tender age—how can a man not yet thirty, not yet married and with no children even *contemplate* the rigors of command? But in these waning days of the kreigsmarine, command was earned through survival, survival through hard-won skill and wily intelligence, in Dutckwitz's case ably demonstrated over three bitterly-fought tours.

"What can I do for you, my learned friend?" asked the captain with a wry, gravelly voice as he gestured the doctor to sit on the edge of the bunk beside the desk. Doctor Oskar Goering smiled, but did not sit.

It was true, at least part of the statement—they were indeed friends. Doctor Goering found himself in the rare position as the one man in *Kapitanleutnant* Duckwitz's command with near total autonomy, a position that allowed him to become the captain's foil and confidant. Mutual trust allowed forbidden discussions on the increasingly erratic instructions from German high command, the confusing, divergent orders, collapsing morale and the unimaginable implications of national surrender.

"It may be the usual malingering," grumbled the doctor. "But two of the crew have been afflicted by a strange illness originating from the aft torpedo room."

The handsome captain nodded, his grey eyes piercing the wall of his quarters. He ran a hand through his brown hair—hair too long for regulations—as he considered the statement. The doctor noticed the captain's hand absent-mindedly tapping a single folded letter bearing a decryption stamp from the radio officer. Another coded communication from the Fatherland—what new and futile insanity could it demand?

"Is this a bad time?" asked the doctor, noticing the captain's distraction.

"For Germany perhaps," said the captain. "We live in difficult days. But you are always welcome in my quarters. I take it you have never seen this affliction previously?"

"I have not," said the doctor. "But diseases manifest themselves differently in every man. There is no reason to assume it is new or unknown."

"If it *is* new and you are the discoverer, it must bear your name," mused the captain. "They'll call it Oskar Goering's disease."

"I've had this illness for years," grumbled the doctor. "It makes one fat and bald and easily annoyed."

The Captain's hardened face twitched once, then broke into an open smile—and yet the smile carried with it such sadness.

"Do you know what we're carrying to Japan?" asked the doctor, steering the inquiry to his concern. "In the aft torpedo room—or in any compartment for that matter?"

"I do *not*," declared the Captain with a hint of righteous annoyance. "The *eierkopf* scientists believe that knowledge above my station."

It went unspoken that the declaration would never leave the cabin. To the crew, the captain must remain God, all-seeing, all-knowing, an ordained instrument of deliverance. But his hand still unconsciously tapped upon this letter.

"Any insight would assist," pressed the doctor. "If the source is some type of toxic exposure, I would recommend we rotate the men's bunks. If it is *infectious*, on the other hand—"

"Then you do not want to risk further infection," said the captain, completing the physician's thought. "I regret I know nothing more than you. In any case, I cannot order a man to sleep in a sick man's bunk; he'd sooner sleep lashed to the keel. I authorize you to distribute rations of brandy to the ill."

"Generous," *harrumphed* Doctor Goering. "We'll soon have an entire company of afflicted."

The captain almost smiled, but it flickered and died upon his tired face. The doctor stepped back for a moment at the uncharacteristic tone. Something troubled the young man, and the sense of discomfort compelled the doctor into retreat.

"We'll speak another time," said the doctor, bowing slightly in deference as he backed towards the cabin door.

"Do not leave," said the captain, apologetically gesturing for the doctor to return as he himself stood up and gently pressed the communique into the interior pocket of his wool uniform jacket. "Accompany me to the command compartment. My learned friend, I will need you at my side, today above all days."

Confused and troubled, the doctor nodded and followed his captain into the main corridor. For the first time, he noticed that the grey-eyed commander had donned a clean uniform typically reserved for return to port, his dress pistol sidearm, had even made an attempt to slick his hair and trim away the more unkempt patches of his scraggly beard.

Today above all days, repeated the doctor to himself. *What could this possibly mean?*

The captain forced a smile and nodded to diesel *obermashinist* Baek as he and the doctor squeezed past in the narrow walkway. Short—and quite fat, despite meager rations—the chief engineer had the ruddy-faced complexion of a gift-laden, bearded *der Weihnachtsmann*. Easily the most popular crewman on the ship, he consistently found no situation above merriment, no comrade undeserving of friendly affection.

"Which sailors are sick?" asked the captain as the doctor followed him towards the command compartment.

"Seaman Lichtenberg," said Doctor Goering. "And his bunkmate, the one whose name I can never remember. The one from Czechoslovakia."

"Damnable *wunderwaffen*. Secret weapons, secret plans. Secrets upon secrets. So secret that even a captain knows not what he carries upon his own vessel. They tell me we carry the weapons that will save the war—but why simply trade them to the Nipponese?"

"We have what they need, I suppose. I doubt their science or manufacturing is within a decade of ours. Their medicine certainly isn't."

"We are selling our future," declared the captain. "God has seen fit to bless their Asiatic empire with natural riches. But on my last porting in Ushant, I saw *our* planes without tires, trucks without diesel. Soon we'll have soldiers without shoes."

To say nothing of women and children without bread, thought the doctor, thinking back to the last letter he'd received from his grown daughter before departing port. Even through her brave, stalwart insistence that all was well, he could see past the thin veneer of state-enforced optimism.

"So we need raw materials from the East," said the captain. "And for this, we must give our technology. I have the U-3531 with a submerged fast-attack speed of more than seventeen knots; I can carry twenty-three torpedoes and sixty men across oceans. And yet we are little more than a glorified oxen. My friend, there was a time when we were *wolves*."

The captain wasn't wrong. For a moment, the doctor

felt himself wondering if the Japanese had designs on the U-boat once it arrived. It'd be easy enough, wouldn't it? Greet their German guests at the docks, lure them in, butcher the crew and take their mighty submarine.

Striding past the radio compartment, the conversation came to an abrupt end as the captain spotted the glance of *Oberleutnant* Boer, the submarine's twenty-three-year-old political officer, an inevitable consequence of the *Valkyrie* assassination bombing attempt on Hitler's life. The ferret-faced sailor was committedly friendless, content in his divine mission. Every casual attempt to engage him in conversation would result in some lecture about sovereign living space, superiority of the German man, the right of Fatherland to assert her will over Europe or the dazzling brilliance of the *Fuhrer*. The few that tried rarely bothered a second time. Boer behaved as a man who'd never invited nor experienced a moment of doubt in his life, a trait that passed the point of admirable conviction and instead situated itself contentedly in the realm of outright parody. With his immaculate uniforms unspoiled by labor and tendency to breathlessly repeat schoolboy slogans and propaganda, even the sympathetic found his devotion to the Reich laughable. But the only truly unforgivable sin committed by Boer was his confiscation of a full third of the ship's razors, allowing the political officer to remain the only consistently shaved man aboard.

The captain briefly paused at the last door before the command compartment. Originally designated as the captain's cabin, the quarters now held two Japanese military attachés. Doctor Goering had seen little of the two diminutive men, they rarely left the small room and preferred to eat their strange rice meals in solitude. He'd only seen them in the moments before embarkation, two gymnast-like, muscled Japanese officers in crisply-pressed khaki uniforms and short beards, sheathed *samurai*-styled blades at their hips. The doctor had watched as the two men eyed the German sailors with a mix of disinterest and contempt, not even bothering with the implied respect of one supposed master race to another.

Captain Duckwitz checked both directions of the corridor and slid a folding oxbone pen-knife from his pocket. As the confused doctor looked on, the captain reached up to the low ceiling and allowed his fingers to find the small wire that went to the intercom speaker inside the Japanese cabin. The young captain slid his pen knife through the wire, slicing it in two. With the thick metal cabin door shut, the interior would be as silent as a bank vault. The coctor did not know what the captain intended to say over the intercom—but whatever was to be said, their Japanese guests were not meant to hear it.

Stepping into the command compartment, the captain and his doctor were greeted by a muffled *captain-on-deck* and salute by the assembled officers. Captain Duckwitz ordered them at ease and turned to his radio operator, leaning low over his station and addressing him with a conspiratorial whisper, the doctor joining the huddle.

"Loss reports?" asked the Captain.

"Not good, captain," said the young man, dropping a single earphone from his head. "Have just received April 30th through May 3rd. Eight losses at minimum."

The captain shook his head. Bad, but not as bad as the air raids of early April. "Read me the designations," he ordered. "But *quietly*."

"U-325, missing with all hands. No cause known.

U-879, sunk by warship patrol. U-1107, lost by aircraft in the Bay of Biscay—"

"Bay of Biscay? More like the valley of the shadow of death," mumbled Doctor Goering to no one in particular.

"U-2359, 2521, and 3032 presumed lost to aircraft," continued the radio operator. "And the U-3502 has been deemed unrepairable from an earlier attack."

"The U-2521?" asked the captain. "That was Heinz Franke's boat, no?"

"I don't know," admitted the radio operator.

"Was he a friend?" asked the doctor.

"Not as such, but I know the family."

"Were you able to decode the message from this morning?" the radio operator gingerly inquired. "I was unfamiliar with the cypher."

"Stop probing," the captain said with a wry smile. "If you were meant to know the message, you would know the message. Doctor—please join me as I address the crew."

Doctor Goering could do little but nod and stand beside his captain, feeling both the pressure of situation and expectation. His young friend was the solid oak core of ever-greater nesting dolls, bearing the weight of command, the pressure of the ocean around their tiny submarine, the hostile airplanes and destroyers that circled like locusts, the massing Allied armies at the Fatherland's borders.

With one deep sigh, the captain took the intercom phone from beside the attack periscope and cleared his throat.

"Crew of the U-3531, come to attention," he began, the intonation of his voice giving no evidence as to his forthcoming message. "This is your *Kapitanleutnant* speaking. We have received urgent orders from Naval High Command that I will now relay to you."

The Captain took another halting breath before continuing, steadying himself against the periscope.

"All *Underseebooten*," he continued. "Attention all *Underseebooten*. Cease fire at once. Stop all hostile action against Allied shipping."

Murmurs whispered throughout the command compartment, turning to hissed whispers. The doctor feared they'd soon turn to a roar.

"The orders continue," said the captain. "It reads as follows—my U-Boat men. Six years of war lie behind you. You have fought like lions. An overwhelming material superiority has driven us into a tight corner from which it is no longer possible to continue the war. Unbeaten and unblemished, you lay down your arms after a heroic fight without parallel. We proudly remember our fallen comrades who gave their lives for Fuehrer and Fatherland. Comrades, preserve that spirit in which you have fought so long and so gallantly for the sake of the future of the Fatherland. Long Live Germany. It is signed Grand Admiral Doenitz. Orders end."

Silence rang through the submarine like a gong, a profound, ear-ringing silence only experienced after a falling bomb has ripped through a city block—or when years of total war come to an abrupt end.

"I will add a measure of my thoughts," said the captain into the intercom. "Men—we have fought like comrades and died like brothers. I am eternally honored to have served with every one of you. We must now steel ourselves to push through this veil, whether that veil be wet with tears or red with hatred. I intend to return us to Germany and place our fates at the feet of our conquerors. Men—brothers—we have survived the war, may we now survive the peace to come."

The dam broke with fifty-seven simultaneous shouts of despair and joy, insistences of disbelief, shattered expectations and uncertainty.

Ferret-faced political officer *Oberleutnant* Boer pushed his way to the foremost of the Captain's congregants, shoving aside ruddy Diesel *Obermaschinest* Baeck and the aghast radio operator.

"Lies!" Boer shouted, waving a finger in the captain's impassive face. "American, British *lies!*"

"I've verified the code personally," said the captain. "The orders are from Admiral Doenitz's hand to my mouth—and *Oberleutnant* Boer, be well advised that I do *not* owe your rank an explanation."

"Orders?" snarled Boer as he nearly ripped open the lapel of his uniform to reach inside his interior breast pocket. "These orders of which you speak? I have orders as well—*secret* orders from the Fuhrer's inner circle! In the event of a collapsing war effort or *sabotage* from within, we are to sail to Argentina to regroup. Captain, *this very vessel* has the weapons necessary to turn the tide of war. Captain, we are the *key* to beating back the mongrel races—but instead, you tell us these *lies* of surrender?"

The captain's mouth had just begun to twitch with an infuriated response when out of nowhere a fist flew into the political officer's face, snapping across the young man's jawline with shattering force, instantly dropping the political officer in a sprawling heap on the floor. Ruddy, affable mechanic Baeck had become a human cudgel, his teeth gritted and brow knotted as he continued the assault, throwing his body atop the political officer and raining down blow after blow after blow. The doctor recoiled in horror—not for the act, but the beloved man committing it.

Shouting officers dragged the two men apart, the political officer now dazed and bleeding, the bloody-knuckled mechanic struggling against the interventionists. In the confusion, the doctor noted a flashing metallic glint in the captain's hand as he drew a Luger pistol and drew aim at the beloved mechanic.

"Striking a superior officer is a capital offense," intoned the captain, cocking the hammer as Baeck's eyes widened in surprise.

"I want him *shot*," shouted Boer, yanking himself free of the two men who'd helped him to his feet. "And *anyone* who sympathizes with his cowardly—"

The captain's face twisted in anger as he shifted his aim from the mechanic to the political officer, pulling the trigger in an instant, the pistol blast ringing through the tight command compartment. Blood spurted from a speck-sized hole under Boer's unseeing left eye as the young, smooth-faced man crumpled to the metal deck.

Silence again took hold as the captain holstered his pistol.

"Release *Obermachinest* Baeck," he commanded to his men. "Baeck, return to your duties at once. As for *Oberleutnant* Boer—perhaps peacetime will elevate fewer such men. Prepare his body for immediate burial at sea."

No one moved.

"I will have order on my ship," growled the captain with an icy voice, the coldest the doctor had yet heard. "We few, we lucky few, have survived all manner of wartime and loss, we have survived unlike so many of our brothers in arms. I would prefer my men to survive the peace, uneasy as it may be. Doctor Goering—I will need you for one final task before you are dismissed."

"Yes, Captain," said Doctor Oskar Goering, following as the Captain turned 180 degrees on one heel and stomped from the command compartment, leaving the political officer's body behind.

"We have a duty to inform our Japanese guests," said the captain as he purposefully strode towards their cabin door, the two men once again finding themselves alone.

"And you require me for this notification?" asked the doctor, not wholly understanding.

"You'll see," said the captain, knocking three times on the door and standing at attention. "Dealing with these Japs isn't like dealing with a proper German. Perhaps *notification* is too strong a word. *Müllschuss* might be more appropriate."

The doctor pondered for a moment. *Müllschuss*, or "garbage-shot" referred to the days' collected trash as it was blasted from an empty torpedo tube and into the abyss. Normally so deft at hiding his feelings, the young captain had revealed his true sentiment of the submarine's foreign passengers—a wish to eject them from the submarine like so much garbage.

The cabin door swung open, revealing the two Japanese officers. Standing at attention as though they'd expected the intrusion, the two short men stood primly, hats cocked, their khaki uniforms unnaturally immaculate in the dull light streaming in from the corridor, beards closely trimmed, hair neatly slicked back without a single errant strand. Try as he might, the doctor genuinely couldn't tell one from the other, the two Japanese could have been brothers or even twins. And then there was the *smell*, too many unfamiliar spices mixed with the slight after-scent of sweet rice wine.

"I have news," said the Captain stiffly, wasting not a

word. "Germany has withdrawn from the war effort. We will return to Europe for an orderly surrender to Allied forces. Gentlemen, I regret that we cannot return you to your homeland."

"Not acceptable," said the foremost Japanese officer, speaking with a faint British-accented German, his face betraying no emotion. "You will complete your mission and return us to Japan."

"The war is over for Germany," said the captain, letting a slight measure of formality slip from his intonation. "I know this puts you in a difficult position, but we would be in violation of our new orders to continue."

"You will complete your mission," repeated the Japanese officer, cold and insistent.

The captain whipped off his wool cap and stepped into the Japanese cabin, pushing his face within inches of the foreign officer, scowling with intense displeasure. The Japanese soldier didn't so much as blink.

"I did not choose this," whispered the captain. "So long as I have breath in my lungs, I would in no way willingly submit myself, this ship, or its crew to humiliation before our enemy. But I will say this—I shot dead the last man to question my orders. I *advise* that you do not make the same mistake."

"My ... *apologies* ... for any offense," said the officer, narrowing his eyes as his twin stood motionless behind him.

"Accepted," said the Captain, stepping back and returning his own cap to his head. "And please understand I must involuntarily confine you to these quarters for the remainder of the voyage."

The foremost Japanese officer nodded, not in agreement but in acceptance of a fact he could not change.

"I request my *katana*," said the stony Japanese officer.

"Whatever for?" blurted out the doctor before the captain could respond.

The Japanese officer tilted his head a millimeter to address the doctor. "There is no German translation for the practice," he said. "We are honor-bound to perform the act of *seppuku*."

Doctor Oskar Goering shivered, remembering the reference from an old pulp-printed adventure novel from his youth. *Seppuku*—the act of honor-bound suicide rather than capture—a self-inflicted stomach-cutting followed by decapitation by an attendant.

"Denied," said the captain.

"A pistol, perhaps," said the Japanese officer. "And two bullets."

"Also denied. Any reasonable requests will be reasonably accommodated. But I will not aid you in your deaths, honorable as your intentions may be. Gentlemen, if there is nothing further, I bid you goodbye."

Without waiting for a reply, the captain took one step backwards out of the cabin, shut the door and locked it from the outside. The doctor followed him back to the captain's cabin, where the pair of men sat down at the small table. The captain reached into his desk drawer and retrieved a cloudy glass bottle of plum schnapps, then poured the dark amber liquid into two tumblers.

"What now?" asked the doctor, accepting his drink with a measure of relief. "You think they'll cause trouble?"

"Denying swords and guns will hardly stop them. These Japanese always carry cyanide salts for such events. Perhaps a pill or powder. But it will be less messy, less of a distraction to the crew."

"We must search the room!" began the doctor, his cynicism falling away for a moment to reveal a zealous young medic from another war long since passed.

The captain shook his head. "We will return in two hours' time," he said. "We will find our Japanese passengers unconscious or dead. You will attempt to revive them—*unsuccessfully*. Their bodies will be interned at sea in accordance with their customs. I'm not of a mood to argue, my learned friend. The matter is closed."

"I *suppose* it is their way," muttered the doctor.

"Good." The captain raised his glass. "Then let's drink."

"To what? The end of this savage war? To our dishonorable survival?"

"Let's drink to the ambiguity of peace."

"I'll let that be your toast," said the doctor with a smirk. "Mine is far less philosophical. I drink to fewer amputations ... and more howling babies."

The glasses clinked together and for one perfect moment the doctor allowed his thoughts to return to home. The local train, chugging merrily along the Warnow River. The sagging green door of his rural farmhouse. His grown daughter smiling for the first time since the invasion of Poland, her husband now returned from the Eastern front. His wife, standing in the kitchen with her daffodil-yellow apron and—

The dim light above them flickered and died. The captain swore as he jumped to his feet, the cloudy schnapps bottle falling to the floor and shattering. He threw open to the cabin door to a darkened hallway, No lights shone from the corridor save for a handful of battery-powered emergency lamps slowly flickering to life in the hands of quick-acting crew.

"Damnable Japs!" the captain shouted to all within earshot. "They've cut the power cables in their quarters!"

How—? thought the doctor as he sprang to his feet to follow the Captain.

"I'm going to *flay* them," shouted the captain, stomping towards their cabin. "And if they live, they'll spend the rest of the cruise in the *torpedo tubes*."

The Captain yelped when he touched the lock to the cabin door, yanking his hand back. Doctor Goering caught a glimpse of the smoking lock, still glowing with a smoldering ember red and realized it'd been *melted* from the inside. The Captain put his hand on the butt of his pistol and kicked the metal door open, revealing the immaculately clean, empty room inside.

"Where are they?" roared the captain to any crew within earshot.

Hearing no answer, the captain shoved a midshipman out of his way as he purposefully stomped back to his unlocked cabin, white-hot anger palpable in every step. The door cracked open before him, light spilling from within. Without warning, a glinting steel blade pierced out of the slit between door and wall, sticking the captain just below his right ear and cleanly exiting the back his neck, expertly severing his cervical vertebra. The captain stood stone-still for a heartbeat, eyes frozen open, mouth stuck in a grimace his hands fell limp at his sides, unable to staunch his own fatal wound. The sword slid out with a gushing of blood, spraying across the walls and the deck as the captain collapsed, his neck spitting gouts of red fluid from the frayed rubbery ends of a severed jugular artery.

The two Japanese officers burst from the captain's cabin and armory, both now clad in black rubber gas masks and brandishing stolen MP-40 submachine guns in one hand and their *samurai* swords in the other, the round glass lenses of the masks flashing with the reflection of the harsh emergency lamps.

The unarmed German crew scattered, channeling themselves down the main corridor as the foremost of the two Japanese opened fire with a deafening fully-automatic burst of bullets. Blinding muzzle-flashes burned into the doctor's retinas as he cowered behind the fleeing men. Three crewmen were cut down in the space of a single heartbeat, screaming as bullets plunged into their exposed backs, their chests bursting open with rents of blood and viscera, twisting and spasming as they fell to the deck.

The doctor opened his mouth, wordlessly, impotently, as the second Japanese locked his glassy gaze upon him. Decided unworthy of a bullet, the attacker cocked back his clenched, sword-wielding fist, then brought the blade down with a deliberate, sudden slash, instantly severing three fingers from the doctor's right hand, clattering across every rib and opening up the skin and fat from his collarbone to the crest of his pelvis. The doctor collapsed, soaked wet with his own warm blood, the slime of yellow fat dripping from his too-generous gut.

Doctor Goering jammed his wounded hand right hand into his armpit, trying to stop the freely flowing blood as the two Japanese officers slowly marched towards the engine compartment, deliberately popping off one dead-ly-aimed round after another as they massacred the retreating German crew.

The doctor had seen slaughters before, yes, but this was something different. Not animalistic, not the deeds of men trapped within the jungle mist of hatred, but mechanical, dissociative extermination without bloodlust or fury, a single-minded focus on utilitarian butchery. The crew might have well be ants under the heel, not of a cruel schoolboy but an unfeeling actuary who'd precisely timed the seconds he'd need to reach his next appointment. No doubt they already had a submarine in the area, preparing to intercept the U-3531 and take her over.

From his prone vantage, the doctor could only watch as Diesel *Obermaschineit* Baeck jumped from behind the battery bank, heavy wrench held high above his head like a war-mallet, only to be felled by a continuous burst of 9mm bullets into his solar plexus.

Swiveling, the first Japanese took aim at the battery bank, the other a seawater pipe, bursting both with a single salvo, electrical arcs and battery acid meeting the foamy white brine of the ocean. Doctor Goering crawled towards his cabin as the influx of water swirled around the base of batteries, already beginning to flood the engine room.

The doctor dragged his girth into his medical cabin and pushed the door closed with a foot, trying to shut the sight of his own bloody drag marks out of his mind. With his one good hand, he reached up to his medical cabinet, swiping his fingers along the wood as glass pill-bottles rained down upon him. Several hit the metal deck and shattered, slivers of broken glass the least of the splendid hell.

Morphine—where was the damnable morphine? The pain, it was too much, he felt as if he'd been sliced in half, only his weary bones holding his feeble, desiccated body together. And then he found it—Temmler Pharmaceutical's methamphetamine pills, already loose on the deck amidst the broken bottles.

The doctor's shaking fingers found three, and then they

were in his mouth with a single shard of glass, all ground up between his teeth and swallowed, burning and cutting their way down his raw throat.

The ecstasy hit almost immediately, a sudden convulsing high that dwarfed the rapture found within a morphine blot. The doctor rose to his hands and knees, his ruined chest and gut spilling down his uniformed blouse and trousers.

An acidic smell burned as it entered his nostrils—metallic pineapple, a fearful odor he'd never thought he'd sense again. Green, low-hanging chlorine gas gathered about the compartment, just like the trenches of the Great War. The burning sensation was the mucus membranes in his nose interacting with the chlorine molecule and becoming a powerful hydrochloric acid. In the nose it was painful, in the lungs it was soon fatal, essentially melting the tissues from the inside until the victim drowned in his own bodily fluids. *But why?* A long-forgotten explanation flashed through the doctor's stimulant-addled mind, battery acid mixing with seawater producing the deadly gas cloud. The Japanese had done this purposefully. Discontent with the labor of methodically shooting the unarmed crew, they'd simply opted to gas them all.

More gunshots, echoing from both ends of the submarine as the Japanese stalked in opposite direction, eliminating the convulsing survivors. Still crawling, the doctor dragged his frame out of the medical cabin door, holding his breath with little gasps. Around him, wounded men clutched their throats and writhed, their lips flecked with pink foam, every choking breath sucking in more of the poison gas.

The doctor grasped a pipe and dragged himself to his

feet, holding in his ruined guts with his two-fingered right hand, pharmaceutical fire coursing through his veins as he stumbled through the engine room, eyes closed against the burning gas clouds, feet wet with battery acid and pooling seawater, muscles twitching as sparks and electrical arcs danced, dead men floating face-down before him.

Yanking an emergency gas mask from the wall, the doctor pushed it to his face and tried to breath, but found no air. He ran a finger through the mouthpiece, finding a thick wad of hardened epoxy over the filter.

The Japanese had sabotaged the mask days ago, maybe even weeks ago.

Uncontrollably shaking, the doctor staggered into the galley, once again collapsing. He reached up to the counter and pulled free a washcloth, spilling a pile of potatoes about his prone form. The doctor pushed the washcloth down towards his crotch, underneath the bloody beltline of his trousers and against his penis. With all his might, he forced himself to urinate, just drops at first, then the warm liquid flowing freely against the washcloth and into his hand. Summoning long-unused willpower, the doctor thrust the washcloth against his face, breathing through the piss-soaked rag, knowing that the water and ammonia would filter out the acidifying chlorine gas. The same trick had kept him alive through the gas-shellings of the Great War. Breathing now, he secured the filthy cloth behind his head with a single hand.

Footsteps—the doctor quickly laid his head upon the ground and closed his eyes as a single Japanese officer passed.

And then a single, brilliant thought entered the doctor's mind.

Wunderwaffen.

The crates in the rearmost torpedo room, the source of seaman Lichtenberg's affliction. The *ray gun.*

Crawling, the doctor single-mindedly pushed his way through heaps of dead and dying men, mouths foaming, broken bodies bleeding from piercing sword and bullet wounds.

Wunderwaffen. Doctor Goering would seize the ray-gun from its crated nest. He would turn it upon the two Japanese officers for this sudden betrayal—maybe even the whole of the Japanese nation. He would roast them, explode their bodies, turn them to blowing chimney ash.

Hope fueling his bled-out body as much as the stimulants, the doctor collapsed a final time before the wooden torpedo-room crate. He pulled seaman Lichtenberg's bed-roll from the box and pried open a corner, hammered-in nails screaming as he forced open the lid with inhuman, drug-induced strength.

Inside lay four identical lead-lined steel boxes. The ray gun—the *wunderwaffen*—this was his prize, his Valhalla reward for survival, his single chance at vengeance. The doctor wrenched open the nearest metallic box in the dim emergency lighting.

Sickly blue light spilled out, illuminating the dim compartment as the lid fell free and clanged to the deck.

Blue powder. Nothing but glowing blue powder lay within.

The doctor ran his hands through the heavy substance and felt a prickling, stabbing *heat* but no other contents within. The cloth slipped from his face, lungs burning, tears now streaming unstaunched from his eyes and down his cheeks, disappearing into the ineffectual glowing powder.

Then something strange happened. It was as if he took a slow step back from his own eyes, experiencing his own sight from a great distance, far-away. A sense of peace washed over him, beautiful and serene. Nothing mattered, not really. He allowed his hands to slip out of the powder-filled box, his other fell from his ragged stomach. The Japanese, the war, the months aboard the submarine, even his wife and daughter seemed so *distant*, so *insignificant* and he wondered why—but even that question held no real significance.

All Doctor Oskar Goering could do was remember a childhood poem. He chanted it again and again in the silence of his own mind as he faded inexorably into nothingness.

There are no roses on a sailor's grave,
no lilies on an ocean wave.
The only tribute is the seagull's sweeps, and
the teardrops that a sweetheart weeps.

CHAPTER 2

Radioactive Exclusion Zone,
Fukushima, Japan
Present Day

Fukushima Daiichi nuclear plant glinted in January moonlight, gentle waves lapping against the snow-dusted rock jetty below the crippled cooling towers. Tall transmission lines and cranes pierced the horizon, thick electrical cables disappeared into the darkness. Only the compound was lit, with dull yellow halogen lamps irregularly dotting the buildings and fences, leaving the abandoned coastal villages surrounding the area only darker by comparison. Behind the three main buildings, endless rows of white temporary storage tanks lapped up leaking irradiated groundwater as it seeped from the crumbling stacks.

The submarine *Scorpion* drifted towards the power plant at dead-slow, her matte-black hull submerged, a single narrow periscope slicing through the dark ocean. The underwater craft mirrored the aesthetic of Fukushima— both stark and utilitarian, both relics of an era since passed.

Dr. Hassan Nassiri stood in a corner of the *Scorpion's* cramped command compartment with arms crossed, trying to swallow down butterflies as the tactical lighting bathed him in thick crimson. It still surprised him that a group of just five could run the entire 250-foot diesel/electric submarine, capable as they were in their individual specialties. He supposed they were lucky the vessel's previous crew of mercenaries had automated and computerized the bulk of the antiquated systems.

Before him, his captain—his friend, though it still felt a strange notion—clasped the periscope handles with both hands as he deftly navigated the submarine into the shallow foreign harbor.

Yes, his friend ... he'd discovered Jonah Blackwell—salvage diver, criminal, man without a country—in a secret Saharan prison. Caught on an illegal underwater mission in Moroccan waters, Jonah had been rendered by the secret police and forced to carve out a tense, often violent life among gangsters and terrorists. But this desert anvil had also forged the only man willing to accompany Hassan into the heart of Somali pirate territory, a man audacious enough to rescue the doctor's captured mother and recruit a crew of hardy survivors and outlaws. Jonah and the doctor created the core of an unexpectedly effective team, their very own wrecking crew, Hassan with his intelligence and medical training, Jonah with his dual capacity for cunning and combat.

But the voyage from Washington State's Puget Sound had been long, long enough for the ghosts that haunted the corridors of their stolen vessel to make themselves known. Whenever he closed his eyes, he felt as though some unseen force spun a wheel until it clicked to a stop upon a terrible or profound recent memory.

Blink.

A proud island metropolis perched upon the foundation of massive oil platforms, its tall skyscrapers toppling into the sea under the impact of a hijacked supercontainer ship.

Blink.

His body wedged within the twisted metal of the *Scorpion* as the last of his air drained from his lungs, his narcotic mind reeling with panic.

Blink.

Seeing Alexis for the first time, the young Texan sitting on the floor of a superyacht engine room and bobbing her head to unheard music, eyes closed and her blonde hair and her freckles and her long, tan legs ...

Blink.

His mother, wrapped in white cloth as their pirate allies solemnly ferried away her pale, electrocuted body for an honored burial in distant lands.

But the one remembrance he forbade himself was his life as an army surgeon in Morocco, the life in which he'd been building a lucrative part-time practice on the side, the life he'd abandoned to find his biologist mother after her plane disappeared over the Arabian Sea. Absent without leave from his military service, he'd been instrumental in multiple savage clashes, hijackings, and the obliteration of an entire island nation; too many lines crossed to ever return home.

Hassan shook his head and ran his fingers through the tousled black hair that framed his dark eyes. He returned his attention to the datasteam steadily marching across his communications console. The butterflies again—but such was life amongst the barbarians. Always some measure of danger, however great or small.

Jonah looked up from his periscope and grimaced,

scanning the red-illuminated command compartment with piercing eyes. Hassan wondered if the American would ever lose his prisoner's affectations or physicality, his intense, almost paranoid attention to detail, and his gaunt, muscled form.

Over the course of the voyage, Jonah had kept his blonde hair close-cropped and beard tightly trimmed. Seeing the scarred-up knuckles and the residual hardening around the American's eye socket and jaw, the doctor had to wonder if the beard covered up further scarring.

"Vitaly—check the readings," Jonah commanded, pointing at the Russian helmsman as he returned his eyes to the periscope. "How bad is our radiation exposure?"

"About twenty mili-sievert per minute," said Vitaly, glancing at a Geiger counter nestled approximately atop his testicles, his answer only somewhat discernible through a thick accent. "We in radioactive containment chamber drainage outflow for sure now. Maybe equivalent of one chest x-ray every two-three minutes. I am detecting Iodine-131, Caesium-134 and ... *da*, Caesium-137. Like Chernobyl, *nyet*?"

"Am I going to grow a third eye here?" asked Jonah.

"For Russian, is no problem," answered Vitaly. "For you, I think maybe not so good news."

"Doc?"

"He's right," said Hassan, trying to dig through the cobwebs of his mind to a short rotation in radiology during his medical residency. "In two hours, we'll be exposed to more radiation than we would in a typical year. I advise we not linger any longer than absolutely necessary."

"Agreed," said Jonah, looking up from his periscope and patting the doctor on the shoulder as he turned to face the main corridor that ran the entire length of the submarine. Yes, *friend* … perhaps it wasn't so strange a notion after all.

Jonah pressed the intercom that lead to the engine room. "Alexis!" he shouted, loud enough to get the engineer's attention over the constant thrumming of the recently overhauled diesel-electric engines.

A static-filled response came back, not clear enough to make the words out.

"How are my engines?" asked Jonah, again speaking into the intercom.

"—good!" said a young female voice from the engine compartment, background noise echoing through the transmission. "We're five-by-five back here."

"You want to come up here for a few, take a look at the harbor through the periscope?" asked Jonah.

"Nope!" said Alexis. "I'm going to stay right here— surrounded by the thickest section of hull. You all can go ahead and get as irradiated as you want up in command."

The doctor couldn't think about Alexis Andrews without allowing himself a tiny secret moment as he visualized her slim form and lively eyes. The fact that she was even on the *Scorpion* was nothing short of a happy miracle. Beautiful Alexis in her cutoff shorts, tank-tops and steel-toed boots, surrounded by engine lubricants and half-disassembled repair projects.

Technically, Jonah and Hassan had inadvertently kidnapped her when they'd stolen the superyacht *Conqueror* under the ruse of a repossession order. Their fates had been linked since finding her stowed away the subsequent day. But what should have been a short, strange week among well-intentioned outlaws had transformed into a fight for survival.

Stomping rang out from the metal deck of the main

corridor, loud enough to make Hassan wince. Somali warlord and former pirate Dalmar Abdi pushed his way through the narrow entrance, rolling in one muscled shoulder after another to squeeze through and into the command compartment. Twin bandoliers crossed his chest like an X, each loaded with large-caliber ammunition. He held an assault rifle on a strap around his neck and a belt loaded with grenades and extra magazines, a small machete and twin pistols strapped to his thighs.

Even after sailing with him for two months, Hassan didn't quite know what to make of the former pirate king. Dalmar's past remained shrouded in mystery, even legend. According to some sources, Dalmar was the son of Mohammed Farrah Aidid, Somali warlord and the illegitimate self-declared president at the height of American military involvement in the country. Supposedly, a six-year-old Dalmar Abdi had taken up arms and lead a company of children against an American rescue convoy during the Mogadishu "Black Hawk Down" incident. Another rumor declared that he was the son of a Somali soft drink magnate, educated in Rome before returning as a humanitarian worker. But upon discovering the state of the war-torn country and the vicious campaign against it by Western powers, he rose up and became the most feared buccaneer in the region.

All Dalmar would say about himself was that he was a 'dread pirate,' a strange attribution that Hassan strongly suspected came from the 1987 film *The Princess Bride*. The one certain fact was that Dalmar and his men hijacked a massive container ship and slammed it into the artificial island city of Anconia Island, and now interests within Western governments wouldn't rest until he'd been caught or killed. Now thought dead, Dalmar's voyage on the *Scorpion* bought him the only three things that mattered anymore—distance, time, and anonymity.

"I don't think you'll need that much firepower," said Jonah, pointing at the bandoliers. "We're having a meeting. We're not assaulting the beaches of Normandy."

The pirate simply crossed his arms and glowered by way of response.

Jonah clearly trusted the shipping heiress who'd set up the meet. Marissa was Jonah's longtime associate and ex-girlfriend, separated from him only when he mysteriously disappeared all those years ago. She'd still found herself willing to assist in a pinch after he resurfaced, even helped retrofit the *Scorpion* at an abandoned dry-dock in Puget Sound, and rehabilitate the submarine after the beating she'd taken in the Indian Ocean.

"I think maybe not so good idea to trust Marissa," said Vitaly, piping up from his navigations console. Jonah and Hassan had inherited Vitaly Kuznetsov with the *Scorpion*. Vitaly had been part of the crew sent to ambush and kill the pair, only to find himself at the wrong end of a pistol when the tables turned. Wounded by Jonah, the doctor saved Vitaly's life and earned his loyalty. "She is ex-girlfriend, no? Woman scorned?"

"See these?" said Jonah, showing Vitaly his bare wrists. "See how I'm not wearing handcuffs right now? We were one phone call away from getting nabbed during the retrofits."

"Could be part of larger plot," said Vitaly. "She gains trust, and then sends you to excruciating death, maybe by torture. Would be very Russian of her."

"I like Marissa," said Dalmar with a massive smile as

he let his arms drop. "She told me all about how I am very famous."

"—*terrorist*," added Hassan. "You're a very famous *terrorist*."

"But I have fan pages on the internet!" insisted Dalmar.

"I still think bad idea," said Vitaly. "So maybe you come back from meeting. Maybe no. Vitaly will see."

"I hope we are ambushed," interjected Dalmar as he inspected his assault rifle. "I have never killed a Japanese before."

"Seriously, lose some of the arsenal," said Jonah, returning his attention to the periscope as they edged ever-closer to the Fukushima docks. "This is a polite meeting among polite company only. No killing."

"Very well." Dalmar frowned as he peeled off his layers of firearms, ammunition and explosives like an ear of corn husking itself. "I will only bring my most polite weapons."

The *Scorpion* slid into the Fukushima docks with a long, low groan and shudder, the metal hull of the vessel scraping along the crushed, sunken cars stolen from the town by the retreating tsunami.

"Sorry Captain," said Vitaly with a grimace as he brought the submarine to a wince-inducing, grinding halt. "I think we maybe hit something."

Hassan, Jonah, and Dalmar watched from the concrete docks as the *Scorpion* slowly backed out to sea, her conning tower and periscope disappearing in a whirlpool of swirling bubbles. Alexis and Vitaly were more than capable of hiding the submarine on the ocean bottom until the party returned, hopefully finding a soft, muddy patch as far from the stricken nuclear power plant as possible.

Jonah nodded as he adjusted his thick parka, zipping it up against the creeping cold of the damp January. All three had long since acclimated to brutal heat, not a winter chill—Hassan's life in Morocco, pirate Dalmar Abdi's home in the scrublands of coastal Somalia, Jonah's long internment in a Saharan prison.

"They're saying this could be this region's worst winter in a century," said Hassan, his breath collecting into a cloud of frost as he spoke. Jonah just nodded.

In silence, the three men followed a single paved road inland. The eerie, moonlit stillness surrounding them was otherworldly, reclaimed by the raging ocean. The first few blocks were stripped bare of any structure, large patches of dried mud and patchy brush bordered by cracked, potholed roads.

Next came the true destruction, buildings torn from their foundations, scattered debris swept and bulldozed into tall towers, stacks of rusting, flattened passenger cars. In typical Japanese efficiency, the wreckage had been carefully transported to designated zones; the roads made clear for traffic that would never again return. And then there were the titans, the massive fishing and pleasure boats too large and difficult to tow back to the beach, some partially disassembled by acetylene torch, others simply left to moor in the mud.

Hassan, his captain, and the pirate journeyed up the winding road connecting the docks to the highway. Only nature had withstood the tidal forces—while the landscape between themselves and the sea had been scraped clean, the stark forest on the other side of a low guardrail still rose tall and ancient.

Jonah led, following the bent and rusted street signs to Futaba Park, a small, snowy city tract more than a mile from the docks. Approaching from the dark, Hassan could see their hosts had already arrived in a half dozen low-slung American Lincolns and Cadillacs of various vintage. The semicircle of headlights illuminated a set of stairs in the center of the overgrown park, the pavement surrounded by thick tufts of dead brown grass.

Yakuza, thought Hassan. He recognized the dress of the dozen collected Japanese gangsters as they sat on the hoods of their cars and smoked, the tiny cherry red of their cigarettes bright in the deepening darkness. As the trio approached, the doctor could see the mix of ages and ranks, a few older men with close-cropped greying hair and expensive dark woolen coats and slacks, young men with bouffants, long, thick sideburns and shiny grey suits. All had tattoos peeking from their folded white collars and the cuffs of their tailored shirts.

Clearing his throat, Jonah waved at the assembled men to get their attention. None so much as looked up. Hassan realized they had all craned their ears towards a loud car radio, over which played a tinny, rapid-fire news broadcast.

"Why are they ignoring us?" whispered Jonah. "I don't want to sit here getting my balls irradiated any longer than absolutely necessary."

Hassan always found the American male's fascination with his testes quite tiring. Still, he had to admit a pre-occupation with his own given the cold temperature and the frighteningly high levels of background radiation. His concern was only increased when the passenger door of the nearest opened, and a figure in a bulky white radiation suit awkwardly emerged from within the vehicle before turning to face the trio.

"Marissa?" demanded Hassan in complete disbelief. He thought they'd left the young woman behind in the Puget Sound after repairs to the *Scorpion* were complete—and yet here she was, standing before them.

"They're not ignoring you—they're listening to a news broadcast," answered the shipping heir, crossing her arms as she stared from Jonah to Hassan and Dalmar, before back to her ex again. Her voice was slightly muffled by the clear plastic face of the blocky hood. "It's about the Japanese whaling fleet in the Antarctic Ocean. The steering mechanisms of one of their harpoon ships failed, it struck the factory ship and sank them both. No survivors have been located as of yet, the search is ongoing. Also, sorry for the surprise—it's not like I can just Skype you guys ahead of time."

Without warning, the mob boss slammed his fist onto the hood of his late model Cadillac sedan and began shouting in rapid-fire Japanese punctuated by what Hassan assumed were expletives. The short man's muscles had long turned to fat, but he still stood an uncontested master of the gangsters surrounding him. Hassan cleared his throat quietly and tried not to remind himself he was the only one that jumped at the sudden sound—Jonah, Dalmar and the tattooed yakuza didn't so much as blink.

"Don't get me wrong—I'm happy to see you and everything," said Jonah, narrowing his eyes. "But should I be concerned about your friend's mood right now?"

"He blames the environmentalists for the loss of the whaling ships," answered Marissa. "Says it has to be sabotage. Been talking about it all night. Calls the activists rich, spoiled children of Western countries. He says Japan used to be strong. He's asking where the Japanese youth are, and why they're not fighting for their traditional way of life. Oh great … now he's saying he'd like to have all of the environmentalists killed."

"Is he quite serious?" asked Hassan, folding his arms as he dropped the question with the drollest tone he could muster.

"Yes and no." Marissa shook her head. "*Livid* is kind of his default mood. Tomorrow it'll be something else ruining Japan or someone else that needs killing."

"Help me out here," Jonah said. "What are you doing with these guys? Didn't we leave you behind before we sailed for Japan?"

"Unlike you," said Marissa, sounding out the words as though speaking with a particularly dim child. "I can fly commercial. I've been in Tokyo for almost a week. Turns out our friends here did a little asking around about you. Some of their associates lost a lot of money when Anconia Island went under, and they were seriously considering shooting you on sight if I didn't show face and make a personal introduction. They gave me the heads-up out of respect for our past business dealing—*legitimate* dealings, Jonah, don't even give me that look. You can thank me later, by the way."

"Pretty remote location for such a flashy crew," observed Jonah, apparently satisfied by her answer. But Hassan was more than a little concerned with the flippant threat to their lives. "Anything I should know?"

"They have style," said Dalmar, his eyes widening as he smiled. "I think style is very important for a gangster."

"It was probably a test," admitted Marissa. "They wanted

to see if you had the *cajones* to come to the radioactive exclusion zone."

Jonah just squinted and nodded, waiting for the boss to turn his attention to them. He didn't have to wait long—the boss reached in through the open window and flipped the radio off. All fell silent, except for the crunching footsteps as the as he sauntered up to Jonah.

"American cowboy Jonah Blackwell!" said the gangster, speaking broken English through a gregarious, sinister grin. Up close, the man's sunken, deep eyes and twin scars across his left cheek made for uncomfortable viewing. Even in the darkness, his nicotine-stained fingertips and missing pinky on the left hand were obvious.

"I would seriously consider *bowing*," hissed Marissa. Jonah snuck a glance at her before giving the boss an obligatory half-bow, just enough to acknowledge his approach. The doctor suspected the sloppy form would have been interpreted as deeply disrespectful if not coming from an outsider.

"Yeah," said Jonah as he rose from the shallow bow. "I'm your American cowboy."

"Marissa say many things about you," said the gangster, tapping Jonah directly in the center of his chest with an outstretched finger. "Some of what she say … not so good."

"We're getting into business, not into bed," said Jonah, ignoring Marissa's annoyed sigh. "So if she told you anything outside of my abilities as a captain, let's put those aside here and now."

The boss frowned at his personal translator, a young man in a slim black suit and thick glasses who went back and forth with him for a moment until he tilted back his head and issued a long, guffawing laugh.

"She say you an asshole," said the boss. "Say we get along very well."

Jonah smirked in reply.

"And who this *kokujin*?" asked the gangster, pointing at Dalmar. Behind him, his dozen men had formed a half-circle around Jonah and the other three, leaning against their cars with their arms crossed or uneasily shifting from foot to foot as they stood.

Dalmar started to speak but Jonah interrupted before the Somali man could launch into his usual *dread-pirate, world-famous-terrorist* self-introduction. It'd be best for all involved if the hulking man stayed dead for the time being, at least on paper.

"Oh, he's just our shipboard events coordinator," said Jonah, pointing at Dalmar. "Shuffleboard, pool parties, bingo, that kind of thing."

"I make an excellent raspberry daiquiri," said Dalmar through gritted teeth, only halfway playing along as his eyes shot daggers at Jonah.

The mob boss just nodded and pointed at Hassan.

"Doctor Hassan Nassiri," the doctor stammered. "Ship's surgeon."

Nodding, the mob boss muttered something in Japanese. "He wants to know why you have so many ailments that you require a full-time doctor," said the slim translator.

"We get our share of stubbed toes and paper cuts," said Jonah. "So how about we hear about the job? You didn't bring us all the way out here for introductions and pleasantries."

The gangster just nodded and gestured to the translator to continue while he leaned against the hood of his car.

"Sorry I couldn't tell you more before you made the

trip, I didn't even have all the details myself," said Marissa. "Apparently they want you as their new cruise line service. Not a lot of foreigners know this, but there's a long-standing community of Koreans in Japan, some of whom have become quite wealthy. They're also well-represented in gangland; the yakuza do a fair bit of business with them. When the armistice was signed in 1954, there were many families trapped in North Korea. Even after more than sixty years, those family ties remain strong, even stronger now that illegal Chinese cellphone have found their way into the border towns. Families are reconnecting, and there are many who want out at any cost. Japanese Koreans are willing to pay top dollar to make it happen."

"You're talking about human smuggling …" breathed Hassan.

"More or less," said Marissa. "Our friends here need a new route and reliable handlers. I told them I didn't know any reliable handlers, but you were the next best thing."

"What happened to the last travel agency?" asked Dalmar.

"Last route was overland, through China. North Korean border guards caught on. They say their men were executed on the spot; the escaping families were placed in prison camps. If they're not already dead, they wish they were."

"Mole in the yakuza?" asked Jonah.

"I doubt it," said Marissa. "More likely they were just unlucky. But they're not willing to risk a Chinese route for the foreseeable future, not until we know for certain."

"So what are we going to be moving? Girls?" asked Jonah. Behind the flippant tone, Hassan could detect the real motives. Jonah wasn't going to accept some bullshit cover for sex trafficking.

"Fuck you for asking," said Marissa, her eyes flashing with anger. "I'm not going to pretend they do this out of the goodness of their hearts—or that they don't have interests in the red-light districts, for that matter. But they're not in the business of turning out North Korean girls—and neither am I, that is for *goddamned* certain."

"Good," said Jonah, glaring right back at her. "But you know I had to ask."

Marissa reached over and pulled a map out of the breast pocket of the slim translator's suite jacket before slapping it into Jonah's chest. "Rendezvous is past the Siberian seamount of the Sea of Japan, near the North Korean port of Rason. Can you accommodate ten families?"

"It'll be tight quarters, three to a bunk or more," said Jonah, sticking the map in his back pocket. "But we can do it. I have to ask this—why not a ship? Why the Scorpion?"

"The port is completely frozen over. It's unprecedented. Can't get a ship in without an icebreaker. Need something that can punch up through the ice—you think the Scorpion can handle it?"

"Sure," said Jonah, but Hassan suspected the American hadn't necessarily considered the logistics of such an operation.

"They're offering five thousand dollars a head," said Marissa. "A hundred and fifty large for less than a week's work. They think there is enough volume to do the run monthly, switch it up to a hidden cove when the ice melts. If things work out, maybe even twice a month."

"A hundred and fifty? That will barely cover Hassan's skin creams," joked Jonah as he reached over to pinch Hassan's cheek. The doctor swatted his hand away. "Just look at this lustrous olive tone. Ten thousand a head, minimum."

"Done," interjected the boss's translator, leaving Hassan to wonder if Jonah should have asked for more—but he knew they could use the money, it'd be enough to refuel and reprovision the *Scorpion* from her long trip across the ocean. If a few runs went well, there might even be enough money left over to start a new life on a distant, non-extradition island nation.

"Great!" said Jonah, rubbing his palms together. "Let's see the cash."

Pushing Marissa aside, the boss's translator laughed as he stepped up to Jonah and shook his head.

"Yeah, so here's the thing …" began Marissa. "They appreciate my referral, but say you have zero reputation in Japan. They want to pay you upon receipt."

It was Jonah's turn to laugh. "Not happening," he said. "We don't work on spec."

"We insist," said the translator, hissing through clenched teeth. "A show of good faith."

"Half up front," interjected Dalmar, resting a hand on the butt of his pistol. "Or no deal."

In a flash, the glasses-wearing translator whipped around and grabbed Hassan from behind, throwing him into a vicious reverse chokehold, a small, razor-sharp silver knife pressed deep against his carotid artery. The doctor barely had time to yelp as Marissa scurried away behind the Cadillac, her bulky radiation suit relegating her swift escape to an awkward waddle. With a sudden clattering of metal, every yakuza gangster had produced an armory of previously unseen weapon, a dozen pistols held at eye level with total commitment. Hassan had no doubt they would not hesitate to pull triggers, though the knife at his throat remained his more immediate concern. The only unarmed man was the boss himself, who stared steely death at Jonah, Hassan and the pirate Dalmar Abdi.

"Remove your hands from your firearms," ordered the Japanese translator, twisting the knife against Hassan's neck. "We learned you have sold tattoos cut from the bodies of dead yakuza. Many wanted to skin you on sight … or if a deal could not be reached. Do not test our patience."

"Jonah!" exclaimed Marissa as she peeked from behind the parked car. "Stop fucking around, make the deal already!"

"I think we can live with those terms," said Jonah with an apologetic grin, letting his hand slip from the handle of his nickel-plated Colt 1911. "Let's not complicate this further."

The boss nodded and cocked his head towards the back seats of the nearest car.

"Good," said the young translator, releasing Hassan. "We will pay half of your fee up front as your pirate requested. But you had better deliver. The world is too small to steal from yakuza."

The doctor gulped and rubbed the corner of his neck where the knife had left a bright red divot. The mob boss reached through his open window and removed a black duffel bag, opened the zipper and threw it at Jonah's feet. It was loosely loaded with bricks of American cash, several blocks of which spilled out before him. Jonah reached down, packed the money away and slung the duffel around his neck.

Everyone turned as flashing red and yellow lights shone from the approaching highway, the police approaching from the distance. Marissa gingerly emerged from behind the trunk and spoke in rapid, low tones with the yakuza boss and his translator, ending the exchange with a hurried handshake.

"Sirens are generally our cue to leave," said Jonah, already starting to back away into the darkness of the night, Dalmar and Hassan at this side. "Anything else we should discuss?"

"Yeah," said Marissa, walking a few steps across the small courtyard to join him as they turned to walk back towards the docks. "My cabin accommodations—because I'm coming with you. Our friends can talk their way past the police so long as they don't have to explain an American woman. Besides, I have to make sure you don't fuck up my twenty-five percent any further."

Jonah scowled. "Fifteen," he said. "And that's dependent on you staying out of the way of my crew."

"Deal. Don't worry—this will be a milk run."

ACKNOWLEDGEMENTS

Great thanks to literary agent extraordinaire Carrie Pestritto for cheerleading this novel all the way to publication. Thanks also to Blank Slate editors Donna Essner for seeing the potential in the story and Kristina Blank Makansi for bringing out the best in every sentence. I've been profoundly lucky to work with such a marvelous team.

I am so grateful to Oki Radic for sitting me down and telling me in no uncertain terms that I must write this novel, as well as all her subsequent feedback. I'd also like to recognize Jonathan Wu for shepherding this story from the earliest drafts—I owe you both so much.

Thanks to first readers John Griffith and Jeremy Mohler for their incredible feedback and support, and to Caleb Gaw and Thierry Sagnier for their amazing help at critical times. Thanks also to my parents, Guy and Susan Zajonc—without your support, none of this would have been possible.

I am so blessed to have Milton Polk, Kelly Polk and Micah Eldred in my corner. And a special thanks to Richard Bernard, for helping me see not only the potential in this work, but also myself.

Writers' groups Arlington Creative Non-Fiction Writers of Virginia and The People's Ink of Portland, Oregon have been phenomenal support networks, and I've been honored to be a member of both.

Most of all, many thanks my incredible wife Andrea. I could never have wished for a more encouraging, insightful and supportive partner as I squirreled myself away in my office with my strange characters and faraway lands. You are amazing and the inspiration for everything I do.

ABOUT THE AUTHOR

As a maritime historian and shipwreck expert, Taylor's real-life adventures parallel those of his fictional counterparts. His fascination with exploration began when he joined a Russian expedition to the deepest archaeological site on the planet, descending nearly three miles into the abyss of the Bermuda Triangle aboard a Soviet-era submersible. Now a recognized expert in his field, his research has contributed to some of the most incredible shipwreck finds in history, including a 110-ton trove of sunken World War II silver.

Taylor lives in rainy Portland, Oregon with his wife and their 11-year-old collie mix, Potter. *The Wrecking Crew* is his first novel.

CPSIA information can be obtained at www.ICGtesting.com
Printed in the USA
LVOW10s2319040216

473772LV00001B/1/P